NICHOLAS KRISTO

By Rick Koestler

First published by Dog Ear Publishing
4010 W. 86th Street, Ste H
Indianapolis, IN 46268
www.dogearpublishing.net

ISBN: 978-159858-465-3

This book is printed on acid-free paper.
This book is a work of Fiction. Places, events, and situations in this book are purely
Fictional and any resemblance to actual persons, living or dead, is coincidental.

Printed in the United States of America

DEDICATION:

This book was written in response to our Heavenly Father's desire for Christians to continuously seek new and creative ways to bring the Good News to the world. The story is dedicated to the Giver of all good gifts, most notably the gift of Imagination

FOREWORD

Everyone has their passions. One of mine is reading. When Rick gave me the first half of his manuscript, I begged him to give me the next section as soon as he could. I couldn't stop reading. I was struck with the originality of what he wrote. It wasn't quite like anything I had ever read before. I think Rick, as an artist, knows intuitively that you don't write something in order to be original. You write something that is deeply true, and originality will take care of itself.

The other thing that struck me in Rick's book was that I put it down and felt inspired, as if I understood myself and God and the world around me in a different, better way. It has been said before that it is easier to write about evil—villains and conflict and wrongdoing. It is much harder to write about goodness without sounding overly sentimental and pedantic. As you read this book, you will find villains and conflict, but you will also see the goodness in characters who take on lives of their own. Such writing is a rare accomplishment and a precious gift to the reader.

So be careful as you read these pages. A strange quality resides in this story. It may change you. It may make you see your friends, your family, your church, your neighborhood in a different way. This book may even spur you, as it did me, to act in a different way. I think that Kafka once said that a book should be the ax that breaks the frozen sea inside of us. Rick's novel may even help to change the flow of those frozen waters to affect the shores which those waters within us touch.

I must say one more thing about the author. Having worked alongside him for many years, I can confirm that he lives the thing he writes about. This book comes from the furnace of his own experiences. I was the pastor of a small mission church in the Lower East Side of New York City. Rick was at a demonstration for life in Atlanta. My supervisor met him by chance there and challenged him to come help the poor in the inner city. Without hesitation he did so.

For years Rick made soup for the pour and brought it in and gave it out every Saturday. In all those years, I have never once heard Rick complain. He talked with people and prayed with people. He saw God heal people in dramatic ways on the street. He made art for the church. He taught other people to make art to give away. He worked with a group who did acts of kindness secretly. He saw prostitutes, pimps, and murderers become followers of Christ. When times were difficult, he kept working. When angry men pulled knives, he stood between them and the innocent. He helped us start a church. He taught the Word of God passionately, and walked with people through the hardships of their own difficult experiences. He is still doing these things today.

I often say that if I am in a battle, I want Rick Koestler in the trenches besides me. He is simply that kind of leader and co-worker. To see his loyalty and hard labor for others has been one of the great gifts and miracles of my life. I don't say these things lightly. When Rick talks about giving or healing or art or standing up to challenges or having a new kind of community or looking out for children, he is not just dreaming. He has lived these things on the hard sidewalks of the inner city.

As you read this book, you enter a world of another place and another time, where characters think and speak in a different cadence, where the scenes seem like something more out of a mural than a movie, like something more out of a fresco than a photograph. But let the reader beware. As you turn the pages, this different world reaches out to touch yours.

Dr. Taylor Field, Ph.D.

Chapter 1. Nicholas.

The winter storms of 1556 A.D. had already taken twenty-three people in the tiny village of Pizal, Italy. It wasn't the snow that most folks couldn't deal with. They had endured storms with massive snowfalls that had left many families stranded. People were shut in for weeks. Instead, the enemy was the bitter cold and the ripping wind.

Nicholas woke and looked out his bedroom window. The storm had slowed some. He hurried to get dressed and put on his bearskin coat, knowing he was risking his life if he left his cabin even for a short time. But there was no choice. By morning, he would be out of firewood. He stuffed some biscuits in his travel bag, then rushed out the door, grabbing his small saw just in case he needed to cut some wood. As he strapped on his snowshoes, he looked up. A tree had fallen and crashed into his tool shed. A sudden gust of icy wind snapped his breath away. He knew he didn't have much time.

He trudged toward the north field next to the fishing pond. As he pushed against the wind, he looked up, slitting his eyes to shield them. Snow had covered many of the stray pieces of wood. He moved farther out, hoping his luck would change, trying in vain to dismiss the knot in his stomach. The heaviness of his numb feet tired him, and the tiny ice pellets blowing off snowdrifts stung his face.

He walked two miles before he gathered enough wood for one more night. By this time, he wondered whether he could make it back to the cabin without getting frostbite.

Nicholas was a rugged man, over six feet with a husky frame. His handsome face sported a hearty beard with an ever-present expression of peace. Six months after he'd left seminary to move back home, his parents died of influenza. That had been three years ago, when he was thirty-three. He now realized his service to God was to be a pioneer, for he deplored the rituals and rote praying so common in the schools of theology. Now, he lived alone on the farm, with the exception of his dog Bolo. He was an only child who had amazed everyone at the age of six months when he stood up on his own and began speaking. Nicholas had been a very special child, with a very special gift; a gift that would soon reveal itself and change the course of his life forever.

Strapping the wood to his back, he hurried back towards the farm. He couldn't feel his feet and his hands were frozen under his mittens. To make things worse, the storm began to pick up again. Fearing that he couldn't make it back, he decided to head for his nearest neighbor's farm. It was only a short walk, and he thought it might be his only chance of survival.

Turning towards the southeast, he spotted a wagon in an open field. A motionless horse stood by the wagon. As he drew closer, he realized that the horse had been embedded in a snowdrift and had frozen to death. When he finally reached the wagon, he discovered a body on the floor next to a cache of supplies. His heart sank. Mr. Pallone, the neighbor from whom he had hoped to beg help, was frozen solid in a fetal position. Nicholas looked up in the direction of the Pallone farm and saw a dark mound at the end of the open field in front of a stand of trees. He thought it could be Mrs. Pallone, who had probably tried to reach her house. The snowfall intensified as he made his way out towards the end of the field, hoping that, by some miracle, Mrs. Pallone was still alive. He would build a sleigh, and with the help of God, get her to the farm before the blizzard claimed two more.

The Pallone family had always been kind to Nicholas, especially after the death of his parents. Every Sunday afternoon Mr. Pallone would come visit him and Bolo, and by the end of the visit, he would always persuade Nicholas to come back to his farm for dinner. Afterwards they would enjoy Mrs. Pallone's wonderful pecan pie. Nicholas would sit and marvel at the beauty of the Pallones' first child, May Rose. She melted his heart with her giggling laughter, rosy cheeks and delightful countenance. By the time May Rose turned a year old, Nicholas still had not heard the child cry.

The snow had now almost entirely covered Mrs. Pallone. Nicholas brushed the snow away. "Mrs. Pallone!" He rubbed her face vigorously and called her name, "Carmella!" He feared she was already dead until he saw her mouth move, and as he leaned closer to her face, he heard her say "May Rose".

As she spoke, a muffled whimpering noise caught Nicholas's attention. He opened Carmella's coat a little and found May Rose snuggled against the bosom of her mother. She was alive but freezing. Carmella looked up at Nicholas and whispered, "Take her to Anna Borelli." And then she closed her eyes in her final rest.

There was nothing Nicholas could do for his dear friend and he had little time if he expected to save May Rose.

He unloaded the wood from his back, then strapped May Rose to his chest under his bearskin coat. He hoped there would be enough body heat to revive her and keep her alive until he reached the Pallone cabin.

Nicholas headed toward the cabin, moving so fast that needles of pain stabbed through his toes as he walked. He had a renewed strength and hope when he rounded the bend in the road and the Pallone farm came into view. His pace picked up even more when May Rose moved under his coat.

As he approached the cabin, he sensed something was wrong. He stopped just long enough to assess the situation. The entrance to the cabin was on the east side, but that side was nothing but a wall of snow. It appeared that a western wind had driven tons of snow up against the entire entrance side of the cabin. The snow all around was very deep as well. To gain entry to the cabin was impossible, because the only other way was through the windows, and the Pallones had secured the storm shutters from the inside.

The barn was their last hope. Nicholas hurried behind the cabin to see how deep the snow was in front of the barn door. At last a break—the snow was low enough for him to pry the door open and enter. Inside the barn were two horses and a cow. It was very dark and cold. He scurried to search for a lantern and some way to make a fire, but all he found were a few plow tools, nails, and a hammer beside an anvil.

He climbed the ladder to the loft. May Rose whimpered. He prayed a lamp with matches would be in the loft, but all he found was a heavy wool rug. He came back down with it and gathered some hay on the ground to make a cushioned area for himself and May Rose. When he finished, he spotted a thick cotton blanket draped over one of the horses. He grabbed it and untied May Rose from his chest. She shivered uncontrollably, but at least she wore all heavy wool clothing. She had mittens and a wool hat that covered her ears, and soft handmade leather boots. Still, the sight of this very young child in such distress put a lump in his throat.

Taking full advantage of the rug and blanket, he wrapped May Rose as well as he could. She continued shivering, calling out softly for her mother. He prayed as he sat beside the child, knowing their time was short and his hope for rescue was long gone. He couldn't feel his hands and feet. All he wanted was to close his eyes and give in to his exhaustion, but he knew this would be his death sleep.

May Rose was already sleeping when Nicholas heard a faint ringing sound, very steady and becoming louder by the moment. The sound perplexed him and he thought he had become delusional as he lay shivering and numb. The ringing wouldn't stop and had reached a level that reminded him of a church bell, only this was a constant pitch. What was happening? Was he losing his mind just before death? He wondered if others who perished this year had experienced the same.

The ringing continued for at least an hour before the room gradually filled with an orange, glowing light. As he struggled to sit up and quench his curiosity, Nicholas noticed that he couldn't see his freezing breath any more. He peered toward the light source, finding, to his astonishment, that the anvil glowed orange with intense heat, and chimed like a bell. How could this be happening? This was impossible! Nicholas gazed at the anvil in utter amazement. As he began to thaw, he knew this strange but welcome marvel would save their lives.

The heat and soft ringing that emanated from the anvil continued as the barn became steadily warmer. Almost hypnotized by the orange light and the soft steady sound, Nicholas lay back and fell into a deep sleep. When he awoke, he half opened his eyes. At first, he thought he was in his own bed at home, but then he heard May Rose giggling just behind him. It all came back to him and he rose to see to the child. May Rose sat up, without her coat on, eating one of the biscuits from Nicholas's travel bag. She giggled again as she took another bite of the biscuit. It was still quite warm in the barn, even though the anvil was no longer glowing and the ringing had stopped.

He pushed open the barn door, grateful to see that it was morning. The storm had passed, and he smiled as the sun melted the ice on the trees, glittering the landscape with what looked like a billion diamonds. He couldn't work out how or why he and the child were still alive, but his main concern now was to get back in his own cabin and find May Rose something warm to eat.

Nicholas knelt down to prepare May Rose for the journey home. Her natural beauty amazed him. Her curly blonde hair fell into ringlets and she had the biggest green eyes he had ever seen on a child. But even more appealing than her beauty was her joyous temperament. Even through this most difficult storm and freezing cold, the two-year-old child had merely whimpered in discomfort.

He put on her coat, then wrapped her in the cotton blanket and fashioned a seat from some pieces of wood he found in the barn. He used the length of cord he carried in his travel bag to tie the seat together. Strapping May Rose in, he pulled her up onto his back, tied the horses and cow in tow, and left the barn.

The deep blue sky was almost cloudless as he headed back to his farm. The countryside looked beautiful with glistening icicles on all the trees and virgin snow everywhere. He thought back over the last twenty-four hours. Remembering Vincent Pallone curled up in the back of his wagon made him wonder what had happened. He knew Vincent had been ill, but his condition must have become grave for his wife to take him and May Rose into Pizal for help. They must have decided to turn back when the blizzard struck.

He remembered Carmella Pallone's last wish, that he should take May Rose to Anna Borelli.

Anna was loved and respected by everyone in town. Her first husband had been Mayor of Pizal, and had died from the same influenza that claimed Nicholas's parents. Anna had been alone until she met and married Michael Borelli just two months ago. She had two children of her own by birth, and four others whom she had adopted.

She had also cared for Ben, the town carpenter who had come to Pizal three years ago, looking for work. He was a huge, burly man standing almost seven feet tall and weighing over three hundred pounds. The Mayor had given him his first job, and since then he'd made many pieces of furniture for the villagers. Every piece was different, made of oak, maple or cherry wood, and ornamented with carved designs.

One day, not long after the Mayor's death, Ben had been working in his furniture shop at the edge of town when he smelled smoke. He ran outside and saw heavy black smoke billowing from Mario Fuso's silver shop. He bolted across the road fearing Mario, one of his best friends, was trapped in his shop. Mario was born without legs from the knees down, so Ben knew he had to help him. He burst through the side door where the fire was not as severe and saw Mario on the floor by his worktable, unconscious. The heat was overwhelming as he grabbed Mario with one arm, covering his face with the other. He managed to escape with his friend, but was badly burned. Everyone thought he would surly die, but Anna took him in and nursed him night and day for five months. He was well enough now to care for himself despite his badly disfigured face, but he couldn't overcome his depression. His face was so badly burned, that people would greet him with disdainful stares and even gasps of horror. For Ben, life had become a nightmare.

When Nicholas finally caught sight of his cabin, he sighed and wondered if Bolo had made it through that chilling night without heat. He pushed some snow away from the front door, and went in. He was delighted when Bolo greeted him, barking and jumping to Nicholas' chest. As he looked down, rubbing Bolo's ears, he said a prayer, thanking God for his home and for saving all their lives.

Nicholas put May Rose under his warmest blankets, gave her some milk and cheese, and headed out again to get wood. Looking over at the tool shed where the tree had come down he noticed that it was dead and perfect for firewood. He could easily snap off enough to last for a week. He wondered why he hadn't noticed it the day before. But if he had, May Rose would not be alive today, so perhaps it was all for the best. After stacking the wood on his supply sleigh, he returned and made the cabin cozily warm, and then cooked oatmeal and biscuits for May Rose. Tomorrow he would ride into Pizal with May Rose and pay a visit to Anna Borelli. Perhaps he could get Ben to come back with him to help give Vincent and Carmella a Christian burial.

Chapter 2. The Messenger

The sky was steel gray and the air still and bitter cold by the time Nicholas saddled his horse, strapped May Rose to his back and began the three-mile trip to Pizal. He moved his horse into a canter, wanting to get the child into a warm house before midday. Images of the night he'd spent in the Pallone barn kept returning. Was this a miracle from God? It had to be! There was no other explanation. But why? Maybe God had a special mission for May Rose when she grew older. Nicholas was mystified by the entire experience.

As he reached his secret forest trail, a short cut to the village, he noticed a dove perched by itself on a naked tree at the end of the bend in the road. He rubbed his eyes. He had never seen a dove so very white. It seemed as if it was glowing. Was it the contrast of the giant black stone rocks behind the tree? Nicholas was approaching it with great curiosity when he heard someone call his name. He turned quickly but there was no one in sight. And then that voice called again.

"Are you speaking to me?" Nicholas asked the dove. He felt foolish to be questioning a bird, but who else was there?

In reply he heard the same voice, sounding directly in his mind. "I am speaking through the dove."

"Who are you?" Nicholas asked.

"I am a messenger."

"A messenger for whom?"

"I am from a kingdom very different from this world," the voice said. "And I have a message for you from our King. He is the Savior of the world, Jesus the Christ. He wants you to know that you were born with a very special mission. You have a gift you are to pass on to the world in which you live."

"I am not aware of a special gift," Nicholas said.

"You have the gift of giving, Nicholas. It is the gift of selfless and noble giving. The world has many forms of giving, but few forms are pure. Many give to receive, to impress, to extort or to manipulate. They 'give' much of the time for strictly selfish reasons. Sometimes they give only to delight themselves, having very little insight with regard to the receiver of their gift. There are others with your gift, but you are the one chosen to affect the world with the honor and nobility in Godly giving. Yours will be a life of moral and thought-provoking example."

"How can someone as common as I affect the whole world?" Nicholas objected.

"You may consider yourself 'common,' but your gift is uncommon. Many give gifts without caring, but you can't care without giving," the messenger said.

"How will I know what to do?"

"I will be everywhere you go," the messenger replied. "I will aid you when you need aid, but I will not make a decision for you. You must think creatively and with discernment. If you do that, you will always be successful. I will be there. Have Faith."

"Were you at the Pallone farm the other night?"

"Yes."

With that, the dove flew away, and Nicholas wondered if he were dreaming. A great peace had come over him as the dove spoke. And still, as he thought about the deep meaning of this strange conversation, he felt a peace and confidence so uplifting that he began to laugh. He knew it was true and became excited over all the possibilities.

When May Rose heard Nicholas laugh, she joined in and they trotted away, tickled by one another's merriment.

All the way into the village, Nicholas pondered the idea of actually speaking to a messenger of God. He was always spiritual but had never thought he would be connected directly with heaven while here on earth. He felt there was much more to God than he had witnessed himself from various church leaders in Pizal. Some of the poorest in the village were spoken down to by the priests, and warned not to come to church until they had the proper attire. Nicholas knew such cruelty was not possible for true lovers of God.

Soon they arrived in the village. As he tied his horse to a post and brought May Rose to the ground, Nicholas heard shouting in the Borelli home. Anna's new husband, Michael, sounded very upset about something. He was demeaning and accusing her. Nicholas rushed to the door, hoping he might interrupt the flow of anger. When Anna came, she was holding back tears, but she burst into excitement at the sight of May Rose. She took the child in her arms, but her smile turned to a look of concern as she questioned Nicholas.

Anna was a big-boned woman without an ounce of extra weight. Her eyes were pale gray and deep set, and her face revealed all of her feelings in an instant. She was the most compassionate woman Nicholas had ever met, and now she listened as he told her all about Carmella Pallone's last request. Anna received the child as a member of her family at that moment. Nicholas thought it would be wise not to try to explain about the miracle in the barn or the conversation with the white dove.

After Anna had cooked a well-needed dinner, her husband left the house to attend an evening business meeting. Anna mentioned that he spent much of his time away on business. Before Nicholas could inquire, Anna asked him to forgive the verbal violence he had experienced when he arrived. She explained that Michael had taken on all the debt and expense of her house when they were married. His business was struggling and he was not accustomed to such pressure. She was such a loving woman that she thought it would do some good if Michael raged at her expense.

Nicholas knew that that was not the answer to the problem, but there wasn't much he could do. He knew they truly loved each other, but that Michael needed his eyes to be opened with regard to how blessed he was to have such a devoted wife and family.

Anna and Nicholas talked for some time as she packed leftover meat pie and fresh bean soup in his travel bag. He said his warm goodbyes to the children. As he was inquiring after Ben, the carpenter walked through the front door. They laughed at the sight of each other and embraced as close friends would. Nicholas told him of the fate of Vincent and Carmella, and Ben volunteered to ride back and help bury them.

Their conversation on the road back quickly turned to Ben's recovery from the fire six months earlier. "I still have enormous pain where my ears used to be," Ben said. "Every time I leave the house I have to wrap my head with this scarf. If I don't, and the cold wind blows, I convulse with pain. Sometimes it's so bad that I fall to the ground." With tears in his eyes, he continued, "I'm so very thankful to Anna for saving my life. I could never repay her for all that she's done, in spite my anguish and self-contempt."

"Don't be so sure of that," Nicholas said.

"What do you mean?"

"Why don't you stay at my farm for a few days and we'll discuss the possibilities?"

As Nicholas spoke, a white dove flew overhead and landed on a tree directly in their path. Nicholas realized he was about to begin his first mission of giving.

After they buried the couple and marked the grave, Ben and Nicholas returned to the cabin for a late dinner, and afterwards retired for the day. Nicholas lay in his bed thinking about Anna and Michael. He remembered how they had impressed everyone with their love for each other before Michael had become overwhelmed with financial troubles.

Like Ben, Michael owed his life to Anna's nursing. He and his best friend, Petro, had been hunting wolves on Bear Mountain. Most people in Pizal avoided the mountain because of its wolf population and other dangerous wildlife. Nicholas himself had spotted several wolf packs, but for some reason animals always dropped submissively to the ground when they saw him. Michael and Petro were not blessed with Nicholas's immunity, though, and the hunt had gone disastrously wrong, leaving Petro dead, and Michael terribly injured. Anna had taken him in, getting Ben's help to set Michael's broken arm and leg. He had been unconscious for six days, but during his slow recovery he and Anna had developed a relationship beyond that of a caring woman and her patient. This had led to the marriage that had at first seemed almost perfect, but just as physical misfortune had brought them together, so fiscal misfortune seemed to be driving them apart. Nicholas was determined to help.

He awoke the next morning with a plan. After a night's sleep, he was refreshed and eager to begin his search for a special piece of maple wood. He knew the location of some large maple trees that had fallen recently on Bear Mountain. He would have set out right after breakfast, but he found Ben in the kitchen with his head down on the table in great distress.

"What's wrong, Ben?" Nicholas said.

"I can't face the world any more, looking as I do. People get upset and horrified everywhere I go. Nicholas, can I stay on your farm until I decide what to do with the rest of my life?"

"Of course. Stay as long as you like, but you know Ben, there are no hopeless situations; there are only people who have grown hopeless about them.* Besides, I have a plan that might lift your spirits. Do you remember yesterday when you thought you could never repay Anna for all she had done for you?"

Ben looked up. "Have you thought of a way I can show my thanks?"

"Yes I have, but I'll tell you on the way up the mountain. For now, let's prepare for a day's work in the forest. You can pack some dried beef, cheese, and bread in my travel bag and I'll grab the tree saw. We'll also need to pull the small supply wagon with us."

Ben's depression lifted as he did as Nicholas requested. He wrapped his head with his long scarf, then hurried up the road to join his friend. "What about the wolves, Nicholas? Shouldn't we have taken a musket?"

"Don't worry, Ben," said Nicholas, "I've been to the mountain many times without incident. Animals are friendly and playful when I enter their territory. It has been this way since I was a boy. I thought it was so for everyone, but I eventually realized it was a gift from God."

The weather was glorious for a day in the forest. The severe chill had gone and it was unusually warm. The sun felt good on their backs as they headed up towards the fallen maple Nicholas had in mind. "How's your carving skills these days, Ben?" he asked as they walked.

"I guess that all depends on what I carve and who I carve it for. For example, if I get a commission to make a piece, I carve in decorations that match the owner of the piece. When I made the cabinet for the Mayor's office, I carved in three owls and vines with grapes and leaves. I thought he made some very wise decisions for our town before he died; that's why I carved the owls. The day he commissioned me to make the cabinet, he invited me over for lunch. He brought out a bottle of the finest wine I've ever tasted. He had only a glass but he savored every sip, so I thought he would like the leaves and grapes as well."

"What do think about carving a gift for Anna?" suggested Nicholas.

"Nothing would please me more. But what would I carve?"

"Over Anna's front doorway is an empty framed panel. It's a perfect place to put a special woodcarving. Today our job will be to find the right piece of wood for the job. Last year I came across a fallen maple tree just past the ravine that Michael fell into when the wolves attacked him. I think you will love this wood."

"But what will I carve?"

"It will be a carving to tell the story of how Anna and Michael came together. You will need to put all your skills to the test for this one. It will be a gift that will have an impact on many lives and bring healing to some. You will make three illustrations on a triangular panel. The first will be a scene that shows Michael shooting a wolf, with another wolf at his ankle. In the background, Petro is surrounded by wolves. The second panel will show Anna at Michael's bedside caring for him. The third panel will show Anna and Michael standing together surrounded by their family. Michael will be holding Anna's hand to his face."

"What a great gift that will be, to me as well as to Anna!" exclaimed Ben. "You know, Nicholas, it's a dark prison to wake every morning feeling as I do. To make this gift will help me to feel alive again. May I do the carving on your farm?"

"By all means," Nicholas said. "You can set up a work area in the barn, and if it gets too cold, we have a storage room in the cabin I think you'll be happy with. When my father built our cabin, he was expecting a large family, so we have any one of three bedrooms for you to sleep in."

Ben was thrilled about this new direction in his life. Ever since the fire, life had become unbearably difficult, but he was sure this project might turn things around for him. As he picked up his pace and pulled ahead of Nicholas, he thanked God yet again for the day they'd become friends.

Chapter 3. A Life-Changing Discovery.

When Nicholas rounded a bend in the trail, he saw Ben standing in the middle of the road stiff as a board. A gray wolf snarled at him from the bush, and two more were easing towards him. As they moved ever closer, teeth showing, they spotted Nicholas and instantly dropped to their bellies. One rolled onto its back, making yipping sounds.

Ben turned to Nicholas, with relief clear on his ruined face. "That's amazing! I've never seen anything like that before in my life."

As Nicholas approached, another wolf came out of the bush. This one was pure white and bigger than the others. Its steel-blue eyes were fixed on Nicholas as it dropped to its belly and crawled its way to him, before rolling over with a soft crying sound. Nick noticed that it was a female and crouched to pet her.

Ben stared, his mouth agape in disbelief, as the she-wolf rolled to her belly again and gently grabbed Nicholas' forearm with her mouth, nudging him in a certain direction. She stood, still holding his arm, and tugged him along a little way before releasing him and pacing onward. Every few feet she looked back to see if he was following.

Nicholas motioned for Ben to follow, and they accompanied the white wolf to the edge of a ravine. Nicholas peered down, and then he heard the crying. A black wolf pup was stranded on a ledge about 20 feet down. He thought it must have slipped over the edge while playing with the other pups.

Grabbing the rope he brought to tie down the maple wood, he threw it around a tree, tied a strong safety knot, and asked Ben to hold the line as he climbed over the edge to help the pup. Halfway down, a white dove flew past him, landing on a branch that had grown out from between the rocks on the other side of the ravine. The dove sat right next to a patch of ivy that spread about three-feet-wide and ran halfway down the ravine.

"You all right, Nick?" Ben called out.

"Yes, Ben," said Nicholas. "Get ready to pull us up when I give the word."

"Nicholas!" Ben shouted. "Do you see the dove? I never saw one so white before! It's beautiful."

Nicholas glanced at the dove, and smiled in recognition. He put the pup in his travel bag, and then asked Ben to start pulling. Even though Nick was a huge man himself, Ben was easily strong enough for the task. As

Nicholas moved closer to the top, he noted that the dove was pecking at the dense ivy patch, cutting some of the vines with its beak. This was curious, but he had a job to do. He pulled himself over the edge of the ravine, freed the pup, and laid it next to its mother. The she-wolf nudged Nicholas' leg affectionately, then lifted her pup by the back of the neck and headed into the bush.

Nick looked for the dove, but it was gone. He thought it must have flown away, but then he saw its little white head peeking out from behind the area it had cleared away. He pointed this out to Ben. "Let's see how far the opening in the ravine goes back. There must be a place to cross to the other side."

"What's on the other side? Is that where the maple tree fell?"

"No. I want to see what's behind that ivy patch, where the dove is sitting."

"But there are only tiny ledges in that spot, and the rocks go straight down to the bottom. It looks very risky to me."

"I know," said Nicholas, "but that white dove is a very special part of my life now and I know it's pecked that ivy away and is sitting back there for a reason. I'll explain about the dove another time, but for now let's just try to get there somehow."

The men followed the edge until they found the spot where the ravine ended and walked the wagon around to the other side. When they arrived at the area where the ivy grew, Nicholas tied the rope around his waist and asked Ben to keep the line tight as he went down to investigate. The ivy had tree roots mixed in, so he held them to steady himself and started the descent.

As he approached the tiny opening, the dove jumped out onto a vine. Nicholas heard a gentle voice say, "Pray to God for wisdom." Then it flew off.

Pushing the vines away, he saw a crude cave hidden behind the ivy. He secured his feet to a tiny ledge and told Ben to keep the line tight. Then he cut off a thick vine with his knife and tied it around the descending vines, pulling them together.

The opening was only about four-feet-wide and ten-feet-high, and too dark to see back very far. Cautiously, Nicholas entered, and climbed over several huge boulders. He glanced up, hoping to gauge the height of the ceiling, but blinked as he saw faint light glittering off the rocks. He stopped, rubbed his eyes, and peered more closely, hardly able to believe in the sight. It was a vein of gold at least eighteen inches wide, descending well beneath the base of the cave. Nicholas stared, incredulously, knowing that his life had changed forever.

"Are you all right, Nick?" Ben yelled down.

Nicholas took a deep breath. "Oh yeah, Ben, I'm very all right."

"What's down there?"

"Ben, when I give the word start pulling me up."

Nicholas found a sharp rock on the cave floor and smashed it into a large protruding gold nugget. A piece the size of a grapefruit broke off, so he brought it to the cave opening for a better look. It was solid gold, pure as it could be. He put the chunk into his travel bag and yelled for Ben to start pulling, but before he began his ascent, he cut the vine that held the ivy together, so that the cave opening was once again concealed. As he began to climb, braced against the rope, the dove's voice seemed to echo in his mind; "Pray God for wisdom."

Nicholas knew he would have to do a lot of praying after finding this vein of gold. He would have to think very carefully about everything he did from now on. Grabbing Ben's arm, he pulled himself over the edge and sat on the ground. He took off his red wool cap, scratching his head as he stared at the travel bag holding the large gold nugget.

"What was down there, Nicholas?" persisted Ben.

Nick reached into the bag, took out the nugget and handed it to Ben.

Lifting the nugget close as he turned it, Ben's eyes grew wide. When he could speak, he whispered, "This is solid gold, Nicholas," then shouted, "solid gold! You're a rich man now, my friend."

"I was rich before I went down there, Ben, but in a different way. Right now I feel more responsible than rich."

"What do you mean?"

"This is just a small fragment of what I found. There is a vein of gold in that cave as wide as your chest. It goes all the way down past the floor of the cave."

CHAPTER 4. A VOW OF SILENCE
REGARDING THE GOLD

olding the giant gold nugget over his head, Ben shouted in excitement and danced in circles.

"Ben, calm down and listen very carefully," said Nicholas, pointing to the gold. "The first thing you need to know is that this discovery cannot be told to anyone for any reason. If people ever found out, the greedy ones would stop at nothing to obtain it. Because of the gold, people would die, lives would be destroyed. The gold would ultimately fall into the hands of evil people and become an instrument of evil. A messenger from Heaven guided us to the cave to do only good for mankind, so this discovery must never be known. You must vow with me today that you will never reveal this gold or its location to anyone for any reason."

Crouching down next to Nicholas, Ben sobered and locked eyes with his friend. "Do not let your heart be troubled," he said. "I vow today to honor your request with my life. And you should know that it is not a difficult thing to ask of me. I am your friend. You are the only one who can look at my mangled face and smile at me. That is worth far more than a vein of gold." He smiled. "I'm really not concerned with money; my skills in carving and carpentry provide me all that I need to be comfortable in this life. What I *am* concerned with is the fact that I can't be among people as a normal person any more. I wish it were winter year round so I would have an excuse to wrap my face in this scarf all day long. And when I think about it, no amount of gold can stop the constant pain where my ears used to be."

Ben unwrapped his scarf to solidify his point. His face was a mass of scar tissue that went right to the top of his head, preventing hair from growing back. The fire had taken both ears, and the flesh in the surrounding area was still red.

"I believe you, Ben," Nick said, his voice husky with compassion.

"What will you do with the gold?"

"I don't see this as *my* gold. That dove gave me the location for a reason." Nick smiled slightly. "This may be hard for you to believe, Ben, but a messenger from Heaven speaks to me through that dove. He has already told me that I've been chosen by the King to bring to the world the true and noble gift of giving. He said that much of the world, including the church, is rooted with ill-conceived perceptions regarding how and why people give. He also said that I was chosen to make a difference. Ever since I spoke to the messenger through the dove, I have felt a great peace and confidence about the message, and it seems to increase on a daily basis."

"What King are you speaking of?" Ben asked cautiously. "The King of France?"

"No, Ben, I mean the King of Heaven, our Savior. I don't know why I was chosen. I've never believed in God the way many in our village believe. I don't like the rituals and memorized prayers. I feel closest to God when I've helped someone in secret or when I'm out among God's creation. It actually feels like I'm in worship when I come up with a way to aid someone in need or even to solve a problem they have. I've always felt this way, since I was a child. I know that the gold we found will be a never-ending resource aiding in the success of the mission."

"What do you mean *we* found? You found the gold, Nick."

"With your help. Would you like to work with me on this mission?"

Ben grinned and said, "I think I would like that more than anything else at this point in my life, but it's becoming more and more difficult facing strangers, and even people that I know in Pizal. Will I hold back your efforts because of this?"

"Not at all. As a matter of fact, I think I have an idea brewing that will help. I'll explain when we're back at the farm. You'll just need to make one more trip to the village to pack your things and get your carving tools. We have a lot of planning to do."

The sun was high, melting the snow on the trees, when they found the fallen maple tree leaning against a bench of snow. It was huge, snapped near the base, and had burn marks on the bark. They thought lightning had probably brought it down. It was a magnificent tree, and after finding a sweet spot on its length, they spent the rest of the afternoon cutting out a slab large enough for the triangular panel.

Ben was an expert with trees. His parents owned a logging company and from his youth, handling wood seemed like second nature. It wasn't until his thirtieth year that he decided to leave home and build his own business. He'd thought Pizal was a perfect place to settle because it was so friendly and only a day and a half's journey from San Marco and his family.

By the time the slab of maple was cut and tied to the wagon, it was late afternoon, and they needed to make haste if they were to return before dark. When they reached the trail that led to the farm, that familiar white dove flew overhead and landed on a thick, three-foot oak stump right in front of them. The men turned to each other in silent question.

Nicholas knew right away why the dove had chosen that particular stump. As it flew off, he grabbed the tree saw and asked Ben to man the other side. As they sawed an eighteen-inch piece off the top, Ben asked, "What's this oak for Nick?"

"It will be the most important part of a special gift for you."

"For me? What do you mean?" said Ben.

"When we were cutting that maple slab I thought of a way to ease your discomfort and at the same time make it easier for you to be among people."

"This piece of oak will do that for me? How?"

As they hurried to finish, Nicholas explained, "The oak will only be a part of the process. For now you just need to tell me if you can remember what you looked like before the fire destroyed your face."

"Yes, I think so, although I never spent much time looking in the glass."

"Do you think you can carve a self-portrait in this wood?"

"I would give it my very best. What are you up to, Nick?"

"I will tell you everything after you do the portrait. You will need to do it before you start carving Anna's gift. And Ben, I want you to take special care with all the proportions of your face. Measure each part. They must measure exactly five percent larger than your face, except for the ears. Make the ears slightly larger, but not so much that it would be noticeable to anyone. You can start when you come back from Pizal tomorrow with your tools."

"You are starting to give me hope, Nicholas," Ben said. "I don't know why, but I feel hope again. I will go to Pizal tonight, so I can start carving first thing in the morning. Besides, by the time I get there, people will be off the streets so I won't have to confront anyone."

It was already dark when they returned to the cabin. Ben didn't even stop to eat. He just asked Nicholas for some bread and cheese, gulped some water down and flew out the door with Bolo jumping and barking, delighted that Ben wanted him to come along. Nicholas, knowing Ben must be exhausted after the day they'd spent, insisted he should saddle the horse and ride into town.

CHAPTER 5. BEN'S FAMILY BECOME FUGITIVES.

E arly on Sunday morning, Nicholas woke to the faint sound of a church bell several miles away in Pizal. The ringing of the bell reminded him of the night in the Pallone barn with May Rose. That had been the beginning of his new mission in life. A clicking sound outside brought him to the window, and he smiled as he saw Ben tapping his chisel into the oak self-portrait. Ben's scarf fully covered his face. Nicholas thought about his plan to ease Ben's pain and rid him of the scarf forever.

After he dressed, he made hardboiled eggs for Ben and himself. When the eggs were cooked, he brought them, the gold nugget and a large platter out to the barn.

Ben had already roughed out the piece of oak. With a crude caliper, he kept stopping to measure his own face and compare it with his sculpture. Nicholas took a seat next to Ben, placing the platter and nugget on a small workbench. Ben finally looked up.

"Good morning, Nick. What do you plan to do with that chunk of gold?"

"How did you fare in the village last night?" countered Nicholas.

"The streets were barren by then," Ben said. "It was very quiet except for the yelling and commotion coming from Anna's house. Michael was shouting, and it sounded like he was throwing things around the house. I would have stopped in, but it was obviously not the right time. I wish I could have helped."

"As soon as you finish the carving for Anna and Michael, you will be helping."

"What do you mean?"

"Wait and see what happens after we install the panel. It will have an effect on the entire family. Now, do you happen to have a heavy rasp in your toolbox?"

"Of course," said Ben, producing one.

Nicholas reached for the rasp, put the nugget on the platter and began to shave the soft gold into tiny bits. "I want to make gold dust of the entire nugget. Whoever we do business with must think we panned the gold from a stream. They must think it took years to attain so much."

While Ben ate the eggs and Nicholas shaved the nugget, a rider approached. It was a messenger with a letter for Ben from his family in San Marco. Ben retired to the cabin to read it, but when he emerged it was obvious that the news was not good. With tears in his eyes, he told Nicholas that his entire family was hiding out in the woods just outside of San Marco.

"How does that come about?" demanded Nicholas, and Ben explained.

Up until recently, Ben's family had owned a prosperous logging business with a sizable piece of land to work the logs. Their nearest neighbor, Andrea Ficci, was a high ranking Captain in the Italian Army. He owned all the surrounding property and wanted to add the Bellicini holdings to his own.

Four days earlier, Captain Ficci had sent three soldiers, as cruel and vindictive as himself, to Ben's parents with an offer to buy the company and land outright. The money offered was no more than a third of its real value.

Jon and Sarah Bellicini were angry and insulted, and an argument ensued. Raven, Ben's twenty-year-old sister, hid herself in the storage room and trembled as she heard her father rage. Two shots rang out, and then came an ominous silence. Raven heard the soldiers say they wanted this to look like a robbery, so they turned things upside down and pulled drawers out of the cabinets. In the course of this, one of them entered the storage room and found Raven. He smiled cruelly, but as he grasped her a deep voice cried out from the front room. It was Ox, Ben's brother, eldest and largest of the family.

Ox burst into the room and saw his parents on the floor in a pool of blood. Enraged, he grabbed the soldier closest to him, and flung him across the room with such force that the man's back was broken. The dead man's companion retaliated, and Ox broke his neck. Hearing Raven scream, the huge man hurried to the storage room, where the third soldier was standing over his sister. The soldier raised his pistol, Raven pushed him away and the gun discharged, hitting Ox in the knee. Ox wrapped his mighty arms around the soldier's chest as he fell, crushing his rib cage into his heart.

Rushing to Ox, Raven removed her apron, tying his leg above the knee to stop the bleeding, then bandaged a wound in his side. Their twin brothers, Lund and Ty, came home to this scene of horror, and they all grieved and wept over the murder of their parents.

That evening the siblings discussed their situation. They knew Captain Ficci would send other soldiers when the first ones failed to report back. When this happened, Ox would be arrested and probably shot. The twins would somehow be implicated, leaving Raven to the Captain's mercy.

Raven was the most beautiful woman in San Marco, but she dressed plainly in a work gown and apron. Her jet-black, wavy hair fell halfway down her back, and she was tall and perfectly proportioned, with brown, almond-shaped, eyes, and a face born of Heaven.

Until that terrible day, her brothers had always made her feel safe, but now the horror of what had happened had sent her into silent depression. Ox had passed out for lack of blood and it was up to Lund and Ty to decide what the family should do. The brothers were fair-skinned, handsome, and identical, tall, but not giants like Ox and Ben.

Painfully, they made their decision. They buried their parents, packed everything of value into their covered supply wagon, then fled through the forest with Ox and Raven. Having traveled all night, they finally found a hidden valley where they could be safe for a while. They set up camp, and then Lund, whose turn it was to keep watch, spotted a close family friend riding along the road beyond the valley. He flagged the man down and explained their situation, then entrusted him with a letter for Ben.

After hearing the story, Nicholas expressed his deep sorrow at the loss of Ben's parents and the extreme situation his family faced.

"I thought fate had landed its final blow the day I first saw my face after the fire," said Ben huskily. "I thought living could not get any more difficult, and now this happens. My family and I are doomed, Nicholas."

Nicholas held up the first bag of gold dust. "You're not doomed, Ben. This gold will help us in many ways, and it will start right now. You keep carving, and I will ride into Pizal and send a messenger to your family. Did Lund tell you exactly where they are?"

"I know where the valley is," said Ben. "I'll write directions for the messenger. But what will you say? What else can I do?"

"I'll send this first bag of gold dust along with the messenger in case they need to buy their way out of a situation. Then they can stay at my place for a few days. It's quiet here, so they should feel safe. When Ox feels better, we'll figure out a longer term plan."

"But Nicholas, you'll be in danger if they come here," objected Ben. "They are wanted fugitives. Captain Ficci will send out soldiers searching for them."

"Ox will die if we don't act now," said Nick. "Don't worry, Ben, if things become too dangerous we'll escape to Bear Mountain. No one dares climb very far up because of the wolves. You know they won't bother me, or anyone under my protection."

Ben pulled his scarf to his eyes. "How could I ever repay you, my friend?"

"No payment is ever necessary," said Nicholas gently. "Just stay with me on the mission, if that is what you wish."

Ben wrote the directions to the hiding place, and Nicholas took his savings from the past two years, saddled his horse and galloped to Pizal.

Chapter 6. A Special Mask for Ben

As Nicholas rode the two miles to Pizal, he considered the supplies he needed to make Ben's special gift of a custom-fitted mask. The oak sculpture of Ben's face was the key if his plan was to succeed.

As he trotted into the village, he reached for his coin pouch. He was relieved that he had no more problems with lack of money. Purchasing anything in Pizal with gold-shavings might attract attention, so using his savings would have to suffice until he found a way to exchange the gold for coins.

The tiny city of Pizal was as busy as ever, with residents and shopkeepers clamoring over prices on the sidewalks and open-air markets. The city had one main, cobblestoned street, which stretched more than a quarter-mile and stopped abruptly at the end of town in front of St. Camille's Church. On either side of the road stood two and three story buildings, most of them having a business on the first floor.

Nicholas stopped at the general store first, buying rabbit glue, down feathers, tanner oils, a yard of blue silk fabric, cyan powered pigment, and two thin pieces of calfskin. He was eager to begin the mask, which would not only allow Ben to move freely among people again, but also relieve some of his pain.

Next he visited the tailor, and purchased two hats, one for summer months and one for winter. He planned to sew in tiny hooks to the mask that attached to small loops attached to the hats, making a single unit of hat and mask. Ben would be able to change head dressings when it suited him.

After buying all he needed, Nick bought fudge for May Rose, then rode to Anna's house, which was located next to the church. As he tied his white horse to the hitching post, patting its neck, Anna and the child stepped onto the porch. May Rose giggled. "Nicki, Nicki!" she squealed, pointing at him. Anna appeared disturbed.

Nicholas climbed the porch steps, took the fudge from his travel bag, and handed it to the child as he knelt to kiss her rosy cheek.

Anna had been crying again, and as she greeted Nick with a hug, her frustration spilled out. "I don't know what to do any more, Nicholas. Michael's always angry and I can't do anything right in his eyes. I really love him and I know he loves me, but I just don't know what to do."

"Anger is the wind that blows out the lamp of the mind," said Nick with a sympathetic smile. "Ben is staying at my place for a while and is making a special gift for you and Michael. I know it's difficult to imagine that a material item might help your situation, but please trust me on this. Meanwhile, I have a favor to ask of you."

He explained Ben's family situation and asked if Anna would be willing to assess Ox's condition when he arrived at the farm.

Anna agreed, and Nicholas spoke to her with so much encouragement that she was laughing with him by the time her adopted son Justus rode up to the front door. He had been fishing for the last two days and had brought his catch home, ready to sell at the market.

Justus leapt to the ground before his horse had stopped. "Nicholas! It's been too long. Will you stay and have dinner? It's all the trout and bass you can eat tonight!"

The young man was delighted to see Nicholas, because it was Nick who had found him six years earlier, beaten, nearly naked and unconscious in a ditch. He had been severely injured, with burn marks on his chest and arms, so Nick had wrapped him in a bedroll, lifted him onto his horse and taken him directly to Anna's house. When Justus finally awoke, he would not relate what happened, but kept repeating, "My name is Justus, because I will have justice before I die."

Anna and Nick had asked again several months later, and Justus simply repeated, "My name is Justus, and I will have justice before I die."

"Justus, are you sure it's not revenge that you will have?" suggested Nicholas, but the boy had not replied.

Justus was only fifteen when Nicholas found him, and in the years since, he had never spoken of his earlier life. Anna nursed him to health and adopted him and he'd been a part of her family ever since. Now full-grown, Justus stood slightly under six-feet and had a slim but muscular frame. He was strikingly handsome with chiseled features, and many people took him for a Spaniard, most notably by the way he pronounced certain words and from his appearance. His silky, black hair highlighted olive skin, and he sported a thin mustache with a small patch of hair under his bottom lip. He was known for his quick wit and skill as a hunter, and through the years he'd trained himself to be an outstanding marksman with the crossbow. He also had deadly aim with the finely balanced dagger Nicholas had given him for his twenty-first birthday. He was a willing student of practical matters, and sometimes helped Anna when patients needed care.

After their greeting, Nicholas rested a hand on Justus' shoulder. "I need a favor, son. What say you?"

"Anything, Nick, you know," said Justus. "As soon as I return from the market we'll have dinner and talk about what you need."

"This is urgent, Justus. I need a rider to travel to the forest south of San Marco, and to deliver a message."

"Sounds like an adventure to me. I'll do it. I'll ask one of my friends to take the fish to market and I'll leave straight away."

"That's perfect, son. Thank you."

Nicholas explained what had happened to Ben's family, and told Justus of the plan to get them to Nicholas' farm as quickly as possible. When he mentioned the soldiers and Captain Ficci, Justus' eyes narrowed, as if there were a connection. In closing, Nick asked if he would consider working for him when he returned to the farm.

"I'll think about it while I'm on the road," Justus said.

"Good. We'll discuss it when you return."

After giving Justus direction to the family's hiding place, Nicholas handed him the letter, the gold dust and a handsome fee for the journey. Justus pushed the coins back and said, "You said it was a favor you needed, right? We'll talk about a wage when I return." With that, the young man mounted his horse and asked Anna to see his friend Rubin about bringing the fish to market, then he rode off in a gallop.

Nicholas consoled Anna again, then mounted his horse, anxious to return to his farm and begin the mask. On the road home he thought of a better way to relieve Ben's pain. The scar tissue around the tiny holes where his ears used to be was still very sensitive. If Ben didn't have his scarf wrapped around his head when a breeze brushed by, he'd drop to the ground in searing pain. That was his most serious problem.

Cantering onto the farm, Nick saw Ben hunched over the large maple slab with his chisel deep into the wood. Smiling widely, he asked, "Did you get tired of working on the portrait, Ben?"

"It's finished," said Ben, wiping wood chips from his chest.

"Already? That's wonderful! Can I see it?"

"Sure thing, it's on the front porch steps. It was more difficult than I thought. I had trouble visualizing what I looked like before the fire. One thing is sure, it's exactly five percent larger than my own head, except for the ears, they're about seven percent. I measured everything with a caliper. Tell me what you think. How did it go in the village?"

Dismounting, Nick joined Ben. "I sent Justus to your family with the letter and gold. I couldn't think of anyone more capable than him."

"I'll bet anything Justus escorts them all the way here."

"Why do you think he'd do that?"

"When he takes one look at Raven, his plans will change. That strong will and stubborn personality of his will melt like ice on a sunny day in July. My sister is beautiful; maybe that's why God provided four very big brothers to protect her." Ben's smile faded. "I'm really worried about her, though. Lund wrote she's been distant and unfocused since the day our parents were killed."

"Time and love will bring her back, Ben," said Nicholas. "And if that doesn't do it, we'll think of something."

Glancing down at the sanded maple slab, Nicholas couldn't believe how fast Ben had worked. All three panels were sketched out in graphite and he'd begun carving the center panel first. The drawings on the wood were so fluid, they could've held up as fine art on their own.

Watching Ben work, Nick felt his heart swell with confidence, for he knew his plan for creating the mask would have the effect he intended. He thought back to his conversation with God's messenger and wondered if his talent for helping the disabled, in body or spirit, could be the primary reason for his commission. One thing was sure, finding the gold had freed him enough to devote the rest of his life to discovering everything God intended him to accomplish.

As Nicholas pondered these things, a white dove flew down and landed on the oak self-portrait Ben had made.

Smiling as he walked to the piece and squatted, Nicholas said, "It's wonderful, Ben. The likeness is amazing."

Nick's spirit lifted as never before, seeing the portrait for the first time. The carving looked very much like Ben before the fire, and had a distinct expression of compassion and strength fixed in the brow. This was the perfect cast from which Nicholas would create Ben's mask.

Chapter 7. Nicholas Creates the Mask.

Ben came over to the porch and squatted next to Nicholas, asking, "You think the portrait really looks like I did before the fire, Nick?"

"You jest, my friend, I'm sure. It's much better than I ever imagined. I didn't know you were that masterful a sculptor."

"I never tried anything like this before. All I can say is that I put my heart and soul into it, and my hands did the rest."

"Your heart and soul indeed. I'm going to make a special mask for you from this sculpture. It will be designed to relieve your pain and allow you a degree of comfort when you're with people. I bought all the things I need in Pizal. I'll start this afternoon."

Ben's eyes welled. "This could really change everything for me. But how can the mask help with the pain?"

"When I'm fitting the mask to your face, I'll explain everything. For now, just concentrate on your carving, and try not to worry about your family. When I was in the village, Anna said things were getting worse with her husband. I know if you put your heart and soul into it, like you did with the portrait, we'll achieve the desired effect."

Tears fell on the panel as Ben picked up his chisel and wiped his eyes. The mysterious white dove flew onto the roof of the barn, watching Ben from above. Nicholas grabbed the supplies from his saddlebags and headed to the far end of the cabin, into his workshop.

He brought out three extra lanterns before beginning work, for he knew he would work through the night until he finished the mask.

He began by bleaching one of the two pieces of calfskin and setting it aside to dry. Then he mixed magenta, cyan and yellow pigment, creating an olive flesh-tone in the grinding jar. He set half the mix aside and made a dye with the remaining pigment, coating the bleached leather until its color matched Ben's skin-tone.

With the unused pigment, he made an unstable tempera and painted three coats onto the face and ears of the oak bust. When the paint dried, he took the un-dyed piece of leather and scraped the underside until it was very thin. After brushing rabbit glue on a small section, he blew on it to speed drying time. When the glue became tacky, he placed the leather over the left ear and began to work it into the contours. Using a metal tool with a small rounded point, he pushed and stretched the leather over and into every shape.

He moved quickly, applying the glue, working it down onto the head until the face and ears were covered. Cutting away the excess leather behind the ears, he repeated the same process, gluing the second, skin-toned piece on top of the first. Two layers made the mask just the right thickness. Nick stopped working to let the glue dry.

At midnight he returned to the workshop to check on the mask. He grinned with satisfaction when he saw the mask had lifted off the head slightly. He knew that when the glue dried, the mask would shrink and lift away from the unstable paint. Since Ben had carved the head five percent larger, the shrinkage would make it a perfect fit.

When the mask was freed from the oak carving, he scraped the paint chips from the underside and cut out the eyes, mouth and nostrils. The ears would be the most difficult part of the task. He cut holes into the deepest part of the ears, then snipped two small pieces of hardened leather, gluing them to the inside of the ear near the holes. This created baffles, able to block the wind from directly entering Ben's ear holes. Ben would never again have to worry about the wind driving him to his knees.

To the underside of the mask he glued a layer of cotton padding, and over that a layer of blue silk, cutting away the material from each hole. Then he sewed in small hooks designed to secure the hat to the mask. Nick completed the mask by sewing leather straps and metal hooks to the sides, just behind the ears. These would secure the mask to his friend's head. After rubbing tanner's oil onto the calfskin face, he gave the mask a final inspection, wrapped the item in blue silk, then headed for his bedroom.

Falling onto his bed, he was exhausted, but beaming inside.

Hours later, a sunbeam angled its way to Nicholas' bed and woke him. He never usually slept this late, and still felt fatigued from the long hours on his project. Looking out the window toward the barn, he saw Ben without his scarf, hunched over the large panel, smiling and talking to himself.

Nick jumped into his clothes and hurried to the barn. "How far did you come on the piece, my friend?"

"The center panel is almost done. What do you think?"

Ben tilted the piece up, brushing wood chips away. When it was vertical, Nicholas came around and stared, incredulous.

"Ben, it's fabulous! How did you get the likenesses so well? It's so sensitive, and at the same time has a distinct style."

Ben had carved the scene where Anna was caring for Michael at his bedside. Michael's forehead was wrapped in bandage and his hand reached out to touch Anna's shoulder. Anna was seated next to the bed with both hands on Michael's elbow. The carved hands were exquisite, with a delicate pinky raised slightly as was Anna's manner.

"To be quite honest, I don't know how I did this," said Ben, holding his hands to his earless head as a breeze swept by. "I've never done formal sculpture before the self-portrait. I used to like to just carve figures and designs into the furniture, but now after this, my thinking has changed some. I know now that Anna will love it. All I've thought about these past two days is this sculpture and my family. I stayed up all night carving. It was a relief to escape from thinking about my face."

"The mask is ready," said Nicholas, patting Ben's shoulder. "From this day forward, you'll never have to wear that scarf or worry about the pain the wind brings. I'd like you to come inside and see how it fits."

When they went to the workshop and Ben undid the blue silk wrapping, and, on seeing the mask for the first time, he burst into tears. The subtle expressions in the brow carried through, and the color matched Ben's skin-tone perfectly. Turning the mask to the underside, Nicholas explained the reason for the baffles in the ears. Then he placed it on Ben's face and strapped it from the back. It rested perfectly on Ben's contours. Nick then adjusted the edges around the eyes and mouth with pliers, enabling the mask to rest comfortably everywhere. He finished Ben's new look with the blue, wool hat, looping the hooks in place, making the hat and mask one unit.

Ben went to the polished metal mirror to see his new persona.

"It's remarkable! You're remarkable!" said Ben, adjusting the three-inch brim on his hat. "People will accept me again, won't they? I'll be able to travel. I'll be able to do anything!"

"And travel you will, Ben. After your family comes here and is safe and sound, I will send you on various missions that will have a deep impact on you and the people you must see. But for now, let's finish up with the business at hand. Remember the ointment Anna used to relieve the pain after the fire? Remember how it had a numbing effect on your skin?"

"Yes, I certainly do. If it wasn't for that ointment, I would have gone mad."

"Well, Anna gave me some a while back, and that means now that you have the mask, you can continue to use the ointment until the scar tissue around your ear holes is totally healed."

Nicholas removed the mask and placed two custom-made gauze pads in the ears, coating them with the numbing ointment. After he had strapped the mask onto Ben's face again, the big man groaned a sigh of relief, "OOOoooouuh...today is a very good day for me. You are God's gift to the world, Nicholas Kristo. At this moment, I feel no pain, and with these leather ears now, sounds are no longer distorted and harsh. I cannot find the words to tell you how very thankful I am."

Nicholas' eyes welled as he put his hands on his hips. "And I can't find the words to tell you how good it is to see your spirit return. Always remember, Ben, we all wear masks, and the time comes when we cannot remove them without removing some of our own skin. The mask, given time, comes to be the face itself."

Ben embraced his best friend, but soon returned to the barn to continue his carving, still wearing Nick's creation. Twenty minutes later, Nick joined him with a long rope and two dozen foot-long pieces of wood. He intended to make a rope ladder and return to the ravine on horseback. He'd make another withdrawal from the vein of gold, but this time he would bring enough back to build a mission on the mountain, if God so desired.

As the men worked, they discussed Ben's family. They wondered if Justus had made it to the hideout without incident. And what about Ox? Would he live, as he'd had to endure the twenty-mile journey to Pizal? How would the situation turn out?

CHAPTER 8. CAPTAIN FICCI.

While Nicholas and Ben hoped and planned, Captain Ficci prepared his men to hunt down and arrest those responsible for the gruesome murder of three of his finest soldiers.

Some days before, in the snow-covered, rolling hills, just outside San Marco, Ficci had sat on the palatial balcony of his house. He had sipped port wine as he wondered why his men hadn't returned from the Bellicini Lumber Company. Early that morning, he'd sent a squad of soldiers to investigate. It was evening now and he wanted answers. Looking toward the barren fields in the west, he saw the silhouettes of soldiers riding toward him as the last of the orange sun fell behind the hazy mountains.

Captain Andre Ficci had served in the Italian Police Force for thirty years. His status as the most highly decorated man on the force meant little to those that really knew him. He'd earned most of the honors in fraudulent ways. Standing six-foot-three, his body hard from constant training, he would take on the challenge of any young man, even though he'd just celebrated his fiftieth birthday. His white hair and beard were thick, and the natural waves and constant grooming gave him a dignified, majestic persona. Under that mask of dignity beat the cold heart of the most ruthless, murderous man in all of Europe.

From the balcony of his forty-acre estate, he watched the soldiers draw near, all the time thinking how perfect his retirement would be after he finally had control of the Bellicini Lumber Company and its land. He would then have possession of seven square miles of property.

Gulping down the rest of his wine, Ficci went to meet the soldiers as they rode up to the front door. "Well, what did you find out?" he barked.

"The men are dead, sir," the sergeant replied, yanking the reins of his horse.

"What? All of them?"

"Yes, sir. We've never seen anything like this before, sir. It was horrible. When we entered the office of the lumber company, Bart was lying dead on the floor by a beam in the center of the room. It looked as though he was thrown against the beam with great force. His back was broken and his body was bent backwards in a U shape. Just across from him Will lay with his neck broken and his head twisted all the way around to his back."

"What about Thomas?" demanded the Captain.

"We found Thomas in the storage room on the floor. His tongue was sticking out and his entire chest cavity pushed in. Someone crushed his chest flat!"

"Did you see any of the Bellicini family?"

"No, sir, but we think some of them might have been killed or injured by our men. There was a pool of blood by the main counter in the office, and also blood on the floor by the doorway in the storage room. The blood trailed all the way back to Thomas' body."

The Captain turned his back and whispered, "This will work perfectly for me."

"What did you say, sir?" asked the sergeant.

Captain Ficci turned and stabbed an index finger toward the lumber company. "It must have been Ox Bellicini who did the killings. He's the only one other than Ben who has the strength to do something like that. Ben's not around any more. Go back to the Command Post and find that lazy brother of mine. Tell him to prepare the men for an extensive search. Have them pack enough supplies for a week, and say they'd better come back with that family in irons.

Chapter 9. The Hideout.

$\mathcal{D}$eep in the forest, south of San Marco, Ty and Lund Bellicini had covered their wagon with a thick blanket of pine branches, making it invisible from the road above. The only good thing about the gully they had chosen for their camp was the thick vegetation and small stream flowing under the road above, twenty paces north of the wagon.

The family anxiously awaited a messenger from Ben. Ty was changing Ox's bandage when Lund came into the wagon with a bowl of mutton for his sister, Raven. Ox's leg had swollen even more, and oozed blood. The pellet was still lodged in his knee, and the twins could only hope Ben would soon come through with a plan. When Ox woke, they begged him not to blame himself for their predicament. He had walked in as the soldiers killed his parents in cold blood. What else could he do but attack?

Holding her mother's favorite lace scarf, Raven sat next to Ty and stared into space, lost in her despondency. She still hadn't spoken to anyone, and when Lund set the bowl of mutton on her lap, she just pushed it around with a spoon.

As Lund stepped out of the wagon to prepare another bowl for Ox, a bear cub ran past. "Ty, come quickly, bear!" he shouted.

Glancing back to the stream, Lund spotted the mother bear running directly toward their camp, apparently drawn by the smell of food. Ty put Raven near the front of the wagon and cried, "Grab your musket, Lund. Run out to the pines, I'm right behind. We need to divert the bear from entering the wagon."

The bear chased them, as they ran, first in the same direction, but splitting up not far away from the wagon. The angry mother chose to go after Ty and followed him into the bush. Ty had run into an enclosed area with heavy brush all around and not a single tree to climb. "If you have a clean shot," cried Ty, "fire now or I'm finished!"

Lund took aim and released the flintlock as the bear stood over Ty, who was scrambling under the bush. The pellet hit its shoulder near the chest, inciting even more anger. The bear came down on all fours snarling, dripping saliva, shaking off the gunshot. Then it stood again over Ty, ready to pounce.

An arrow whizzed past Ty, plunging into the bear's throat. The bear roared. Its head jolted back, and it lost its balance, front legs flailing. Another arrow zipped past, sinking under the bear's jaw, through its mouth and into its brain, killing it instantly.

Ty stared, incredulous, as the bear fell to the ground with a thud. Forty paces away, Justus reloaded his crossbow with another bolt. Next to him stood his shiny, Spanish black stallion, hooking its hoof to the ground.

Ty saw him and called out, "That was some shooting, friend. Who are you?"

Justus moved closer, leading his horse. "Is your name Bellicini?"

"Yes, I'm Ty Bellicini, and that's my brother Lund," responded Ty. "How did you get that second arrow off so fast?"

As Justus jumped over the bushes, he extended his hand. "Practice, practice, practice, my friend," he said. "My name is Justus, and I was sent to deliver a letter to you. It's from your brother Ben and his friend, Nicholas Kristo."

Lund stretched out both hands in welcome. "Thank you, my friend! We are twice indebted to you."

The twins perused the letter, then invited Justus back to the campsite for refreshment. At the wagon, Lund poured the ale. The brothers were hesitant to impose on Nicholas, but they had no other options, if Ox was to have a chance.

Justus handed them a sack of gold dust, telling them the safest route to take to the farm. He explained that Nicholas wanted them to use the gold if they were forced to buy their way out of a situation, or on any other need that would get them to the farm safely.

He had mounted his stallion for the ride home when Raven stepped out of the wagon. He froze, and seemed to lose his breath. Raven stared back with no emotion, then quickly turned into the wagon.

Lund and Ty thanked Justus again for all he'd done and bade him farewell.

With the sight of Raven burning in his mind, Justus rode about a hundred paces, then turned his horse and yelled, "Wait; I know the way back much better than you. I could scout the road ahead and make sure there are no surprises, then bring reports back to you. What do you think?"

Ty shouted back, "We're already in your debt, but we do appreciate your offer, and we accept."

Justus smiled and rode ahead, promising to return soon. Being familiar with the area, he could guide them through shortcuts and save them a day or so.

Lund and Ty packed their gear and cleared away the camp area, preparing to travel all night. When dusk set in, they began to move south towards Pizal on a road used mostly by traders. The letter from Ben and Nicholas sternly warned them to avoid the slave traders at all cost, but fate had little regard for warnings, and the Bellicinis would soon find themselves in yet another quandary.

CHAPTER 10. ANOTHER VISIT
TO THE GOLD MINE.

$\mathcal{N}$icholas rode through the forest, once again taken by the beauty of God's creation. Only minutes from the ravine, he rounded a bend and saw the mysterious white dove perched on a branch low to the ground. Next to it sat a wildcat. He was pondering the message in this when he heard a voice saying, "Nicholas, teach the creatures to know your people."

The dove flew off, leaving him to wonder. He'd been thinking of building a mission on the mountain, but what did that have to do with the message? As he neared the ravine, he realized that if he were to build a mission here, people would need to come up the trail without fear of wolves, bears or wild cats. Was this what the messenger meant?

The carnivorous animals needed to be trained somehow to identify the missionaries, allowing them to come and go without fear. If this could be achieved, the top of the mountain would be an ideal site, providing privacy for their work. Nicholas had, from childhood, preferred to give his gifts in secrecy. He preferred the gift to seem to come directly from God. He had seen enough vainglory in giving as a boy when the rich had dropped their coins so ostentatiously into the brass plate at church.

Stopping close to the edge of the ravine, Nicholas dismounted and secured the rope-ladder to a tree, lowering it down near the cave. He then retrieved a three-inch pulley from his travel bag and tied it to a thick tree branch directly over the cave. Putting a long rope through the pulley, he let both ends drop to the cave opening. He climbed down the ladder with two saddlebags over his shoulder, praying the small pulley would hold the weight of the gold once the bags were packed and hauled up.

Once inside the cave, he lit a lamp and worked with a pick ax and hammer for three hours, filling the bags with the purest gold nuggets he'd ever seen. With that much gold, he would not have to return to the cave for many years.

When the bags were full, he tied one end of the pulley-rope to the bags, grabbed the other end and hauled the load to the top. Then he tied his end to a large jutting rock with a slipknot and made his way up the ladder. He guessed there must be two hundred-fifty-pounds of gold as he lifted the bags, one at a time, over the horse's back. After undoing the pulley and collecting his gear, he walked the horse down the mountain trail, knowing the perfect hiding place for the gold.

Three wolves emerged from the bush, next to a bend in the road where Nicholas had seen the dove and wildcat. When they saw him, they dropped to their bellies, panting, with their tongues drooping. He released the reins of his horse and approached them. One of the wolves rolled onto its back, whining. Nick squatted, turning his palms up, showing his empty hands. Then he stood and squatted again, palms up, and then a third time. He would begin teaching the animals the gesture of squatting with palms up meant the humans before them were non-threatening, and were linked to him. He stopped several more times on the way down, repeating the same gesture with other wolves and even a bear.

When he returned to the farm, Ben was sitting on a stool with his back to the barn door, eating an apple as he studied the panel. The mask had a remarkable effect on Ben's appearance, as well as his demeanor. His confidence had returned. Nick even heard him laugh to himself several times the first day he wore it. But there was a certain undeniable dignity about the expression on the mask. It had an uplifting effect on Nick every time Ben looked at him. He thought, *If it affects me that way, it will surely do so with others.*

"Hey Nick!" Ben called out. "Those saddlebags are bulging at the seams. Was it hard to mine the gold alone?"

"Yes indeed, it was a hard day's work. I'm just thankful I brought enough back to last for years. There must be two-hundred-fifty-pounds of the purest gold you'll ever see. I though of the perfect temporary hiding place."

"Great," said Ben. "After I finish the panel, I shall build a false bottom into the window seat by the fireplace. Then, with the floor in place and the gold hidden, we'll pack the seat with winter clothing."

"Splendid," said Nick. "In the meantime, I intend to dig a hole right in the middle of the pigpen. We'll bury the gold there for the time being, but right now I'd love to see what progress you've made on the carving."

"I was just taking a break, thinking about the last panel," Ben said, as he walked to the sculpture, lifting it vertical. "I want to make it really special. The first and second panels are just about finished. I carved in tall, slender pine trees to divide the three scenes. What do you think?"

Nicholas gasped. "The likenesses are stunning. How did you carve that so fast?"

"It's almost as if there is someone else in my mind guiding my hands. I've never done anything remotely as refined as this. Sometimes I can't believe it myself."

The men studied the first scene and recalled Michael's local fame after he survived the wolf attack. Nicholas planned to use that fame to bring Anna and her husband closer together, and also give a boost to Michael's failing business.

As he walked his horse into the barn, Nicholas asked Ben to take a break from the carving and ride into Pizal with a message for his friend Mario Fuso. He also directed Ben to stop at the tailor's to be fitted for special suits he'd wear when riding on the missions Nicholas had planned for him. Ben's eyes grew wide when he saw the watercolor sketches Nicholas had prepared. They were dignified, but simple in design, and would match perfectly with his hats. Both summer and winter outfits were black with a red pin stripe bordering each lapel and the hem of the breeches, and there was a black wool, double-breasted, full-length overcoat for the cold winter months. That also had a red pin stripe around the lapel, and was decorated with gold buttons down the front.

Before Ben left for Pizal, Nicholas handed him two bags of gold dust he'd shaved the night before. "Take this, Ben. Stop at the bank's mortgage office and buy the Pallone estate outright. Tell the banker your family had a thriving business in San Marco and wanted to relocate farther south, closer to you. If any gold is left after signing the deed, open a trust fund for May Rose and deposit what remains for her."

As Ben mounted Nick's white horse, Nicholas reminded him how important it was not to discuss mission affairs and transactions with anyone.

Ben was nervous about being seen in public again, and all along the road to Pizal he wondered about how people might respond to his new appearance. Could his life ever be normal again, or would people be as frightened by the mask as they were by his face?

CHAPTER 11. MAKANDE.

$\mathcal{A}$s the Bellicinis surged forward on the traders' road, Ty rode far behind the wagon to ensure they would not be caught by surprise. Justus returned twice that night to report on his scouting. He also, secretly, hoped to speak to Raven, but she remained inside the wagon.

Lund drove all night until Justus appeared a third time to guide them to a safe camping place. This was reached by a small road leading to a clearing a quarter mile into the forest. When they were settled in, Lund changed Ox's bandage. The wound appeared infected and Ox, though stoically silent, was obviously in agony. His wound troubled him, but he was also troubled in spirit that he could not help his family.

Ty set up camp, then cooked the wild boar he'd shot just after dawn. It was on the spit when Justus bolted into the camp.

"What's wrong, Justus?" cried Lund. "Did you spot a search party?"

"No, no!" Justus drew his horse to a halt. "I heard some commotion on the road about a half-mile south and went for a closer look. It was a wagon carrying seven or eight slaves. I saw a huge man with a very long beard drag a black man into the wooded area just outside their camp, and I think he was taking him to be whipped. Lund, may I borrow a half-pound of the gold dust? I'll pay it back with my own earnings."

"Well, it's a five-pound bag," said Lund. "We won't miss it, I'm sure. What are you planning?"

"Nicholas said to avoid slave traders, but I'm afraid they're going to kill that slave. I want to buy him. Ty, will you ride back there with me? I'll need help, because there was an armed man with Longbeard. Looked dumber than a cockroach pie, so who knows when he might cut loose and shoot?"

"I owe you my life, my friend," said Ty simply. "Let's go."

They poured about eight ounces of gold dust into another sack, and set off. They arrived at the slave camp to find the black man tied to a tree not far from the wagon. His face was pressed against the bark and his arms hugged the tree, tied at the wrists to the other side. His ragged shirt was stuck to his back with blood, and he appeared to be unconscious, but the slave master continued the whipping.

Ty raised his flintlock and fired into the air to announce their arrival, and the slave master turned angrily. "What...what's this all about? And who might you be? Why did you fire your weapon?"

Justus raised the loaded crossbow to his hip. "If you keep beating that slave, you'll kill him."

"So? I own the worthless slug."

"What did he do to deserve such punishment?" asked Ty as he reloaded.

"I bought him on my way through San Marco. The Captain said..."

Justus broke in. "What Captain is this?"

"Captain Ficci. He said this slave was an exceptional specimen. He said he could cook and manage an estate unlike any of the others, but when he gets to me he's a bump on a stump. He tried to run away twice now, and he can learn his lesson or die. It's all the same to me."

"This Captain Ficci, was his hair and beard white?" asked Justus, barely restraining his anger.

"Yes, do you know him?" asked the slave master.

"You could say so, in a strange sorta' way. What will it cost to take that slave off your hands?"

"A woodsman like yourself surely could not afford him. Ficci got three times what he paid for him, and that's what I intend to get...three times. You could start by offering that beautiful white horse your friend is riding."

"The horse is not for sale," Ty said shortly.

Justus held up the sack of gold. "I'll give you eight ounces of gold dust if you cut him down right now and give him to me."

The slave master's eyes widened with greed, and he signaled to his partner. The man reached for a pistol.

Before he could lift it, Justus had his crossbow ready to fire. "Do not try anything foolish, gentlemen. If I were not a fair and just man, you and your partner there would be dead already."

The slave master's partner lunged for the weapon, and Justus fired. The bolt hit and split the gun-handle, knocking it to the ground. Ty drew his own pistol and pointed it at the slave master's head.

"We don't want trouble. We'll just buy the slave and move on," Justus said coolly.

"Cut him down," cried the slave master to his partner.

Justus tossed the sack to the angry man, then reloaded his crossbow. Ty dismounted, and ran to help the slave. As the obese partner cut him loose, the slave moaned. He appeared half-conscious as Ty caught him under the arm and helped him onto the horse. They left as swiftly as they had come.

Only minutes later they were in their camp. When Lund saw the slave, he climbed into the wagon and laid several blankets on top of supply crates, providing a place for the man to lie. Ox was so huge he occupied most of the space on the floor of the wagon.

Ox moaned, "Wha...what is it, brother? What has happened?"

"Not to worry, Ox. Justus and Ty have just saved a slave. He'll be your company until we arrive at the farm."

After they'd placed the man next to Ox, Raven entered the wagon carrying a small bowl of water, bandages and salve. She silently tended the man's welts, waving off Justus when he would have helped.

Justus left the wagon smarting from the rejection, but he returned at sunset just before they were ready to start their second night's journey. Ox was asleep when Justus entered the wagon and seated himself near the slave's feet.

"What is your name, friend?" he asked.

"My name...uhh...from homeland?" the black man asked, and moaned softly.

"Yes, the name you were born with."

"Makande, they call me Makande. It mean Holy Dance. Thank you for saving me."

"How could I not do it? I know what it's like to be tortured. How long were you with Captain Ficci, Makande?"

"One year maybe. They teach me many things."

"How did he treat his slaves?" asked Justus.

Makande sat up. He was obviously still in pain, but was anxious to cooperate with Justus. "When he have guests we safe, but when they leave, he cruel," he said. "The women he take for his pleasure. Every month a slave is missing. He say they run away, but we all know truth. One reason he sold me, I see him kill important man who won't accept his deal. He stab man in throat. He force two slaves to bury body. He no trust me now, he sell me. Do you know Captain Ficci?"

"Let's say I have a score to settle with him," Justus said.

At this point, Raven brought a plate of food for Makande, shooing Justus away so the slave could eat in peace. Justus backed out of the wagon with a smile, but Raven refused to look at him. Rather piqued, Justus asked Ty if he had somehow offended the girl. The explanation for her reserve left him reeling, but no less eager to gain her attention.

Soon after, the wagon was on the move again. They were only hours away from Nicholas's farm, and the Bellicini family began to hope and believe Ox might survive. They knew they could not stay with Nicholas forever, but at least they might have some time before Captain Ficci located them and sent them back on the run.

Chapter 12. The Chill under Ben's Mask.

etermined to put an end to the logging family for good, Captain Ficci sent his brother Manuel to lead the search for the Bellicinis. Before the squad left the Command Post, the Captain instructed his brother privately. "The Bellicini brothers must be dead before you return." He promised fifty gold coins to Manuel if he was successful, and insisted Raven be taken alive, as he had special plans for her. Captain Ficci warned his brother that the girl was not to be violated by anyone, including him.

The squad rode out early morning, south, on a tip they received that a wagon and several riders had been spotted leaving a valley on the outskirts of San Marco. When they found the Bellicini campsite that afternoon, it was deserted. Sergeant Ficci was relentless, thinking of the fifty gold florin reward, and ordered his men to ride south through the night toward Pizal.

The odor of fresh baked bread wafted to Ben and his growling stomach as he approached the outskirts of Pizal. His hands were sweaty and his nerves unsettled as he made his way to Anna's house across from the church. Tying his horse to the front gate, he glanced up over the door to the area where he would soon install the maple carving, realizing all the possibilities of Nicholas's plan.

Anna appeared at the door, her eyes wide, wearing a warm smile. "Ben! You look amazing! That handsome mask, and hat, where did you get them?"

"Nicholas made it with the help of a self portrait I carved in oak," said Ben, "but don't mention that I told you. You know how Nick is about his gifts. Do you really think it looks good, Anna?"

Tip-toeing to touch his mask and hat, Anna giggled with delight. "It's wonderful, Ben. I recognized you at once. And as I see it now, up close, the brow causes the face to look... compassionate but also regal or dignified, yes, dignified. And with the hat and stylish brim, you are a pleasure to behold. The mask gives you an air of mystery too. I wouldn't be surprised if the ladies start to wonder about you."

"Nicholas thought of everything. He put baffles and pads in the ears. The baffles protect me against the painful wind and the pads have your famous ointment on them, keeping me pain-free until my skin is totally healed."

Anna hooked her arm into Ben's and led him to the kitchen. "Nicholas is special, isn't he? Years ago, when my first husband broke his leg falling off a ladder, Nicholas made a pair of crutches for him and left them secretly on the porch early one Sunday morning. My daughter saw him from her bedroom window, and told me, but Nick never mentioned it. We always pretended we didn't know who had left the crutches, and that seemed to make him happy.

"But, Ben, though I'm so pleased to see you, what brings you to the Pizal?"

"I need to prepare a place for my family to stay when they arrive. Does anyone know they're coming?"

"As far as I know, no one knows except me. Nicholas told me to keep it hush. When the time comes, I will tend to Ox."

Reaching for Anna's hand, Ben kissed it. "I owe you my life, Anna, but I can't stay right now. I have many errands to run before my family arrives."

Anna led him to the door, fixing his hair on the side of the mask. "Come to dinner tonight, Ben. Michael will be working late again. We'll catch up."

"I'll be there if I can, Anna, and I'll leave my horse here for now."

As Ben walked down the street toward the tailor shop, all the people he knew recognized him. They waved and smiled, pointing to the mask in pleased surprise. People he didn't know greeted him politely as they passed, saying, "Good morning, sir," and "Excuse me, kind sir."

Ben was delighted and relieved. In one day his life had turned around and people welcomed him back as if he'd never been disfigured.

After being fitted and leaving the sketches and instructions with the tailor, Ben stopped at the bank, as Nicholas had directed. While he waited for the bank manager at the scales, the room became silent. When he turned, all eyes were on him. Ben tipped his hat as they smiled saying, "Hello, sir," and "Good day, kind sir." He graciously replied in kind.

The bank clerk, a balding, squinty-eyed little man, finally stepped up to him. "Can I help you, sir?"

Ben instructed him regarding his family's wishes to relocate and buy the Pallone estate outright. Reaching into his travel bag, he placed two sacks of gold onto the scales at the counter. The moment the clerk placed the counterweight on the opposite scale, a chill came up under Ben's mask. And then another chill shot down his spine. The clerk's eyes widened as he asked, "I didn't know there was a mining stream in this area. Did your family live far from here?"

The chill under Ben's mask grew intense as he scrambled for a response. "They lived in a town up north. I'm not at liberty to discuss my family or their plans to settle in Pizal. And I would appreciate if you would keep what we've discussed today confidential, as we are a private family."

When Ben had the Pallone deed in his hand, and had secured a trust fund for May Rose, he made for the door. The chill under his mask ceased as soon as he stepped outside. At that moment, he knew the bank manager would somehow bring trouble to his family. The minute he returned to the cabin, he would discuss the strange phenomenon with Nicholas.

Ben walked a few doors down, to Mario Fuso's Silver Shop. The front door was boarded up and a donkey stood out front, packed to the hilt with all of Mario's belongings. A neighbor leaning out the window said she heard Mario was at the Bear Mountain Inn, and he'd already drunk no small amount of ale.

Hurrying to the Inn, Ben entered and caught sight of Mario sitting at a table, talking to a maid, pointing to his stumped legs. Everyone grew silent when they noticed a giant man in a mask filling the doorframe. Mario turned to see, then shouted, "Ben, is that you? Of course it's you! Will you look at that mask; it looks just like you...what a piece of work that is! I need a great favor from you, my old friend. I want you to shoot me dead!"

"How long have you been drinking?" Ben said, moving closer.

Spilling ale onto his jacket, Mario held out his jug. "Long enough to know my life is over. Our esteemed new Mayor has managed to make all of Pizal think he is a savior from heaven, and at the same time take everything my family has worked for since I was born...with this pathetic body."

"Did he evict you from your shop?"

"Better than that. He now *owns* my shop and has plans to change it to a business of his own."

Ben's heart ached for Mario. His dear friend was now not only without legs, but also without a home.

With a sarcastic twist, Mario asked, "Will you carry me just outside the door, Ben? I'll finish this ale and use the jug to start my new job...begging for coins."

With that, Mario dropped the jug, leaned over and passed out.

Born with legs that ended just above the knees, Mario had to be carried everywhere, which was why he spent so much of his life in the silver shop his parents bought when they married. Mario had become an expert silversmith, making fine commissioned pieces and jewelry. He'd sit in the workshop for days designing new silverware, working on new styles of architecture. His favorite pastime was designing new types of buildings, but he had not yet received a commission for this kind of work.

Ben picked up Mario under one arm and walked out the door. Hurrying back to the silver shop, he untied the donkey and led it to Anna's house. Anna stood out front with her hands on her hips and dishtowel over her shoulder. "Is Mario drunk again, Ben?"

"That's an understatement, Anna. The bank seized his property. I'm taking him to Nicholas' farm. There's plenty of room for him to stay for a while. Sorry about dinner, but we'll eat together when my family arrives."

After tying the donkey in tow, Ben rode back to the farm. He wondered about the letter Nicholas had written to Mario. He knew Nick had a master plan for the mission, and only hoped Mario could somehow be included.

CHAPTER 13. HANNAH.

Nicholas spent the entire spring-like day on the mountain, searching for the perfect location to build his Mission. As he thought more about it, he reasoned that one or two buildings would not be enough for what he had in mind. He would need a small community with a special purpose, keeping the very existence of it a secret. His commission from God was to bring hope to the world through giving. Just as the Savior *gave* His life as a *gift* to the world, bringing a message of hope, Nicholas would bring his message of hope through Godly and creative gifts. These would be gifts designed to have a deep impact on people, and since hope was his theme, he would call the community Hope Mission.

All the way up the mountain trail, Nick encountered an unusual number of animals. Perhaps there were so many because spring was approaching, but it presented him with the opportunity to teach more of the wildlife to recognize people connected with him. Persisting with the same gesture; squatting, with palms up, he prayed that his training might be ordained of God because of his unusual needs.

The mountain itself was not high; a three-hour ride to the top. There was only one main trail, but lots of little paths branching off to streams and ponds. Nicholas had never been to the top, and to his delight, when he arrived, he found a beautiful lake next to a huge open field about half the size of Pizal.

He rode around the water to the end of the field and discovered a sheer drop, almost straight down, the length of a cathedral, angling out half way to the bottom. The view from the field was breathtaking. From where he stood, Pizal and all the roads to San Marco were in plain sight. Looking to the north, gray clouds lay low on the mountains around Rome. The countryside was inspiring, with its lush green landscape and rolling hills, dotted with villages and church steeples on the north, south and west. This, decided Nicholas, was the place to build Hope Mission.

As he reached in his travel bag for a pad to sketch the layout of the land, he noticed a huge black bear coming toward him from the lake. The bear stopped twenty paces away and sank to its belly. Then, lifting its head in a turning motion, it groaned softly. Nick squatted to the ground, palms up, in his gesture of goodwill and friendship. A white dove flew down onto the back of the giant bear. Gladly, Nicholas perceived this as a sign from Heaven that his teaching would be effective.

Nick approached the bear, and gave it a vigorous rub on the neck as the dove flew onto his shoulder. The bear reacted as a dog might have done, stretching and groaning in contentment at the caress. Afterward, Nick sketched the layout of the field and lake, then hurried down the mountain wanting to be home before sunset.

All the way down, he considered different ways to grind the large gold nuggets into dust. He remembered their foot-pedaling tool sharpener and its very coarse grinding wheel. His father had put the coarse wheel aside years ago because there was never a need for it. Now Nick decided he would replace the fine wheel with the coarse one and grind the nuggets into tiny chunks. This process would bring ease and speed to the huge task ahead.

Arriving at the base of the mountain, Nicholas had only a short ride to his cabin. He wanted to try out the grinding wheel before Ben returned from the village. At the fork in the main road, he saw a nun sitting on a boulder where the road divided. She wore a brown, peasant work dress and a habit to indicate her order, and was accompanied only by an over-packed mule. She rose to greet him, and Nick saw she stood only as tall as the mule's back. Her light blue eyes sparkled in a constant smile, and she spoke in soft tones. "Good day, sir. Is this the road to Pinzolo?"

"Yes, Sister, it is. Where exactly do you want to go? Maybe I can help," Nicholas answered, dismounting.

"There is a large valley two leagues north of the Pinzolo, not far from the city dump. I've been there many times, but I tried a different road this time and I wasn't quite sure of my direction reaching this crossroad. Thank you for your offer, but I'm sure I'll find it just fine now. What is your name?"

"I'm Nicholas Kristo. And yours?"

"I am Hannah. Do you live far from here?"

"Only a short ride. I own a farm. Would you like to rest at my home for a while?"

"Thank you, but I must get to the colony early tomorrow."

"Colony?" asked Nicholas.

"It's a leper colony, Nicholas. Three times a year I make the trip to bring supplies, which are donated by certain families who have relatives living there. Mother Gabriela always tells me to leave the supplies before they come, fearing I'll become infected. I can never obey her. I bring it right to them, and then remain in the caves and help for several days. Heaven knows, I would never tell Mother Gabriela that."

"You don't fear the disease?"

"Not any more. I've been helping them a long time and never even had so much as a sore. It is an awful disease. There must be at least forty adults living there, but I only know of three children. Many of the adults are missing limbs and have oozing sores. They are in great agony and shame. When I stay with them, I go to the children first. None of them has lost any limbs yet, but the disease will also catch up to them too eventually. I pray constantly for them."

"I know a man who cares for such people," Nicholas said. "He is very wealthy and I know he would consider some way to help if he heard about the colony. I will send a message to him and make a case for the lepers."

"That's so very kind of you. What is this man's name, so we can thank him when the time comes?"

"The man wishes to remain anonymous in his gifts, but I will relay your thanks if he decides to help in some way. You will know the wealthy man's messenger by the mask he wears on all such missions."

Sister Hannah smiled. "The work of an unknown good man is like a vein of water flowing hidden underground, secretly making the ground greener." She told him more about the colony and the children, and Nicholas was touched by the love and courage of this tiny woman with a giant heart. He conducted her to a nearby stream, where they talked until dusk, and then made their farewells.

As he mounted his horse and rode away, Nicholas resolved that helping the leper colony would be Ben's first official mission. As soon as his family settled safely, Ben would go to Pinzolo.

Nick cantered all the way home, where he saw to his horse before hurrying to the barn to adapt the grinder with the coarse wheel. He dug up more than half the gold buried in the pigpen, washed it clean, and then returned to the barn to begin the grinding.

Chapter 14. Gold Dust Flying Everywhere.

As the Royal Guard soldiers rode along the traders' route at dusk, Sergeant Ficci made no effort to hide his frustration at their failure to locate the Bellicinis. The trail had gone quite cold when they came upon a slave master hauling seven slaves in a wagon. The soldiers surrounded the wagon, forcing it to stop.

"I'm Sergeant Manuel Ficci. We're Royal Guard from San Marco in search of a fugitive family named Bellicini. They are wanted for the murder of three soldiers. Have you seen a wagon traveling this road with three large men and a young woman with black hair?"

"Are you related to Captain Andrea Ficci?" asked the slave master.

"Yes, he's my brother. Now, answer the question. Have you seen a wagon this day?"

"No wagon has passed this way for the past two days."

"Did you see any riders at all?"

"Yes, we did," said the slave master, scratching his matted hair. "Two riders stopped at our camp long enough to buy one of my slaves. I haven't had a deal that sweet in a long time. One of the men had a crossbow. He was the one with the gold dust..."

"Gold dust?"

"He paid for the slave with eight ounces of gold. Funny thing, I bought that slave from your brother last time I was in San Marco. Glad to get rid of him though—worthless animal."

"Was his name Makande?"

"I don't know. I'm just glad he's sold. I sure wish I could have made that big white horse part of the deal."

"What white horse?"

"The man next to the man with the crossbow was riding a beautiful white horse. I could've turned a pretty profit with that one."

"Did the horse have a black spot on its chest?"

"How'd you know?" said the slaver suspiciously.

The Sergeant turned to the others, saying, "That's Ty Bellicini's horse." Then turning back to the slave master, he asked, "In which direction did they ride?"

"North, up this road."

Sergeant Ficci thought it didn't make any sense for the fugitives to travel back toward San Marco. He knew the traders' road south would leave them close to Pizal, and he'd heard Ben Bellicini lived near there. The family had to be headed for either Pinzolo or Pizal. With the trail hot again, Ficci turned the soldiers south and rode toward Pizal.

It was dark and had just begun to rain by the time Ben arrived at Nicholas' cabin. Mario was still passed out as Ben lifted him off his horse and carried him inside to the guest bedroom. After throwing a blanket over him, Ben returned to the horse and donkey, and led them to the barn. Inside, Nicholas was seated at a spinning grinding wheel, holding a giant gold nugget to it. Tiny chunks flew everywhere, sparkling their way out onto the ground. Ben laughed aloud, thinking Nicholas must have been at it for hours, because the gold dust was piled up under the wheel all the way up to his ankle.

"This is a sight to see, Nick! I've never see so much gold in my entire life!"

Nicholas stood up, laughing, shaking gold dust from his pants and shoes. "He he ho...I guess this *is* a sight to see. There must be a hundred pounds of it on the floor. I haven't heard you laugh like that in a long time, Ben. We'll need to put the gold into sacks, but for now we'll use hosiery."

"Hosiery?"

"Yes. I went through the house and gathered up all the hosiery I could find."

"Last night I built the false bottom in the window seat," Ben said.

"Good. But what happened in Pizal today? How did people react to the mask?"

"It was incredible. I stopped to say hello to Anna and she thought it was wonderful. Then on the streets, people I didn't know were overly friendly, saying, 'Good day, sir,' and, 'How do you do, sir.' Everywhere I went the reaction was the same. People stopped what they were doing and stared, but not like they used to. They were so very respectful toward me. I'm rather stunned by it all."

"Bravo, Ben!" Nicholas said. "I can't tell you how happy I am for you. Did you make it to the bank?"

"I stopped at the tailor first. The suits will be ready in two days. Then, when I went to the bank, a very strange thing happened. When I lay the gold on the scales to be weighed, and glanced up at the clerk, a very cold chill came up under my mask. The chill went right down my spine and stayed that way until I stepped outside onto the street. I had a distinct feeling the clerk would hurt my family somehow when they arrive."

"Did he ask about the gold?" asked Nick, concerned.

"Yes, indeed, but I was evasive. I asked him to keep the transaction confidential. He agreed, but the chill under the mask remained. Then I opened a trust fund for May Rose and left."

Nicholas sat down at the grinding wheel, and rubbed the back of his neck. "You see what I mean about the gold, Ben? We can never be too careful about how we conceal the source. You did well, though. As for the mask, it's the first gift given from the Mission, so I wouldn't be surprised if what you experienced was help from above. I was told we'd have divine help, and to have faith. I've chosen you to be a representative of Hope Mission, and I'm sure you'll receive help from above from time to time. Having people greet you with trust and respect is part of that help."

"Hope Mission? We're Hope Mission?" asked Ben. He had known Nicholas was planning some major undertaking, but he had not asked for details until now.

Nick smiled. "Yes. I rode to the top of the mountain today and found the perfect place to build a mission community. It will be the secret workplace for all our projects. Our theme is 'hope', and so we'll simply call it Hope Mission."

"If it is to remain a secret, how will people know the gifts are ordained of Heaven?" Ben squatted and scooped some gold in his hand, letting it slip through his fingers.

"Good question. Once a gift is set in motion, it will be out of our hands. That's where faith comes in. Heaven is watching with a keen interest and you can rest assured that the forces from above will be working behind the scenes. It's at that point you must exercise faith. Once the gift is given, we must not force its success. We must observe how God works through it. That will be our greatest lesson, our greatest reward. There are many different missions ordained of God that are active in the world today. Ours will somehow work in concert with them." Nicholas stood and stretched. "Did you give my message to Mario Fuso?"

"No." Ben explained Mario's drunkenness and homelessness, and that Mario was now sleeping in Nick's guest bedroom.

"Excellent," said Nicholas. "I will talk to him in the morning. Now, shall we conceal this gold?"

Together, the friends weighed gold dust and poured it into hosiery, which they concealed in the false bottom Ben had installed under the window seat. After this, they went to bed, mindful of the fact that Ben's family could arrive at any time now.

At morning's first light, Justus rode up to the cabin, dismounted and walked around to Nicholas' bedroom window. Tapping on the shutter, he called, "Nicholas, Nick, it's me, Justus."

Nicholas came to the window, opened it, and rubbed his eyes. "Justus... are they here? How's Ox? Is everyone all right?"

Justus explained. "They're about two miles behind. Ox is in bad shape; his leg is turning black. Everyone else is fine except Raven. She hasn't spoken to anyone in days. Oh, and we have an extra guest with us. Don't be angry, but I bought a slave with some of the gold."

Nicholas smiled. "You bought a slave? I can't wait to find out why."

"I can't explain right now, it has to do with justice. I'll pay you back, I promise. His name is Makande, and he was on a slave wagon en route to be sold somewhere... that's if he survived! The slave master would have whipped him to death if we hadn't come along, and buying him was the only thing I could think of. I plan to set him free. I know our goal was to just bring the Bellicinis but—"

"Don't worry about that now, son. Fulfilling a goal is fine if you don't let it deprive you of interesting detours. I need you to work with me a while. What say you?"

"What would I do?"

Nick grinned, knowing what he had in mind for Justus perfectly suited his adventurous nature. "It's a dangerous job. You would need to travel, and to be responsible for large sums of money. Oh, and you would be sworn to secrecy."

"Look no further, Nick. I am the man for the job. When do I start?"

"Right now. Saddle an extra horse and ride into Pizal. Don't let anyone know about Ben's family. Go to Anna's and tell her the Bellicinis have arrived. She is prepared, and will come back with you. Try to ease out of the village without being noticed. Got that?"

Justus nodded.

"Good. After you return, ride to the Pallone farm. You will need to keep constant watch on the roads leading from here to there. A search party may come to Pizal and we need to be ready. Whatever you do, Justus, do not confront the soldiers if they come. You must use your wits and not your crossbow for the time being. Let's try to stay one step ahead of them."

"How can we move Ben's family into the Pallone farm? It doesn't belong to us."

"Don't worry, Justus, we took care of that yesterday."

"Can you use another scout, Nick?" Justus asked. "My friend Rubin is a lot like me. He would just love this job, and you can trust him as you do me."

"By all means, bring him. We'll need all the help we can to keep everyone safe. Now off with you."

Chapter 15. The Bellicinis Arrive.

he moment Justus began his ride to Pizal to fetch Anna, Nicholas thought, *Better wake Ben, his family will be here any minute.*

They prepared the kitchen table with hard-boiled eggs, biscuits, cheese, dried fruit and nuts and cider.

When the wagon arrived, Ty and Lund rushed to Ben, embracing him, weeping for the loss of their parents, and the dire times they were facing. Touching Ben's mask at the same time, the twins were amazed at how much it resembled him.

After bringing Ox and Makande into the cabin, and settling them in rooms, Ben introduced Nicholas to his brothers, and they thanked him for his life-saving hospitality. Then Ben led everyone back to Ox's bed to see his injury. Ox was delirious, moaning and sweating in a half-conscious state of agony. When Ben pulled the bandage back, they all sighed, recognizing gangrene.

"Anna will be here within the hour," said Ben. "Let's hope she can do something to relieve his suffering. Hey, where is my beautiful sister, Raven?"

Ty answered, "She's still in some sort of shock, Ben. She won't leave the wagon."

"It's all right," said Nick, "she's been through a lot. After you've had something to eat, Ben will take you to the Pallone farm. You'll be able to rest there, and Raven will adjust in her own time."

After they'd eaten, Ben grabbed his maple carving and tools, and drove them in their wagon to the Pallone farm, only a mile away. What they all needed most was a good long rest in a warm cabin, and Ben would see to that.

Not more than an hour later, Justus, Rubin and Anna rode onto Nick's farm. Justus and Rubin barely stopped as Anna dismounted and hurried into the cabin. The two young men didn't want to waste a second securing the main road north and south of the Pallone farm.

Anna entered the cabin with a large bag filled with everything from bandages to surgical instruments to baking soda. After hugging Nick, she looked around the room. "Where's Ox?"

"We have a full house today, Anna," Nicholas said. "Ox is in my room, Mario Fuso is in the guest bedroom, and Makande, a slave Justus bought coming here, is in the room Ben was staying in. Ox is in bad shape, Anna, but I have faith in your healing hands. And there will be a wonderful surprise for you in a few days."

"You mean the panel you said Ben was carving for Michael and me?"

"Yes, he couldn't stop working on it for days. More than anything, he wants to show his thanks for your care and kindness."

"Did you see the carving?" asked Anna.

"Yes, but I won't tell you any more. You must see it yourself."

"You've got me all excited about it already. But let me get to work now—show me to Ox, and please bring some boiled water in a basin."

Ox was groaning and half-conscious, with sweat drenching his shirt, when Anna entered the room. She removed all the bandages and cut off the pants leg at the thigh. Twenty minutes later, after cleaning his leg and seeing the gangrene, she told Ox she had to remove his leg from the knee down or he would die.

Ox cried out and rolled over in bed, smashing his enormous arm on the nightstand, cracking its top panel.

Reaching into her bag, Anna pulled out a jar, explaining to Nick the special powder was given to her recently by a Chinese doctor. It was an extract from the poppy flower, able to relieve pain. She mixed a tablespoon into hot chicken broth and spoon-fed Ox. Then she sprinkled some directly on the wound. Not long after, Ox passed out and Anna removed his leg at the knee with a saw she borrowed from Nicholas.

After Anna had packed the stump with bandages, and seen the bleeding slow, she went to Makande's room. She removed his old bandages, and cleaned his wounds, putting her famous numbing ointment on the whip stripes.

Mario was still sleeping when Nicholas entered his room with a breakfast tray. "Mr. Mario Fuso, it's time to wake up to your new life!"

Groaning and holding his head, Mario rolled to the wall and sat up. "Where am I? What's going on?"

"Ben brought you here to my place after you told him to shoot you," said Nicholas with a cheerful lack of sympathy. "Do you remember?"

"I don't want to remember," said Mario, "but I do now. Yes, it's a new life all right, a life of begging in the streets. That's probably why I was born with these stumps for legs—it was my destiny to beg."

"Ben told me all about what the new mayor did to you, but things will be better now. Don't worry about your things. Ben put the donkey in the barn last night. And if you're hungry, here are fresh biscuits, eggs and cheese," said Nick, placing the tray on the dresser.

"Thank you, Nicholas. You know I've lost everything, and I don't know what I want more—to really hurt the mayor or just to kill myself. I'm so torn up inside I want to die. The funny thing is, I can't even kill myself without someone's help. I'm a joke—a pathetic joke, so how can you say things will be better?"

Taking the food to the bed, Nicholas sat down, resting his hand on Mario's shoulder. "One of the reasons Ben went to Pizal yesterday was to give you a message from me. I want to offer you a job designing a community of buildings on the mountain. I saw some of your designs sitting around your shop before the fire and I was very impressed. Do you think you might be interested?"

"You're just trying to cheer me up, right, Nick? Or do you really want plans drawn up?"

"I really do, Mario," smiled Nicholas. "But before I go on, you must vow an oath of secrecy to me and to God for what I'm about to tell you. The lives of many good people will depend on the strength of your vow."

"A vow is not necessary if you need me to keep something hidden. I would go to my grave to keep from betraying either you or Ben. But if you insist, I will give my oath."

"I think you've just made that vow from your heart, and I believe you, Mario."

Nicholas explained everything, from the messenger dove to the entire concept of Hope Mission. The only thing he left out was the gold. Only Ben, Justus, and he would ever know about the gold.

Astonished, Mario said, "It's an amazing story, and somehow I believe you, but who has the money to build this mission? I know for sure you're not a wealthy man. Do you have a sponsor?"

"I can't tell you everything, but I will say you can trust God to provide the resources as we need them. In the meantime, the mission will pay you an architect's wage for as long as the construction lasts. And one more thing, Mario; no one must learn of anything we do on the mountain. No one will ever see the buildings you design either, except the people who live and work there."

"That's all right with me, as long as I eventually earn enough money to buy back my Silver Shop. My parents died in that fire, but our shop was very special to them, and it held all the memories of us working and creating beautiful things together as a family."

"We'll find a way to do that too, Mario," said Nicholas. "In the meantime, we'll set you up in this room. I'll bring in all of your drafting supplies and tools and we'll make this your workplace. As soon as Makande recovers from his wounds, I'll ask him to look after you and Ox when Anna leaves."

Mario blinked. "This sounds wonderful, but who in the world is Makande?"

Chapter 16. Makande Meets Nicholas.

$\mathcal{S}$pring was fast approaching as the morning sun warmed the budding trees. The crisp mountain air filled the cabin as Nicholas went through the house opening windows.

After setting up Mario Fuso with materials he needed to begin drawing plans for the mission buildings, Nicholas searched the house for Makande, who was not in his room. Stepping outside, he found the black man squatting down by the water trough, scrubbing Ox's bloody dressing. Makande glanced up, smiled and stood, wringing out the bandages. From out of nowhere, Nicholas watched his friendly white dove swoop down and land on Makande's shoulder.

Makande stood as tall as Nick, and, despite his recent mistreatment, he had a muscular frame. He had no facial hair, and near blue-black skin, and his perfect white teeth seemed to glow when he smiled. His manner was humble, but at the sight of the dove he laughed aloud, touching the bird's breast with a gentle index finger. "This bird so white, you think? It look like it shine next to my black skin."

Nicholas smiled, unsurprised. "Lately that dove has become my best friend, and now it's your friend too."

The voice of the messenger spoke in his mind. "This man has no guile."

"Did you hear that?" asked Nick.

"Hear what?" Makande sounded puzzled.

Nick extended his hand in greeting. "Oh, nothing. Welcome to my home. My name is Nicholas Kristo."

"In my country they call me Makande. It mean Holy Dance."

"Why did your family choose that name?"

"My father changed name to Makande when I seven. My mother sick and sleep too many days. She not get up. I love her so much, one day I lay my head on her hand as she sleep and ask Love God to bring her back. I told Love God I would not eat 'til she come back. After three days she wake. I knew Love God heal her. I so happy I get up from her side and dance round bed. My father comes in and sees my mother awake, and me dancing round bed. He change my name to Holy Dance that day."

"Why did you pray to Love God and not some other god?"

"Love is most powerful thing, so I pray to Love God."

"Did Justus mention that he talked to me and intends to set you free?"

Makande grimaced. "No. Why he wants to see me die?"

"He wants to set you free so you can live, not die," said Nicholas, puzzled.

"In this country, a man with black skin like me, and whip scars like me, he is run-away slave. I will end up dead, sure. Please say not to set me free. I can cook and do many things. Please, Mr. Nicholas, ask if I can stay slave."

"If you had the chance, would you go back to your homeland and be free?"

"All of my village and my family killed or taken as slaves. I only know this life now."

"How would you like to work with me as a free man?"

"I afraid be free. What it be like?"

"You would have your own living quarters. You would be able to come and go as you please. And as your employer and friend I would protect you from being seen as a slave or from ever being treated harshly again."

"That sound good to Makande. I stay with you. I work hard."

Having remembered the messenger saying he had no guile, and listening to Makande's story, Nicholas knew the former slave would play a key role as plans for Hope Mission moved forward.

Anna appeared outside with her carpetbag and told Nick she'd done all she could for Ox, and needed to return to her family. After thanking her, Nick promised to visit soon with Ben and her special gift. Smiling, she kissed him on the cheek and before she mounted her horse, Makande bowed before her. "Thank you, Miss Anna. My back like new again."

A tear welled in Anna's eye as she mounted her horse and rode away.

Nicholas led Makande inside, and gave him two shirts, a pair of breeches, a pair of old shoes and a jacket. Makande never ceased smiling as Nicholas explained how he was to care for Ox and Mario while they were his guests. Wasting no time, the former slave went into the kitchen, familiarized himself with the cookware and foodstuffs, and began to prepare a meal.

The Pallone house still had all the comforts of home when Ben, Ty and Lund entered, assessing what provisions they might need. They found dried foods, firewood, and everything else they needed to settle down after their ordeal in San Marco.

Raven came in and quietly began searching the kitchen for cookware and food. When her brothers saw her moving about, they were encouraged she might finally be coming out of her despondency.

After helping unload the wagon, Ben set up a work area outside and began to carve. Lund and Ty came out and had their first look at the panel. They couldn't get over Ben's newfound skills as a sculptor. As they watched him carve, they discussed the effect losing his leg would have on Ox. Ox was a proud and quiet man, and the thought of existing with only one leg would be unbearable for him.

As fate would have it, the Bellicini family would have some time to adjust to their new home. Sergeant Ficci was forced to return to the Command Post in San Marco after two of his men fell violently ill with food poisoning. The Sergeant seized a wagon from a nearby farmer, laid his men in the rear and traveled back to San Marco. On the next search, he would ride directly to Pizal and begin an investigation. Ficci thought, *Pizal will never be the same when I'm through.*

CHAPTER 17. ONE THOUGHTFULLY PLANNED GIFT.

itting on his porch, admiring the way the setting sun peeked through purple and pink clouds on the western mountains, Nicholas made a decision about converting the gold to coin. He went into the cabin and removed ten sacks of gold dust from the hiding place, then stowed these in his saddlebags.

Whistling on his way to the chicken coop, he made a withdrawal, and returned to the cabin. He walked into the kitchen with the squawking chicken and handed it to Makande, asking if he'd mind cooking dinner for everyone. Makande smiled and nodded, taking the bird behind the house.

With his saddlebags filled with gold, Nicholas mounted his horse and cantered out toward the Pallone farm to see Justus. Halfway there, he found him sitting on boulder at the side of the road making new bolts for his crossbow.

"Hey, Nick, how's Ox holding up?" Justus said.

Nicholas dismounted and joined him. "Anna had to take his leg off at the knee. He was still sleeping when I left. We'll see how he reacts when he wakes in the morning. Justus, I need you to go on your first assignment. It will only take two days."

"What about keeping watch here?"

"Ask Rubin to keep watch while you're gone."

"What's the assignment? Where do I go?"

"I have sixty pounds of gold dust in my saddlebags. Tomorrow morning I need you to take it to the bank in Pinzolo and exchange the raw gold for coins. Carrying a fortune like that will be very dangerous, so think about a strategy that will bring you back safely."

Justus whistled aloud. "Sixty pounds of gold? How did you get it?"

"I can't tell you everything now, Justus, but it was come by honestly, and without harm to anyone."

"Well, of course!" said the young man, surprised.

Nick grinned at this evidence of trust. "Then let's just say God provided the gold for us to build a Mission on Bear Mountain. You must vow an oath of secrecy about everything concerning the gold and the mission, son. No one must ever know the location of the Mission or that the gold even exists."

"On my life I swear, Nick," Justus said.

"One more thing; should you run into trouble, keep your eye out for a friendly white dove. If you're in danger, watch what it does very carefully, and it will show you a way to safety."

"How do you know such a thing?"

"I can't answer that, because I don't know myself. Just trust what I say is true. It may save your life."

Nicholas turned over the saddlebags to Justus, prayed to God with him for protection, then rode back to the cabin. All the way, he couldn't help thinking about Ox and Mario. Neither could walk, and he was determined to create a way for them to improve their mobility. In the morning he would begin with Ox, since he had suffered the most recent traumatic experience.

The next morning, as the sun rose behind the Pallone home, Ben was already at work brushing on a light coat of varnish to the maple panel. The carving was finished. He decided not to stain the piece because it already matched the wood around Anna's door. He set it out in the sun, hoping it would dry before he made the ride to Nick's. This would be a day to remember, he resolved, as he rubbed a coat of oil into his mask, giving it a slight shine. As soon as the panel dried, he strapped it to Ty's white horse and rode to Nick's farm.

Nicholas woke to the smell of fresh baked bread mingled with apples and cinnamon. Makande knocked on his door and then entered. Mario was strapped to his back, looking over the black man's shoulder. Both were smiling when Makande asked, "You hungry, Mr. Nicholas? I make fresh raisin bread and apple sauce."

Nicholas grinned, scratching his head. "How could one resist the smell of fresh baked bread, Makande?"

Mario chimed in a high tone, "This is one amazing man, Nick! I'm getting to know what it's like to walk around like normal people. He's had me on his back from first light."

"Is Ox awake?" asked Nicholas.

"Yes, he's sitting up," said Mario, "very quiet, looking at his stump. When he saw me with Makande he turned his head away. You'd better go in and talk to him, Nicholas."

Nicholas went into the kitchen, heated up some chicken broth, then cut three slices of raisin bread and laid it on a tray with a bowl applesauce. When he knocked on Ox's door and stepped into the room, the big man's deep voice broke the morning air. "Nicholas, I've been wanting to talk to you since we arrived, but the pain was unbearable."

"How are you feeling now?" Nicholas said, setting the tray down next to Ox.

Ox sighed. "It's not nearly as painful, but it feels like my leg is still there."

"Your brothers and sister are fine," said Nicholas. "A friend is patrolling the north road in case a search party should show up."

"What a mess this is," Ox sighed, disgusted. "One day we were a happy family building a business we all loved, and then it all changed when I opened the door and saw my mother and father on the...we can't stay in Pizal, Nick. They will eventually find us here. We'll head south until we are too far for them to bother looking."

"This Captain Ficci is ruthless," said Nicholas. "Ben told me that he's been after your business for a long time, and now that you're on the run he has a perfect excuse to get rid of your family permanently."

"Maybe I should just turn myself in. After all, it was me alone who killed those soldiers. I can make a case that no one had the strength to mangle them the way that I did."

Nicholas reasoned with him. "Odds are that if you convinced a court that it happened that way, then the business would go back to your family."

"Exactly!"

"But you would go to the firing squad and Ficci is back where he started—still trying to get your business. And who would protect the others with you gone? Ox, he won't stop until he's rid of you all."

"There must be something we can do. It just seems hopeless."

"There *is* something we can do. I came up with an idea that might work, but I want to wait until all the Bellicinis are here before discussing it."

"Thank you, Nicholas," Ox said. "We can never repay you for all the good you've done."

"No payment is ever necessary. In the meantime, we have to get you walking again."

"That's not going to happen unless there's a miracle. I'll be stuck with crutches the rest of my life."

"Not if I can help it," said Nicholas. "I'm working on something that might give you hope, but whatever I come up with, promise you'll tell no one you received anything from me, but rather from Hope Mission. I would prefer if people see it that way, all right?"

"I promise."

Ben burst into the room, rushing to Ox, hugging him, delighted to see him on the mend. Then he told Nick he'd finished the panel and that it was strapped to Ty's horse.

After breakfast, Nicholas and Ben went outside to see the finished carving. Ben removed the straps and leaned it against the water trough. Makande came out and squatted in front of the piece, nodding his head in delighted appreciation.

Ben had carved the last scene with the most exquisite style. Michael held Anna's hand to his face, while his other arm was over her shoulder holding one of her hands, and their children were standing beside them. The triptych carving was truly a masterwork.

"In my country I make river canoe from tree," said Makande. "We hollow out tree with hook ax and shape it into canoe, but I never see nothing like this. Mr. Nicholas, this most beautiful wood piece I ever see."

"I feel the same way, Makande. Ben has become a great artist, and now I know for sure this piece will change lives once we install it over the doorposts. It will be interesting to watch what happens."

After Ben strapped the panel onto the horse, they set off to Anna's house.

"When we return to the cabin later, we'll need to have Lund, Ty and Raven come to my house to discuss a plan to hide your family away for a while," said Nick as they rode.

"I don't think I have to hide," said Ben, reaching back to steady the panel. "I moved to Pizal over two years ago. Surely they're not seeking me."

"I wouldn't be so sure of that. If Ficci doesn't get all of you out of the picture, he'll be unable to seize the land. So, we meet this evening and I unveil my plan."

"How can we travel with Ox? His leg is no way healed."

"He'll be on crutches in no time, but not for long. You and I are going to build him a new leg, but not just any wooden leg. It will be one of a kind, something never done before. But I'll need your help."

"I'll do anything to see him walk again. What should I do?"

"When we return from Pizal, stop at the fallen oak tree by my wood shed and saw a piece as large as Ox's leg from his knee down. Bring it home with you and wait until I come before you start carving. I'll explain what to do after that."

When they arrived at Anna's and Michael's house, Ben untied the straps and brought the panel carving up to the front door. Anna and the children hurried onto the porch to see Ben's gift to the family.

When Anna saw it, her mouth dropped open. "Oh my heavens, Ben, it's so beautiful! How did you do that? I didn't know you were—you're a genius! The likeness of each one of us is incredible. I have never seen anything more beautiful in my life. You carved the story of Michael and me. It's wonderful!"

The children giggled, pointing out themselves on the panel, looking at the last scene. People from all over Pizal came to see what the commotion was about. At first sight, some gasped with delight, and others sought out the artist, patting him on the back with compliments. By the time Ben and Nick climbed up to install it over the doorposts, seventy-five people flooded the porch and walkway, buzzing about how the couple had come together and how Michael had been injured in an heroic attempt to rid the area of ravenous wolves once and for all.

The panel was fastened in place by the time Michael appeared at the front gate on his way home for lunch. Seeing him, the crowd exploded with applause. Michael stared at the panel in disbelief, then tears welled up in his eyes as he reached for Ben, hugging him. The crowd broke out in applause again while Anna blew her nose for the third time.

Joy flooded Nicholas' heart as he watched the initial result of his plan. The effect of the carving on people was much more intense then he'd imagined. But even Nicholas couldn't know the long-term effects. In time he would hear that from the day the panel was installed, people came from everywhere to see it. Every time Michael came home from work, people were standing in front of his house, gazing at the panel, waiting to get a look at the hero in the first scene. Always gracious to his admirers, Michael told the story again and again of how the wolves attacked him and how Anna had saved his life. Again and again he described the extraordinary love and compassion she possessed. Each time he'd finish telling the story, the love for his wife was rekindled, as it had been when they first married, and he'd enter the house smiling, looking for Anna's affection.

The marriage improved on a daily basis, and when word traveled to Rome about the quality of the piece, an important art dealer visited Pizal in search of its owner. He informed Anna and Michael that two museums in Rome were considering the purchase of a reproduction of the panel. In time, a cast was made and three reproductions produced, each piece fetching as much as two years' wages. Michael came out of debt and regained a whole new perspective on life, all from one thoughtfully planned gift.

Chapter 18. God's Gold.

*L*ate the next morning, dark storm clouds threatened Justus's ride to Pinzolo. His first assignment from Nicholas was to exchange ten sacks of gold dust for coin at the city bank of Commerce. After mounting his black horse and pulling up his jacket collar, he thought, *It'll take a lot more than any threat of stormy weather to stifle or slow ME down.*

With his crossbow strapped to his back, Justus set out for the big city, knowing he wouldn't arrive there until late afternoon at the earliest. Spring showers along the way only made his mission that much more exciting, as he looked forward to spending the night in a city known for its 'entertainment'.

Justus' clothes were nearly dry by the time he passed through Pinzolo's city gate, and walked his horse down the crowded main street. The sound of merchants haggling with people, and wagon wheels on cobblestones, made him feel right at home. As he rode along asking strangers the location of the Pinzolo Bank, someone pointed to the other side of the street next to a cathedral.

Music filled the air as he crossed the street, and he saw a gypsy wagon opposite the bank, set up for a sideshow. As he drew closer, his eyes widened at the sight of a woman dancing in a crowd of people, most of them men. Directly behind the dancer was a brightly colored wagon with the word 'Assanti' written in bold, green script across the side. Two men accompanied the dance, one playing the violin, the other a Spanish guitar.

Justus stayed on his horse, which enabled him to see over the crowd. As he inched closer, he froze in his saddle, transfixed by the music and the whirling beauty before him.

The men played a slow, enchanting melody with impeccable timing, their eyes fixed on the dancer. Justus glanced at the wagon again, and saw the words, 'See Rosalina Dance', in smaller, red script.

She wore a bright green dress, tight at the waist with a thick black belt, and a red leather vest. With raven-black hair and sparkling eyes, she mesmerized the crowd with her tempting smile and sumptuous movements. She was wildly beautiful with an olive complexion and a tiny beauty mark perfectly fixed on her chin near her mouth. Her thick, red lips, and gold, hoop earrings with matching necklace, titillated Justus as she danced barefoot; gold anklets accenting her feet. Justus had never before witnessed such a sight, and was transfixed by her beauty and every erotic move.

Rosalina turned with slow, sensuous motions, each time casting her eyes on someone else in the crowd. Bending low and rising as she turned, she tilted her head and her eyes found Justus. Smiling constantly, she lifted her dress to the knee, elbow jutting, and spun around. Then, reaching to the sky, fingers spread, she fell to the ground, ending the dance.

The crowd was silent for a moment, then burst into a vigorous applause. The dazzling temptress hypnotized all who watched, including Justus.

As the musicians collected coins from the crowd, Justus walked his horse across the road toward the bank, looking back every few steps to catch another glance of Rosalina. He noticed her laughing, caressing the face of a well-dressed businessman. Then, losing her smile, she glanced up and away, locking eyes with Justus.

With the saddlebags over his shoulder, he dismounted and entered the busy bank. As he emptied the bags on the counter with the scales, he felt eyes on him. The teller weighed the gold and recorded the figures in a ledger, and Justus suddenly realized the danger of the public transaction. As soon as the weighing was done, and the teller handed him the bags of coins, Justus shoved them into his saddlebags and left.

Dusk had arrived as he mounted his horse in search of the nearest hotel. He wouldn't risk traveling at night with so much gold.

Riding to the end of the main street, he found a decent place just across the road from an Army Command Post. Thinking he'd be safe there until morning, he went directly to the restaurant next door, saddlebags in hand, and ordered a hearty bowl of venison stew and a jug of ale.

After dinner and a second jug of ale, Justus went straight to the hotel, paid for a room, and locked himself away for the evening. Exhausted from his non-stop day, he fell asleep before his head hit the pillow.

In the morning, he awoke to a loud banging on the door. "Open up! This is the City Police!"

Rubbing his eyes, Justus leapt from his bed and opened the door. "What's going on?"

The soldier scanned the room. "Someone has attacked the night manager, so we're questioning everyone in the hotel. Did you see or hear anything for the past hour or so?"

"No, sir, I was asleep until you knocked. Is the manager all right?"

Still looking past Justus into the room, the soldier replied, "He'll be fine. He was unconscious when one of our men found him. He's awake now and has a nasty cut on the back of his head. We need to move on now. Good day, sir."

As he shut the door, Justus turned to where he'd left the saddlebags. They were gone! He frantically searched the room, but found nothing. His heart sank. What would he tell Nicholas? How could he show his face ever again?

He walked to a chair next to a window facing the street and sat, thinking carefully about everyone who'd seen him in the restaurant and lobby the night before. He could think of no one suspicious and began to lose hope of ever finding the gold—God's gold! His heart sank deeper yet, remembering that the stolen fortune was to be spent on a Mission—a Mission that would help really hurting people.

Leaning his elbow on the windowsill, looking down on the street below, Justus raked his hands through his hair and cried aloud, "Please forgive me, God." Despondent, he glanced across the street to a restaurant window on the second floor and noticed a white dove landing on the windowsill. He was struck with how unusually white it was, and immediately he recalled that Nicholas had promised a dove would help in a time of trouble.

Watching the bird intensely, Justus felt a glimmer of hope as it flew up and back several times. Someone came to the window and opened it. It was the gypsy dancer, Rosalina Assanti! What in the world was she doing on the other side of the city so curiously close to him? Justus believed the dove was a sign from Heaven. The gypsies must be responsible for attacking the night attendant, and stealing the pass-key to his room.

Justus stayed in his room watching the front door of the building. When the gypsies finally emerged, one of the men staggered as they walked into a nearby alley. *Their wagon must be hidden there,* thought Justus.

He quickly left the hotel and followed the group out of the city onto an unfamiliar eastbound road. They traveled another hour before they stopped at an abandoned campsite deep in the forest.

Justus stayed out of sight until they had built a fire and begun drinking again. Then, as they sat on the ground with their backs resting on the wheel of the wagon, he rode into their camp with his crossbow trained on the men. He stopped thirty paces away and saw Rosalina step out of the back door of the wagon.

Raising his crossbow, he turned to Rosalina. "Did you really think you would get very far stealing God's gold?"

Rosalina laughed. "God's gold? We don't know anything about any gold. Such a sweet-looking man as yourself should be careful not to come into someone's camp greeting them with accusations."

"Oh, I'm sorry. Let me start again," Justus said. "Hello, my name is Justus. It seems I've been careless and lost saddlebags filled with sixty pounds of gold last night while I was sleeping. Please don't take this the wrong way, but would you mind very much opening the back door of the wagon so I can take a peek in and reassure myself that you're an honest family?"

Rosalina's smile vanished. "I think you should turn around and leave this camp before one of my brothers takes offence to your insolence."

Out of the corner of his eye, Justus noticed one of the brothers lunge for his rifle. Justus fired instantly, striking the man's hand, pinning it to the wagon wheel. Before Rosalina realized what happened, Justus pulled a dagger from his belt, ready to throw.

"You fool!" Rosalina screamed. "You shot my brother's hand! I can't believe it. You shot his hand! How will he play his violin again?"

While the impaled brother screamed in torment, Justus yelled to the other brother, "Lie down flat with your face to the ground, and put your hands on the wagon wheel so I can see them. Rosalina, your brothers may never play another tune unless you march into that wagon right now and bring out my saddlebags."

Rosalina walked backwards towards the wagon, then ran up the steps and disappeared inside. Justus finished reloading his crossbow and yelled, "If you don't come out with those bags right now, the next thing you hear will be the sound of your other brother in abject misery."

Rosalina appeared with the bags, which hung close to the ground because of the weight. With one hand under and one over, she dragged them down the stairs to his horse and set them down. In the hidden hand was a small flintlock pistol. Aiming it point blank at Justus' head, she fired.

Justus flinched back and the horse reared up, knocking Rosalina to the ground. The pellet skimmed off his forehead, leaving a good-sized gash pouring blood down over his cheeks.

Justus kept one eye and his crossbow trained on the brothers as he slid from his horse. "Stay on the ground and rip a piece of your shift off for a bandage," he said to Rosalina. "Then come here and tie it to my head."

She sat stone-faced, tearing a wide, long piece from her lace petticoat, then rose and marched to him. Justus made her stand to his good side as she tied the bandage in place. He ordered her to sit on the ground again while he unhitched the wagon horses and tied them in tow to his horse. Then, squatting down, he checked the saddlebags to make sure Rosalina had not replaced the gold with something else. As he opened the second bag, a snake leapt up and bit him on the underside of his arm.

He dropped the bag while Rosalina rose unhurriedly, and laughed, shouting, "I see you've met my little friend. It's all over for you now, pretty boy. My pet is an adder, very poisonous. You won't last two hours with your 'God's gold'."

Justus pulled the dagger from his belt and cut his skin behind the bicep, directly on the snakebite.

"It appears I'm not done with you, Tippy Toes," he joked. "You will have to draw out the poison."

Stamping her bare foot to the ground, Rosalina cried, "I will not!"

"Then it looks as if you'll be hiring new musicians. In two seconds I plan to sink this bolt into your other brother."

Rosalina hissed, "My brothers will kill you some day for this."

"It's not your brothers I'm worried about—it's you. You've tried to kill me twice now in the last five minutes."

Justus sat on the saddlebags as Rosalina placed her mouth on the cut and drew out the venom. Then, spitting it out, she asked, "What will you do with us?"

"I should've made you swallow that venom, but because this is God's gold, no one will die. You will find your horses three miles up the road."

As he admired Rosalina's stunning face up close, he said, "Someone once told me that the devil was considered the most beautiful angel in heaven. Somehow, that all makes sense to me now."

After making another bandage from her petticoat, she wrapped his arm and sat down on the ground where she watched sourly as Justus threw the saddlebags on the horse and left the camp with the gypsies' horses in tow. Looking back, he saw Rosalina running towards the impaled brother and thought how blessed he was to have come out of the encounter alive.

CHAPTER 19. NICK'S PLAN OF ESCAPE.

A low, eerie fog clung to the ground that night as Nicholas went behind the barn and dug up Ox's severed limb. Bringing it into his workshop, he placed it on the table, washed it off, then mixed a large vat of plaster. The mix was thick as he packed it all around, covering the calf and foot. After it dried solid, he sawed the inch-thick cast in two from top to bottom and removed the leg. Then, after coating inside the mold with grease, he strapped the two pieces back together and poured another batch of plaster into a hole he'd cut at the top of the mold. When it dried hard, he un-strapped the mold and freed the plaster leg, finishing the cast by rasping the rough edges.

Nick returned Ox's limb to its grave, and carried the duplicate into the house, where Ben had just arrived with the family to discuss their plan. As they all gathered in Ox's room, Nicholas put the plaster leg aside before he welcomed his guests.

"Good evening, my friends," said Nick. "I trust you're all feeling much better than the last time we met?"

Raven still seemed detached as she peered uninterestedly into the next room. Ben spoke first. "Nicholas has met with us tonight to discuss a plan to survive Captain Ficci's efforts to be rid of us all."

Everyone turned to Nicholas in silence. "The most important thing right now is to hide you away in some secure place, where no one ever goes. You will have to hide for a time, at least until things change in San Marco. That could mean some years."

"We would have to leave the country to find a place like that," Lund said. "We might never get there once Ficci sends word to the borders."

"I propose that you don't leave the country, and for that matter, that you don't even travel very far at all," said Nicholas, grinning. "Prior to your arrival, I had plans to construct a Mission on the top of Bear Mountain. We will build a house for you there first, and then work on the Mission construction. There is a lake next to a huge open field on the other side of the mountain. That will be the location of your new home."

"Won't people eventually know who we are and our location?" asked Ben.

"No one dares climb the mountain with all the wolf activity. I've been up there numerous times and the wolf population has increased dramatically. Smaller animals are dwindling, which means the many wolves are hungry, and will attack anything to survive. Not even a military patrol would make it to the top."

"So what would the wolves do to us? How could we be protected?" Lund asked.

Ben broke in, "Nicholas has a gift from God when it comes to animals. They drop to their bellies when he comes into view, even wolves. I was there. I'm a witness."

"What happens when we don't have Nicholas around?" Ty asked. "We'll be exposed to danger just like anyone else."

"That was the biggest kink in my plan until a few days ago," said Nicholas, "but I believe I have found a way for you all to be safe when you're up there without me. Tomorrow, at first light, we'll ride to the main trail and see if what I have set up is effective. In the meantime, if you knew you had safe passage from now on, would you consider living there for a time?"

Ox answered, "I'm sure we've all thought long and hard for a plan to insure our safety, but I believe yours is the best and the only one for now. Unless anyone in my family objects, we're with you, Nicholas. One thing though, I'll have to stay here until I can walk on crutches, and even then it might take a while for me to get to the top."

"I'm working on that Ox," Nicholas said. "I'll have something far better than crutches to get you up that mountain when the time comes."

When the meeting ended, everyone sat in the dining room to a hearty venison stew Makande had been working on all day. Before the Bellicinis left that evening, Nicholas wrapped the plaster leg in a blanket and gave it to Ben, along with a set of calipers. Using calipers would insure the wooden leg matched the plaster model. He asked Ben to go to the shed before he left and saw a piece of the fallen oak the same size as the plaster leg.

Ben stayed up half the night carving the oak leg. When he finished, he carved two words on the bottom of the big toe; 'Love, Ben.'

Early the next morning, Lund, Ty, and Ben returned to Nick's cabin, highly anticipating the journey up the mountain. Raven showed signs of improvement, wanting to stay at home and knit lace, one of the things she loved to do most.

When the Bellicinis arrived carrying muskets, Nicholas raised an eyebrow, then took the oak leg from Ben, placed it in his workshop and mounted his horse.

They rode to the trail at the base of the mountain. A new wooden sign had been posted on a tree reading, 'Danger. Do not enter—numerous wolf packs'. Nicholas turned to the others, and said, "This is as far as I go."

The twins panicked. Ty cried, "What are you talking about? We can't go up there alone. We'll get torn up before you make it back to the cabin."

"If I go with you, you'll never know if there will be safe passage without me," Nicholas explained. "You must do exactly as I say and you won't be harmed. As soon as you see a dangerous animal, dismount and squat down to the ground, turning your palms up, showing them empty hands. Move slowly and calmly, giving them time to see what you're about."

Nicholas showed them by squatting himself, then continued, "I have been up and back on this trail teaching the animals for quite some while, and now has come the time to test the result in faith."

"Faith?" Lund and Ty cried simultaneously.

"I've seen wolves roll over on their backs when Nick arrived," Ben said.

"But Nick won't be around," Ty argued.

"Listen," urged Nicholas, "just go in far enough so that if it doesn't work you won't be far from here. Pick a spot and wait there. This place is teaming with wildlife. You won't have to wait long. When they come, and you squat, they will become docile and let you pass. Keep going until you get to the top. Stay on the trail and you will come to the spot I told you about. You'll see a beautiful lake next to an open field—that's your new home, Hope Mission."

The white dove swooped down, landing on Ben's hand. Looking down, he smiled beneath the mask and said, "We will be safe, brothers. I know it."

"I like the idea of staying as close as we can to this spot," said Lund. "But I think we must risk going up the trail a ways. If this works, our family has a chance."

Nicholas removed his red cap and held it to his heart. "Trust what I say about the animals. It is ordained of God."

When he rode off, the brothers left their horses and, with their flintlocks ready, walked up the trial looking this way and that. Only a hundred paces in they found a small clearing that offered several ways to exit if they had to. The men were silent as they sat around a boulder, constantly looking around. Lund held his flintlock, white-knuckled.

"This is insanity," Ty whispered.

They heard a noise in the bush behind and turned to see. Twenty paces away, a black bear came around a bush, rolling its head from side to side, grunting.

"May the Saints protect us," Ty whispered. "Another black bear, only this one's bigger than the one Justus killed."

Lund raised his musket, but Ben put his hand on the barrel and lowered it. "Let's just try what Nicholas said while the bear is still at a distance."

The men stood up and faced the bear. Then, at the same time they squatted, slowly, turning their palms up. The bear stopped, staring at them, then shook its head left and right and settled on its belly, with its chin tucked between the front paws.

"Now that's the most amazing thing I've ever seen," Ty said. "I think this thing really works."

"Now let's see what happens when we stand," Lund added.

The brothers stood, watching the bear closely. Ben heard something from behind and turned. Five wolves had approached, flanking them, working their way closer. The men instantly squatted again, showing their palms. The wolves stopped at once and dropped on their bellies, with one of them rolling over, whining. When the men stood, the bear and the wolves remained down, as peaceful as the white dove that had just swooped down and landed on Ben's shoulder.

Lund laughed, saying, "That Nicholas is something else! How'd he do that?"

The animals remained down until the men returned to their horses and began the ride to the top. Now that they believed Nicholas's gesture to the animals was indeed ordained of God, new hope sprang alive in their hearts. Perhaps their family would survive the ordeal after all, and perhaps their future was no longer in a black cloud.

When Nicholas returned to the cabin, he uncovered the oak leg and brought it in for Ox to see. Makande had Mario strapped to his back when they entered the room and joined them.

"You'd have to carve a whole tree to get me walking, Nick," Mario joked.

They all laughed as Nick turned the leg so Ben could see the 'Love, Ben' signing on the big toe.

"What are you going to do with it, Nicholas?" asked Ox in a husky voice.

"I will build you a moveable leg," said Nicholas. "I hope, by the time I'm done, that you'll be able to walk like you did before, with perhaps only a small limp."

Mario looked at the leg with envy. "Can anything be done for me, Nicholas?"

"Yes, indeed, Mario, but I'm still thinking on it. Right now, you need to make a design for the first Mission house. Makande will help you with what you need. I will get to work on Ox's leg and Ox can start moving around on the crutches Makande made for him yesterday."

Nicholas went directly to his workshop and began by cutting the leg at the ankle. He beveled each side so the foot swung freely on a hinge. Then he drilled holes up into the front and back of the ankle and foot, placing heavy springs into the holes. He joined the foot and leg at the ankle with a hinge. When Ox walked forward, the spring in front would push together and allow the foot to bend up. When he stepped with his good leg, the wooden foot would spring back into a natural position.

Next, he cut the toes straight across the joint where they bend up when walking. Then, he beveled the topside, allowing the toes to turn on a hinge. Nicholas completed the leg by screwing half of a heavy-duty hinge to the top of the knee and the other half to a thick leather cup socket he'd made from an old saddle. He made the base of the socket flat in front and beveled in the rear, allowing the leg to swing back but not forward. Finally, he sewed two leather straps with buckles to the socket, allowing Ox to secure it firmly to his thigh. The leg was finished.

Lifting the prosthesis over his shoulder, he grabbed an oilcan and went in to see Ox.

Makande was busy putting numbing powder and extra padding on Ox's leg when Nicholas walked in.

"Well, Ox, here it is, your new leg. I wonder if you would try it on. I may need to make some adjustments."

Ox's eyes grew wide. "I've never seen anything like that before. Do you think it will work?"

"We'll find out right now, Ox," said Nicholas. "It will be painful at first because your leg is still tender, but you'll get used to it in time."

"I can deal with the pain if it means I'll walk again."

Ox moved up to the side of the bed, and Makande helped Nick strap the leather cup socket in place. Both men helped Ox to his feet. His huge body left his head only six inches from the ceiling. Resting his arms on their shoulders, he hopped one step and then another. "Hey, this can work! Ooooccch...Ohh... I can't believe this—this—this thing really works!"

As Ox slowly walked out into the main living room, leaning on Makande, Nick dashed oil into the squeaking springs and hinges. They all knew Ox was in pain, but he laughed all the same time, tears running into his thick beard, thanking Nicholas for restoring his ability to walk.

Chapter 20. Raven Cares for Justus.

At dusk, rolling peels of thunder and flashes of lightning in the hills of Pinzolo startled Rubin as he turned up his collar and made his rounds for a third time. Riding north and south past the Pallone farm, wondering what happened to Justus, Rubin worried. His best friend should have returned from the city eight hours ago.

As he rounded the first turn past the farm, a rider appeared, slumped on his horse not far down the road. Rubin gave his horse a kick, and as he drew closer, recognized Justus's black.

With his head down, tilting sideways in the saddle, Justus lingered a moment, then fell to the ground.

Rubin leapt from his horse and ran to his friend, turning him face up. Looking at his bandaged head, he cried, "Justus, what happened? There's blood all over you!"

Barely audibly, Justus mumbled, "Rubin, my friend...Rubin. She shot...me. My arm...a snakebite. Beautiful... gypsy did it... Rosalina, Rosalina."

"A woman did this to you?"

"Yes," said Justus, holding his throat. "I...I'm so thirsty...my arm... the poison. I'm burning... fever... can't stop shaking. Take my saddlebags to Nicholas. Do... not look inside." With that, Justus passed out.

Rubin struggled to lift him over his saddle, and walked the horse to the Pallone farm. Stumbling up the porch steps, carrying Justus over his shoulder, Rubin slammed on the front door. When Raven appeared, she gasped, seeing Justus unconscious, wearing bloody bandages on his head and arm.

Rubin knew Raven spoke to no one because of her recent ordeal, so he carried Justus to Ty's room and laid him on the bed. He explained that Justus had been bitten by a poisonous snake and was burning with fever. "It's urgent that I get to Nicholas with Justus's saddlebags, Raven. Will you care for him?"

Raven waved him off, and Rubin hurried to his horse. When he had gone, she quickly removed Justus's leather jacket, shirt and boots, then peeled free the bloody bandages, and washed his wounds. Fetching two cotton blankets, she covered him and placed a cool, damp cloth on his head, replacing it every few minutes with a fresh one.

Raven found herself smiling for the first time in a week, distracted by Justus and the need to break his fever. She realized that sitting alone soaking in the memory of her murdered parents only caused deeper pain and longing.

As the bloody bandages soaked in hot water, Raven noticed lace on the fringe and knew instantly it was torn from a woman's petticoat. After heating a cup of barley soup, she sat in a rocking chair next to Justus, admiring his smooth face and silken black hair as he lay sleeping. When she had removed the bandage on his arm, she'd seen oily red lip paint on both sides of the cut and fang marks. She thought, *A woman drew out that venom.*

Raven wondered for quite some time what her patient had gone through and who the mystery woman might be.

"No, Rosalina," Justus moaned, sweating, his voice thick with fever. "Over there, Rosalina!"

Doting over him, changing his cooling-cloth a bit too often, Raven thought about the scars on his chest and rib cage and what horror he must have endured to earn them. She was taken with his handsome face and full lips, and found herself thinking about life and love for the first time since the family left San Marco.

It was already dark and raining in sheets when Rubin met Ben, Lund and Ty on the road to Nicholas's cabin. As they rode up to the front door, the rain hissing around them, Ox stood under the porch portico. He waved, and Lund shouted, "How in the world could you be standing...walking, Ox?"

Ox hopped two careful steps forward on his own and pulled up the leg of his breeches. "Hope Mission built this leg for me. Take a look at this thing. It's a movable leg, springs and everything. Hurts worse than a hernia, but I'm walking."

"Nicholas built it, didn't he?"

Ox watched as the men dismounted and ran under the portico, "From now on he prefers us to call any gifts given by any of us, a gift from Hope Mission, location unknown."

"My mask is a gift from there," Ben added. "And the carved maple panel given to Anna and Michael is also from the Mission. No matter who does the actual crafting, the gifts are from and of God, working through his newest Mission."

As the brothers marveled at the new leg, they told Ox about their encounter with the animals and their ability to travel safely on the mountain.

Meanwhile, Rubin went into the cabin and gave the wet saddlebags to Nicholas. He told him all that he knew about Justus and that Raven was looking after him.

Asking Rubin to wait, Nicholas took the saddlebags into his bedroom and shut the door for a minute, then came out with ten gold coins. "Rubin, I need you to go on another important assignment. Are you willing?"

"Yes, sir," Rubin said, and smiled. "I like adventure far more than accounting. My father wants me to help him at the bank eventually, but I'd rather ride with Justus while I'm young. What do you need me to do?"

"Ride into Pizal and set up a watch for the soldiers. Take a room at the hotel facing north. You'll be able to see them miles before they reach Pizal. Before you check in, stop at the church and find Brother Taylor—he's a monk on sabbatical, so he could be anywhere. Tell him I wish to see him about an urgent matter." Nicholas reached in his jacket, pulling out an envelope. "Then go to the tailor's and give him this letter. Ask if Ben's suits are ready, if they are, send them to me with a messenger."

Handing Rubin the coins, Nicholas continued, "This should cover all our expenses. You've become a valuable member of our family, Rubin. I only see good things down the road for you. Keep two gold for yourself as a wage, son. Now off with you."

Rubin smiled all the way to his horse.

Nicholas gathered the brothers in the dining room for another meeting. "We don't have much time. Soldiers are bound to show up soon. I sent Rubin into Pizal as a watch. Tomorrow, at first light, we must take all necessary tools, climb to the top of the mountain and build a temporary shelter. Now that you have safe passage, you can take Raven with you. Mario's working on plans for your house. When he's done, we break ground for Hope Mission."

Chapter 21. The Journey to the Summit.

Early the next morning, after the sun dried the morning dew, Nicholas glanced out his workshop window to see Justus riding onto the farm full stride. Nick dropped his hammer, and went out to greet him.

"Had enough adventure yet, Justus?" laughed Nicholas. "Rubin told me what happened, but not in detail. Up and about already? Rubin said you were in horrid shape last night."

"I'm great, Nick. I'll have to tell you what happened another time. Did Rubin bring the gold? Did he look in my saddlebags?"

"I have the gold, son. I don't think Rubin peeked. Why are you in such a hurry?"

"I need to know what to do about Raven."

"What do you mean?" Nick's eyes narrowed in surprise.

"Last night when the fever broke and I awoke, she actually made eye contact and smiled at me. I think I love her."

Chuckling, Nick asked, "That's all it took, a smile and a glance your way? I think you're already in trouble."

"How can I get her to talk to me?"

Nicholas paused a minute, seeing the Bellicini wagon off in the distance. "Raven went through an ordeal that damaged her mind and trust in men. A man tried to rape her after she watched the other soldiers kill her parents. It won't be easy finding a single answer to your question. However, there is one thing you might try."

"What is it, Nicholas? I'll do anything."

"Really? Anything?"

"Yes, anything."

"Remember years ago when I pulled you out of that ditch naked and beaten up, with burns all over your chest?"

"How could I forget?"

"You never told anyone what happened to you, or who your family was, or anything about your past life. And no one tried to force it from you, right?"

"Right."

"Raven suffers just as you did. She can't speak or stop the images that keep barging into her mind. If you find a moment when she looks receptive, take the opportunity to ask for her help. Tell her what happened to you all those years back, and in so doing she will gain a trust in you, knowing you suffered in a similar way. If she shows compassion for others, it will heal her. You probably don't know this, but if you succeed, you will have given her a special gift from Hope Mission."

"How's that, Nick?"

"Being an instrument in the healing process for anyone is a gift of compassion. The question now is whether you have the strength and courage to share what happened to you."

Justus grimaced. "That's a stiff poke in the eye. I didn't expect that. I'd rather deal with gypsies trying to kill me than look back at my past, any day. I'll have to think on this a while before I try anything. What's that?"

"Hmm?" Nick's gaze followed Justus's pointing finger. "The wagon, you mean?"

"No, the rider that just passed it."

"It must be the messenger Rubin sent, with Ben's new outfit," said Nick, leading Justus in for a bite to eat before their journey up the mountain.

When the messenger arrived, Nick put the clothes in Ben's bedroom, then set up Mario for completing the plans on the Bellicini house. Makande would stay behind and help Mario.

When Ben's family arrived, Justus and Nicholas led the way to the base of the mountain. Rigging two additional horses to their wagon, they turned onto the trail leading to the summit, encountering wolves several minutes later. As Nicholas led the way, and the wolves laid themselves down in submission, he notice how lean they were and surmised that many of them were starving.

Three hours later the group arrived at the summit without incident. Everyone bolted into action, gathering logs and clearing a spot in the field near the lake with the best view of the countryside. After helping secure support beams and laying in a roof for the shelter, Nicholas and Ben mounted and made their way back down the mountain.

Bird song and trees rustling in the wind provided a pleasant ambiance to their descent, but an eerie absence of smaller wildlife rankled Nicholas, and he suspected the many wolves would soon turn their ravenous appetites toward larger prey.

"You look worried, Nick. What's got you?" said Ben, adjusting his mask.

"It's nothing, Ben, not yet anyway. Your new suits came by messenger this morning. How do you feel about going on your first mission? It would only be a few days at most."

"I don't see why not, now that my family is safe up there. Ficci will be after me as well, so if I'm away doing something for Hope Mission, all the better."

A white dove suddenly swooped down, landing on a bush off the main road in front of them. When they stopped to observe, the dove pecked at an odd-looking berry bush neither man had ever seen before. It pecked until it held a berry on a stem in its beak, then flew to Nicholas, landing on his wrist. When Nick turned his other hand, the dove dropped the berry in his palm. It flew off and repeated the action, bringing another berry, dropping it in his hand.

Nicholas handed a berry to Ben and they inspected the tiny fruit, wondering what the dove meant for them to do. As small as a pea, the fruit was purple, dotted with yellow spots. Nick ate his with curiosity, waiting for a word from the messenger, but none ever came. It tasted more like a sweet nut then a berry. The flavor lingered on his palate. It seemed like a great treat for anyone, but more for a child because of its sweetness. Both men dismounted and picked a bagful before they continued down the trail.

"So, Nicholas, where am I off to?" Ben asked.

"I want you to go to the outskirts of Pinzolo. There is a leper colony living in caves down in a shallow ravine just before the city dump. Go to the top of the ravine and call for Sister Hannah. She's visiting there now and expecting something from Hope Mission. Don't go near the caves, Ben, or you may come back with that dreaded disease."

"Is Sister Hannah a leper?"

"No. I met her on the crossroads to Pinzolo. She seems to be immune for some reason. Stop at Anna's on the way and ask for the medicine she uses to help leper sores. It's like a soda powder that foams up when mixed with water, so don't get it wet. When you arrive at the colony, give Hannah the medicine and ask what their needs are. Buy them enough supplies for a year and tell her we'll return from time to time. She already knows a masked man will be coming to help, so don't worry about frightening her. After you leave the colony, go into Pinzola and buy a fair amount of land deep in the woods. We are going to have decent housing built for lepers. We'll fence it off and warn people to keep out for obvious reasons. Hire a construction company and tell them to expect plans in a few months. Give them half the cost for supplies, and say the other half will come on completion of the project. When all that is set in motion, you can return home."

Ben nodded, absorbing the list of instructions. "How much gold shall I take, and when do I leave?"

"I figure ten pounds should do it. Leave tomorrow morning. When we return to the cabin, you can try on your new outfit. Tonight I want to create three special gifts for the leper children. Would you be willing to help?"

"I'd love to."

"I need you to carve a small horse in full stride. When you're finished, just leave it outside my workshop. I'll show you what I made tomorrow before you leave."

Chapter 22. A Conversation with Brother Taylor.

The moment Nicholas and Ben returned from the mountaintop, Mario called Nick into his room to review the finished plans on the Bellicini home. Nick had to step over the drawings and notes scattered everywhere, but he was soon kneeling next to Mario, studying the drawings. He was expressing his approval when there was a knock on the door.

Ben answered and welcomed Brother Taylor, inviting him into the living room. Nicholas came out when he heard his voice.

Brother Taylor was a fair-skinned monk with a bowl haircut. Rather short and stocky, clean-shaven with a round face, he wore a brown, hooded robe with a white rope tied around his waist.

As he led him by the arm to the den, Nick's voice bubbled with joy seeing his friend. "Ah, welcome, my brother. How are you enjoying your sabbatical?"

They settled in cushioned chairs, and Makande brought in apple juice, handing them each a jug.

Taylor answered, "It's so good to see you again, Nicholas. The sabbatical is slowly becoming torture. I thought when I left the seminary, that God would surely guide me to the next step in my spiritual journey. I want to serve Him but cannot return and obey church leaders who want me to abandon the very people they sent me to help. It just all seems so political. I am a simple monk, with a simple command from above—to Love. Why did *you* leave seminary, Nicholas?"

"Well, for me it was a little different. I think the churches are good, but the leaders need to expand their thinking a bit. Lay people must learn to believe they are an important part of God's message to the world. Instead, they are led to believe that following rules and saying many prayers is all that God is interested in. That's why I called you here today. I believe you are on the crossroads, and want to honor God with a service you really believe in."

"That's true. I feel I've been sitting on the crossroads for quite some time now, and while I've been sitting there, nine other monks have joined me. They all believe as I do. We want love to be the focal point of our service to God. The other brothers are simple, hard-working men as well, and are waiting for a sign from God, as I am. We're talking about starting a new order."

Nicholas summarized the events that had occurred since the snow-storm and the miracle that had saved May Rose. He also explained about the messenger from God that spoke to him through a dove, and about the Bellicini family and their ordeal.

Brother Taylor sat mesmerized, with a smile as wide as his face as Nick told him about plans to build a secret Mission on the mountain to aid the hurting and disabled.

Barely able to contain himself, Taylor leaned in. "Brother, I must join you! Hope Mission leads me to the road I am to travel."

Nick beamed. "I was hoping you would say that! One reason that I think this is perfect for you, is that our community will be away from the influences of the rest of the world. Children born there would be taught the ways of love from childhood, and then when they're older and choose to leave, they will bring a true message, rooted in God, to the rest of the world. There are three attributes to our mission statement; faith, hope and love. And when you join us, brother, I believe you would supply much of the love."

Taylor gulped down his apple juice. "Did you know there was a man in the fourth century also named Nicholas who became known for his abil-ity to give godly gifts?" he enquired.

"No, but perhaps that's why my parents gave me this name. They always believed I would do something special for God. Maybe God has sent me to carry on the work the first Nicholas began."

"Why not?" said Taylor. "Hope Mission sounds like a very good start. I will go back to the brothers and tell them this fantastic story. I believe they will join you in a heartbeat. What would you have us do?"

"The Bellicinis are at the top of the mountain preparing to build the first house for the Mission community," said Nick. "If you come back with others, you can begin by helping with construction. But what that family needs most is love and encouragement after the ordeal they've been through."

Brother Taylor inhaled. "What is that wonderful aroma coming from the kitchen?"

"Makande has roasted chicken, fried vegetables and apple pie. Would you stay for dinner? I want you to meet Mario. He's an architect and expert silversmith. I'm sure you'll enjoy his company and find much to talk about."

Brother Taylor accepted the invitation, and at dinner Mario reviewed his sketches of the first building with everyone. Taylor promised to return the following day with an answer from his brethren, then left the farm, whistling hymns all the way down the road.

Standing before the bedroom mirror, Nicholas straightened Ben's collar on his new double-breasted, silver-buttoned overcoat. "How does it feel, Ben? Is it too tight?"

"It's fine. Everything fits fine, and all the black with the red pin-stripes around the lapel looks great. They match my hat, but still... something is missing."

Nicholas went to his room and came back holding a black leather sash, with a thin red trim on its border. He smiled as he laid it over Ben's head. "Let this fall down across your chest. It will be the official symbol of Hope Mission."

"That did it, Nick. Now it's perfect." Ben smiled.

Nick's eyes narrowed. "Remember, Ben, this assignment could get dangerous. You'll be carrying ten pounds of gold coin. Try to observe everyone and everything—stay one step ahead of danger. Use your wits and be watchful for our friendly dove as well."

Confident Ben would do well on his journey to Pinzolo, Nicholas went straight to his workshop, intent on making toys for the leper children. The first toy he created was a hunter, made of wood about three-hands-high, having hinges on swinging arms and legs. He carried a bow with dagger in his belt, and was modeled after Justus. Next, Nick fashioned a dancing girl in a flowing red dress that spun on a base. Both figures were painted with bright colors and smiles on their faces. They were not sculptures of the kind Ben would carve, but simple designs with a clever touch only found in Nicholas.

While the paint dried, he stepped out the door and found the wooden horse Ben had created. He stained it chestnut, then built a wagon to the same scale, rigging the horse to the wagon with tiny leather straps. Along the side of the wagon, he painted a black panel with red trim, reading, 'Hope Mission', in gold-leaf script. He took the small sack of purple and yellow berries they'd picked on the mountainside and placed them in the back of the wagon. The children would eat the sweet treat as they played with the other toys. He thought the leper children had probably never seen a toy before.

His work done for the day, Nicholas went to bed blessed and fell into a dreamless sleep.

Chapter 23. Highwaymen.

The next morning, on the top floor of the Pizal Inn, Rubin awoke and went to his window to take in the fresh spring air. His heart jumped as he saw six riders on their way to Pizal in a gallop. The riders were too far away for him to tell if they were soldiers, so as he dressed, he kept one eye out the window until he was sure who they were. As soon as he saw a soldier's red cape lifted in the wind, he flew down the stairs, leapt on his horse and hurried to Nicholas's farm.

The citizens of Pizal stared as six soldiers rode through main street with their shiny boots and wide-brimmed, black-feathered hats. Sergeant Manuel Ficci led them straight to the village inn, where they'd stay until he'd made a thorough inquiry regarding the murder of three of his own Royal Guard.

It was dusk when the soldiers walked into the tavern as if it belonged to them, sitting down at a dining room table, tossing their flintlocks and gear everywhere. Sergeant Ficci planned to eat and drink for the rest of the night, waiting until morning before conducting any official business.

Not quite as tall as his brother Andrea, Manuel Ficci wore his long brown hair greased back and tied off in a bunch. It always made him feel more appealing to the ladies, though none ever told him so. The sight of his patchy beard and the greasy face with a deep scar under the left eye usually left women trembling.

"Inn keeper, send us some ale, and be quick about it!" commanded the Sergeant.

The innkeeper's wife soon appeared with pints of ale and a loaf of bread with sausage and cheese on a large platter. As she laid the tray down, Ficci groped her, pulling her onto his lap, joking about her abundant cleavage and narrow hips. The maid broke free and ran to the arms of her husband, the innkeeper.

Heavy drinking ensued as the soldiers demanded more of everything, referring to the innkeeper as the maid's grandfather. As the night wore on, a drunken Sergeant Ficci followed the young maid into the kitchen, cornering her. "We'll have a really... special time tonight, my innocent little love toy."

"Get your hands off me, sir, or my husband will come and teach you some manners!" the maid warned, backed against the wall.

Smirking, Sergeant Ficci stroked the maid's neck, ogling her cleavage. "I will not take my hand from where it is pleased to be. And furthermore, if you do not come to my room tonight, you will not have a husband in the morning, and this quaint little inn will be ashes."

The young girl ducked under his arm, running in terror to her husband, silent about the Sergeant's threat.

As the night wore on, the soldiers staggered to their rooms, leaving the Sergeant alone, passed out, his head on the table. The innkeeper grudgingly carried him to his room, dumping him on the bed.

Approaching the outskirts of Pinzola, Ben knew two men were following him. They were quite a way back, almost out of sight, but a warning chill came up under Ben's mask. He suspected the riders were highwaymen in search of an easy mark. Ben carried a flintlock pistol and dagger under his coat, but would never use them unless his life was in danger.

When he rounded a bend in the road, and was briefly out of sight of the men, he led his horse into a small clearing on the side of the road and dismounted, hiding until they had closed the distance. When they were a stone's throw away, he undressed from the waist up, and removed his mask and hat. Reaching into his travel bag, he opened the sack of the soda powder medication Anna had given him, and scooped a handful into his mouth. This, mixed with his saliva, formed a massive foam drizzle that poured down his chin and neck, onto his bare chest. When he heard the horse's hooves, he stepped from behind his horse and raised his arms, groaning like an animal, and lunging at their horses. The riders' horses stopped and reared back.

"Oh my god—what is it?" gasped one of the men.

"He has no ears!" said the other.

"Look at his face!"

"What face? He has no face! He's a mad man—foaming at the mouth! Look at the size of him! I don't know about you but I'm—"

The highwaymen bolted back in the direction they'd come, holding their hats to their heads, too scared to look back.

Ben laughed a good long time, then cleaned the foam from his chin and dressed, thinking about the fun he'd have telling Nicholas.

As Ben mounted his horse, the wind blew a horrid odor his way, indicating that the city dump and leper colony couldn't be far. When a ravine appeared off the road to the east, Ben dismounted and walked his horse. He was both nervous and curious, for he'd never even seen a leper, let alone a colony of them. Stepping to the edge, he called down, "Hello! Can anyone hear me?"

Peering down into the dark cave openings, he saw shadowy figures moving slowly behind massive boulders that lay in a barren field of garbage and debris.

A small voice cried out, "Go from this place, sir. We are lepers. Go now, sir."

A nun emerged from one of the caves. As she walked toward Ben, she called out, "Greetings, sir. You must leave at once, this is a leper colony."

"I am a messenger sent from Hope Mission, come to help," said Ben. "Can you come up so we can talk?"

While she climbed the crude, stone stairs, three children walked onto the field, curious to see the giant man wearing a mask. Squinting, Ben saw sores and scabs on their tiny faces and limbs. He wept.

As the nun climbed the last steep step, Ben reached for her hand.

She smiled. "Hello, I'm Hannah. That mask...are you sent by that wealthy man who wishes to stay anonymous?"

Looking down at the children again and then to Hannah, Ben replied, "Yes, and this good man has now created a community to help the sick and disabled. He's called it Hope Mission. My name is Ben Bellicini, and it's a pleasure to meet someone with a heart like yours."

"You couldn't have come at a better time," said the nun. "I've decided to stay here indefinitely, which would make it difficult to obtain supplies. Some in the colony are not only suffering with leprosy, but are physically sick from lack of food. I assure you that *any* help will be most gratefully accepted."

Ben glanced into the ravine again, noting that the children wore rags and had no shoes. Behind them were two women, each missing a hand.

He took a deep breath. This was indeed a fitting recipient for Nick's mission of hope. "Sister Hannah, I want you to write down everything you need to improve living conditions here, and that includes clothes, shoes, blankets, and anything you can think of that might help these people." He removed the medicine from his travel bag and held it out. "You must take this powder. It will ease the open sores. As soon as I have your list, I will go into Pinzolo before evening and buy the supplies you need."

Reaching into a sack on his saddle, Ben smiled beneath the mask, then set the toy hunter, dancer and horse and wagon on the ground. "In the meantime, I would like you to give these toys to the children. The founder of Hope Mission made them himself."

Surprised and delighted, Hannah asked "Oh! Aren't these the most clever toys you've ever seen? The founder made them especially?"

"Yes," said Ben. "See the sack in the wagon? It's filled with a sweet, nutty treat for the children. Things will start to brighten right away if we can make the children smile, don't you agree?"

"Yes, indeed. This is a blessed day for everyone living here. I will begin writing the list right now. And by the way, that's a very handsome mask you're wearing. I'm almost afraid to ask why you wear it."

"Don't be!" said Ben. "I was burned badly in a fire trying to save my friend. It left my face a horror to behold. I lost both ears in the process, but this mask has enabled me to come back into society and live a nearly normal life. The mask is also a gift from Hope Mission, and again, was made by the founder himself."

After Hannah completed the list, she brought the toys to the children, and Ben rode away with their delighted cries ringing in his ears.

He hurried into the heart of Pinzolo and purchased a large wagon with a wooden roof to which he hitched his horse. Then he set about filling Hannah's list. The nun had been thorough, but not excessive, and after stocking the wagon with blankets, pillows, fabric, and leather, Ben added other practical comforts. Next, he stopped at the market where he spent more of the gold on baskets of fresh fruit and vegetables, fish, sausage and pasta. On the way back, he bought a lactating cow and five chickens, so the lepers would have fresh milk and eggs.

It was dark by the time Ben returned to the spot where Hannah and he had spoken. He decided to stay in the wagon for the night, waiting until morning to carry the supplies down to the colony.

He was woken abruptly by the sound of Hannah's, high-pitched, excited voice as she knocked on the back door of the wagon. "Ben! Ben! Are you awake? Something wonderful has happened! It's a miracle!"

Rubbing his eyes under the mask, Ben opened the door. "What is it, Sister?"

"The children are healed! I can't believe it. They're healed, all of them! Their skin is now pink where the sores were. It's as if they have new skin."

"How can that be? Do you think the soda medicine did it? Could that have helped so much and so quickly?"

"I don't think so," said Hannah. "I've used that medicine before, and I'm delighted to have some more, but it helps the sores in a limited way. No, Ben, this cure must have been God's hand."

"I believe also, but why just the children?" Ben considered. "Wait, were the children the only ones who ate the sweet berry treats?"

"Yes, I think so. They loved them."

Ben smiled widely behind the mask. "Those berries were pointed out to us by a messenger of God! N- the founder of Hope Mission and I tasted them, and we thought they were an ideal treat for youngsters. That's why I brought them here. I can't explain it all now, Sister, but the berries could hold some sort of medicine that fights the effects of the disease. I think you should pass any that are left out to everyone here and let's see what happens. I'll bring the supplies down and then return to Pinzolo on unfinished business. When I return, we'll see if there's been any change."

Ben emptied the wagon and hauled the supplies down into the ravine. The lepers remained in the caves until his last haul. When he waved farewell and made for the steps, they emerged from the shadows, weeping, and thanking him.

Back in Pinzolo, he finished the business of buying land and hiring a construction company by late afternoon, then returned to the ravine. At the stairs leading down, Sister Hannah stood holding hands with the children. "Fear not, Ben, they're totally healed," she laughed, showing him their new pink skin. Tears of gratitude replaced the laughter as she embraced Ben, praising God, and thanking Ben for bringing the healing berries and supplies.

"How about the adults, Hannah? Have they improved any?"

"It's not as effective on them, as the disease was much more advanced, but some see some signs of improvement. Please send more berries when you return to the Mission."

"I surely will, Hannah. In the meantime, Hope Mission has bought a patch of land close to here. I've arranged for a construction company to start building a home for the colony. If this berry is indeed a cure, you can use the housing for those with lost limbs and for orphans. When the founder hears what's happened here, he'll send me back with instructions."

After embracing Hannah in fellowship and placing five gold coins into her hand, Ben began his journey home. He was unable to stop thinking about what had just transpired. He knew Nicholas would be as thrilled as he with the miracle, even if Ficci had arrived in Pizal, eager to find and arrest them.

CHAPTER 24. SERGEANT FICCI INVADES PIZAL.

$\mathcal{B}$y mid-morning the next day, a shaft of sunlight had worked its way across Sergeant Ficci's bed, striking his eyes, waking him rudely. With his head pounding, he rose from bed, dunked his face in the water basin on the nightstand, then hurried downstairs, where his men had been waiting an hour.

Sergeant Ficci was determined to find the Bellicini family, even if it meant turning Pizal upside-down and sideways. More than anything, his mind rested on the fifty gold coins his brother promised if he was successful in arresting the Bellicinis and bringing them back dead or alive. The investigation began at the town hall.

Ficci and two soldiers entered and approached a clerk at her desk. "We are Royal Guard conducting an investigation for the San Marco authorities. Where is the mayor this morning?"

"He hasn't come in yet, sir. Is there something I can help you with?"

"Are you familiar with the Bellicini family?" Sergeant Ficci asked.

"No, sir," said the clerk. "I'm not aware of any family with that name in Pizal. But here is the mayor. He may know more than I."

With a warm smile, the obese, well-dressed mayor stepped up to the counter, accompanied by a man who had the look of a clerk. "Good morning, good morning, gentlemen. How can I help you?"

"My name is Sergeant Manuel Ficci, second in command of the Royal Guard in San Marco. I'm conducting a murder investigation. We have reason to believe a man named Ben Bellicini lives in this area. Do you have this name in your city records?"

"I will have someone look," the mayor replied. "It may take some time."

Ficci grimaced. "Time is one thing I don't have, Mayor. Please have someone look through the records NOW."

"Uh...I'm the banker," said the man Ben had taken for a clerk. "Is there a reward or anything for this information? Much of the information we receive at the bank is highly confidential."

Sergeant Ficci glared at the small, squinty-eyed bald man. "Yes, there is a reward. Is there somewhere we can go privately to discuss this?"

Sergeant Ficci and the bank manager stepped into a small empty office, shutting the door.

"How much reward is involved, Sergeant?" asked the manager.

Ficci pulled a dagger from his belt very slowly and pushed the manager against the wall. He placed the point under his chin, inserting the blade into the skin only far enough to draw blood. "Your reward will be your life, little man. I will sink this blade all the way into your brain if you don't tell me everything you know in the next five seconds."

With his chin angled high, blood running down his neck onto his jacket, the manager stuttered, "B..b..en Bellicini came into the bank not long ago with no small amount of gold dust. He bought the Pallone farm outright. He said his family was relocating, but he wanted to keep the transaction confidential."

With the blade still in place, Ficci asked, "Where is the Pallone farm?"

"A twenty-minute ride up the north road out of town. If you don't find him there, he could be with a man named Nicholas Kristo. His farm is not far north of the Pallones', near the base of the mountain."

"If they wanted to hide, little man, would they choose the mountain?"

"No, sir, for it would be their deaths to try."

"How so?"

"Can you take the blade from my neck? I'll tell you what I know."

When Sergeant Ficci released him, the manager pulled a handkerchief from his jacket to stop the bleeding.

"No one climbs that mountain now, Sergeant. There are signs warning people to stay out. In the past, folk have gone up there, never to return. There is an overpopulation of wolves and other dangerous animals, hungry for any meat. They stray down here all the time. We've had hunting parties, but it was no use—there are too many animals and too many dead and injured hunters."

Sergeant Ficci rushed from the building with his men and joined the others at the inn. They gathered their guns and gear and rode to the Pallone farm, cantering the horses all the way. After seeing the home deserted, they found oil in the barn and poured it over the house and barn, burning them down.

Next, they rode north to Nicholas Kristo's farm. When the soldiers arrived, Makande was standing in front of the cabin with Mario strapped to his back.

Sergeant Ficci recognized him at once. "Makande, what in the world are you doing here? Who owns you? Did you run away?"

"No, Mr. Sergeant. I swear, no. Mr. Nicholas made me free man. I work on his farm now. I am free slave, sir."

Mario spoke over Makande's shoulder, noticing black smoke rising to the south, over the tree line. "May I ask why you've come here, sir?"

"I am making inquiries regarding the Bellicini Family. They are wanted for the murder of three Royal Guard soldiers. I am told Nicholas Kristo and Ben Bellicini are friends. Has any member of that family been here? Has Ben been here? Where is Nicholas Kristo?"

"As far as I know, Sergeant," said Mario, "Nicholas is away on a business trip and I haven't seen Ben for quite some time."

The sergeant glared at Mario. "If I find that you're lying, you will be arrested with the others, and you won't be treated any differently just because you have stumps for legs." Turning to his men, he barked, "Search the cabin. I'll check the barn."

When Ficci entered the barn, scanning the tools and equipment, he saw something glitter on the ground. Walking to a round object covered by a sacking, he squatted, scraping gold dust from the floor. After removing the sack, his eyes widened as he saw gold deeply embedded into a coarse grinding wheel. He thought, *There's enough gold embedded in the stone to buy a herd of horses and then some.* He suspected the gold dust Ben had used to buy the Pallone farm came from this very spot, and that Nicholas must have been the one grinding down nuggets.

A surge of lust enveloped Manuel, and he was determined to kill anyone standing in the way of his finding Nicholas's cache of gold. Nicholas Kristo was his main interest now, the Bellicinis only an excuse to get to him. Smiling at the gold dust on his finger, he thought he might just retire early and live the good life like his older brother, Andrea, only richer...much richer.

CHAPTER 25. THE MISSION IS UNDERWAY.

E arlier that day, with Ben on his way home from Pinzolo, and the Bellicinis preparing the land on the mountaintop for construction, Nicholas awoke with a smile. Slipping into his clothes, he thought, *Hope Mission is no longer a dream, it's a reality, but Ficci and his men are within reach. We'll make haste to the mountain right after breakfast.*

The smell of fresh-baked biscuits wafting into his room was accompanied by Makande's pleasing voice. "You hungry, Mr. Nicholas? Got fresh fruit, biscuits and cider."

"Yes, indeed, Mr. Makande," said Nicholas, opening the door, "but how'd you learn to cook so well?"

"Captain Ficci had old slave who had special magic when it come to cooking. She taught everything to Makande. I learn many things from other slaves in San Marco too."

"Did Mario have breakfast?" asked Nick, headed for the kitchen.

"Hour ago. He want to see you when you have time."

When Nicholas detoured to Mario's room and opened the door, Mario sat on the floor with drawings and draftsman tools all around. "Good morning, Nicholas," said Mario, looking up, scratching his leg stump. "I've finished with the plans for the first house and started designing a fence that will surround the entire community. What do you think?"

Squatting down, Nick reached for the drawings, nodding as he studied them. "What I think, Mario, is that I found the right man for the job. These drawings are so imaginative and different compared to the more common architecture we see in Pizal. How did you come up with the ideas?"

"Believe it or not, it was the easiest thing I've ever done. Ever since my first night here, I've been literally seeing these buildings in my dreams. The dream could be about this or that, but while it's all happening, I see these buildings in the background. As soon as I wake up, I draw a sketch, then refine it later. I can't explain it, but only wish the same thing would happen when I want to design something in silver. Now, take a look at this one. It's the first house."

The outside view showed Gothic influence on the windows, with a mixture of Romanesque style molding all around the roof, an over-all modern approach to building design. The house was huge, having six bedrooms and a grand living space with two fireplaces. The kitchen was large enough to prepare a banquet for fifty people. Mario had also designed a guesthouse directly behind, adjoined to the main house. It could accommodate an extra twenty people.

"It's larger than I thought," said Nicholas, "but that works to our benefit."

Makande stepped inside the room, "Mr. Nicholas, many holy men stand outside wanting to see you."

Nicholas found twelve monks and three nuns waiting by the barn, along with two donkeys and a horse packed with personal belongings.

Brother Taylor stepped onto the porch, hands outstretched in greeting. "Good morning, my good friend. When I returned to our boarding house last night, the brothers and sisters were just finishing a prayer meeting. They all listened to your story, and when I was finished, half the brothers hurried to their rooms to pack. Some prayed for the rest of the night, seeking God's will. This morning when I stepped outside to finish packing, they, and the sisters, were all ready to go. Do you think you could use us all, Nick?"

Overwhelmed, Nicholas answered, "Goodness! I'm—I don't—yes, yes, by all means, every one of you will be helpful."

Taylor indicated the group. "I will introduce each one to you later, but for now let me say all the brothers and sisters can teach and the brothers are very good with construction. They say they pray just as well, if not better, with a hammer in hand."

"God has smiled on Hope Mission today," said Nicholas. "I never expected such a response. Let me explain what I'm thinking in terms of how this could all work together. My work will be to bring hope to people by the things we do and the special gifts we create. *You* will oversee everyone's spiritual needs. The heart of the Mission is complete now—we have faith, hope and love. The second house we build will be a house of worship and housing for the brothers and sisters. It will be in the center of Hope Mission."

"If I may ask," ventured Brother Taylor, "who will finance the construction?"

"God has already taken care of that, Brother Taylor. You need never be concerned, for all of our financial needs have been provided. Are any of the brothers adventurous?"

Brother Taylor grinned. "Brothers Dominic, Thomas, James and Jude like to travel and are seen as feisty and opinionated by the rest. I believe they will fit your description." He called the men over and introduced them to Nicholas.

Nicholas intended to send the four on a special mission all over Italy. They were to ride in pairs on horseback, two to the north and the other pair south. Taking the young men into the cabin, Nicholas gave them drawings he'd made of movable wooden arms and legs, and even a sketch of a chair with wheels for the crippled.

They would seek out the blind and promise to return with dogs, trained to help them make their way around. And for those that were deaf and dumb, they would send a missionary to teach new ways to communicate with people.

They would stop at every church and show the sketches, taking the names of people who were disabled, visiting them with encouragement and taking measurements for their prostheses. If they found disabled non-believers, Nicholas added, these were to be included as well.

The missionaries were to promise to return to those disabled no later than eight months later with a special gift from Hope Mission. After instructing the four to keep the Mission location a secret, Nicholas provided them with horses and enough gold coin to keep them housed and fed for a year. The brothers took the horses but refused the money. People were always more than willing to feed them or give them what they needed for the day, they said, and Nicholas should keep the coin for more urgent needs.

"After all," said Brother Dominic, speaking for them all, "it is blessed to give, and why should we deprive the charitably-inclined of God's blessing?"

Brother Taylor prayed with them before sending Dominic and Thomas to the north and James and Jude south. As the brothers rode off, they were laughing on their horses, all of them promising to come back with the most names.

As the traveling monks moved down the road and out of sight, Nicholas turned to Brother Taylor. "As soon as I collect the plans for the building from Mario, we'll make haste up the mountain trail. Ficci's within reach. Makande will stay behind for now to look after Mario."

Ben had arrived in Pizal early that morning. After seeing soldiers in front of city hall, he snapped the reins of the wagon, trotting his horse to Nick's farm, not realizing Rubin had warned him the night before. When he arrived, only Makande and Mario were there, so he rode on to the base of the mountain attempting to catch up with the others.

Three hours later, after reaching the summit, Ben marveled at the work already completed. He was surprised to see monks working with the Bellicini brothers, and nuns gathered around Raven. The Mission had become another world.

The men finished the temporary shelter and cleared the field where they would build the Bellicini home. Ben saw large beams and trusses being erected as he rode through the camp, and his heart was filled with joy.

Everyone greeted him with smiles, with one sister reaching up and kissing his mask after he dismounted. They all gathered around laughing as Ben told the story of the frightened highwaymen. Some began to weep as he described the leper colony and the children in rags with no shoes, and the women with no hands. The crying turned again to delight when he gazed at Nicholas and said, "It had to be those berries, Nick. There's no other explanation. The children's skin was as pink and soft as a new baby. And by the time I left, some of the adults showed strong signs of improvement."

"Did you get to take care of all the Mission business?" asked Nicholas.

"I took care of everything. I even bought that wagon over there. It has a wooden roof so we can bring supplies wherever needed."

"Well done, Ben, well done." Turning to the others, Nicholas laid a hand on Ben's shoulder. "This evening we will all give thanks to God for Ben's success and safe return. And then we'll celebrate at dinner. Perhaps Lund and Ty can sing some of the tunes that made them famous in San Marco."

CHAPTER 26. JUSTUS REVEALS HIS DARK PAST.

While Ben kept the missionaries mesmerized with his adventures in Pinzolo, Raven ducked away from the crowd and ran to the lake. The white dove flew overhead and landed on a tree next to her.

Seeing the dove land, Justus sensed it was the right time to attempt a confrontation. He glanced at Nicholas, who nodded his approval.

Slowly, Justus drew near, wondering if he was able to share his own dark past. Up to that point, no one knew what he'd endured, not even Anna or Nicholas, both of whom had been instrumental in saving his life.

Raven sat on a wide, flat rock, her bare feet dangling inches from the water, looking out over the pristine lake to the hills surrounding Rome. She turned as Justus sat beside her, looked in his eyes, then lowered her head. The breeze across the lake lifted her black, wavy hair off her shoulders, and she smiled faintly, telling Justus she'd accepted his company. Then, apparently distracted, she scratched at her arm.

"Why are you scratching?" asked Justus, reaching for her arm. "See here, that's Stinging Nettle. Try not to scratch. I have an alkaline powder that will help. I'll be right back."

Running near the shelter, he found Nicholas's horse, knowing he'd brought medical supplies before he left the farm. Finding the powder and a bandage, he ran back to her thinking, *She's starting to respond. Maybe, just maybe....*

Still scratching when Justus knelt, Raven folded her legs under and turned to him.

Justus reached for her arm, after pulling a cork from a small bottle. "People say when you put this medication on it looks like leprosy, so I'll put a bandage on until the rash goes down."

After tying the bandage off, Justus looked into her eyes and made a leap of faith. "I know that what you went through back in San Marco was the single most traumatic experience of your life. We are all concerned about you."

Turning her head, she stared out across the shimmering lake.

"I spoke to Nicholas not long ago, and he thinks you may be able to help me, and I you."

She glanced at him, raising a curious eyebrow.

With a glimmer of hope Justus continued, "I've never told anyone what you are about to hear. Seven years ago I had an experience that was very much like yours in San Marco."

With her gaze now fixed to his, Raven nodded for him to go on.

"My father's name was Raphael Cruz. He was the Trade Ambassador for the Spanish Government when he met and married my mother Elizabeth. Twice a year they traveled to San Marco, trading Spanish-made firearms at the Government Command Post. My father was paid well for his job, so each time we made the trip, he rented a beautiful home in the countryside just outside the city. People said my mother was the most beautiful woman in all of Barcelona. Everywhere we went, people would stop and watch as she passed. The last time we were at the chalet, she was six months pregnant, but men never tired of seeking her attention, most of all Captain Andrea Ficci."

Raven put her hand to her mouth, leaning in to listen intently.

"Yes, the same Captain Ficci whose soldiers made a surprise visit to your parents' business that horrible day. Captain Ficci would make unannounced visits to our home when my father was away on business, always trying something new to charm my mother, but nothing ever worked. One day my father didn't return home on the day planned. My mother made inquiries right away, employing Ficci's police force, of all people, to launch an investigation. I suspected, even then, something underhanded happened to my father. It left my mother vulnerable and lonely."

Raven rested her hand on the rock next to Justus, touching his pinky. He paused for a moment, realizing that this was the first time she had willingly made contact. This gave him the courage to go on.

"One night soldiers came, forced their way in and locked me in my room."

With a furrowed brow, Raven rested her hand fully on his.

"My mother screamed as I pounded the door, ordering them to leave the house. Then it became quiet as the men began to laugh, and then quarrel about who was next. Right then I knew they were violating my mother."

Raven's eyes welled with tears as she squeezed his hand.

One of the soldiers said very clearly, 'The Captain said to kill them both.' When they came into my room one of them said, 'Not yet, let's play a little game with him first.'

"They grabbed me by the feet and dragged me out of the room, past my mother, who was lying on the floor, dead. As my head scraped the floor next to her, I saw her belly had been slit, and her unborn baby lay in a pool of blood..."

"Oh, God, no!" Raven cried out. "God save us, Justus, how have you lived with this for so long? I at least..." She swallowed. "I at least had my brothers."

Justus continued, scarcely noticing that Raven's silence had finally broken. "The first thing I think about when I awake each morning is how they will die. I don't care if it's wrong. I must have justice for my mother and father. I feel I will honor their lives if I kill the men who murdered them."

Raven wept, reaching out to stroke his face. "Hatred will eat you up. In the end, you will die in misery."

Justus went on, his voice cracking, his tears falling into Raven's hands. "They dragged me to the other room and kicked me in the head, knocking me out. When I awoke, I was tied to a chair, with blood running into my eyes, unable to see. After a few minutes it became obvious they were playing cards, and the winner would get another opportunity to burn my chest with a lit cigar. When they'd had enough to drink and tired of the game, they threw me in a wagon and rode to the outskirts of Pizal. After they dumped me into a deep ditch, I thanked God they were drunk. Both fired their flintlock pistols and missed, each bragging it was he who'd gotten the head shot.

"In the morning, Nicholas found me and brought me directly to Anna Borrelli's. She took me in as her son, and that's when I changed my name to Justus."

"What is your real name?" asked Raven, aghast at the story.

"My real name is Ricardo Alfonzo Cruz, but you must call me Justus until those men pay for what they did."

Raven leaned closer, and began, haltingly, to relate her own story.

Squatting by the campfire, Nicholas smiled as he glanced toward the lake and saw Justus and Raven sitting so close, sharing their deepest hurts. His thoughts shifted to what Ben had said about the berries and their amazing ability to cure the leper children. He wondered if the adults could be healed if they continued a steady dose. After a time, he called to Justus who presently came to the campfire, hand in hand with Raven.

Poking a branch at the burning embers, carefully ignoring the apparent breakthrough Justus had made with the girl, Nick asked, "Would you be willing to travel on another Mission, son?"

"Yes, sir. When would I go?"

"First thing in the morning, but we must find someone very good with plants to accompany you. This is—"

"I love plants," Raven said. "It's one of my favorite things—my garden. How can I help?"

Grinning, Nicholas laid a hand on her shoulder, and winked at Justus. "It's good to have you back with us, Raven. This is the first we've heard your lovely voice. Tomorrow, you'll both go to the location Ben and I found the berries. Gather as many as you can, then uproot one of the bushes whole, with its surrounding soil. Raven can bring burlap to keep the roots and soil together and moist. From that point, Justus will ride alone to the leper colony in Pinzolo. He'll give Sister Hannah the berries and tell her to plant the bush in fertile soil somewhere near the ravine, then return home."

"I'm there for you, Nicholas," said Justus. "I'll pack my saddlebags now so we can leave at first light." Turning to Raven, he reached for her hand. "You'll be ready then?"

"For certain, Justus." Raven smiled. "I want to work with this Mission more than anything right now. After all, this will be our new home and new family."

CHAPTER 27. WOLVES… STARVING WOLVES.

hen Justus hurried off to prepare for the journey down the mountain, Raven remained by the campfire confiding in Nicholas. "Justus told me the most horrid story about his past. I don't think he wants me to share it with anyone, but I need your advice about what I've just heard."

"If I can help, I will, Raven. Justus is like a son to me."

"Well, as he explained the horrible thing that occurred, he changed into another person right before my eyes. When he spoke about getting justice, I know he meant revenge. His face became hard and I grew frightened, but I didn't let him know."

Nicholas grinned, poking the burning embers with a branch. "You are the first one in all those years to hear his story. We all wondered what happened but he wouldn't budge. Perhaps now that he's told someone, there's a chance his heart can heal and open to receive one of God's greatest gifts."

"What's that?"

"The giving and receiving of forgiveness."

"I can't see how he could forgive what happened to him and to his loved ones. How will he ever come to it?"

"Raven, un-forgiveness entraps a person, and more so if the offence is great, as it was with Justus and yourself. Bitterness often lies beneath our inability to forgive or be forgiven. It's a corrosive culprit that denies our peace and destroys our relationships. Bitterness is always destructive and never constructive. I'm sure you feel you have the right to be bitter after what those soldiers did to you and your family."

"Yes, I do."

Nicholas dropped the branch and walked Raven out to the lake. "So you give yourself the right to be bitter and what starts to grow down in your heart as a result are the roots of bitterness. Those roots have fine tentacles that reach out and grow, eventually attaching themselves to everything and everyone in your life. We can even lose our physical health if we nurse those roots.

"Though we can't see what's happening on the inside, often we see the outer results. Bitterness is like a continually running machine that uses our body for its energy source. It runs when we're sleeping, it runs when we're talking to our friends, and it runs when we're simply sitting and being quiet. It keeps operating and draining energy. I'm sure if you asked Justus how many girlfriends he's had, he would say none. Why? Because bitterness and un-forgiveness have dominated his life and has destroyed his ability to have a normal, loving relationship. I can see you and he enjoy each others' company and would make a fine couple, but until these deep hurts are dealt with, your relationship with him will probably be filled with uncertainty."

"What should I do then?"

"As life unfolds up here on the mountain, God will provide various opportunities for you to help him see what is destroying him. You've bonded with him and now you're his chance to experience true peace and love in this life. And as you make these discoveries, they will have a healing effect on you as well."

Raven thanked Nicholas, embracing him, then hurried off to the shelter. She would hold his advice close to her heart as she thought about her first Mission assignment with Justus in the morning.

Not long after sunup the next morning, the buds on the trees had just begun to sprout. Crisp, pine-scented air and bird song brought a smile to Raven as she prepared breakfast in the shelter. Justus attempted to sneak up behind and scare her, but was foiled when Nicholas and Ben walked in.

"Good morning, all!" said Nicholas, "Are you ready for the journey Justus?"

Handing Raven a sheet of cloth, Justus answered, "Yes, sir. I've even found some burlap for Raven to wrap the plant in."

"Great," said Nick. "As soon as you've had breakfast, ride down the mountain trail until you see a fallen maple tree in front of a massive boulder. That's where the purple and yellow berries are. Gather as many as are on the bushes, then dig up and preserve a healthy bush. Raven should not go any farther down. She'll return after Ben and I come to meet you."

Soon after, Justus and Raven had saddled their horses and started down the trail.

At the base of the mountain, Sergeant Ficci had awoken earlier than his men and walked a good bit up the trail. An eerie feeling rankled him, but he neither saw nor heard any forest activity.

Returning to his men, pushing aside his reservations, he kicked their shoes, ordering them to get up and move out.

After their horses were saddled, the soldiers began their way up the trail. Their anxiety mounted, because of the warning sign they had just passed, and the stories they'd heard about wolves. Sergeant Ficci feared little, for he always carried two pistols, a dagger and his sword.

They moved slowly up the quiet trail for a time until the lead man stopped, turned to the others, and cried, "Wolf pack!"

Cocking their flintlocks and forming a circle in a small clearing, the men stood ready. Ficci drew both pistols as no fewer than fifteen lean wolves moved through the bush, surrounding them. As several of them closed in, snarling and showing teeth, Sergeant Ficci shouted, "Fire!"

The soldiers fired, hitting some of the wolves, but they had no time to reload, so the starving beasts leapt at the rearing horses, bringing several down.

Sergeant Ficci fired both pistols, then stood on his saddle and grabbed a low branch, making his way onto a tree, as the frenzied wolves swarmed around the screaming soldiers.

A giant white wolf leapt up, biting onto Ficci's boot. Shaking his leg in a panic, he grabbed a higher branch, pulling himself up, until the wolf finally dropped to the ground and scurried to the feast.

More wolves ran down the mountain, smelling the blood, hearing the screams. No fewer than thirty of them now surrounded the bodies of five soldiers and two horses.

High up in a tree, Sergeant Ficci looked on in horror as he reloaded his pistols, seeing the beasts ripping flesh and fighting one another for the best meat.

Justus and Raven had just finished packing the berry plant on the saddlebags when they heard the sound of shooting not far away. Justus told Raven to stay behind while he went to investigate.

"Please don't go," Raven cried.

"I—"

"Please!" begged Raven.

Justus reached for her as she trembled. "I have to," he said, pulling her into his arms. "I'll be all right."

When she reluctantly agreed, he set off on his horse in the direction of the gunfire. Minutes later he heard growling as he dismounted and walked into a small clearing. Justus gagged at the sight and smell of the carnage before him. Five wolves were still feeding. On seeing him, they growled, so he dropped into a squatting pose, with his palms turned upwards. The wolves, instead of dropping belly-down as usual, ran away.

Walking through the slaughter, Justus dropped his crossbow, and vomited.

A voice from behind commanded, "Stand up, boy, and kick that crossbow over this way."

Justus wiped his mouth and looked up, seeing a soldier aiming a pistol at his face.

Kicking the crossbow forward, he asked, "What do you want?"

"Why did those wolves run when you came?" countered the soldier.

"I don't know," said Justus. "Maybe they had their fill. It certainly looks that way."

Raven's voice echoed down from the trail. "Where are you? Are you all right, Justus?"

The soldier limped closer, warning, "Don't say a word."

Raven appeared, and gasped in horror.

Holding his aim on Justus, the soldier laughed, "Well, look who it is, Raven Bellicini. You know, you look beautiful even when you're horrified."

Justus turned to Raven. "Do you know this man?"

"He is Sergeant Ficci of San Marco," said Raven. "He's the brother of Captain Andrea Ficci."

Justus glared at Ficci, knowing he must be associated in some way with his parents' deaths. He could even possibly be one of the soldiers who tortured Justus the night they murdered his mother. Before killing Sergeant Ficci, Justus would find out everything possible about the Captain.

"Where is Ox, Raven?" the sergeant asked. "I've come to arrest him and your other brothers for the murder of three Royal Guard soldiers."

Justus broke in. "I found her wandering around up here on my way back from a hunt."

"Where is he, Raven?" demanded the Sergeant. "Is he on this mountain somewhere?"

"I don't know where he is," Raven answered, weeping.

Limping closer to Justus, Ficci's face wrinkled in pain. "This is how it will be. You, boy, will lead the way out of here. The wolves seem to be afraid of you. And you, little Raven darling, are my insurance that your brother will turn himself in. Now, get off your horse and see what you can do to patch up this foot of mine. We're going to get real close, you and I. Let's go, right now!"

"I don't think you want to do that, Sergeant," Justus cried out. "I think you want to be as far away as you can from that little wench."

"What are you talking about, boy?"

"I was just about to have my way with the pretty little thing when I saw that bandage on her arm. She's hiding *leprosy* under there. Aren't you, wench?"

"No. I swear it's only a rash. I swear!" Raven cried.

"She's lying, Sergeant," Justus declared. "I saw part of it under that bandage. It's leprosy. Why do you think whoever she was with abandoned her? I saw it. See for yourself—it's a grayish-white rash."

"Take the bandage off," the Sergeant commanded, "now!"

Sobbing, Raven undid the bandage and raised her arm. Moaning loudly, Justus cried, "Of course it's leprosy. Sometime tomorrow she'll probably have open sores on that pretty little face. A damn shame, don't you think, Sergeant? Such a waste."

"Turn your horse around and go back up the mountain," Ficci ordered. "You're doomed anyway. All I have to do now is find your brothers, and that I'll do when I come back here with enough fire power to wipe out the entire village of Pizal and these mountain wolves. Now, boy, lead the way out."

CHAPTER 28. THE POISON OF REVENGE.

After Sergeant Ficci confiscated the black horse, he held Justus at gunpoint, forcing him to lead the way down the mountain trail on foot.

"Sergeant, are you really the brother of Captain Andrea Ficci?" asked Justus, half turning as he walked.

"Aye. Why do you ask?"

"Well, my father said he once met Captain Ficci in a brothel in Rome, and the Captain told him of a fantastic woman in San Marco. He said she was the most beautiful woman he'd ever seen and he made her husband disappear just to have a chance with her. Is that true? Did such a woman exist?"

Ficci laughed. "Oh yeah, boy, I remember that one real good. She was a sight to behold. It's a pity."

"What is, Sergeant?"

"If she had just compromised a little she might have been happy with Andre. But she was stubborn and persisted in finding out why her husband went missing. She got too close to the truth, so my brother had to find a way to stop her from meddling."

"Did he?"

"He paid a visit on her one night, took some of us with him. She became much too loud and feisty and tried to fight us off. See this scar under my eye? Well, she's the one who left it there." He chuckled. "I would take a scar under the other eye for another night like that."

"Did she keep quiet in the end?"

Sergeant Ficci shoved his pistol into his belt. "In the end, that's all there is, boy, quiet."

The moment the end of the trail came into view Ficci kicked the horse, cantering south toward Pizal.

With blood pulsing in his veins, Justus stood watching Sergeant Ficci ride away, the man who had done the most to destroy him and his family. He assumed after his mother scratched the gouge under his eye, the demon had cut her open.

Running back to the scene of the carnage, Justus planned to retrieve his crossbow, find a stray horse and ride to Pizal. He'd follow Ficci on his return to San Marco, then at dusk, on the road alone, he'd sink a bolt into his chest.

Raven met Nicholas and Ben on the way to the summit, telling them all that happened. She wept, pleading with them to find Justus before the Sergeant killed him. Ben took the berry plant and sack of berries from her horse, urging her not to worry. "Just hurry back to the shelter, we'll find Justus."

After Raven turned her horse, they rode down the trail and into the clearing with the carnage. Vultures swarmed the carcasses, thrashing wings bobbing up and down over the bodies. The stench was overwhelming.

As the men dismounted, Justus ran in from the south trail panting and shouting, "I was... just with the man who... killed my m...mother. Where's my crossbow? I... must follow him while he's alone.... I'll hide in Pinzolo when... I will—"

"Slow down a minute, Justus," Nicholas broke in. "Let's talk about this as we ride to the base of the mountain. Jump up on my horse, son."

When Justus found his crossbow, and they'd begun the ride down, he told them the horrific story of his mother's rape and murder. When the mountain trail ended, they dismounted, giving the horses a rest.

"We can't stop now, Nick, I don't have much time," said Justus, pacing on the road, looking toward Pizal. "I really need to find him."

Nicholas and Ben sat on a fallen tree by the side of the road. Stretching his arm out, Nicholas reasoned with him. "Justus, let's try to take a closer look at this whole situation. What is it you want, justice or revenge?"

"I want three things. I want justice, because unless I do this, justice for them will never happen. The government will not indict itself. I want honor for my parents. When I kill them, I will have honored the memory of my parents. And I *do* want revenge. I want to pay them back for leaving my unborn baby brother or sister twitching in a pool of blood, and for torturing me."

"The whole responsibility for getting this done is on your shoulders, right?" Nicholas asked.

"Yes, sir, and I don't mind one bit. I live for it."

"That's just the problem," said Nicholas, "You live for it. Ever since this happened it's consumed your life. You can think of little else. Revenge has robbed you of the joy of life. Hatred for these men has rooted itself deep in your being and its fruit has poisoned your sense of reason. Before you took a liking to Raven, how often did you enjoy the company of a lady? And I know myself you had many opportunities."

"Well, never. I was much too busy practicing with my crossbow and dagger."

"When you were practicing, what were you thinking each time you shot a bolt?"

"All the arrows were meant for them."

"When you go to sleep, what are you thinking about? When you awake what are you thinking about? Do you think you'll ever have a normal relationship with Raven while you have only one passion in your heart? Your heart's all filled up with hate. There's no room for Raven."

"Maybe," said Justus. "But when this is over, a new life will begin."

"Although you are an expert marksman, your desire for revenge may end your life. Things may turn out very differently from the way you expect. When the wolves attacked the soldiers and you came afterwards, did you expect Ficci would come down out of a tree with a pistol aimed at your head?"

"No, sir, but I thought of a way for Raven and me to escape."

"There will come a time when these evil men will back you into a corner and you'll have nowhere to turn. They are experts in murder and deception. It will take careful thought and strategy to outwit them at their own game. Right now, your mind and heart are blinded by revenge. You will make a fatal mistake. You must trust what I say, and that I have a plan."

"And what is that?"

"I'm still working out the details, but rest assured in the end the very thing they lust for most will be their demise. In the end, you will have the justice and honor you desire, but revenge is reserved for God. I want you to observe how things unfold, and as they do, you will clearly see the hand of God at work. Are you with us, son?"

Justus hesitated. "I thought it was the most difficult thing I'd ever done when you asked me to share my story with Raven, but this tops that by far." After taking a deep breath, he faced Nicholas. "I will do this. I'll give it my all. I'm just glad you didn't ask me to forgive them on top of everything else. You weren't going to ask me to do *that*, were you?"

Nicholas smiled. "I think we covered enough for one day."

Ben laughed and added, "That time may come, my friend. That time may come."

"I'm telling you both right now," said Justus, throwing his arms in the air, "that will never happen. I will never, never forget that they deserve a cruel fate."

"We'll deal with the soldiers soon enough," Nicholas said. "So while we have some time, let's stay with the mission at hand. Justus, you'll go to the leper colony as planned, and give Hannah the berries and the berry bush. Ask her about the condition of the lepers." Reaching into his travel bag, Nick continued, "Give her these coins. Tell her she is to use the money to send a messenger once a month to Anna Borelli, reporting the condition of the people and the progress with the construction of their new home.

Then you can return home. Ben, I need you to take the new wagon and travel to Rome. Take what you think you need from the coins in my saddlebags."

"Why am I going to Rome?"

"We'll be building an orphanage on the Pallone farm, now that the soldiers have burnt it down. Mario sent a messenger last night to give word. Brother Taylor will come into Pizal and hire Michael Borelli to find local workers to do the job. Mario will work on the plans as soon as I return home and go over it with him."

"Is that why I'm going to Rome?" asked Ben. "To get orphans?"

Nicholas instructed Ben to go into the city streets and find as many homeless children as would fit in the wagon. The youngest would be his first priority. He was to tell them they would be loved, provided for, and given surrogate parents until they were old enough to begin a life of their own. On his way back, he would stop at the leper colony, and if the children there were completely healed, they would come too.

Ben asked, "When I return, where will they stay until the orphanage is built?"

"They can stay on my farm," said Nicholas. "There's plenty of room. I will soon go into Pizal and announce I'm moving away and that I am turning all property rights over to the Brothers. From now on, I will stay at Hope Mission, and its location and my whereabouts will remain secret."

CHAPTER 29. AN INSPIRING SPEECH BY NICHOLAS.

*L*ate that afternoon, Nicholas cantered onto the farm on his great white horse, with Justus riding double. They were surprised to see a crowd of priests, nuns and monks milling around on Nicholas's front porch. Standing in the midst of them, Brother Taylor waved, running to greet them. Nicholas had asked him the day before to meet him there to discuss plans for the new orphanage.

"Greetings, my brothers," said Taylor, smiling. "The word spread fast among the brothers and sisters in Pizal and San Marco. Twenty more have decided to help with Mission construction. They've been waiting all day to see you."

"They could not have come at a better time," said Nicholas, dismounting. "I will greet each one after dinner tonight."

Nicholas led Taylor into the cabin, while Justus walked Nick's horse to the barn.

Once in the den, Nicholas gave Taylor enough gold florins to buy the building supplies needed to complete construction on the Bellicini house and church. Then he asked if he'd go to Pizal and hire workers to begin building the new orphanage at the Pallone farm. Taylor would need to choose some of the new nuns to stay at his farm and wait for Ben to arrive from Rome with the children.

After the conference, Nick found Makande in the kitchen with two brothers, cooking the evening meal. They had prepared pounds of pasta with olive oil and garlic, some with tomato sauce and basil. They also baked five loaves of hard crust bread.

Sitting around the dinner table that evening, Nicholas met each new missionary, welcoming them warmly, and cautioning about the secrecy of the Mission's location. Then, picking up a piece of bread, he held it out and stood.

A hush fell over the room.

"A great saint once said, 'There is a hunger for ordinary bread, and there is a hunger for love, for kindness, for thoughtfulness.' These words sum up what this Mission is all about. We are simply here to feed the hunger I've just mentioned. Whatever there is of God and His goodness in the universe, it must work itself out and express itself in part through us.

"Part of our mission is to give noble and godly gifts to a hurting, divisive world. We'll give gifts that will encourage and inspire. They will be both material and spiritual. The material gifts must have deep meaning for the ones receiving them. The spiritual gifts will have even more importance, such as teaching to forgive and receive forgiveness, or even teaching people how to forgive themselves.

"An act of goodness is of itself an act of happiness. No reward coming after the event can compare with the sweet reward that went with it. Some may say it's impossible for any one group to make a difference in the world. Well, I like what St. Francis of Assisi said regarding that, 'Start by doing what's necessary, then do what's possible, and suddenly you are doing the impossible.'"

Everyone said 'Amen' simultaneously, then looked at one another surprised at their united response, laughing along with Nicholas.

Makande leaned in, mentioning to Nicholas a package had arrived from Pizal earlier that day.

"Oh, they must be your new clothes, Makande," Nicholas said.

"What you mean, Mr. Nicholas?"

"I had outfits made for your new job. There are three suits in the package. Try on one of the work suits and meet me in my workshop with Mario in about two hours. I'll explain everything then."

Nicholas excused himself and brought his favorite oak armchair into his workshop. Cutting the rear legs halfway down, he glued and nailed in a thick oak platform under the seat of the chair. Then he drilled a hole straight through the length from the left to right. This would be the chassis of the wheelchair. Then, he removed two-foot-wide wheels from his small supply wagon, slid the axle through the chassis and fastened the wheels to both sides. Without stopping to rest, he removed two, hand-length wheels from the play wagon his father built when he was a boy, setting them aside. Then, he cut a fist-length off the front legs of the chair and drilled holes in each, attaching the small wheels with tiny axles. He finished by tacking a red cushion his mother had made to the seat.

As he sat in the chair testing it, Makande knocked on the door. "Mr. Nicholas, can we come?"

"Come on in, Makande. Let me see the new you!"

Entering with Mario strapped to his back, Makande proclaimed, "I feel like different man, Mr. Nick. These suits will last my life, to the end. I take real good care of them. They mine to keep?"

"Yes, sir, Mr. Makande," said Nicholas. "You are a free man now, with a great future before you. As soon as we try out this new wheelchair for Mario, we'll talk more."

"Is that chair for me?" Mario asked.

"It is, Mario. Makande, un-strap him and sit him on the chair."

Mario wept aloud, slapping his stumps excitedly as they lowered him onto the new wheelchair. Grabbing the spokes of the wheel, he moved slowly at first, but then in no time became familiar with what he needed to do to turn and go backwards. He would move forward three paces, then stop to wipe his tears, then move backwards. "Nicholas, could you adjust the left wheel?"

When Nicholas stooped down to look, Mario grabbed his head and kissed him on both cheeks. "Thank you, my dear, dear friend. I will work with you the rest of my life. I will design all the buildings for Hope Mission. If you will have me, I will live here."

Nicholas rested his palm on Mario's face. "We love you, Mario. You are welcome here as long as you like."

"So I guess you won't mind if I design the floors and doorways in a way that's easy for me to get around?"

Nicholas smiled. "There will be others in chairs like yours, Mario. It's a great idea."

Mario backed up, then wheeled his way around the workshop, practicing his turns and working his hands on the spokes of the wheels.

Turning to Makande, Nick chuckled, "Just look at that new outfit. You look like quite the gentleman now, Makande. We'll have to get you new boots and a hat for traveling next time we're in Pizal."

Makande's work suit was a three-quarter length, dark blue wool jacket with silk runners on the shoulders and silver buttons in front and on the sleeves. The shirt was blue cotton with a silk collar and white pearl buttons. His mid-length breeches matched the shirt with thin silk runners on the outside leg.

Makande walked to a small mirror next to the workbench, smiled and said, "I am happy like Mario. Love God lives in this house, I know."

"Yes, He does, Makande," said Nicholas, "only I call Him God of love. Did you know he has a Son?"

"He has Son?"

Reaching into his work apron, Nick answered, "Yes, He was born in Bethlehem. I will tell you all about Him next time we travel together. In the meantime, I want you to take these two gold coins as a wage for taking care of the house, the guests, the cooking and everything else. I don't know how I got on without you. Your new job will be to take care of all the internal affairs of Hope Mission. You will hire whomever you need to keep things running smoothly. Work closely with Brother Taylor; he has many with him that may be helpful to you."

"This is important position, yes?"

"Yes. This job can only be given to a man with a clean heart. The God of love told me you have a clean heart."

"Love God talk to you?"

"He sends his messenger. His messenger speaks to me."

"Mr. Nicholas, you hold money for me. I want save, buy freedom for wife."

"Your wife?" said Nicholas, truly astonished. "You have a wife?"

"Yes, and new baby soon too," laughed Makande. "Last winter I pray to Love God with Bell. We married after prayer."

"But why have you waited until now to tell me?"

"It takes long time to feel free," said Makande. "I feel like free man today. Time coming I want to bring wife and new baby to freedom, to Love God."

Nicholas hesitated, then said, "I'm almost afraid to ask where she is right now."

"Captain Ficci own her."

Nicholas walked to the workbench, paused another moment... "Well, we'll just have to buy her from him, won't we? Are you worried for her because she's always around the Captain?"

"Love God protect her till I come. One year, maybe, then I come."

Nicholas approached the former slave and laid a hand on his shoulder. "As soon as I see Rubin again, I'll send him to buy her freedom and bring her here so she can give birth to a free child."

"Captain ask too much when he sells slaves. He will ask much gold if he knows I buy her."

"Rubin will take care of the sale. Don't worry about the cost, Makande. God will provide the gold."

Makande smiled, fixing his eyes to Nick's, holding his hands on his heart. "We will work together for life, I know." Walking to Mario, he wheeled him to his room, saying, "You hear, Mario? You meet my Bell soon. She cook like angel from Love God... from God of love."

Returning to the workshop not long after with blankets and pillows, Makande reminded Nicholas there was no room left in the house, so they would have to sleep on the workshop floor for the night.

Chapter 30. Joseph Solo.

The next morning after breakfast, eighteen priests, nuns and monks gathered outside the cabin, preparing to make the journey up the mountain. Brother Taylor kept two nuns behind to help Makande manage the cabin, and to wait for Ben to return from Rome with the orphan children.

As Nicholas emerged from his workshop, eager to set off for Pizal, he opened the front door to the sight of a man no taller than a fence post, pacing the porch, biting his nails.

"Good morning, sir. How can I help you?" asked Nicholas with a friendly smile.

"And a sunshine morning it is, sir," said the tiny man. "My name is Joseph Solo and I am looking for Nicholas Kristo. Have I come to the right place?"

"Yes indeed. I'm Nicholas."

"Very good, very good," said Joseph nervously, picking at his thumb. "Is there a place we can speak alone? I won't take too much of your time, I promise, I promise."

"Of course, Joseph. Let's go to the barn."

As they walked past the monks and nuns packing their gear, Nicholas smiled, noticing Joseph's clothes and his quick, short stride as he hurried ahead. He wore a beret, and his thick, frizzy brown hair covered his collar. His burgundy overcoat fell all the way to the ground and pooled around him. He had a round face with large, pale blue eyes, and was clean-shaven, except for a patch of hair under his bottom lip.

The moment Nicholas opened the barn door and they stepped in, Joseph began to explain himself in a jittery, high-pitched voice. "The most important thing you should know right now is that I work alone, and I live alone. That's just the way it is. It must be this way."

"Wait, Joseph, slow down. Why are you here?" asked Nicholas grinning. "What brought you here?"

"I am sorry. I should tell you what happened. Two days ago, I woke up in my cabin and a brilliant white dove sat on my bedpost. I don't know how it got in, but there it was, almost glowing."

"Where do you live?

"I live alone in the mountains, just north of Rome. I only leave there when someone needs my help or to buy supplies. Anyway, I woke up and this dove was on my bedpost, and then I heard a voice in my head that I know is not my own. It said, 'Find Nicholas Kristo. He lives in Pizal.' And then the dove flew into the other room and waited by the front door."

"Are you a priest?"

"No," replied Joseph, beginning to pace the floor. "I wanted to be, but I realized because of my short stature no one would ever take me seriously. Some people laugh when they see me. I hate it when the ladies say, 'Oh, isn't he cute?' as if I'm a little puppy or something. Anyway, I love God and have a special relationship with Him, and that's all that really matters...to me."

Taking a seat on the grinding wheel, Nicholas asked, "So, tell me what happened next?"

"The bird stood by the door waiting for me to come find you. I knew it was a messenger of God because of the peace that came over me as the dove watched me prepare for the journey. Well, I set out for Pizal, asked around and so here I am, Nicholas. It was a two-day trip and I don't know why I'm here. Maybe *you* can tell *me*."

"Why do you live alone?"

"It must be that way, it must. God has given me the gift of healing, but it's different from the gifts of others. It seems God wants me to relate to the sickness or disability of the person who is to be healed. For example, if I am about to lay hands on a blind man, I will become blind temporarily. It's frightening. Before I lay hands on a leper, I break out in leper sores for a time. Too frightening! That's one of the reasons I live alone. If I'm among too many people for any period of time, all sorts of things start happening."

"Don't you get lonely?"

"Loneliness always *needs* something. In sweet solitude I'm never alone. God is there, always loving me."

Nicholas reached out to the man's shoulder. "Well, my friend, have I got a story to tell you."

Nicholas started from the beginning and told Joseph all about the messenger dove and Hope Mission. By the time he'd finished, Joseph sat transfixed, not wanting it to end.

"It's not the end, Joseph," said Nicholas, "it's just the beginning. We could certainly use a good man like you. Your gift is very rare and would be extremely valuable to the Mission."

"I cannot live around a lot of people," said Joseph, shaking his head. "It's just impossible. As much as I would like to join you on this tremendous adventure, I can't. I must be alone."

"We could make that happen. You could live close by, but still have privacy."

"What do you mean?"

Pointing toward the mountain, Nick explained, "A half mile from where the Mission will be built is a huge rock that juts up from the ground, past the tallest trees. It's flat on top and is the perfect spot to build a look-out cabin. From there, you can see in all directions from San Marco to Rome. It's the most scenic location on the summit."

"I would be away from everybody?"

"Most of the time, if you choose."

"Don't get me wrong. I love people. It's just that I have no control when I'm to lay hands on someone."

"I understand completely. You could stand watch alone most of the time, and if we really need you, we'll send a messenger. By the time you come back here with your things, the cabin would be built. We have many people up there right now willing to help."

Joseph flashed a smile. "This could actually work, couldn't it?"

"Indeed it could, if you're willing."

Reaching out his tiny hand, Joseph promised to return within a week with all of his books. He said that was all he owned of any value.

Nicholas thanked him and wished him a safe journey, then saddled his horse and set off to Pizal to announce his departure.

So much was happening with the Mission. Nicholas prayed as he rode towards the village, asking God for wisdom. So many people were turning to him for answers.

A call from behind broke his prayerful meditation.

"Nicholas, Nicholas, wait for me!"

Pulling the reins, Nicholas stopped and turned the horse. "Rubin, how are you, son?"

"I'm well. Any word from Justus?" asked Rubin, pulling the reins to a stop, patting his horse's neck.

"By now he must be returning from Pinzolo. Soon I'll send you on a mission together, but for now I have an important task. Are you up to it?"

"By all means, sir. Where are you sending me now?"

"San Marco," said Nicholas. "This is a dangerous mission and I need someone intelligent and business-minded if we're to be successful."

Reaching into his saddlebags he came out with a sack containing fifty gold florins. "Take this and ride to the Command Post in San Marco. Leave most of the gold at the Magistrate's office until your business is finished. You are going to confront two of the most dangerous men in all of Italy, so be extremely cautious and do exactly as I say. Ask for Captain Andrea Ficci. When he comes, you must be deceptive and tell him you're from the north, because he'll come looking for you after you make a deal. Tell him his name is renowned all over Italy, and you've heard from various slave traders that he has some of the finest, most skilled slaves. You're interested in a slave named Bell who is an expert chef. Tell him your employer wishes to stay anonymous for his own reasons, but will pay a handsome price for her. If he invites you to his estate or anywhere else immediately, tell him you left your money at the Magistrate's office and you'll finalize the sale later that day, when you sign ownership papers."

"Why are we buying a slave?" asked Rubin, placing the sack in his saddlebag.

"She is Makande's pregnant wife. At some point Ficci will probably invite you to his estate to sample her food. You can go, just make sure he knows you're not carrying the gold. Try to sign the ownership papers and have Bell with you by sunset. Tell him you'll be staying at a local hotel for the night and you'll be traveling home first thing in the morning. After you've paid the hotel fee, wait an hour, then pack your things and ride through the night back to Pizal. Don't stop until you're at the Mission."

"Why not just leave in the morning?"

Nicholas maneuvered his horse beside Rubin's and laid a hand on his shoulder. "I know it will be a very long day for you, but this man would think nothing of finding you on the road back, slicing your throat and taking his prize slave back home. He just wants the gold. Your life doesn't matter to him."

"What price should I pay?"

"Because you're so young, he will try to squeeze as much as he can right away. Just turn around and start walking. He won't let you leave if he knows you have a substantial sum. When he gives his second price, offer him slightly less; that should do it. Now, before you leave, go back to my farm, saddle another horse and take it in tow for Bell."

Rubin straightened his white banker's collar nervously. "Don't worry, Nicholas. I'll bring her back. Although I have no crossbow or dagger like Justus, I can broker a deal. That's my gift, Nick. Father said I could sell Rosary Beads to the Devil."

Smiling, Nicholas agreed, "I know, son, that's why I chose you. One more thing; this won't make any sense to you, but if you see a shining white dove at any time, watch it very closely. It will help you in a time of trouble. Don't ask me how, just trust what I say is true."

"Justus mentioned something about that dove. I will keep my eye out for it."

Nicholas said a prayer of protection, then a moment later Rubin was off, galloping toward the farm.

CHAPTER 31. BUT WAS IT CIVILIZED?

*W*hen Ben reached the outskirts of Rome, he gazed down from the foothills, in awe of the scope and breadth of the city. With the Coliseum and St. Peter's dome dominating the horizon, and hordes of wagons gone to market, this truly was the 'center of civilization'. But was it civilized?

With a good hour's ride before he entered the city, Ben slapped the reins and moved the horses down the country road. Wondering where he might first begin to look for homeless children, he felt a chill of warning beneath his mask. He stopped the wagon and stepped out to look around, suspecting some kind of trouble. A white dove swooped down and landed on a tree next to a narrow path leading into the woods. It flew up again and then down some fifty paces in. Ben followed it for several minutes before he spotted a woman pulling a small wagon towards the edge of a cliff. When the woman looked over the edge, hauling the wagon closer yet, Ben called out, "Hello, hello, do you need help?"

Weeping, the woman said, "Go away. You'll ruin everything. Just go away!"

As she moved behind the wagon, and pushed it to the edge, a rock stopped the wheel.

Ben hurried toward her crying out, "Whatever it is, Miss, I will help you. I promise."

Pointing into the wagon, she stepped to the very edge and moaned, "No one could ever help with this."

"Stop, please! Just let me see."

When he approached the wagon and looked inside, his heart sank. Two girls, about eight years old, lay on the floor convulsing wildly with palsy. It was the worst he'd ever seen. They were twins, and their eyes rolled while their tongues, dribbling with saliva, slid over their cheeks and chins. Their arms and legs were bent and twisted in un-natural ways, constantly convulsing, jutting this way and that.

The woman stopped crying and, looking into the wagon with bitterness, said, "Today is their eleventh birthday. They look much younger because they cannot straighten their bodies. Eleven years of torment is enough. It will be over soon, daughters."

The dove flew over and landed on the wagon, facing Ben.

"Were they born this way?" Ben asked, as calmly as he could.

"No, it happened about a year after. It's been a living nightmare since then. My husband left me, saying they have demons and I am cursed. From that point on, it's just been them and me. I cannot manage another day—not another hour. To watch them suffer and have no life at all is unbearable. We will all stop suffering this day... but I'll wait until you leave."

Ben broke in, "God has a—"

"Don't you dare mention God to me," the woman hissed with narrowed eyes. "Don't you say a word about Him. How could you look at these children and say He exists? And if He does, that He... cares?"

Ben squatted down next to the wagon and petted the dove, then reached in and touched the children's feet. They instantly fell into a deep sleep.

The woman looked on in amazement. "Who are you, sir? They hardly ever sleep, and never in the day. How did you do that?"

"My name is Ben Bellicini and I am a missionary working with Hope Mission. I don't know why they fell asleep, but I think there is still hope for them and you. The founder of our Mission is an extraordinary man of God. He will find a way to help you."

"If he's anything like the ones around here, just forget it," said the woman. "There is no hope and there is no God. Now that they sleep, they won't feel any pain when they hit the bottom. I thank you for this! Now, if you'll excuse me . . . "

"Wait, please wait. What if you're wrong? What if there is a chance for them? You will be the one taking it away from them. I know you love them and wish to die with them, but I beg you to wait for just a while longer."

The woman sighed, and wiped her eyes on her worn sleeve. "I cannot wait, sir. They are not only suffering from palsy, but we are all starving as well. Look how thin they are!"

"If you come with me into Rome," Ben pleaded, "I will take care of everything. I have a big wagon with a roof. You can have food and shelter there until we return to Pizal. We have a fine new orphanage, with kind sisters in charge. We'll take the children there until they see Nicholas. Please do give yourselves this chance. If nothing else, it will offer you some days of comfort."

The woman stared at him, with hope dawning in her exhausted eyes. Then she turned abruptly to the wagon.

Ben made a move to delay her, but she gave him a sudden smile. "We will come with you, for a feel a spark of hope."

"A great fire may follow a tiny spark," said Ben, and smiled back under the mask.

The woman stared at him for a few seconds. "I think it's that mask you're wearing," she said. "The expression...it makes me think you care and that you're an honest man. Imagine how silly that sounds—but it's true. Why do you wear it anyway?"

Ben told her everything as they settled the sleeping children in the wagon and continued on the way to Rome. He felt, rightly, that to hear a tale of misfortune overcome and a life renewed in hope would strengthen her.

Her name, she told him, was Maria, and her twins were Daisy and Rose. As the children slept, Ben and Maria drove on, drinking cider and eating bread and sausage. He even made her laugh once, when he told the story of the highwaymen who had sought to steal his gold. For the first time since the fire, Ben felt attracted to a woman.

Maria was his own age, thirty-two years old, and when she smiled, it was magic to him. While she was plain looking, he came to think her personality extraordinary. Could she ever, maybe by some miracle, grow to have feelings for him? As quickly, he dismissed the thought when he imagined what her reaction would be if he ever removed his mask. But still, it was good to have her company.

When they entered the city, Ben explained that his mission was to gather up as many homeless children as would fit in the wagon, and bring them back to the orphanage. Maria told him that she had spotted young ones at the city dump the day before while she searched for scraps of food.

After Maria guided him to the spot, Ben rode upwind of the stench and found a place to stay until morning. As they waited patiently for homeless children, they talked until night fell, totally engrossed with each other. Daisy and Rose remained asleep.

When the clouds moved away from the moon, Maria pointed to several children moving over heaps of debris toward a shelter of sorts, on the other side of the dump. Several minutes after the children disappeared from view, an enchanting sound came from that direction. Someone was singing and playing a stringed instrument.

"Whoever's singing has the most beautiful voice I've ever heard," Maria said. "You agree, Ben?"

"Yes indeed. Let's walk over and see what's going on. If Daisy and Rose awake, we're sure to hear them."

Ben leapt from the wagon, turned and reached for Maria, helping her step down. As they made their way over mounds of debris, they drew close to a shelter made of doors, planks and pieces of fence. Ben reached for Maria's arm, whispering, "Let's stop and listen."

A deep velvet voice, with perfectly timed vibrato, accompanied by harmonic chords plucked on strings, filled the air. He sang,

"Listen child, don't fear the night,
The God of love will bring His light,
To guide you through without a tear,
To draw you close and keep you near."

"Go around the front and ask if we may join them," Ben whispered, "I'm afraid I might scare them wearing the mask and all."

Maria peeked in and saw a dozen children sleeping around an old man with a long beard. He was dressed, in rags, and playing a guitar, completely unaware of her presence. She spoke through a crack in the door. "Good evening, sir."

The old man stopped playing and replied pleasantly, "Who is it? Who's there? I am blind."

"My name is Maria, sir. My friend Ben and I heard you singing. It was so lovely we had to see. May we come in?"

"Yes, you may," said the old man, "but my songs are finished for tonight. I can tell the children are asleep."

Maria called to Ben and they entered, seeing the sleeping children but very little else in the flickering candlelight. Ben had to kneel because of the low ceiling.

"Good evening, friend. My name is Ben. What's yours?"

"I am Giovanni, and I sing for the children."

"Are all of these children homeless?" Ben asked.

"Sad to say this is true, sir. I know there are many others in Rome, but these children have been with me now for some time. They bring me scraps of food and I shelter them here at night. They say they feel safe with me. I don't know why. I'm blind. How could I possibly protect them?"

An older boy awoke and gently replied, "We feel safe because your songs stop our fears and we all sleep through the night, Giovanni. We get to hear about God too. Your songs bring us hope."

"Would you sing just one more tune for the night, Giovanni? We've never heard such a wonderful voice. God has truly gifted you," Ben said, glancing around at the children cuddled beside one another in the shelter.

Giovanni began picking the strings of his worn guitar, singing a lullaby about King David's Psalms. Midway through, Maria started to nod, and Ben's eyes became heavy. It was true. Giovanni's voice was so soothing it could enchant anyone.

After the song, Ben asked Giovanni if he would consider relocating to Hope Orphanage with all of the children. He would have his own room, new clothes and would work closely with the brothers and sisters to care for the young ones. "You would be most welcome, and your presence would be a blessing for all."

"I thought the city dump would be my final resting place," Giovanni replied, a tear falling from his sightless eyes. "Thank God I was wrong. God bless you, we will come."

Ben and Maria left, promising to return in the morning to meet the children and take everyone who was willing to begin a new life at the orphanage.

The next morning, as Ben stepped out of the wagon, Giovanni and fourteen children greeted him with smiles and hugs, anxious to hear more about Hope Orphanage.

The younger children joined Daisy and Rose in the wagon, while the others walked alongside, singing Giovanni's songs. Ben walked beside them while Maria took the reins of the wagon, with Giovanni at her side with his guitar. They would have a full day's journey before they arrived at the leper colony, and then another day to reach the outskirts of Pizal.

All along the way, Ben's prayers did not cease, as he hoped that Nicholas could do something to help Maria's children. He knew she would fall deeper into despair, and maybe become suicidal again, if Daisy and Rose suffered much longer.

CHAPTER 32. COUNSELING JUSTUS.

J ust before the changing of the guard, Sergeant Manuel Ficci limped into the San Marco Command Post with his arm in a sling, looking for his brother. Andrea sat at his desk. His jaw dropped when he saw Manuel in such disarray. "What happened to you? Where're your men?"

"All the men are... dead," said Manuel, lowering his head. "I'm the only one who made it out alive."

Manuel summarized the whole story, from the time they started the investigation, to his encounter with the ravenous wolves, to meeting up with Raven Bellicini.

"Are you positive it was leprosy? Was it a grayish rash?" asked the Captain.

"Yes," said Manuel. "I made her take the bandage off. I saw it myself."

"What happened to your horse?"

"Coming up a hill, it stepped into a rabbit hole and broke its leg. I had to shoot it. I sprained my arm when I fell," said Manuel, breathing a sigh of humiliation.

"It's hard for me to believe that I sent a fully armed and trained patrol out to arrest an unarmed family, and only one comes back... and he's half-dead," the Captain mocked.

"There is some good news to all of this, Andrea."

"I can't wait to hear it."

"When I went into Nicholas Kristo's barn looking for clues, I found a grinding wheel. There must have been a pound of gold embedded into the stone. He obviously has found gold nuggets somewhere and is grinding them down to gold dust to avoid being noticed."

"Finally something worthy for my brother to bring to the table," said the Captain. "Who is Nicholas Kristo?"

"Ben Bellicini's friend. I went to his house looking for the Bellicinis. I didn't find them, but you won't believe who I did find." The Sergeant paused for effect. "Makande, your former slave. He was there carrying a man with no legs."

"How did Makande end up there?"

"When I was on the traders road leading to Pizal, I met a slave trader who said a young man with a sack of gold dust bought Makande from him. He was with a man on a white horse. When I questioned him further, I found out it was Ty Bellicini's horse."

"So everything leads back to this Nicholas Kristo."

Manuel nodded.

The Captain stood and paced around his desk. "While you were gone I did a lot of thinking about the Bellicinis and their property. They will be on the run for the rest of their lives. In time, I will seize the property anyway. But for the sake of the gold, we will still pursue them. Where do you think they are?"

"Up on that mountain somewhere with Kristo... surrounded by wolves."

"So we just need to get past the wolves?"

Manuel's eyes grew wide. "Those wolves overwhelmed us. There must have been thirty or forty of them. We shot at least ten, but they flanked us on every side and attacked before we could reload. They were lean and appeared starving, and fought one another for the meat. I watched them devour two of our horses as well."

"After we get you patched up, we'll have a training session with the Royal Guard. When we go back there, it'll be with overwhelming force. We'll not only ultimately find Nicholas Kristo and his gold, but look like heroes by ridding Pizal of the horrid wolf problem and a murderous fugitive family."

Manuel sat on the desk, pulling his injured foot onto his lap. "It may take a few weeks. I can barely walk right now. That wolf almost took off one of my toes."

"Don't worry, Manuel, we have all the time we want. As it stands, they think they are safe on that mountain so they'll probably remain there. My question is, what keeps them safe from the wolves? They must have some sort of barricade. Whatever it is we'll soon find out."

Manuel finally smiled.

After his visit to Pizal, Nicholas returned to the farm and asked Makande to prepare himself and Mario for the journey to the top of the mountain. He guessed Ben would return from Rome with a wagonload of children and wanted only the nuns in the cabin to begin the orphanage. In the meantime, he rode out to the burnt-down Pallone estate to see if the new construction had begun.

He found Brother Taylor sitting on the ground studying Mario's plans. The burnt debris had been cleared and the frame of the large house was already in place. Nicholas waved as he recognized some of the fifteen men Michael Borelli hired from Pizal to work on the building.

Nicholas dismounted, smiling. "Brother Taylor, I see things are moving right along."

"Hello, Nicholas. They sure are. Wait until you see what they've done on top of the mountain! It's going so well up there that I decided to get things moving here at the orphanage. Has Ben returned from Rome yet?"

"Not yet," said Nicholas, "but he should be here any time now. How much work is completed on the Bellicini house?"

"Ox is amazing," said Taylor. "He has his hands in everything—he never stops. Sometimes he works into the night. When I saw how well he handles people and the construction, I left him to oversee in my absence. The others are just as helpful and hard-working. There are over forty people living up there now. I had the brothers buy milling equipment, a hundred pounds of nails, sheets of glass and a host of other hardware and raw material, as we are well past midway in construction."

Nicholas instructed Taylor to build a lookout cabin on the huge rock that jutted up past the trees. It was to be anchored to the rock, with baffles all around, because of the treacherous winds. "In the meantime, Mario should be done with the plans for the church building and the housing for all of you. I will bring them up this afternoon."

"We'll be waiting," said Brother Taylor, with a smile.

When Nicholas returned to the farm, Makande and Mario were packed and waiting. They put all of Mario's drafting supplies and silversmith tools and clothes on one side of his donkey and the new wheelchair on the other. Makande had Mario strapped to his back and they would be riding together, eager to see the new building.

Justus was at the base of the mountain waiting when Nicholas arrived with Makande and Mario. When they approached, Justus walked his horse to them.

"Everything went very well with Sister Hannah. The berries we sent are having a tremendous impact on the colony. Hannah said the people have come to life again, and are looking forward to the new housing. Even though she doesn't know who's doing all the good, she wants to say 'thank you.'"

Justus maneuvered his horse beside Nicholas as they moved onto the trail. "Nicholas, may I ask why you choose to remain anonymous?"

Cantering slightly ahead of Makande and Mario, Nicholas explained, "Our Savior and King said that when we give to the poor and needy, we should not be like hypocrites who want attention for such giving. It can become a prideful thing and therefore bring dishonor to our God. The chance of this happening to us is even greater because 'giving' to the poor and hurting is our main objective. Our gifts must ultimately glorify God, not us. Sometimes we cannot avoid being open when we help someone, and if that's the case, we should give with humility and grace, never expecting anything in return."

"I think I understand now," said Justus. "You know, you were right about the problem I have with being revengeful and unforgiving. All I could think about on this past mission trip was how to kill the Ficci brothers. I started to realize how those thoughts dominated my life. I couldn't even think of Raven, whom I adore. I came to realize that I'm not free to think as I choose, because too many bad feelings have taken over. The thing is; I don't know how to get out of it. I want to be free to enjoy thinking about the pleasant things in life, but how?"

Nicholas grinned. "Well you've made the first, most important step already, Justus."

"I did? What's that?"

"You've acknowledged the fact that you have a problem. Not only that, but you've nailed down the nature of the problem. You're not free. Makande's heart and mind were always free, even while he was in slavery. Your slavery is self-imposed. Your master is hatred and bitterness."

"If that's the case, how can I be freed?"

"When you've accepted that what I've said is indeed the truth, you must forgive the Ficci brothers and then let go of everything attaching you to them."

Disappointed, Justus replied, "I knew you would get to that 'forgiveness' thing sooner or later. I just dread it."

"But it will give you your freedom," Nicholas said. "Your hatred doesn't hurt the Ficci brothers. As a matter of fact, if they knew you hated them, they would probably enjoy it. You would be giving them pleasure by hating them. The only one it's hurting is you."

"The offence is too great for me to forgive."

Nicholas pulled his reins and stopped the horse. Justus did the same, leaning on his saddle horn, locking eyes with Nick.

"Everyone will receive justice in the end. There is one God and Judge over all of us, and His Justice is fair and true. No one will escape it. Let me ask you a question. Are you innocent of wrongdoing?"

"Not by any stretch."

"Our Savior was. Not once did he offend or do wrong. Yet, He was mocked, scourged and spat upon, worse than you were by the Ficci brothers. When religion nailed Jesus to the cross, He asked His Father to forgive the offenders because they didn't know what they were doing. It was a mindless act. Evil and selfishness have consumed the Ficci brothers and in the end they will eat the fruits of their own way."

"But I can help God implement justice."

"God does not need our help for that. You must trust that He is true to His word. That's what's missing Justus—trust. You don't trust anyone but yourself to get the job done. As this situation with the Ficci brothers unfolds, you will see the hand of God at work, and you will have to make choices regarding your willingness or unwillingness to forgive. Just remember this, a society can forgive a criminal for the most heinous crime, but the Judge will still make him pay for his crimes. If you ever find the strength to forgive those brothers, they will still have to face eternal judgment before a Perfect Judge. Trust Him."

"You've given me much to think about," Justus said, his voice thick with emotion. "I know I want to be free to love, but my feelings are still too strong."

"Just think on the things I've told you, and in time you will start to see life in a new light. When that happens, your freedom will be at the door, and will taste...sweet. And by the way, it's because of your intense feelings that I had to send Rubin to San Marco and not you."

"You sent Rubin to San Marco? Why?"

"I found out that Makande's married, and that Captain Ficci owns his wife. I sent Rubin to buy her and bring her here."

"That's one job I wish you had given to me."

"You wouldn't have been able to contain your hatred and contempt. Perhaps when you gain more control of your feelings there'll be another opportunity. Before you can face the Ficci brothers, you have to master what you think and how you think and feel. If you slip and make one mistake, they will kill you without batting an eyelid."

Justus thanked Nicholas and urged his horse forward, saying he missed Raven and would meet Nick at the top.

CHAPTER 33. RUBIN CONFRONTS CAPTAIN FICCI.

*A*t the Command Post in San Marco, the Ficci brothers interrupted their conversation only long enough to look over the young man who'd just come through the door inquiring the whereabouts of the Judge Magistrate.

Rubin was handsome but short and skinny, with a ruddy complexion. He sported a thin mustache over pencil-thin lips, and dressed in the clothes his parents provided, dark suits befitting an accountant.

Rubin took a saddlebag in hand, wiped the road dust off his jacket, adjusted his white collar and walked up two steps to present himself at the Magistrate's desk.

"Good day, sir, my name is Oscar Grosseto. I am from the beautiful city of Benevento, in the north, and have come in search of a certain Captain Andre Ficci. Do you happen to know where I can find him?"

"Well, young man, you won't have to look very far," said the Judge. "He's sitting right across the room with his brother. He is the one with the white hair. Will you be staying long in San Marco?"

"No, sir," said Rubin, glancing at the Captain. "I have instructions from my employer to return as soon as my business is finished. May I leave gold florins here with you during my stay?"

Smiling, the Judge stroked his beard. "Yes, you may, young man. I see someone has instructed you well."

Rubin removed a leather sack from his saddlebag. "I will send a messenger to you advising how much and whom you should release the money to, as I don't want to travel with these coins more than I have to. If there is anything left after the sale, I will pay to have the balance sent on to me. Is this acceptable to you, Judge?"

"Yes, of course," said the judge, pulling a ledger from his desk. "Sign the book and I will arrange the rest."

After Rubin signed in and turned over the gold, he approached Captain Ficci's desk, overhearing Manuel say, "Don't worry, Andre. I'll be well enough to travel again in a week. By then I won't need this stupid crutch. I'll just stay on my horse more often."

Glaring at Rubin, Manuel barked, "Is there someone you're looking for, boy?"

"Yes, sir. I'm told this is the desk of Captain Andrea Ficci."

The Captain rose from his desk and stood beside his brother. "I'm Captain Ficci and this is my brother, Manuel. What brings you here?"

With a lump in his throat, Rubin rubbed his sweaty hands onto his breeches. "Let me begin by saying what a great honor it is to finally meet you, Captin Ficci. My name is Oscar Grosseto and I'm from the northern city of Benevento. Your name is renowned all the way to Sicily, sir. I pleaded with my employer to commission me for this business proposition."

Smiling, the Captain moved closer. "All the way to Sicily, you say? What do they say about me?"

Rubin put on his most admiring voice. "They say you are the most honored soldier in the Royal Guard, and are destined for high government positions. I've even heard a lady of means mock her husband's manhood by comparing his to yours."

"Is that so?" asked the Captain, lifting his chin. "So what is this business proposition you're interested in?"

"My employer, who wishes to stay anonymous for personal reasons, hears that you have some of the finest slaves in Italy. He is a very successful businessman who entertains important people on a daily basis. He is in search of a slave he believes to be in your possession. Her name is Bell. Do you own her?"

The Captain scratched his chin. "How did he come to know that I own her?"

Rubin paused a moment... "I don't know, sir. My employer did not privy me with that information. I only know that I'm not to return with a substitute if you have already sold her. May I ask if you still own her, Captain, sir?"

"Yes, I own her. She is my finest slave."

"On behalf of my employer, may I ask if she is for sale and at what price?"

"She's a fine specimen and I could not take anything less than thirty gold florins for her."

"Sir, forgive me, but why do you ask over double the normal rate for this slave?"

"Because she is with child. If you buy her, the child will be yours as well."

"I'm sorry, sir. I have strict instructions not to spend more than twenty florins. I hope I've not taken too much of your time, but it was indeed a pleasure to make your acquaintance." Rubin turned and walked toward the Magistrate.

"Wait, please, we can work something out, Mr. Grosseto. I may be able to reduce my price. Bell has not performed nearly as well since her husband was sold. If you think your employer could do better with her, I'll let her go for twenty-six florins."

"Twenty-four and it's a deal, Captain Ficci. My employer will be well pleased, and I will get a bonus because of the child."

"Twenty-four it is then. Tomorrow you may visit my estate and Bell will cook your favorite meal."

"Again," said Rubin, smiling, "forgive me, but I must be on my way first thing tomorrow. Is there a way we can close the deal tonight?"

"Of course," said the Captain. "Let's leave right now and I'll have Bell make you a late lunch before you sign the ownership papers and take her. You can pay me and be on your way this very evening."

"Perfect, Captain. I left the gold with the Magistrate. In the morning, before I leave, I will tell him to release the monies to you."

"Your employer sent the right man for the job. Our Royal Guard cannot protect everyone from would-be criminals seeking to relieve visitors of their saddlebags."

Rubin pretended to be relaxed and content after the business transaction, but his nerves were on edge. Sergeant Ficci did not take his eyes off him the entire time.

The Captain took his brother aside and whispered something, then returned with a crooked smile, promising Rubin the best meal he'd ever had.

After they left the Command Post, riding toward the Captain's estate, Rubin began to have visions of Manuel Ficci ambushing him on the road back to Pizal. He had to escape with Bell in the dead of night, just as Nicholas advised him, if there was any chance of success.

Entering a private winding road onto Captain Ficci's estate, Rubin kept praising the beauty of the property and estate in an effort to keep his mind from freezing with fear. When they arrived at the impressive white mansion, a pregnant black woman stood straining a smile under the portico, stroking her swollen belly, waving at the Captain.

"That's her, Oscar. Isn't Bell a prize?"

Bell was a light skinned African with Asian influences somewhere in her genealogy, showing in a small nose and high cheekbones.

Touring the mansion, Rubin was amazed at the wealth the Captain had amassed. From the fine paintings and sculpture that dressed the walls and corridors, to the gold and silver dinnerware and candlesticks glimmering on the dining room table, he'd never seen so many things of value in one place. Unlike his brother Manuel, Captain Ficci was well groomed and had the slaves keep his home impeccably clean. From all he'd seen, Rubin was almost fooled into believing the Captain might not be as bad as his reputation warranted, until two frightened girls walked into the dining room.

These beautiful slaves, not more than fifteen or sixteen, brought in trays of fresh fruit and cheese, laid them on the table, and asked the Captain what else he desired. While Rubin sipped his port wine, he observed the Captain devour the girls with his eyes. He noticed a strange twitch on one side of his mouth as he ordered them to stand at the window until Bell called them to help with dinner.

"Where did you get those lovely creatures, Captain?" asked Rubin, lighting a cigar the Captain gave him.

"Oh, you like them young, do you, Oscar?"

"Actually I've never had one as young as these, but my employer would melt with envy if he were here right now. He has a taste for the young and innocent. They don't appear Italian. What nationality are they?"

"They are Spaniards," said the Captain. "Rosa is fourteen and Linda fifteen. I bought them from their father when I was in Barcelona last year. He was about to lose his tavern, so I made him an offer, and before I could finish the sentence he pushed the girls to my side. I guess I was in the right place at the right time. Anyway, the hardest part of owning them is deciding which one will warm my belly in the evening."

As the young girls stood by the open window, with their heads down and their arms crossed, a white dove flew onto the windowsill between them. Rubin recalled what Nicholas had said about the dove, and a plan popped into his mind.

"You're a lot like my employer, Captain Ficci. He would be tickled to have a choice like that. You're a lucky man. Let me ask an insane question. Would you ever consider selling them? I know I wouldn't. They're so lovely."

"Everything has a price, Oscar," said the Captain, "But I doubt if you brought enough gold to afford them. Besides, I haven't quite tired of them yet."

"It would be fun to explore the possibilities, don't you agree? Can I make you an offer?"

"By all means, young man, but it better be good. If you managed to take them, I would be without any females in the house, and that would leave me more than a little perturbed come bedtime."

"Then I'll be bold and make only one offer," said Rubin. "I've left forty-five gold florins with the Magistrate. I've spent only a small amount for my lodging at the hotel. I will give you all that the Magistrate is holding as well as what is in my possession for those sweetmeats."

The Captain turned towards the girls, and scratched his chin in thought. Finally, he smiled and turned to Rubin. "After we have that roasted duckling, I'll have the girls pack their things. You have a deal, young man."

"Wonderful! Wonderful! My employer will be beside himself," Rubin said, laughing.

With a salacious smirk, the Captain said, "I'm sure this evening when you're in the inn room you'll be tempted to test what you've purchased for your employer."

"Let's put it this way, Captain," Rubin said, imitating the Captain's smirk. "I'm going to become very close to all three ladies before they even know my employer's name. Tonight will be very interesting."

When the sound of horse hooves clamored in the distance, Captain Ficci went to the open window. A patrol of soldiers had come with reports of the day's activities. "Why not have some more wine, Oscar? I'll be only a few minutes with my men."

The Captain hurried away, leaving Rosa and Linda alone with Rubin for the first time. The young man assured the girls that all would be well, and then went to the window. The Captain stood in front of the house, stabbing his finger into a soldier's chest while the others looked on, expressionless.

Rubin spent the time remaining by sifting hurriedly through the documents on the Captain's desk. When he stooped to pick up them that had been dislodged by his hasty perusal, he noticed the corner of a paper sticking out from behind the desk, upright against the wall. He retrieved it and began to read.

Rubin had seen many such documents while working with his father at the bank. This was a purchase order for ten racehorses, and the signature appearing next to Captain Ficci's was that of the Duke of Guise. This, Rubin recalled, was the man his father said was sent by Henry II of France to invade Italy. Apparently, Captain Ficci was acquainted with the Duke and had bought the horses with government monies. This one document could finish Captain Ficci's illustrious career, for it revealed not only his collaboration with the enemy but also that he was stealing from the Italian treasury.

Rubin put the document in his jacket pocket and gulped down his wine. This would surely give them leverage when the time came to confront the Captain regarding the Bellicini family.

"Come, girls," Bell called, stepping into the room. "It's time to help with dinner."

As the girls left, Captain Ficci returned. Sipping his port, he remarked, "Smell that, Oscar? That's what your employer will enjoy every night, the moment you deliver Bell. Let's relax in the dining room. We're finished with business and it's time to savor Bell's delights."

"Forgive me if we leave just after dinner," Rubin said. "We will want an early start in the morning. It's already getting dark and at least a day's ride to Benevento. A signed release form for the gold will be awaiting you at the Magistrate's office tomorrow."

After dinner, Bell looked on curiously as the men signed ownership papers for the slaves. Rosa and Linda had already packed their things, and were at the front door. Bell slowly made her way down the stairs with a carpetbag and half-knitted, multi-colored baby blanket. With their gazes to the ground, the women said their hollow goodbyes to Captain Ficci.

The Spanish sisters rode double on a horse that the Captain provided as part of the arrangement. Bell took the horse Rubin had brought in tow and the foursome began their way into San Marco. Smiles appeared on the slaves' faces as Rubin explained why he had come, and that they soon would be free, and Bell would be reunited with her husband. Leading the way, he heard the women giggling behind.

He thought of the purchase order he'd 'borrowed' from the Captain. If used in the right way, it could change everything for the Bellicinis.

As he let his horse fall behind, Rubin witnessed such joyful hope emanating from the women that he couldn't think of a career more gratifying or fulfilling than the one he'd chosen.

When they arrived at the hotel in San Marco, Rubin noticed Sergeant Ficci with two soldiers across the road, waiting.

After entering the hotel, he paid for two additional rooms and told the former slaves to be ready to leave in the dead of night at a moment's notice. Then he signed the release form for the gold, telling the hotel manager to bring it to the Magistrate first thing in the morning.

Rubin waited for a good hour after Sergeant Ficci had left the scene before waking the women. They left, heading north, but doubled back on a different southbound road as soon as they were out of San Marco.

Sergeant Ficci and his men arrived at the hotel at 6 am, inquiring as to the whereabouts of Rubin and the slaves. The manager turned over the Magistrate's release form, explaining that Rubin had left with the women some time during the night, and was heading north. Sergeant Ficci and his men bolted from the hotel office and rode toward Benevento. By the time they realized they'd been deceived, Rubin and the women were riding into Pizal.

CHAPTER 34. A LETTER OF DISTRESS.

When Nicholas rounded the last turn on the trail leading to the summit, the lake to the east was spotted with missionaries, fishing for the evening meal. To the west was an open field with two construction projects underway. A dozen men working in the center were clearing the ground, preparing for the church construction. Where the trail ended and field began stood the Bellicini home. Monks and priests were busy on the roof, working hard to complete Hope Mission's first building.

Makande rode up from behind, while Mario, strapped to his back, reached in his leather binder and handed Nicholas plans for the church. As Nick sat reviewing them, Ox stepped out of the front door of his new home. With a wide smile and hearty laugh, he waved them over.

"Hello, my friends; welcome home. Mario, we've set aside a large room for you on the first floor. One of the brothers made you a bed, cabinet, and drafting table." Pointing to the house, Ox asked, "What do you think, Nick?"

Nicholas looked to the roof, with its double chimneys, and then to the adjoining guesthouse. "I think you've all done a marvelous job, Ox. It's beautiful. Let's have a look inside."

Both fireplaces were ablaze in the grand room as Ox led the way. Some construction was still ongoing in the stairwells and kitchen, but most of the work was complete. After touring the massive kitchen and second level bedrooms, they returned to the grand room. While Nicholas praised Ox and the others for a job well done, he noticed a white dove sitting on a silver tray across the room on the fireplace mantle.

"How long has my friend been sitting there?" he asked.

"Since this morning," Ox replied. "It's sitting on a letter that arrived from Anna Borelli. One of the brothers brought it here, saying a messenger delivered it to her with hopes it would somehow reach you, since no one knows where you live any more."

As Nicholas walked to the silver tray, the dove flew up onto his shoulders. On the front of the folded page were the words, "To the Founder of Hope Mission", in the most beautiful script he'd ever seen. Thinking the letter must be of extreme importance for the dove to take such keen interest, he excused himself and sat on a cushioned chair by the fireplace.

Dear Founder of Hope Mission,

It has come to my attention that you are building a mission somewhere to help those of the world who are missing limbs and others that are hurting. Two of the most delightful young monks have come to my home and added my mother's name to their list so she will receive a special shoe. She's always limped, having been born with one leg shorter than the other.

I don't know if you are able to help, or would even want to. I'm a wealthy woman owning a villa in Rome, and a mansion estate in Cosenza, where I'm residing now. My father recently passed on and left me a great inheritance, but it does me no good, having the disabilities that have of late consumed my life.

I live in a constant state of depression and unhappiness. Since last year, fear seizes me day and night, causing sleeplessness for long periods. I don't have the slightest idea why I've come to this morbid state, but it has become unbearable. Doctors have tried all their antidotes and therapies, but I just seem to be getting worse. I have become reclusive, rarely going out any more, for fear of personal injury or suspicious someone may have designs on my wealth.

Sitting here with all the worldly goods I could ever hope for, I envied those young monks. The joy present in their eyes as they spoke of their mission, and their refusal to take money for the gift they earnestly desired to deliver, made me weep at their genuine goodness.

The monks have said you are an extraordinary man of God; and if anyone could help, it's you. I have always been Christian, but my family never took an interest or thought that a spiritual education was necessary for a family of such means. I believe God exists, but don't believe he's as interested in the wealthy, having been given so much already. If you have any thoughts on the matter, I would indeed be thankful and would give a considerable donation to your Mission. You may be my last hope for a cure.

Sincere Regards,
Bernadette LaViano.

One of the things Nicholas loved most to give was a gift that money couldn't buy. This letter would create a mission for him to do just that. He would ride to Cosenza and visit Bernadette LaViano himself. In the morning he'd stop at his farm to check on the children Ben brought from Rome, and then go off to Cosenza. Nicholas smiled, loving his job.

CHAPTER 35. A MIRACLE IN THE BARN.

The next morning at Nicholas's farm, Sister Mary peered out the kitchen window and saw a strange little man sitting on the porch steps. As he read his book, he twirled a lock of long, curly hair, jouncing his knee up and down faster than a nervous woodpecker. Behind him stood a Shetland pony and a mule packed with mostly books.

Stepping out the front door, the nun greeted him. "Good Morning, sir. May I ask what brings you here?"

"Good day, Sister, good day. I am Joseph Solo, and have come at the request of Nicholas Kristo to serve as official lookout for the mission...uh... Hope Mission."

"Oh, so you are Joseph," Mary said, and smiled. "Nicholas told me about you. Please come in and have something to eat and drink. You must be famished after your journey here."

"Are there many people inside?"

"Only Sister Margaret."

Relieved, Joseph replied, "Yes, I'm hungry, thank you. Will Nicholas be here today?"

"He usually checks in once a day. He spent the night on the mountain."

Looking nervously from side to side and behind, Joseph followed the nun into the kitchen. She went to the oven and pulled out a tray of freshly baked berry tarts, then poured cider. While they ate breakfast, the sound of children laughing filtered into the kitchen. Sister Mary hurried to the window and saw that Ben had arrived from Rome with some children and several adults.

"The children are here! They're here!" Mary sang, laughing. "Sister Margaret, come, let's welcome them to their new home."

Joseph asked if he could wait in the barn. This seemed a strange request, but when Sister Mary agreed, he quickly slid past the others, grabbing his book and what was left of his tart.

After greeting Sisters Mary and Margaret, Ben introduced Maria, Giovanni and the children. Soon after, the boys and girls scurried into the cabin to inspect their new temporary home. Ben guided the nuns to the back of the wagon, where Daisy and Rose lay on the floor, convulsing in their palsy.

Putting her arms around a tearful Maria, Mary whispered, "You'll have all the help you need here. Come on, let's take them inside."

By the time they had the twins settled in one of the bedrooms, the children had emptied the tray of tarts and sat on the porch, surrounding Giovanni. He plucked his guitar, and began a song of thanksgiving. The children joined in, knowing the tune well.

Nicholas arrived not long after and immediately won the affection of the children. He told clever stories and promised to take them to the construction site of the new orphanage when he returned from Cosenza. Ben told Nicholas about his mission to Rome, and explained why Maria and Giovanni had come with the children.

After giving them a hearty welcome, Nicholas went into the cabin to see Daisy and Rose. When he entered the room, the children's convulsions strengthened, as though they were excited by his presence.

Nicholas stared at them, his chest heaving with compassion. Mumbling a prayer, he reached down with a handkerchief, wiping saliva from their faces. They fell into a deep and peaceful sleep at his touch.

Sister Mary entered the room and quietly relayed that Joseph Solo was waiting in the barn. Nicholas went to greet him.

"Mr. Joseph Solo, welcome, welcome!" he cried, as Joseph peeped cautiously from the barn. "Tell me, how was your journey?"

"Greetings, Nicholas," said Joseph. "Can we talk in the barn...in the barn? The journey here went well, not too many people on the road...not too many. The nuns were very nice to me when I arrived. They're in perfect health, you know."

"I have good news for you, Joseph. Your cabin is already built on that mighty rock, and after toying around with a small and large magnifying lens in my workshop, I came up with what I call a magni-tube. When you look through it, it magnifies everything in the distance. You can see all the way to the mountains around Rome. At night you can gaze at the moon and stars and let God fill you with the mystery of His creation."

"You must know how very thankful I am for this opportunity to work with you and still live alone. There's only one thing wrong," said Joseph, putting his hands to his head.

"What's that?"

"I can't see right now. I'm blind. While you were speaking, I lost all vision. Everything is black. It's very frightening. Too frightening. The Lord must want me to lay hands on a blind person. Did one like that arrive on the wagon?"

"Yes, his name is Giovanni. Ben brought him back with the children. Should I take you to him?"

"No, not yet. I need to explain a few things about my gift. The reason I have such odd ways is a sort of protection to my relationship with God. I have seen healers lay hands on people in public places and because some are weak or prideful, they enjoy the adulation. And though they're directing people's attention to God, they take some glory to themselves, forgetting they are only an instrument and have no power at all. I prefer to do the Lord's work in private. He never desired an audience, and neither do I."

"I believe there are few who think on your level," said Nicholas, "but I agree with your thoughts, Joseph. I believe God works with people, much of the time, on an individual level. When He heals someone, it's a very intimate event and has everything to do with the life and faith of the one He's turned His attention to. I believe as you do. God has no need to impress anyone."

Relieved, Joseph pointed upwards. "Exactly. I'm glad you understand. Not many people do these days. If you could bring this Giovanni in here now, alone, I would like to talk to him."

Nicholas went to the porch and guided Giovanni into the barn, all the time thinking about Joseph and how God had blessed this tiny man.

Hearing them come into the barn, Joseph waved his arms out, his eyes rolling uncontrollably. "Bring him next to me, Nicholas."

Nick led Giovanni to stand before Joseph, just beyond reach of those flailing arms. Joseph looked unnerving and comical, but his voice was kind as he greeted the blind man. "Hello, Giovanni, my name is Joseph Solo and today is a very special day for you. How long have you been blind?"

Giovanni replied in his musical voice that he had been blind for most of his life. "I think I was five years old when the light in my eyes began to dim, and then in six months there was no light at all. It's been over sixty years now."

"Do you believe God can give you sight again?"

"For most of my life, I would have said no, but since I've been living in that shack at the city dump with the children, I've come to realize that God's been providing for me my whole life. I was just too bitter and resentful against Him for taking away my sight. The children and a man named Jives healed me of that bitterness. Now I believe nothing is impossible for Him."

"Nicholas," Joseph whispered, "could you get me something to stand on, and put it in front of Giovanni?"

As Nicholas went for a work stool, Joseph nearly gagged at Giovanni's dank odor. All the years of living in the city dump without clean clothing or a place to bathe, had left him in rags, with his gray, matted hair and beard falling down near his rope-belt.

Nicholas placed the stool in front of Joseph and guided him onto it. "What's going on?" Giovanni asked. "What are you going to do?"

Joseph felt for Giovanni's shoulders and asked, "How would God be glorified if you could see again?"

"God is glorified every time I sing about His love or His Son, but if I could see again I would write new songs about hope and His grace. If I ever see again, I will sing about every wonderful thing he has created and everything my eyes behold."

Joseph reached for Giovanni's face and felt for his eye sockets, placing his thumbs on them. "God has chosen to restore your life today. Receive your sight now, in the name of Jesus Christ."

Giovanni fell to the ground with his hands to his eyes. "It's burning! It burns so badly! What did you put in my eyes?" Curling into a ball, he cried, "God help me!"

Joseph rubbed his eyes, smiling, as he stepped down from the stool. "Praise God, thank you, Lord! I can see again. My vision has returned."

Nicholas stooped down to Giovanni, who was cautiously pushing himself into a sitting position. He was breathing heavily, almost gasping. "I see... light! I... can see light again." Tears streamed down his face onto his beard as he lifted his head and whispered, "Oh my merciful God, I can see. This is just . . . " and he wept, thanking God.

Nicholas rose and shot Joseph a strange look of wonderment.

"Now don't look at me that way, Nicholas," said Joseph irritably. "Don't look at me as if I had the power to do one single thing for this man on my own. You know it was God. You know!"

"I know, Joseph. I've just never seen anything like this before, and I'm so swept with joy at this moment. I know you are God's instrument and it was He who worked this miracle."

"If I hadn't gone blind myself, and been in need of your help," said Joseph, "I would have made you leave the barn before I laid hands on him. But now I can see that you are praising God and know it's Him who heals. I'll sleep well tonight. Please don't point people in my direction when they ask how his sight was restored."

"All right. Before you do anything else, ask Ben to show you to your new cabin home. He will explain how to make safe passage to the top of the mountain, and will get you settled."

As Giovanni sat gazing at his hands, Nicholas helped him to his feet and took him into the house. Everyone surrounded him, praising God for the miracle. Giovanni couldn't help telling them it was Joseph who laid hands on him, but when he hurried to the barn with the others to thank the small man, he was gone.

CHAPTER 36. BERNADETTE LAVIONO.

*A*fter giving Giovanni some of his old clothes to replace the rags he wore, Nicholas mounted his great white horse and headed east towards the Tyrrhenian Sea. Bringing the horse to a canter, he wondered why the dove had chosen to sit on Bernadette's letter, and what purpose she might have regarding Hope Mission. Ahead of him, the dove appeared on a tree and swooped down onto his shoulder. A voice said, "Turn Bernadette away from herself."

Nicholas understood that he had to find a way to inspire Bernadette to become more interested in others.

Night had fallen by the time he arrived in Cosenza. A low, thick fog clung to the ground as he rode past an old church and cemetery on the edge of town. Looking ahead, he saw an inn not far down the road. The sign over the door read "The Crow Tree Inn". As a wind blew across the fields sweeping away much of the fog, Nicholas entered the inn and inquired the whereabouts of the LaViono Estate.

The innkeeper directed him to a private road leading to the coast of the Tyrrhenian Sea, where the LaViono mansion looked out over the horizon. Nicholas rode for another mile or so, watching a storm front move in from across the water. The wind picked up, and the rain began to fall in sheets. With the mansion in sight, Nicholas kicked his horse to full stride and rode for the shelter of the veranda at the side entrance.

Drenched to the bone, he left his horse, ran under the portico of the mansion and knocked on the door. The wind and rain coaxed him forward, just as an older gentleman opened the door and waved him in, eager to close the door.

Nicholas introduced himself, still out of breath and dripping. "Good evening... sir. My...uh... name is Nicholas Kristo and I...huh... thank you for inviting me in out of that wicked storm. I am here representing Hope Mission at the request of Miss Bernadette LaViono. Have I come to the right estate?"

"This is the LaViono estate," said the butler, "but I am not aware of any request of Miss LaViono. Please wait here until I inquire."

Nicholas looked around, astonished at the opulence of his surroundings. He'd never seen such a display of affluence and status before. There were marble sculptures and paintings with gold leaf baroque frames everywhere. The shiny marble floors and dark wood-paneled walls made him feel as if he were in a king's palace.

Several minutes later the butler returned. "Miss LaViono asked me to apologize for her, and requests that you meet with her in the morning. She wants you to know she is quite indisposed at the moment due to the weather, but wishes you to stay this evening in the guest room on the second floor. I will have someone bring your horse to the stable and you can relax in the sitting room. Would you like some refreshments?"

Nicholas glanced up and saw a shadowy figure move past the second floor staircase as thunder pealed in the distance. "Please express my appreciation to Miss LaViono for her hospitality. I would be delighted to be her guest. If you'll show me to my room, I can put on some dry clothes. Some hot broth might be nice, if you would be kind enough to bring it to my room. This has been a long day and I think I'll retire."

They climbed the winding marble stairs, and the butler led him through the east wing to his room. When the servant lit the lamps, Nicholas was stunned at how beautiful and spacious it was, having its own fireplace and bath. If this was the guest room, he could only imagine what the master bedrooms must look like.

He put on his nightclothes, then sat by the window thinking about the love and simple motives of everyone involved with the mission. Indeed, that was what made him rich, not the gold he had found in the ravine. The gold was only an instrument.

This mansion, with all its ostentatious wealth and beauty, was impressive, but it paled in comparison with the miracle Nicholas had seen earlier that day. After sixty years, Giovanni could see again. Nothing was more beautiful than the expression on Giovanni's face as he saw once more, and nothing made Nick feel richer than to have been able to witness the event.

As the storm passed over, a tremendous cracking and boom of thunder shook the windows and floors. A woman screamed. Then came another crack and boom, followed by a shrilling screech from down the corridor. From the window, Nicholas actually saw the lightning strike a large willow tree near the servants' quarters, bringing it down, with fire near the base. Knowing the blaze would soon be extinguished by sheets of rain, Nick took a lamp into the corridor and walked to where he heard the screams.

"Miss LaViono," he called out, "are you all right? Miss LaViono?"

Two tall, white doors stood at the end of the corridor. He opened one a crack and softly called, "Miss LaViono, are you in there? Are you all right?"

Soft weeping caught his attention before another boom of thunder made the woman scream again. He entered the room, holding the lamp high.

A woman lay in a fetal position on the floor in a corner next to the bed. Crying and shivering, she moaned, "I'm so terrified, I cannot move. I cannot move."

Nicholas approached and squatted down in front of her, smiling as if he could calm the storm himself with his innate and overflowing peace. "Don't worry, the storm has almost passed over. Soon it will be far away. I must say, this is a most peculiar way to have met you. Miss LaViono, I presume?"

She wore silk nightclothes and had covered her legs with a dark woolen shawl. She held the end of the shawl over her nose, concealing her face. "Are you the founder of Hope Mission?"

"Yes. My name is Nicholas Kristo and I've come in response to your heartfelt letter. Why don't we go to the sitting room in the center of the house? There you won't be quite as startled by the thunder, and we can get acquainted by the warmth of the fire. Here, take my hand."

"I beg your pardon?"

"Don't be alarmed, I only wish to help you. Take my hand."

Keeping her face covered, Bernadette reached out a trembling hand and as Nicholas took hold, she pulled away a moment and shivered. When she reached out again, Nicholas held her tightly, but she pulled back once again. Each time she touched his hand, her fear evaporated and a great peace took its place, but when she pulled back, the fear and anxiety returned.

When she finally let her hand remain in his, Nicholas brought her to her feet and led her to the sitting room.

Still holding the shawl to her face, she held onto his arm all the way down the corridor. The peace and absence of anxiety overwhelmed her and she became increasingly perplexed and curious as they entered the room and sat in front of the fire. As she let go of his arm, fear gripped her again. She let the shawl drop to her neck, revealing her face in the warm golden light of the fireplace.

Nicholas stared, transfixed by her beauty and movements. She appeared no older than thirty, having silver-blonde hair with long flowing waves resting below the base of her neck. Her face was angelic with a perfect complexion, and though there were dark rings under her eyes from lack of sleep, it didn't diminish her beauty as she gazed at him with a hint of hope.

"Why did you travel all the way to Cosenza, rather than just return a letter to me?" she challenged. "I imagine it was rather foolish of me to have revealed even the slightest notion that I was a woman of means."

Nick inclined his head, not taking offense. "I am inclined to speak from my heart, madam. May I do so?"

"By all means, sir."

"Wealth and status are not, and never will be, a motivation in my life. My interest is in people, especially those who are hurting and are in need. My mission is to bring hope to the world."

"Then why come all the way to the east coast of Italy to see one lonely rich woman who has everything anyone could ever hope for?"

"Forgive me, Miss LaViono, but in my humble opinion you are in more need of hope and peace than almost anyone I've ever met. You are living in a self-imposed prison, trapped in a dreadful state of mind and spirit, and all the money in the world cannot help you."

"And I imagine you think you can help. For a price, of course."

Nicholas swallowed his annoyance. "Why would you want to insult me when I have come to offer my help? I do not work for money. I work for God. I would not accept any payment from you anyway, and now I must also refuse any monetary contribution you may want to offer Hope Mission."

Bernadette gulped back tears. "I *am* sorry if I've offended you, but I've been shut away in my room now for more than six weeks and I feel worse than ever. Please forgive me."

"Take my hand," said Nicholas.

Bernadette quickly pushed her hand into his. She felt such a comforting peace when he touched her that her tears became tears of gratitude, relieving her temporarily from the darkness and fear that had dominated her life for so long.

Holding her hand with the palm up, he said, "This is a hand that has not worked at anything its entire life. This hand has always been pampered and cared for by others. It is a hand protected from problems and the worries of the world."

As he let go, Bernadette began trembling once again. "If I may, sir, what's wrong with being protected from problems? My parents loved me and wished to see me live a comfortable life."

"That's just the problem. You've had *no* problems and were always made to feel comfortable. You see, adversity may seem harsh at the moment, but in the end it becomes a wonderful teacher. We learn how to deal with life through adversity. We learn how to have compassion for others through the adversity we experience in our own lives. Adversity builds character and even teaches us wisdom, if we look deeply enough. No one wants to suffer, but for those who are not privileged, the greatest lessons learned are through suffering, in one form or another.

"You were protected from adversity, but also denied the most important form of education one can receive. There are no schools to teach the hard lessons of life. Living a privileged life has left you self-consumed, in a constant state of anxiety and doubt. Tell me, how often during the course of a day do other people cross your mind?"

She shrugged. "I think of others in a negative way—as if they would do me harm. My father felt that way all his life."

"It is your way of thinking that needs to change if you are to live without fear," explained Nicholas.

"Mr Kristo—"

"Perhaps you might call me Nicholas," he suggested, "and I, in return, shall call you Bernadette."

She nodded absently. "But how should I change my way of thinking?"

He laughed. "The answer is simple, but the remedy difficult to achieve for a woman in your position."

"Tell me."

He said gently, but still with laughter in his voice, "You need a job, Bernadette. That's the first step in your journey to a normal life."

"Oh, impossible! What would I do?" asked Bernadette.

"You can work with the Mission," said Nicholas readily. "I've created the perfect job for you."

"And you think scrubbing floors and keeping house for poor and desperate people is the answer to my problem?"

"Not in your case. I need someone to record everything that has happened and will happen at the Mission in a journal. When the journal is complete, it will find its way to the New World. I will send those who feel called to begin other branches of Hope Mission in the New World."

"How is it that you think *working* will change my mind about anything?"

"You will put your mind to the task of replacing the darkness and fear with challenges and goals that will benefit others. In this way, your mind will become renewed with a sense of meaning and purpose you never dreamed could exist. This will happen by your own efforts and by God's love."

Bernadette stood and warmed her hands by the fire. "I believe God has ordained the right man for His Mission, Nicholas Kristo. Almost, you almost give me hope that what you say is possible. But I am afraid to leave this house. How can I travel to who knows where? What if I fail, and become a burden to others as well as to myself?"

"Hold on to the hope that you may come to know happiness, and the faith that you will succeed," said Nicholas. "Think on this tonight and tomorrow. If you decide you would give it a chance, I will take you safely to Hope Mission to begin your work. If you cannot find happiness with us, I will escort you back here myself and you can resume life as you know it. You have my word on this." He smiled at her, and added, "But if you only have faith, all of what you're going through now will have been like a bad dream and you will find sunshine again, and joy, and discover God anew."

Bernadette took his arm and gave him a wry smile. "I will surely think on this, but doubt I have enough courage to change my life so dramatically. Kindly see me to my room, for the storm has passed and perhaps I will sleep for a change."

Chapter 37. Bernadette and Nicholas.

$\mathcal{I}$t was mid morning by the time Nicholas woke and found himself in the elaborate, decorative bedroom with windows facing the Tyrrhenian Sea. The butler knocked on his door and invited him to breakfast, but also offered to bring something to his room if he so desired. Nicholas said he'd come down shortly and asked if Bernadette had woken. The butler said she was still sleeping, which pleased Nick, because he knew she would need a refreshed mind to make a life-changing decision.

After having fresh-baked pastry with the butler, he walked around the property, enjoying the lush landscape, wondering what might persuade Bernadette to trust him. On his way back, he entered the stable to check on his horse. Passing by an empty stall, he found a half-bred female poodle lying in the hay, feeding her four-week-old pups. One of the pups was separated, on the other side of the stable, whining and limping on three legs. Picking up the white fuzz bundle, he noticed blood on its front leg. Upon closer inspection, he saw a good-sized splinter had lodged itself firmly into the pup's tiny paw. He thought, *This pup is perfect to illustrate what Bernadette needs most.* Taking it into the house, he found Bernadette and her mother having breakfast on the second floor patio, outside the dining room.

"Good morning, Nicholas, this is my mother, Elizabeth. I was telling her about the terrible storm last night. She can't hear very well and missed the entire event. She's very good at reading lips though. Just speak slowly."

Stroking the pup's head, Nicholas smiled warmly. "Good day, Mrs. LaViono. You have a wonderful home here by the sea."

Elizabeth did not respond, and quickly rose to her feet with a grimace, limping into the dining room and out of sight.

Nicholas asked, "Did I say something wrong?"

With a frustrated sigh, Bernadette replied, "Not at all, Nicholas. I told her of your proposal and she became stone-faced, as is her most common reaction regarding anything that is suggested concerning me. Sometimes I think she is partly responsible for my father's early death. I don't ever recall hearing her laugh. It's strange that I should think about that."

As the sunlight lit up Bernadette's violet eyes and glittered off her silver-blonde hair, Nicholas noticed the dark rings under her eyes had faded. The exceeding beauty and grace of the woman astounded him. Forcing himself to take his eyes from her, he asked, "When was the last time you heard your own laughter?"

"I can't remember. Where did you find that adorable little pup? Why is it crying?"

Nicholas handed the pup to her. "I found it in the stable. It has a splinter in its paw and I'm not very delicate with little animals."

Bernadette took hold of it and found the splinter embedded in the paw. "Let's go to the kitchen," she said.

Nicholas followed her there where she gently soaked the paw in a basin, loosening and preparing the splinter for removal. Calling one of the maids to find pincers, she stroked the pup and spoke to it as if it were her own child, reassuring its full recovery and reunion with the rest of its family.

Taking the pincers from the maid, Bernadette removed the tiny piece of wood, and while she bandaged the little paw, Nicholas asked, "How did you sleep last night?"

"Now that you mention it, I can't remember falling asleep, only that it was the longest sleep I've had since my father's passing two years ago."

"Have you had time to consider what I said?"

Tying the dressing off, Bernadette held the pup to her breast, "I can't get away from the horrible dread that comes when I think of a future where anything can happen at any time. The way I look would draw the most unwelcome men after me. Fears flood my mind, even now."

Nicholas drew near, changing the subject. "What did you think the moment you knew the pup was injured?"

"Well, I was concerned and alarmed and determined to help the precious thing."

"Did you have any fear as you soaked its paw and removed the splinter and put on the bandage?"

"Why, no! Isn't that peculiar? No, I only felt...what is it...what is it?"

"Compassion?"

"Yes! That's it. Compassion."

"Now, if you take that experience and imagine filling your life with situations like that, but on a larger scale, you will have turned your mind away from itself, leaving fear to live somewhere else. Compassion for the pup saved you from your fears while you were tending to it. It's not only compassion that will save you from yourself, but also love and kindness, and forgiveness, and a host of other fine and noble gifts from God. The problem is that much of mankind chooses not to use these gifts but to turn in toward their own desires instead."

Bernadette laughed. "I see! I can see it now! You're so right, Nicholas, but the future..."

"The future has not come yet and the past has left us forever. All anyone ever really has is right now, this very moment. All life is contained in this very moment, and then the next, and then the next. Think about it. You cannot hold a future moment and the past is only a memory. The only thing that is real and exists is now. If we can learn to fill our lives every waking moment focused on kind and noble things, and create a plan for the future, we'd be fulfilling our lives in a way that not only glorifies God, but frees us to be happy and content in a way that money cannot buy. When you were tending to the pup, did you feel contentment? Did you feel happy?"

Bernadette paused a moment. "When I think back, I felt happy when the pup licked my hand and played with me after I put his bandage on. At that moment I felt contentment. I see what you're saying is true, but I have little courage to make such a great change in my life so soon. I honestly hope you can understand."

Nicholas took the pup, and as he headed out to the stable, he turned and smiled. "I understand what you're saying, but I disagree. I think you *do* have the courage. You just need to search deeper for it. After I return the pup to its mother, I must go home. I will come to say goodbye after I've saddled my horse. Don't let yourself feel bad about anything. You can always write another letter and come another time if you change your mind."

Bernadette's mind flooded with a new fear that the only person who'd ever come close to helping her was leaving forever. She feared she would lose the peace and comfort she had gained from his touch.

Running to the front window, she watched him saddle his horse. He laughed as the puppies poured from the barn to surround him, jumping onto his boots and rolling onto his feet.

When he returned to say goodbye, Bernadette had a handkerchief to her mouth. "Must you go now? Why not stay a day longer?" she pleaded.

"There is much going on at the Mission right now. Some of our people are in danger, while other newer members need my attention and counsel. I was reluctant to come here for even a day, but I'm glad I did. You have been a most gracious host and I think you're beginning to understand what you need to do to come out of the darkness." He smiled, and held out his hand in farewell.

The instant Bernadette took his hand, an indescribable sense of well-being and ease flooded her mind. She said, "I can't thank you enough for riding all this way to help me, even though I think my case is hopeless. But I'm still curious to know why you would come to help the rich when the poor need you so much more."

Nicholas grinned. "God loves the rich as well as the poor. It's just that the poor know they are in need. Many rich people, not suffering as you are, make their money and comfort a god, forgetting about the true God and His Son. It's sad, because this life is only the beginning. Afterwards, when we wake from the sleep of death, we will spend an eternity in conscious bliss where there is no fear or pain or evil of any kind."

"You truly are an extraordinary man of God, Nicholas, and you have succeeded in bringing hope to a hopeless case like me. I wish I could find the courage to come with you. Before I became ill, writing was a favorite pastime of mine. I even kept a journal of my boring life, just for the joy of writing."

Smiling, with a sparkle in his eye, he said goodbye and went to his horse.

Bernadette stood frozen in terror from the moment he pulled his hand away. This was the strangest course of events she'd ever encountered, and after she found courage to flee to her bedroom, she lay on her bed weeping and condemning herself for turning away her only chance to make something of her pathetic and miserable life.

Nicholas had ridden several hundred paces down the road when a white dove swooped down, landing on his shoulder. A voice said, "Please wait, Nicholas."

He waited, for what, he did not know.

Bernadette drew the curtains in her room as if to blanket herself from the outside world. When she glanced outside and saw Nicholas some distance away, sitting on his motionless horse, she wondered why he waited. She stared, and suddenly it occurred to her that she still had time to change her mind. She flung a cloak around her shoulders, rushed down the stairs, and ran down the road to him.

"Nicholas, what's wrong?" she panted, severely out of breath from the short burst of exercise. "I saw you from the window." She smiled.

"I was wondering when you'd do that," grinned Nicholas

"Do what?"

"Smile. You have a wonderful smile," said Nicholas. "But regarding your question, as I rode down this road, Heaven asked me to wait a while. Now you are here, will you not reconsider my offer? Hope Mission's journal needs to be written by someone with intelligence and a neat hand."

Bernadette's heart raced as she realized Nicholas was her only hope to live a happy life. "Yes, I'll come!" she blurted. "I don't know how. Yes. Please come back and wait. What shall I take? I need to tell my mother. Am I crazy? Please come back, Nicholas."

Nicholas dismounted and walked her to the house, telling her not to take too many things and there was no need of formal clothing. He explained that she was free to leave her position at any time, and that if she chose to leave the Mission for any reason, he would provide an escort or bring her home himself.

Bernadette's mother was furious at what she termed her daughter's desertion. As Elizabeth raged, Bernadette realized the pain of staying was far greater than the fear of an unknown future.

Elizabeth demanded to know her daughter's destination and the duration of her stay, and when Bernadette said she could not reveal either, the woman locked herself in her room. Bernadette pleaded for her under-standing and blessing, but when no response was forthcoming, she gave up and began packing.

One thing kept her moving forward, and that was the mysterious gift of peace Nicholas gave each time they touched. She thought, *This gift he has must remain a most guarded secret. If he ever came to know the effect of his touch, he would soon take advantage of me, in one way or the other.*

As she put on her riding clothes and boots, her hands trembled as she plotted ways to enjoy that touch. She didn't want to appear unseemly or for-ward, but there *was* a way to insure he would often have to be in contact with her.

With a weighed-down horse in tow, they began their journey to Pizal. Bernadette took care to pack various medicines, bandages, and any other remedy she could find in her medicine cabinet. She might unexpectedly fall from her horse, or stub her toe, or sprain her arm, or become ill with fever, or be attacked by a swarm of bees. Maybe she'd see a poison plant, and not knowing what it was, pluck its leaf admiring its lovely color. Any number of unexpected accidents would insure close, personal attention from her companion.

CHAPTER 38. BERNADETTE'S FALL.

After riding west for several hours on a country road outside Cosenza, Bernadette began trembling again as past memories, and uncertainty of the future rankled her. As Nicholas led the way, her eyes remained on him as the only real cure.

Nicholas spent the time in giving her an account of the events since the first day of his commission. He began with the deadly blizzard earlier that year, and how the anvil had flooded the Pallone barn with heat, saving him and May Rose. Bernadette reasoned he was keeping her pre-occupied with stories to focus on anything but herself. It worked to a point, but the only real relief she attained was at his touch. Something mysterious dissolved her fears completely when he drew near, and she was determined to find out the source.

In between stories, Bernadette managed to plot an accident she would initiate a little farther up the road. She would trip and fall while bringing her horse to water, causing enough minor injury to bring Nicholas into physical contact.

Riding just behind him, Bernadette called out, "Nicholas, I'm sorry to interrupt your story, but I'm quite thirsty and I think the horses are as well. Might we find a stream?"

As she spoke, a snake slithered across the road in front of Bernadette's horse. It reacted by rearing in terror. Bernadette held fast at first, but finally lost her grip and fell to the side. Her foot caught in the stirrup as she fell headlong to the ground, knocking herself unconscious.

Nicholas leapt to the ground, grabbed the reins and settled the horse. He freed Bernadette's foot from the stirrup, then dug into her saddlebags for bandages. Smoke rising above the trees just around the bend suggested a habitation, so, after bandaging her head, he draped her over her saddle and led the horses toward the smoke.

There was no house, but Nicholas found a recently abandoned campsite with enough wood for the night. Here, he decided to stay. He laid out Bernadette's bedroll next to the smoldering coals, then settled her as comfortably as possible.

Nicholas rarely felt guilt, but on this occasion his heart and mind were soaked in it. He had promised Bernadette peace and happiness, but now she was injured, with no care but his.

Bernadette was still unconscious as he rolled his coat into a pillow, placing it under her head. While he adjusted the bandage, his gaze lingered on her face. Even pale and insensible, she was the most beautiful woman he'd ever seen.

But then—how very different they were. The thought of marriage with a woman like Bernadette, raised in affluence, with preconceived notions of superiority, repelled his spirit and forced his mind to the problems at hand. If ever a woman won his heart, it would be one with an intense compassion for people - it must be a woman flooded and overflowing with love for God. He presumed when he met that woman, he would know it at once... there would be no question.

His attention shifted to her swollen ankle, and he realized the boot was so tight that he should cut it off at once. As he sliced the soft leather with his dagger, Bernadette began to stir, raising her arm to her forehead.

He removed the boot just before she woke, thinking, *Even her swollen ankle looks attractive. Get hold of yourself, Nicholas.* This was a total contradiction to his common sense, and he determined not to let his emotions dictate his thoughts.

Bernadette blinked and attempted to sit up, then gasped. "Oh... my head!"

Nicholas explained, "Your horse reared, and you fell. Your ankle is sprained, so we'll have to stay here for the night and in the morning see if you're able to travel. Don't worry. I'll tend to you and make things as comfortable as possible."

Bernadette whispered, "That's just perfect for me."

"What did you say?"

"I've made a perfect mess of it all, haven't I?"

"None of this is your fault, Bernadette. It was sheer mischance, or perhaps I startled your horse in some way. Now, just hold still while I bandage your foot."

Bernadette said nothing of the snake on the road, but watched dreamily as Nicholas finished the bandage. "May I ask you a question?"

"Ask anything you like, Bernadette."

"You already know my sad state of mind, but what's it like to be Nicholas Kristo?"

Nicholas considered. "The most dominant thing in my mind is my love for God. It causes me to do the things I do and say."

"But do you never become afraid, or confused, or upset?"

"Since I was a little boy, there has been a resounding peace in my heart and mind. At first I thought everyone felt that way, but now I know it's God's love for me and mine for Him. Not long ago I found a scripture that best describes how I feel. It says, 'And the peace of God, which passeth all understanding, shall keep your hearts and minds through Christ Jesus.'"

Bernadette thought, *That's exactly what I feel when he touches me; a peace that passes all understanding. Somehow, without his knowing it, he's able to transfer that peace to me.* Not thinking, she said, "I would pay anything to have that state of mind and heart every waking moment."

Nicholas threw several small logs on the hot coals, rekindling the fire. "You don't have to pay anything for it. It's a gift from God...it's free. You only need to have faith and trust in God's Son. When we reach the Mission I'll introduce you to Brother Taylor. He'll teach you all about God's love. But how have you handled your fears up to now?"

Bernadette looked surprised. "It hasn't been difficult at all! I wonder why?"

"You've been listening to my stories, and your mind was so engaged and engrossed that you 'replaced' thinking about yourself and your fears with something else."

"Is that why you haven't stopped telling me stories from the very start?"

"Yes. I wanted to divert your attention, and from what you've just told me it worked pretty well. You need to know what works so you can practice it on your own. The sooner you start the journal the better. Writing will keep your mind focused on your job, not on your fears."

Bernadette pointed to her horse. "I put a new, almost empty writing tablet in my baggage before we left. I'll begin at—" Her voice broke off in a gasp of fear, for a huge wild cat emerged from the bush, sauntering its way toward them. Just before she screamed, Nicholas said, "Please don't worry. It means us no harm."

The moment he turned toward the creature, it dropped to its belly, rolled onto its back and made a purring sound.

Bernadette stared, mouth agape, as she witnessed Nicholas approach the pregnant cat, stoop down and rub its belly. Glancing up, he told her about his special relationship with animals and about the wolves on the mountain, and how to gain safe passage.

With wide eyes, she watched Nicholas guide the wild cat to a private spot in the bush near their camp where she would give birth to her litter. From that moment, Bernadette realized Nicholas was the most remarkable and interesting man she'd ever met. Her heart glowed watching him leave the cat and return to the campsite wearing a parental smile, as if he'd tucked his own child into bed for the night.

After tossing more wood on the fire, Nick found her writing things, grabbed some bread and cheese from the baggage, and returned to

Bernadette. As he changed the bandage on her head again, she began to laugh. Nicholas raised his eyebrows. "After all that's happened to you in my care, you're laughing?"

She forced herself to stop. "That's just the point. After all that's happened to me in your care, here I sit, with a badly sprained ankle and lump on my head, entertaining wild cats in the wilderness with a man I met only the day before. At this moment, I feel more wonderful inside than on any Christmas morning as a child. None of it makes any sense, but I don't care...I'm only thankful you came to help when you did."

Her laughter mixed with tears of gratitude as she continued, "I'm laughing because I don't think I've ever felt such joy about life than at this very moment, and all of my father's money could never buy the freedom I feel right now. Is it God, Nicholas? Is it He who's doing this?"

Nicholas knelt before her. "God is interested in your life, Bernadette. He always has been. He has a plan for you, but you must renew your mind with His ways. I think you just received your first lesson in the 'School of Adversity and Suffering.'"

Bernadette pushed herself over to a large stump next to Nicholas's bedroll, leaning her back against it. Wiping tears with her sleeve, she reached for the quill and ink and began to record the stories Nicholas had told her on the road from Cosanza. Little did she know, the world she was about to enter would soon reveal a life she only thought existed in fables.

Chapter 39. Ben Removes His Mask.

*L*imping only slightly now, Sergeant Ficci, aided by Sergeant Vance, ordered forty-seven top-line soldiers onto the grid in front of the Command Post. The sun was rising through crimson clouds in the eastern mountains as they lined up in four rows waiting for Captain Ficci to give final orders before their march to Pizal.

Sergeant Manuel Ficci was always envious of Andrea's success and ability to acquire anything his heart desired. He secretly hated him, not only for his success, but because, from the time they'd become interested in the gentler sex, Andrea had mocked Manuel's women, maliciously pointing out their inferiority.

Manuel also feared his brother, knowing he was more skilled in the art of combat, but he was determined to make this march to Pizal a turning point in his life. He plotted a way to not only seize all the gold they found, but in the end, to retain all of Andrea's property and slaves. For the first time, the thought of killing his brother became an aspiration. As the Captain came out of the Command Post to address his men, Manuel's heart surged with bloodlust.

Captain Andrea Ficci mounted his golden horse and walked it slowly to his men, now standing at attention. Looking more like a General than a Captain, he began his speech. "Men, this will be one of the most unusual missions your government has ever assigned to any group of soldiers. You are all handpicked for this mission and I have the utmost confidence that we will return victorious.

"What's different about our enemy is that this time we'll be fighting wolves, not men. Yes, wolves, lots of them. As you know, I recently sent a five-man patrol to the mountain to arrest the Bellicinis and only Sergeant Ficci survived to return. There are scores of starving wolves on the mountain behind Pizal and it will be our mission to exterminate them, ridding the people of their scourge forever. Before we leave, Sergeant Ficci and Sergeant Vance will give instructions about the wolf traps, poisoned meat, and extra firearms. We leave in one hour, and if any of you fine soldiers are wondering where I will be as we ascend the mountain, wonder no longer. I will be out front, leading the way."

The soldiers swelled with pride, and were captivated with the courage and confidence of their commander.

Seeing the reaction of the men, Sergeant Ficci seethed with envy, and in a pale attempt to show his admiration and support, he turned with a fictitious smile and bowed toward his brother.

Meanwhile, at the orphanage, the children seemed to take on a new life as Giovanni, having regained his sight, became more than just a comforter-entertainer to them. He brought them on special hikes into the forest, teaching them about plants and insects and animals. He expounded on every subject he remembered from his parents' sincere efforts at education.

In the evening, he kept his tradition of lullabies, but now he sang with perfect vision, beholding a glowing fire, and children snuggled in clean, fluffy beds, safe from the rats and disease of the city dump. So soothing and enchanting was his evening songs, that the nuns were unable to continue their work. They'd stop, sit back and close their eyes, listening, thanking God for Giovanni's miracle of sight and gifted voice.

Ben decided to help with the construction of the new orphanage at the Pallone farm, giving him an excuse to visit Maria at Nicholas' farm only a short ride away. Each day, tender thoughts of her invaded his heart, but he was tormented with visions of her possible rejection when the time came to take off his mask.

He knew she was fond of him, but how would she react?

A gentle breeze brought the scent of honeysuckle under Ben's mask as he approached Nicholas's farm. Maria was hanging clothes on a line beside the east side of the cabin, with Daisy and Rose on a blanket beside her. Some of the other children were amusing them, making them laugh, bringing excitement and even stronger convulsions.

Dismounting at the front door, Ben waved to her and thought, *If I ever manage to survive this day, the rest of my life will be easy in comparison.* He decided not to torment himself another day. As soon as they were in the cabin he'd remove his mask in her presence, come what may.

Ben brought Daisy and Rose into the cabin to Sister Mary and asked Maria to meet him in Nicholas's workshop, saying he had something very important to show her. When they were alone, he bolted the door and sat her down on a stool. She looked exceptionally fine, happier and healthier than he had ever seen her. This only caused him more anxiety.

"What is it, Ben? What's wrong?"

Sitting opposite her on a small work stool, Ben explained. "Maria, I cannot go another day without revealing to you what the fire did to my face. What you've been seeing is only this mask. You already know I have feelings for you and I hope and believe you have become fond of me. We already have a wonderful friendship, but nothing will ever be real or truthful until you see the damage on my face."

"Ben—"

"Wait! Let me finish."

She smiled uncertainly, then folded her hands in her lap.

"I have no ears and half a nose," continued Ben. "I have kept my eyes, but the only part that's not scarred is my mouth. If you can bear the sight of me and not be repulsed, then our relationship will grow. If not, then I will forget my hopes, and wish you well as you move on with your life."

"I'm more than fond of you, Ben," said Maria, smiling. "How could I not love you? You saved the lives of my children and myself, and gave me hope that life is worth living after all. The way you live your life is exceptional and inspiring. The hope you bring supports the poor and suffering. I will always love and respect you no matter what lies under the mask. I am sorry for your pain, but I will see you with eyes of love."

Tears fell as Ben's trembling hands loosened the straps that held the mask in place.

Maria reached out and stopped him. "Wait, Ben, please let me do it." She stroked the cheek of the mask, then rose and moved behind him.

Ben sat on the stool flooded with a thousand different emotions. His chest heaved as Maria unbuckled the straps and gently pulled away the mask and hat, showing the back of his head. Leaning forward, she kissed the scar tissue that surrounded the hole where his ear once was, then moving to the other side, she kissed the scars very gently, whispering softly, "Don't worry, Ben. I love you. I love you. These scars were formed saving the life of one of your best friends."

Moving around to face him, she stepped back, considered for a moment, then reached out and touched an area still red and sensitive. "It all healed fairly well, don't you agree?" she said.

Ben could hold back no longer and began weeping as she embraced him, kissing the most damaged areas, promising her feelings had not changed a shred. Ben regained his composure, and replaced the mask, asking Maria to buckle the straps from behind.

"You know, Ben," she said as she complied, "I've been meaning to ask you about the mask. The strangest things are happening lately."

"What do you mean? What things?"

"Yesterday I noticed a very subtle change in the expression. At first I thought it was just my imagination, but then it happened again when you laughed along with the children. Now mind you, they're very subtle changes, but they're changes nonetheless."

"You mean the mask physically changes with my feelings?"

"Exactly. I don't know how that's possible, but something very real happens when you laugh or become serious or when you're thinking about something. It was most noticeable yesterday when you laughed."

Moving around to face him, she put her fingers on the mask, pointing to specific areas. "I could swear I saw the eyes squinted slightly and the cheeks rise up a bit, causing two tiny dimples to appear on the upper sides, right about here. You see, even now it's changed again...it has a slight wrinkle in the brow as if you're studying something. And it's true, you're very focused on what I'm saying. I don't know if it's because I look at you more than most people, but it really happens.

"Just last night when you went in to see Daisy and Rose as they slept, you looked at them with compassion in your eyes. I could see it, but then the eyebrows on the mask seemed to adjust, making you look altogether filled with love and concern. And that's another reason why I love you. Masked or not, you show your true self in your face."

Ben grinned, reaching for Maria's hand. "I have to believe what you say is true. When I was a boy, people would always grab my cheek when they saw those dimples. From the very beginning, the mask has done strange but helpful things. When a situation is dangerous in some way, a chill comes up under it. The more severe the situation, the colder it gets." Ben drew her near. "Now, when you come into the room, I feel a warmth under there. It never happens with anyone else. This mask is the first gift given by Hope Mission, and Nicholas told me he wouldn't be surprised if Heaven itself had something to do with its strange properties. It is a true miracle to me."

As Ben held her head to his chest, she asked, "Do you think there's any hope for Daisy and Rose, Ben?"

"Nicholas will be returning soon. We'll talk to him and Joseph Solo about it. If God restored Giovanni's sight, then there's always hope for the twins. But before I'm sent on another mission, there's something I need to talk to you about."

"What is it?"

"I don't think I've ever met anyone quite like you before. Your heart is so good and your compassion for people is remarkable. Perhaps it's because of all that you've gone through and the daily adversity you've had to struggle with, but whatever it is, you have won my heart. I don't want to live another day without you in it. I was terrified you'd reject me after you saw my face, but when I looked into your eyes after you moved around to face me, I saw only love. It was as if you didn't see what everyone else does."

Maria pulled back and laid her hands on Ben's mask. "All that I see are scars of love. Every mark on your face has love written on it. If people could see your heart as I do, their eyes would adjust and they would see the face of true courage. If you had died in that fire trying to save Mario, the pain would have been over. In some ways your sacrifice is more than death, because living in pain and isolation, you die a little every day. Believe me, I *know*. When people saw my Daisy and Rose, and made remarks about demons and curses, it tore my heart and I died a little right there. And then the next day it would happen again, and I would sink deeper into despair. If you had not come, I would have surely jumped. The pain and hunger and constant misery took me to the edge of that cliff.

"I don't want to live another day without you, Ben. Since we arrived here, I've come to love you, and with the help of the nuns, life has become a blessing, for me and my girls. God is in this place. God is in your heart as well, and now I know God will work everything out in His time."

Lifting her chin to his face, Ben kissed her lips and then her cheek, and whispered in her ear, "Would you be by my side forever? Would you live with me here on this mountain forever? Would you be my wife and love me as I am forever? It would be my greatest honor."

Slipping her fingers under his mask, she whispered, "Yes, Ben, forever. I'm yours forever. And loving you will be *my* greatest honor."

Chapter 40. Bell Goes into Labor.

As Ben and Maria discussed wedding plans in Nicholas' workshop, there came a knock on the door.

"Ben, I hate to interrupt," said Sister Mary outside the door, "but Rubin just arrived with Bell and two young girls. He wishes to speak with you."

Ben kissed Maria and hurried out the front door. Two teenaged girls and Rubin were helping pregnant Bell down from her horse. Holding her belly, she appeared distressed, as if she would deliver the child any moment.

While Ben carried her luggage, Rubin introduced Bell and the girls, Linda and Rosa, as they moved into the house. When Sister Mary took over, Rubin led Ben down the road explaining how, after buying the slaves, he had deceived Captain Ficci and escaped with them in the middle of the night. Handing Ben the critical document that implicated Captain Ficci as a traitor, Rubin told him how important it was that Nicholas keep it in a secure place. He explained how it tied Ficci to the Duke of Guise and their sordid relationship, and also how it proved Captain Ficci was covertly making withdrawals from the Italian treasury.

A warm feeling came up under Ben's mask as he smiled and slipped the document into his jacket. "Outstanding job, Rubin. This purchase order will shift the balance of power to the Bellicini family, once it finds its way to Rome and the powers that be."

"Thanks, Ben, but now I need to tell you about Linda and Rosa. Their father sold them to Captain Ficci in Barcelona. He was deeply in debt and about to lose his tavern, when he made the deal. As soon as Ficci brought them home he violated their youth."

"I'm surprised the Captain let you buy all three," said Ben, brushing dust off Rubin's black jacket.

"That was a ploy to seize our gold. His brother, Manuel, intended to follow us after we made the deal, and kill me on the road somewhere, then take the slaves back to the Captain. The girls want to return to Barcelona, but not to their father. Their grandmother owns a loom, and designs different fabrics sold at the market place. They want to work with her until they're old enough to build a life of their own. I hope to escort them to Spain, Ben. Can I borrow from Mission funds for the trip? I'll pay it back, I swear."

Ben had never really appreciated Rubin's true potential until that very moment. To skillfully change his identity and deal with the most dangerous men in Italy without a hitch was simply remarkable. He knew Nicholas would agree with Rubin's request, so he gave the young man more than enough money to accompany the girls home and then return.

In the morning, after a good long rest, Rubin and the girls would begin the long journey to Spain.

Later that evening Nicholas arrived with Bernadette, who had ridden most of the way sidesaddle to minimize the pain in her ankle. Blinking fireflies and the sweet aroma of honeysuckle filled the cool evening air as they approached the cabin.

Nicholas lifted Bernadette from her horse and carried her to the porch. No one had heard them arrive, so they sat on porch chairs by the window, listening to Giovanni's evening lullaby. The children began to settle in beds all around him, while the nuns sat by the fireplace holding small logs in their still hands, engulfed in the old man's velvet voice.

Inspired, Bernadette opened her journal and began to write as Nicholas went inside looking for Ben, wanting to prepare a room for his new guest. He went straight to his workshop and found Ben carving a secret wedding gift for Maria.

Ben told Nicholas all the remarkable events that had occurred during his brief absence, and just as he finished his update, a scream pierced the walls of the house.

Giovanni stopped singing. Nicholas and Ben hurried to Bell's bedroom, meeting Sisters Mary and Margaret on the way. Bell had gone into labor and the nuns went to work, bringing hot water and towels to her bedside.

When Nicholas went outside to inform Bernadette, he found her introducing herself to Justus, who'd just ridden down the mountain.

"What's going on in there, Nick?" Justus asked.

"Bell, Makande's wife, went into labor and it's going to be a long night. I need you to help me tonight, Justus."

"No problem, Nick. Besides, Raven is still angry with me, so with luck, by the time I return, she'll be cooled off. What do you need me to do?"

As Bernadette smiled at Justus' dilemma, Nicholas asked, "What happened with Raven? Was it something you said?"

"Exactly, but it was more the way I said it that bothered her. One minute we were happy, discussing our feelings for each other, and then as soon as I mentioned that nothing would ever change until the Ficci brothers were dead, she turned her back. She said I loved my hate for them more than my love for her. She wouldn't speak to me after that. I'm right back where I started, Nick."

Bernadette leaned forward, intensely interested.

"Do you think there is a shred of truth in that?" Nicholas asked.

"Probably, but the problem overwhelms me. I can't control my feelings when it comes to hate *or* love."

Nicholas glanced at Bernadette with a grin, then replied, "If you can't control feelings of love, it's probably a good thing. In the end, your love for her will cause you to sacrifice something of yourself. But uncontrolled hate is a deadly trap. Why do you think Jesus said, 'Love your enemy'? He, of all people, knew the vile effects of hate in a person's heart. I believe if you could see what hate and revenge has already done to you, you'd begin to think differently about it."

With a hint of reproach, Justus replied, "As far as I know, it's done nothing but drive me to seek the satisfaction of justice for my family, who were murdered by the Ficci brothers."

"The effects of hate have already stolen years of your life, Justus. You have no control because you can't see the truth of it yet. Once you see clearly that the hate you feel works as a disease, eating away every good and virtuous attribute you possess, you'll gladly dismiss it from your life. Only then will you have the ability to take back full and complete control of your volition. Hate is God's enemy, and the Devil's handmaiden, and your master. Hate is the last thing in the world I'd want pushing *me* around, dictating my every action and stealing joy from my life every chance it had. You open your heart up to the worst possible influences when you allow yourself to feel hatred. That's right, Justus, it's a choice. It will not enter your heart unless you let it. The trouble is, you let the energy of hate drive you toward satisfaction, not knowing its consequences but, unbeknown to you, that end is anything but satisfying."

"Then I shouldn't dwell at all on the Ficci brothers, right?"

"You're starting to see, but you've been sleeping with hate many years now. Start by observing your own feelings. The moment you become aware that hatred or vengeance wants to take over your will, make a conscious effort to let the thought go, knowing it means to harm you. Take control! Proclaim 'hate' as an invader, wanting to steal Raven and every other good thing God has placed in your life."

"I trust you, Nicholas," Justus said. "You've always looked out for me and now I know I need to make some changes if I hope to be with Raven. I can see your point about letting this dark and miserable emotion 'push me around'. When you put it that way, 'hate' becomes a wicked bully who's just out to ruin my life."

"You've got it now, son," smiled Nicholas. "Now think about all we've discussed on your way up the mountain. When you get there, tell

Makande his wife has arrived and is in labor at my place. You can also inform Brother Taylor and Lund that most of us will be joining them after Bell gives birth. They will need to make preparations for a handful of new guests. According to Rubin's report, he overheard Sergeant Ficci telling his brother he was well enough to ride again, and by now the soldiers should be half way here. Everyone involved with the Mission must be on the top of the mountain before they march into Pizal."

Justus thanked him, mounted his horse and rode up the moonlit mountain trail, realizing for the first time that his uncontrolled emotions were his greatest enemy, not the Ficci brothers. For the first time, he prayed that God, not himself alone, would insure justice was served for the murder of his family. His heart grew warm at the thought that after Raven heard his new views she might smile again, and that was something he couldn't live without.

Nicholas carried Bernadette into a guest bedroom and made her comfortable. He told her that after Bell delivered the child, he would formally introduce her to everyone as Hope Mission's first journalist. Leaving her to her writing, he went directly to his workshop and began making her crutches.

As she lay in the meager room with humble furnishings, listening to Bell cry out in pain, Bernadette began to think of her new life. Amazingly, she had ceased to think of her wealth, and the fear that had dominated her every waking moment was absent.

Nicholas was right, she decided. From the time they'd left the mansion, her mind had been occupied with matters beyond herself, and this had left no room for dwelling on fear.

Hearing the nuns lovingly comfort Bell with hopes of a healthy child bathed her in a belief God dwelt in Nicholas' house, and she felt safe. If living modestly with simple, struggling people was the price she had to pay to continually feel fearless and vibrant, she was more than willing to pay. Besides, this was the most exciting thing she'd ever encountered. She had an occupation she had loved as a child and a chance to be close to a man she now regarded as the most extraordinary individual she'd ever met. How could she not rejoice?

Chapter 41. Fleeing Again to the Summit.

*A*fter saying good night to Bernadette, Nicholas grabbed several blankets and an oil lamp and headed out the door. With his house overflowing with people, the barn was his best option for a good night sleep, since at least it had hay for a mattress.

Opening the barn door, he heard sounds of shuffling and moaning. He held the lamp high to peer at something rolling around on the hay near one of the horses. Moving closer, he recognized Joseph Solo, bent and twisting in convulsions. His jaw was forced open and his tongue twisting, in uncontrolled spasms. Joseph moaned toward Nicholas as if to say something, but apparently had no muscular control to do so.

Squatting, Nicholas reached for Joseph's hand. At the moment of contact, Joseph fell into a deep sleep. Nicholas hung the lamp on a stall, and bent to examine the dried blood spread on Joseph's face and neck. He hurried into the house for a towel, surmising the injury must've come with Joseph's first convulsion, when his muscles locked, throwing him to the ground.

As he cleaned away the blood, it occurred to him that this must be the time ordained by God for Joseph to lay hands on Daisy and Rose. How wonderful it would be to see the young palsied girls join the other healthy children, and then see their mother begin a new life with Ben!

Nicholas covered Joseph with a blanket, then made himself a bed in the hay, put out the lamp and lay down.

As he closed his eyes, exhausted from the busy day, images of Bernadette's beautiful smile floated into his mind. Reason and logic struggled to convince him he could never settle for a woman who had been spoiled from birth, but another voice defended Bernadette. *She's not the same person you first met only days ago. You can't deny you've noticed.*

Nicholas turned in his hay-bed, pulled the blanket over his head and refused to think about it another minute. He must save his energy to get the loaded wagon and all the Mission family up the mountain to safety in the morning.

Nicholas woke to the sound of Makande's laughter as he stood in the barn doorway holding his new baby, wrapped in Bell's multi-colored blanket. "Mr. Nicholas, wake up to see my baby girl! I don't know how you get them here, but I am thanking you in my heart forever."

He laughed again as Nicholas rolled off the hay and joined him. "How beautiful, Makande! She looks like an angel of Love God...God of Love! What have Bell and you decided to call her?"

Carefully handing the infant to him, Makande said, "We call her Hope. We name her after Hope Mission, place where God of Love lives. Place where we find freedom and be happy. Place we will stay forever and work for Love God."

As they argued over who the infant looked more like, Joseph woke and sat up staring into space, seemingly despondent. Nicholas handed the baby to Makande and went to Joseph. "When I came here last night you were convulsing. What happened?"

Rubbing the cut on his forehead, Joseph replied, "It was the worst experience of my life. I came down the mountain to find you and talk about my job as lookout. When I entered the barn, I lost all control of my muscles and went into extreme convulsions. I lay here God knows how long before you came. It was ghastly. I was mentally aware of everything happening but unable to control any part of my body. While convulsing, I asked God why He could let anyone suffer so. I questioned why He gave me the gift of healing, but with suffering. I had no answer and became angry with Him. As saliva dripped down my neck, my anger caused me to sin against God and now I know what I must do."

"What must you do?"

"It's obvious that someone in your home has palsy and God wants me to lay hands on them, but I cannot while I'm in this state of confusion. I will fast for three days and seek an answer from God."

"I will fast as well, Joseph," said Nicholas, patting Joseph on the shoulder, "and I will pray God speaks understanding to your heart. In the meantime, you must hurry to your lookout post and watch for soldiers. We'll be preparing to leave at once."

Nicholas instructed Makande to organize and prepare everyone in the orphanage for the journey. He helped Ben and Maria put Daisy and Rose into the wagon along with some of the younger children. Bell and her newborn sat in front beside Makande.

Bernadette appeared at the front door on crutches, looking for Nicholas. When he came out of the wagon, Nick lifted her onto her horse and tied her supply horse in tow.

Within the hour, they were at the base of the mountain ready to make the journey to the top. Getting the large supply wagon up the first steep incline would be a challenge.

As the caravan moved up the mountain trail, the incline appeared not far ahead. Bernadette pulled her reins back, pointing up the mountain to the east. A large black bear made its way down over the rocks toward them. Bernadette guided her horse backwards until she was at Nicholas' side. As she reached out her hand, Nicholas held her, reminding her about the pregnant wildcat and reassuring her that she was safe. As he spoke, everyone stared at them, then shared surmising glances.

"What is it?" demanded Nicholas, his tone soft but stern?

His friends smiled simultaneously, turning their heads away, saying quite casually, "Nothing, no... nothing."

Ben approached Nicholas. "We need to get up this steep incline. I don't know if those two horses will be able to carry the load. Have any ideas, Nick?"

Nicholas gave Bernadette a smile of assurance, turned to the curious onlookers with a lowered brow and dismounted. Taking a coil of rope from his horse, he asked Ben to follow him. As they walked out over boulders toward the bear, it rolled onto its back, grunting. When they reached it, Nick squatted, vigorously rubbing its neck and belly. The children laughed as if at a circus and Giovanni's jaw dropped, never having seen or imagined the like of this.

Nicholas motioned for the bear to come to its feet, leading it toward the wagon, all the time talking, while rubbing its neck and ears. When they reached the wagon, everyone sat quietly staring as the men tied the rope into a bridle, placing it on the bear. Then they tied the bridle onto the hitch and led the bear, horses and wagon up the steep incline, arriving at the top with relative ease. Applause broke out as Nicholas untied the bear and fed it all the dried beef he had in his saddlebags.

Bernadette clapped twice as fast as the rest, while Maria went to Ben, stepped up on a rock and kissed his mask. Looking toward Maria, Nicholas could have sworn he saw Ben's mask turn a blushed shade of red when Maria kissed him, but he put it aside as a product of his imagination.

Sisters Mary and Margaret stood with the children, confirming to each other the notion that the spirit of St. Francis was indeed behind Nicholas' ability to calm the wild beasts. Giovanni overheard them and, after seeing how the bear obeyed his every coaxing, thought them quite correct.

Once they were past the steep incline, the mountain trail took a less drastic angle. It became more like a walk in the forest, only continually moving upwards. Nicholas moved a little ahead of the wagon while Bernadette nudged her horse with her good foot to catch up.

"Nicholas, do you mind if I ride with you a while?"

Nicholas' stomach fluttered, but he answered calmly. "By all means, Bernadette. How is the journal developing?"

"I have written more in these past few days then in my entire life. It's a wonderful occupation for me and every bit of advice you've given me has helped. I feel I've been born again to a whole new way of life."

"Born again?" Nicholas smiled. "We'll speak of this again, but for now, how are you faring with your fear?"

"I have a confession to make about that, Nick."

Holding his smile back at her frank tone, he replied, "I'm ready, Bernadette. Please tell me."

"Remember that stormy night when you came to my aid after I screamed?"

"How could I forget? I never saw anyone more terrified for less solid reason in my entire life."

"When you touched my hand all my fears evaporated in an instant. But when I pulled my hand back, the terror returned. Each time you touched me, the fear would vanish. At first I thought you were casting a spell. I kept it to myself because it had such a powerful positive effect and I didn't want you to know what power you hold over me. I'm not afraid of that now, as I know you for a truly good man. Ever since I stayed in your guest room, peace has come, and I don't understand why. I know part of it is a result of the redirecting of my thoughts, but that cannot be all. Can you explain the effect of your touch?"

"I knew nothing of that until now," said Nick. "My only explanation is that I've always carried a sense of peace and calm, which has increased since God sent me on this mission. I've come to the conclusion that love is behind it all."

"Love?" Bernadette blushed as she spoke.

"The scriptures say, 'perfect love casts out fear,' and if that's the process sent from Heaven, then it makes sense that resounding peace abides in the absence of fear. I have an indescribable love for my God and His creation. What you experienced at my touch could only be God sharing with you what He's given me. I can't think of any other explanation." He paused, marshalling his thoughts. "What you experienced when I touched you is only a sample of what He wants to give you, Bernadette. The scriptures say, 'For God hath not given us a spirit of fear; but of power, and of love, and of a sound mind.' "

"I've been a Christian my entire life and never has a person spoken to me of such things. If this is all true and written down, I must search the scriptures myself. Where can I obtain a copy?" asked Bernadette.

"I have a New Testament that I copied in the scriptorium before dismissing myself from seminary. You can read it when we arrive at the Mission."

"Thank you, but—"

"But?"

"There's more I wish to ask, but I feel I cannot take all your attention. So many others need you more than I."

Nicholas looked back over his Mission family, and smiled. "All is well at present. Ask what you wish."

"Why did I continue to feel the peace when I was alone in the guestroom?"

Nicholas laughed. "My home is now taken over by people who love God as much as I, and I never doubt the Holy Spirit rests in such places. Darkness and fear flee from the presence of the Spirit. Now, after seeing you grown happy and dauntless so soon, I trust you will stay with us a while?"

"I will surely stay. A life of consternation and anxiety is no life at all, in spite of the wealth and status. It's a wonderful thing to smile again."

"And your smile is a wonderful gift for all who see it." Nicholas found himself so contented that he began to surrender to the possibility that Bernadette might be God's choice for him, as well as his own, but he resolved to reveal nothing until he was certain of God's design.

Half way up the mountain, Nicholas found a clearing and bade everyone rest. He helped Bernadette dismount, and pulling her crutches from the saddle, she made her way to the baggage horse and retrieved a small, leather-bound journal. Finding a cozy place under a cherry tree, she rested her ink jar on a flat rock and continued the personal diary she'd started when they left Cosenza.

April 27, 1556

It seems as though confusion has taken the place of fear and trepidation these past days. How, in one day, a man can enter my life and so totally revolutionize my thinking completely mystifies me. Instead of apprehension and foreboding in a past time, I find myself drawn to thinking about this man for reasons unlike any I've ever known. And though his handsome face and charming smile would allure any woman's heart, it is none of that which draws my thoughts to rest on him. Somehow, his selflessness and compassion shine brighter than any physical attribute, and if he looked as a horrid beast I would find myself no less comforted and invigorated in his presence. But questions arise as I write these thoughts and consider him further. Will his devotion to God prevent him from ever accepting the love of a woman? And though his blue eyes sparkle when they meet mine, do they not yet even shine when he pets the bear? Or when he speaks his mind? Or when he searches mine?

Nicholas stood on the blind side of his horse, pretending to adjust the saddle straps, transfixed on Bernadette's every move as she wrote in the small unfamiliar journal. It was as though her every movement glided gracefully into the next, as she dipped her pen, and fixed her hair, and bit her lip, moving the pen across the page like a dancer on the stage. He could only smile in surrender when he realized how totally out of control his feelings were becoming and how at the sight of her, involuntary emotions overwhelmed his senses and seized his faculties.

CHAPTER 42. SUFFERING.

*M*oments before Nicholas intended to give the signal for everyone to mount up, Maria stepped out of the wagon weeping, calling for Ben. When he came she embraced him, saying Daisy had bitten her tongue again and was bleeding.

Sister Mary went to aid the child while Sister Margaret joined Ben in comforting Maria. Until then, Bernadette had not seen the palsied children and wanted to investigate what so upset their mother.

Calling Nicholas to aid her, she threw her arm over his shoulder and limped to the wagon.

As Nicholas lifted her onto the back steps, Bernadette gasped, holding a hand to her mouth, watching Sister Mary wipe blood and saliva from the child's face. Tears formed as she witnessed the children convulse and moan with sounds that wrenched her heart, pulling her further away from herself than she'd ever been. Looking on in dismay and pity, she motioned for Nicholas to take her away.

Nicholas ignored her request momentarily as he reached for a towel, then climbed into the wagon to wipe the children's faces once again. They fell into a sound sleep at his touch.

"I don't understand," said Bernadette as Nicholas swept her up and stepped off the wagon. "After seeing the twins in that horrid state, and knowing they've been living like that for most of their lives, I can't understand a single reason God would permit such a thing. Why does He allow such misery to the innocent?"

Nicholas lifted her onto her horse, then mounted his and gave the signal for the others to follow. "You should speak to Ben about this first. Ask about what happened to him, and how he came to wear the mask. Ben was right there, at the inception of Hope Mission, and by speaking to him you'll gain a deeper understanding. When you record all the things you see and hear, I promise you'll come away with a rich knowledge of the character of God. But you must know that some things God allows will always remain mysterious. We cannot presume to know the mind of God."

Bernadette nodded and reined back, waiting until Ben caught up.

"Hello, Ben. Could we ride together a bit and talk? Nicholas tells me how vital you are to the Mission, and since it's my job to record everything, and you were there from the start, I thought you might be willing to help."

"By all means," said Ben, smiling beneath his mask. "So you're Hope Mission's new record-keeper. What is it I can help you with?"

"Nicholas wants me to understand the subject of suffering, and said you might be able to help by explaining how you were burned and life afterward."

Ben told her about his ordeal, praised Anna Borelli for her skills in keeping him alive, and then explained how his life had degraded from there.

"When I first looked into the glass after they removed the bandages, I thought I would faint. I appeared as a monster, and was thrown into a state of despair and misery so dark that if I'd died on the spot I would have thought it a kindness from God. When I went outdoors without covering my face, children ran screaming to their parents. People gasped in horror at the sight of me, and my heart became bitter against God for having rewarded my effort to save my friend with a life of anguish.

"Beyond my appearance, the pain I experienced was unbearable. When a soft breeze glanced over the holes where my ears used to be, it brought me to my knees in a searing pain I wouldn't wish on my worst enemy. As time went by I lost all hope—until Nicholas gave it back."

"What did he do? What happened?"

"The first thing he did was turn me away from myself by asking if I'd like to carve a gift for Anna Borelli. I was pleased to do so, for she is a fine person for whom life has not been easy. As I worked on a sculpture for her, Nicholas planned and made the mask for me."

"He helped me in the same way. He made me turn away from myself, and as soon as I did my condition improved," said Bernadette, glancing ahead toward Nicholas.

"God has given Nicholas a special way with people," said Ben. "His gifts bring people hope. Before I finished the carving for Anna, he asked me to carve a portrait of myself, and from that he created the mask. I never dreamed it would serve me as well as it has. To start with, my ears are protected from the wind and thus I have no more pain. Further, because Nicholas told me to make the ears slightly larger, I can hear Giovanni's beautiful voice singing to the children walking near the wagon."

Arching her eyebrows, Bernadette said, "I can't hear anything. He's singing? That's amazing!"

"It gets better," said Ben, grinning to himself. "There are mysterious things about the mask I cannot explain. When evil is present, a chill comes upon my face under the mask and warns me to beware. And how does the mask cause people to respect and admire me far more than before I became scarred? Also, Maria tells me she sees subtle changes in the appearance of the mask, changes that reflect my moods and emotions. It's almost as if it were becoming a real face."

"It's true!" exclaimed Bernadette. "When I first saw you, the mask appeared to have a lowered brow, and now the brow is relaxed and expresses a calmness or tranquility."

"Now that you've heard my story, you should ride back to the wagon and ask Giovanni about his life with blindness," suggested Ben. "His is the most remarkable story I've ever heard."

Bernadette thanked him and walked her horse back to the wagon. As she drew near, she realized Giovanni was indeed singing. She was astonished Ben heard him from such a distance.

Following the wagon, she was enchanted with the song and taken by his words and gentle guitar picking. A sense of wonder overcame her as she looked about and saw wolves and other wild creatures playing or sitting pensively as the group moved ever closer to the mountaintop.

When the singing stopped and Giovanni moved to the front of the wagon next to Makande, Bernadette trotted alongside. "Mr. Giovanni, may I speak with you a while?"

Placing his index finger to his lips, he warned, "I'd love to, but let's be as quiet as possible, as the twins need to sleep."

Bernadette moved closer to the wagon, "I'm Bernadette LaViono, Hope Mission's new journal-keeper."

"I am pleased to meet you, Bernadette." The elderly man smiled. "I am also stunned by your beauty. It is as much a gift from God as my newly-opened eyes are to me."

Bernadette smiled back, warmed as much by his tone as by the compliment. "Nicholas mentioned something of your experiences. Would you tell me more?"

"Well, praise God, He's blessed me with vision after sixty years in the dark. I am more thankful to Him than words can express. I've written two new songs about the day Joseph Solo put his tiny thumbs on my eyes. Two minutes later, I saw light. Then in another minute, I had perfect vision."

"What was life like before the miracle?"

"Well now, *that's* a story. When I was about five, I lost all vision. I became totally dependant on my parents and lived with them a good long time. They read to me on every subject, every day until the day they died, my mother living only a year longer than my father. I was forty when I found myself cast into the streets of Rome, singing to survive. Daily living became difficult, as evil young boys stole what little alms I collected from my day of public songs. This went on for a long time and I became ever more bitter toward God and the lot He'd given me.

"I lived in the streets near death, weak from lack of food, homeless, and in constant darkness. Then, one day, the stealing stopped. When the young thieves approached to take what little I had, they seemed to be scared away by something. Then, each morning when I woke in my shelter under a wagon, I found bread or cheese or fruit in my hand. As time went by, I perceived someone was near all day long, listening to me in secret, chasing the thieves and providing the food as a kindness for my songs.

"One day when I sensed someone about, I called to him, wishing to thank him for bringing a bit of relief to my wretched life. A voice, deeper than mine, came from an alley directly behind me. He said, 'No, thank *you* for sounds from Heaven in this wicked city.' I asked him to come forth but he would not and said he would visit me late in the evening when all were asleep. He said he could help make my life a little safer and would explain later. Then he was gone.

"Late that evening he came and woke me, and led me to his hidden shelter in the city dump. It was warm and spacious, having a small, iron stove and a place for me to make my bed. He led me around, making me familiar with where the dried foods were, and then we sat by the warmth of the stove and he began to explain about himself and why he wished to help.

"He said his name was Jives and I should be thankful I couldn't see him, for he was born with a host of birth defects leaving him with the appearance of a hideous troll. The bones in his face were misaligned at birth and his spine refused to straighten from childhood, leaving him with a hunch, and a face he could not bear to look at in the glass. It was this man who taught me how to love God and appreciate every day of life. After he accepted the fact he was seen as a monster, he resigned himself to a life of solitude and introspection. Aside from his encounters with me, he would sleep in the day and only come out in the dead of night to attain provisions for himself and for children seeking his protection.

"One night, years ago, a monk spotted him searching the garbage behind his church and allowed him to have free access to the basement under the church library. He'd spend entire nights copying the best literature. After some years, Jives had managed to copy a dozen books, and from the Bible he copied Psalms, Proverbs and the New Testament. Reading the scriptures led him to thinking about why, and for what purpose, God permitted a creature like him to ever see the light of day.

"Before Jives continued, he groaned a deep sigh and lay down in his bed to rest. As he directed me to the firewood, instructing me how to keep the stove constant, he became ill, and before the pitch of night he was in a grave state indeed. Sitting on a stool by his bedside, I reached out my hand and he took it, holding it to his chest. With a feeble voice and a desperate grip on my hand, he thanked me for reaching out to him and explained that no one had ever done that before in kindness. He said he knew he was to die that very night and wanted me to come into possession of what little he'd managed to acquire over fifty-one reviled and dejected years.

"His hand trembled in mine, and his voice declined to a whisper as he continued to explain what he came to believe about suffering and God's reasons for it. He first looked for meaning in his life and could find none save his books and the homeless children he cared for in the city dump. He came to reason the purpose of his life rested fully on the lives of the children, and that keeping them safe and fed validated his own wretched existence. He reasoned God placed those children in his care, and protecting them was the only source of true happiness he'd ever encountered.

"While in repose, deeper in thought, he said after thinking about it many years, he pondered what life would be like without suffering and hardship, beyond the obvious answers. There would be no need for compassion, or empathy, or sympathy. What need would we have for hope in a perfect world, and how deep could we love without all those attributes? How much faith could we muster in a God who could not identify with His own creation? If Christ had not suffered Himself, and chosen to live as we do while He was here, how could He have learned compassion and empathy? Would we not trust His testimony less if He had chosen to waive His own hardship here on Earth?"

"After an hour, his hand became still and cold, and there was a long silence, and I knew he'd died. Lying in bed that night, across the room from Jives' body, I began to reflect on my own life as he had on his, and pondered the notion of how my blindness might have aided and tempered me according to God's design. At first it seemed a cruel lesson, but probing deeper into the providence I suspected God had prepared for me, I came to see my pride in spite of my blindness and self-pity. I saw extreme pride in my voice and the profound effect it had on people. I searched deep within and saw the life I might have led if I had been allowed vision along with a gifted voice, and a disproportionate degree of pride - a pride that would've driven me daily toward fame, fortune, and comfort, and finally self-consumption.

"As I lay in bed blind to the outer world, I received vision of the inner world, and came to realize that even having had the hardship of blindness, I was yet prideful and conceited, and I thanked God for revealing the source of my reproach toward Him. Perhaps it was the providence of God that I should by no means see outwardly, before I beheld inwardly the vainglory that would ultimately blind me spiritually from seeing His light. I came to see that I was destined to replace Jives as the children's protector and caretaker in spite of being blind, and I was glad to do so. In time, I came to feel the same validation Jives did, and all at once my soul did rest and my life had true meaning.

"When I woke the next morning a young boy came into the shelter asking for Jives. When I told him what had happened, he burst into tears and stayed by his side all day. He told me how Jives taught him to read and write, and how he had cared for and loved the homeless children, allowing them to stay in his warm shelter while he searched the night for food and other useful necessities.

"Now, Bernadette, if you turn and look to the end of our caravan, you will see a boy of about fifteen, marching as a soldier, watching over the other children that are walking and playing in front of him. His name is Roberto and he is the same boy whom Jives taught to read and write, and now he is teaching me."

Bernadette turned and saw the boy marching as a rear guard. Turning back to Giovanni with childish anticipation, she asked her final question, "And what of the pride now that you can see, Giovanni?"

"From the day Joseph laid hands on me, and light came into my eyes, I have become extremely sensitive to pride. When it's near I see its darkness and am aware of its danger to my spirit. It has no part in me now, and when I sing, I sing to God, for it is He who imparts all good gifts. As I see your exceeding beauty with my new eyes, I have a question for *you*."

"And what is that, Giovanni?"

"As you behold your beauty in the glass, who receives credit for that gift? Do you see it as I do, as a gift from God?"

"The very next time I look into the glass I will, with deep humility, ask that question of myself. You are an extraordinary man, Giovanni, and I shall record your story with a tenderness and nobility proportionate to the spirit from whence it came."

Trotting up toward Nicholas, Bernadette organized the stories in her memory and began to understand, at least to some degree, the reason God permitted suffering. But she wanted to go deeper yet and hoped Nicholas would take her there. As she slowed her horse beside him, Nicholas asked, "How did it go? Did they help to understand?"

"Yes, indeed, Nicholas, both Ben and Giovanni shed light on the question and I'm starting to understand the matter in a deeper way, but maybe you can add to their insight."

Nicholas gazed at her for a long moment before answering. "Everyone struggles with this question, Bernadette. Wars, famines, diseases, natural disasters and untimely deaths are never easy to rationalize. But miseries of this nature are less troubling than the ones that happen to us personally, such as Maria's struggle with her palsied twins, and Ben with his scarred face, and Giovanni with his sixty years of blindness, and even Makande and Bell with their lifetime in slavery. The human spirit is capable of withstanding enormous discomfort, including the prospect of death, if the circumstances make sense.

"Many war heroes, martyrs and political prisoners have died for their cause in confidence. They knew, without question, the consequences of their sacrifices. A soldier in battle sees the reason behind giving his life, if it's a just and noble cause. By contrast, good people, such as those you've spoken to minutes ago, have no such consolation. It is the *absence of meaning* that makes the situation so intolerable. As you look into the lives of the people who surround you, God's providence will become apparent, but still much will remain a mystery until He reveals it at the end of time."

Chapter 43. Captain Ficci Plans his Assault.

*A*s the caravan turned the last bend up the mountain trail, the new log fence surrounding the Mission came into view. Approaching from the east came Joseph Solo on his Shetland. He rode directly to Nicholas and gave his report. "The soldiers are at the base of the mountain. As soon as I returned to the lookout cabin, I peered through the magni-tube and saw them coming from a great distance. Wonderful invention, that thing you made. There are about fifty soldiers, ten on horseback. I watched them bypass Pizal and turn toward the mountain trail."

"Good job, Joseph. How are you feeling? Any better than the last time we spoke?"

"I'll let you know everything in two days when my fast is over. In the meantime, could you direct me to the individual stricken with palsy?"

"If you ride back to the wagon, you'll find Daisy and Rose. They are eleven-year-old twins and have had the condition for ten years. Will you lay hands on them now, Joseph?"

"No, no, not yet. But I need to see them before I return to my cabin."

Joseph rode back to the wagon and as he dismounted, Ben introduced him to Maria. With a distant look, he greeted her and went directly into the wagon. He stayed for several minutes and then emerged, wiping his eyes with his sleeve. Acknowledging no one, he mounted his pony and rode toward the lookout cabin and solitude.

Nicholas had previously informed everyone about Joseph's odd ways and his need to be alone, so when the healer left abruptly, talking to himself, no one was shocked.

When the caravan arrived at the south gate, Nicholas entered and stood gazing silently for a long time, pleased with the progress since his departure less than a week ago. A patchy fog was forming as he looked toward the center of the Mission, where the nearly-completed church stood. There were three brothers up on the steeple, dangling on ropes with pulleys and buckets of white paint.

Ox and Brother Taylor greeted him, and explained the amazing progress they'd made since the recent additions to the workforce. There were now ninety monks helping with construction. Brother Taylor explained that many of them had come to help temporarily and would return to their specific orders when the Mission construction was complete. They had vowed to keep the location secret.

As the nuns came and guided the group to their living quarters, Ox pointed toward the west gate where a large, half-built home stood. It was to be Nicholas' house, and directly behind it, to the left and right, were two more frames. They were to be the homes of Ben and Makande.

The air was thick and it began to rain as Ox pointed to the trenches and drains they had built, leading floodwater out the north side of the mountain and over the edge. When the rain began to fall in sheets, they hurried into the Bellicini home and finished reviewing the new construction.

Bernadette, now able to walk without crutches, limped to a cozy spot near the fireplace in the grand room and began to write in her journal. Makande disappeared into the kitchen to prepare a grand meal, and Nicholas went to the second floor after asking Ben to find Justus and meet him in the den. Now that the soldiers had arrived, there wasn't much time before they'd have to confront the Ficci brothers and put an end to the quest to arrest the Bellicini family.

At the base of the mountain, Sergeant Ficci organized the men in an open field near the mountain trail. They'd already had their tents pitched when the rain began, and now it was coming down in torrents.

Captain Ficci was standing alone in his huge tent, looking up the mountain, when he noticed his brother glaring at him from the neighboring tent.

Manuel quickly turned, pulling the flap shut.

The Captain suspected his brother would betray him if enough gold was involved, so he called his Staff Sergeant into the tent for a conference. Sergeant Nathaniel Vance was in charge of the second squad, which numbered twenty-three soldiers. Vance had just been transferred to San Marco the week before, after fighting the French in Genoa for a fortnight. His regiment had driven the Duke of Guise back into French territory, and after being highly decorated for his valor, he now found himself in an altogether different kind of battle. Captain Ficci ordered him to keep a close eye on Sergeant Ficci.

Suddenly a loud rumble ended their conversation, and looking up toward the mountain they witnessed a massive mudslide. Trees, bushes and boulders came roaring down a steep incline covering the mountain trail.

When the rain eased, the Captain ordered his brother to take several men and find an alternate road around the fallen earth back on to the main trail.

Reluctant to go any distance up the mountain with so few men, Sergeant Ficci persuaded his brother to wait another day until the ground dried and they had better footing.

The Captain ordered Manuel instead to take ten men on a hunt and, after killing the game, butcher it and poison the meat. The hunters caught an elk and two deer, and discovered a path leading around the mudslide toward the main trail. By mid afternoon the following day, they expected to make their first attempt to the summit, slaughtering and poisoning as many wolves as possible on the way.

Nicholas grabbed a jar of apple cider and three mugs from the Bellicini kitchen and went to the den. Ben and Justus were already there when he entered. Pouring the cider, he turned to Ben. "Is it just my imagination or does your mask change its shape with your feelings?"

"Maria tells me the same thing. I can't really tell, but it appears to be true," Ben said, and smiled.

Justus added, "I noticed just today and it's true. The brow gives it away. Right now it's relaxed, but when you came into the room it had a wrinkle above the bridge of the nose."

Handing them mugs of cider, Nicholas grinned, "When Maria kissed you after we made it up that steep incline, I could've sworn your mask blushed. I could be wrong, Ben, but I know I didn't paint the outer layer of the calfskin red when I created the mask. Whatever's happening I count as good, because it's bringing you even closer to the way life was before you were burned. Have you and Maria chosen a date for your wedding?"

"Not just yet, but it will be soon. We want to be the first couple married in the new church. I think we'll wait until this matter with the soldiers is over and we can relax."

Nicholas turned to Justus. "And how are you and Raven?"

"We are in love, but she won't even discuss a future with me until she sees what happens with the Ficci brothers. I think she'll turn from me if I lose control and kill one of them."

"Well, men, that's why I've called this meeting," said Nicholas. "Ben, you need to go outside the Mission fence and search for a way down the other side of the mountain. Should the soldiers somehow make it here, you'll have an escape route.

"Justus, I think you should go down the south side of the mountain, in stealth, and bring back a report on the soldiers' activities. I stress, by no means should your crossbow go off by accident, if you spot the Ficci brothers. We must find ways to avoid bloodshed. This will be our greatest trial, so let's keep our wits about us and be in constant prayer."

Justus turned to Nicholas and asked abruptly, "Is Bernadette in love with you?"

Nicholas froze for a second. "Why do you ask, Justus?"

"With all due respect, Nicholas, it's pretty obvious."

"It is?"

Ben supported Justus. "We all noticed it first when Bernadette saw the bear coming and reached out for you. It was obvious by the way you looked at each other."

Nicholas paused. He felt a faint stirring of anger at his friends' persistence, but then, had he not just quizzed them on their romantic affairs? "To be honest, I do have feelings," he admitted, "but I don't know what to do with them. This never happened to me before. Anyway, I'm probably the last thing on her mind."

"Not so, Nick," Justus declared. "Every time she looks at you her face lights up, and looks almost as beautiful as Raven. I say she loves you."

Nicholas' heart swelled, but he acknowledged the comment with a jest. "Your words are like your arrows, Justus, taking no detours, sinking right to the heart of the matter." He left the room, and glanced down over the railing into the grand chamber below, where Maria, Bernadette and Raven sat by the fireplace, with the twins on a blanket beside them. Bernadette was feeding the girls dried fruit as Maria and Raven sewed Maria's wedding gown. Descending the staircase, Nicholas noticed Bernadette talking to the children with the same endearment and assurance she had shown the pup before they left the mansion.

When he joined them, they all smiled, pointing out the fine lace Raven had offered to finish the neckline of the dress. Nicholas reached out to Daisy and Rose, causing them to giggle. The women turned to each other, amazed at the effect of his touch.

"You ladies seem to be having a rousing good time. May I steal Bernadette away for a while?"

"Yes, sir, you may," Maria answered, "but not for too long. Bell and Makande have prepared a grand meal for everyone. The aromas filling this house are so delicious. They're preparing roasted quail, fried bass, and an assortment of vegetables fit for a king, not to mention the berry and apple pies cooling on the kitchen table as we speak."

"We won't be too long, Maria," said Nicholas. "I must see Joseph Solo before it gets dark."

As Bernadette rose, Nicholas asked her to find her journal, and to walk him to Joseph's cabin. When the time was right, Bernadette would record an eyewitness account of the healing of Daisy and Rose. Nicholas had to persuade Joseph to break his rule about never having an audience when the Lord called on him for a healing.

Chapter 44. A Visit with Joseph Solo.

he rain had stopped and the crisp, moist spring air invigorated Nicholas and Bernadette as they left the south
gate heading east towards Joseph's cabin. Limping along, Bernadette
stopped, squatted down and rubbed her ankle. Nicholas offered to take her
back and saddle a horse, but she refused, asking only to hold his arm as a
crutch to relieve the weight.

When she rose, Nicholas grabbed his belt and Bernadette slipped her
arm through his, drawing close to him as they proceeded. Walking in
silence, a host of curious emotions rankled Nick. When the wind lifted her
silver-gold hair onto his shoulder, he made the distressful discovery that her
natural scent had the ability to weaken his knees and completely eradicate
his ability to think.

As they strolled casually, Nicholas looked out across the lake and
wondered if his voice would sound the same with the now present lump in
his throat. "So, Bernadette, you seemed to be enjoying yourself as you fed
Daisy and Rose earlier. I thought that type of mission work disturbed you."

"I had a preconceived idea about what a Mission is, and about the
work that goes on here. Feeding the children didn't feel like work—it felt
like love. I've been thinking a lot since my conversation with Ben and Giovanni. I've come to realize their endeavors with adversity and hardship led
them to ask some very interesting questions about suffering.

"Even though the answers were not complete, there was consolation
in their hearts and revelation in their spirits. As I considered their words,
and thought about my own life, I discovered it was the very absence of conflict and hardship that bred in me a life deeply afflicted with apprehension
and fear. And to complete the darkness, there was my father, who never
trusted a soul and never forgot to remind me of it. And my mother, who
drilled my mind into believing that no man was good enough, and no
endeavor worthy enough for their gilded offspring."

"Is that why you never married?"

"Yes, but now my life is new and I'm seeing more clearly every day.
An important lesson I've learned lately is that *meaning* is the most funda-
mental and essential food for the soul."

"Hearing you speak such things shows me you'll write our journal
with inspiration and insight. You see, the journal is to uplift and motivate
future generations of Missionaries like us. I'm confident in you now,
Bernadette."

"Thank you, Nicholas. You know, I love this work so much, it doesn't feel like a job. Now may I ask *you* a question?"

"Anything."

"I told you why I never married. Would you answer the same question?"

Stunned, Nicholas paused a moment... "My heart has never stirred for a woman until recently. I thought it was my fate to be single-minded my entire life, but I was wrong."

"May I ask who she is, Nick?"

Ignoring the question, Nicholas pointed to the cabin atop the giant jagged rock. "That's Joseph Solo's lookout cabin. It's about fifty paces up. The brothers carved out makeshift stairs that wrap around the rock leading to the cabin. Come behind me and wrap your arms around my neck. I'll carry you up."

Her eyes searched for an answer to her last question, but when none came, she sighed, "Thanks. It looks steep, but I trust you, Nick."

Nicholas was amazed at her fearless attitude and willingness for adventure. Was this the same women he'd met that stormy night in Cosenza? He thought how true it was she started life anew and how delightful it was to witness a new character blossom. But still he realized the need for caution. He could not ask her to be his wife until he perceived her new path was set, and was indeed God's will.

Leaning over the safety railing, Joseph appeared and waved them up. The monks had built the railing to keep the strong winds from blowing Mr. Solo's small body clean off his porch.

When they arrived at the top, Nicholas introduced Bernadette and asked if Joseph would direct them to the magni-tube first. It was located atop a tower built behind the cabin. Nicholas and Bernadette climbed the ladder, and when they reached the top and looked out across the countryside, they ooed with delight. The orange sun was about to kiss the top of the blue mountains, west of the lush rolling hills behind Rome. They turned round and round, able to see a full 360-degree panoramic view of their beloved Italian countryside.

Nicholas manned the magni-tube, and searching to the east, found Cosenza. Backing off from the eyepiece, he guided Bernadette to the scope and, peering through the lens, she gasped with such abandon Nicholas began laughing. They drank in the glorious view until the sun was halfway behind the mountain, then climbed down and joined Joseph in the cabin.

Everything in the cabin was scaled down to accommodate Joseph's miniature frame, including the front door, so they both had to duck as they entered the living room. As Nicholas turned to shut the door, he noticed the wind baffles installed around the cabin. Looking down, he saw bolts coming through the floor, fixing the cabin securely to its foundation. On the ceiling were metal fixtures securing the roof trusses to the walls, should the wind play havoc and attempt to separate the frame from its most essential protection. It was one of the most secure structures Nicholas had ever seen.

Bernadette took a seat by Joseph's tiny bed and huge bookshelf, writing in her journal as the men stood by the front window. With his stomach growling from fasting, Nicholas rested a hand on Joseph's shoulder. "How is your fast going? Have you spoken to the Lord?"

"Tomorrow my fast will end and I'll get to taste some of that wonderful bread someone baked today," said Joseph. "The aromas have made their way up here and tempted me. But for now, the lack of food has made me reconsider some questions I struggled with while in that horrid convulsed state. First, I prayed about the question of why the Lord gave me the gift of healing, with suffering attached.

"The answer is so simple and yet I missed it all of these years. God has seen fit to have me suffer along with the one I lay hands on, that I may gain a deep compassion and empathy for all who struggle in the world. When I pray for them, I need to identify with them as Christ identified with our suffering, being naked, nailed to the cross, scourged and humiliated. Now, for Christ's sake, I welcome the affliction that accompanies the healings, and from now on I shall have a more thorough and complete empathy when I petition the Lord regarding an illness."

As Bernadette struggled to write it all down, Joseph continued, "After having suffered on that barn floor only a fraction of what those little girls have had to endure for so long, it will indeed be an honor to be the instrument God uses to lay hands on them and see them healed."

Bernadette stopped writing and glanced up, unable to believe what she'd heard.

"When will this happen?" asked Nicholas. "What can we do to help?"

"The first thing you can do is not tell the rest of the Mission what God is preparing to do."

"But, Joseph, they've never seen a miracle. Would it not build their faith and bring them closer to God?"

"I knew you would ask that when it came time, so here's my answer. Did their faith not increase when Giovanni came out of the barn with new eyes? Living with this Mission family will always afford opportunities to build faith and bring us closer to God. As for healing Daisy and Rose, people only need to see them cured. It's not necessary to see the process."

"For the sake of future generations, would it be possible for only Bernadette to witness the healing? She's recording everything that occurs at the Mission."

Seeing Bernadette with her mouth agape, Joseph smiled. "You just don't stop, do you, Nick? Before this is all over, you'll end up persuading me to break all my own rules."

Nicholas laughed. "Does that mean she can be there when you lay hands on them?"

"Yes, but only her. Tomorrow night after everyone's asleep, I'll come down from this rock and meet Bernadette in the children's room around 2 a.m. Tell only Maria what I'm about to do. She should stay in bed and pray. Tell her in the morning her children will be healed, but tell her not to seek me afterwards. I will be drained and will want to return to my cabin. She must see it was God who cured her children, not me."

Glancing at the open cupboard and sparse food supply, Nicholas said, "Tonight I'll ask Makande to put aside some of Bell's home cooking for you. You can also take milk and butter when you return. But why not come down earlier and listen to Giovanni sing his nightly lullaby?"

"Are you trying to make me a social creature, Nicholas? You know it'll never work. I've never been like that, you know. The idea frightens me."

Bernadette glanced up and smiled. "I know all about fear, Joseph. Nicholas is a master at teaching people how to rid themselves of fear."

"Let me ask you a question," said Nicholas to Joseph. "How often have you had visitors in your home?"

"You're the first...ever!"

"Were you afraid with us here at any time? Was it not a pleasant visit? You'll soon come to see that life on the mountain, although not perfect, is shrouded in the peace of God and you are a part of that peace. Soon, of your own volition, you'll want fellowship with others, because we're all likeminded. Part of the problem you had before was, along with your extraordinary gift from God, you were mixed in with a society filled with a thousand different world views and a thousand different gods."

"Your visit has been quite pleasant, I admit. I hope you're right, Nick. I'm weary of the anxiety and fear."

"Why not come down earlier than you planned? You won't have to be near anyone and you'll hear a most gifted singer."

Joseph smiled. "You see, Bernadette, he just doesn't give up! I will consider it, Nicholas, but in the meantime, if Bernadette doesn't mind, may I have a word with you alone?"

Bernadette rose from her seat, wiped her pen clean, thanked Joseph for his hospitality and excused herself. She left the cabin, and stood on the front porch, looking out over the wind baffles to the mountains in the west, thinking about what Joseph said. Could Joseph, make those poor children's lives better?

"What is it, Joseph?" asked Nicholas, when they were alone.

"She's quite beautiful. Will you marry her?"

"Why does everyone assume I'm destined to be with this woman?"

"It's as clear as the wind beating against the window, my friend. I must confess, from the time you came out of the west gate, I used the magni-tube to spy on Bernadette and you. If she had got any closer, I would have thought you two were already married."

"Her ankle was in pain, she needed me as a crutch!"

"You're a very stubborn man, Nick. At some time you must admit to yourself and everyone else you love her."

"What gives you the notion I love her?"

"The magni-tube you created is very powerful. As you walked towards the giant rock, past the open field, I saw your face as you spoke to her. Though I've never been in love myself, I knew what love looked like when I saw your face. It's nothing to be ashamed of. I wished I could look as happy and content as the two of you."

"You mean she had the same look?"

"Absolutely! She loves you. Didn't you know?"

"I was too busy struggling with my own feelings to notice, but God has given me hope more than any other gift, and that's what I feel when I look at her. I hope and pray I'll be convinced that she can live as I do, for and in God."

"So you admit you love her?"

"I love her, but I'm entirely unprepared to deal with that fact."

Joseph giggled. "This is getting so interesting. You've got me actually enjoying having guests in my home." He touched Nick's arm in a rare gesture. "Come, Nicholas, are you not forever drawing secrets from others? Now it is your turn to submit to the same treatment and understand how naked it makes one feel."

CHAPTER 45. NICHOLAS EXPOUNDS ON LOVE.

*A*s Nick and Bernadette returned to the Mission from Joseph Solo's cabin, the sun had dropped behind the mountains, and as darkness set in, Nicholas looked to the torches lighting the west gate for his bearing. Bernadette clung to his side in silence, and as they approached the open field, Nick squinted at a white figure emerging from a wooded area to the north. As it drew closer, a smaller shadowy figure came into view. He stopped and squatted when he realized it was the large, white female wolf, and the black pup he had met before. The pup had grown to half the size of its mother.

When they were twenty paces away, the wolves simultaneously sank to their bellies and waited for Nicholas to approach. Bernadette's eyes grew wide as he took her hand and walked over, rubbing the mother's neck and ears. As he explained how he had rescued the pup from the ravine, the she-wolf jumped to her feet, walked out several paces and began running in circles. Then, all at once, she dropped to the ground, playing dead. The black pup ran to its mother and howled as if she'd really died.

Nicholas frowned at the curious sight.

"She might be trying to tell you something," Bernadette said.

"I don't exactly know," said Nick, "but what I do know is Captain Ficci and his men are at the base of the mountain with guns and traps. After the wolves killed five of his men, with his brother as witness, I suspect they've already killed some of these wild creatures in an effort to get to the Bellicinis."

"What will you do if they make it all the way up here, Nick?"

"I don't know just yet, but my instincts tell me they'll never make it. I'm not saying it won't become difficult for us, but I know God has His hand directly over this Mission. So the Captain will be fighting God, and that's one battle he cannot win. It's very important for you to record all of these events, Bernadette, because in the end, when we read how everything unfolded, we'll see God's providence."

Scratching the black pup's belly, Bernadette said, "I've written down everything that's happened since we left Cosenza. You can rest assured I will not sleep until the ink is dried and the journal is updated and complete."

As the wolves escorted them to the west gate, Bernadette, now barely limping, held Nick's arm and walked in silence as she rallied her courage to speak. "Nicholas, you mentioned earlier your heart was never really stirred by a woman until recently. Can you tell me more?"

Nicholas smiled. "Love for God brings my joy for life, and I would be content with only that for the rest of my life. However, a new and different love has sprung up and grows increasingly stronger, as if it were a flowered vine growing around my love for God. Love for our parents is one thing and love for people is yet another, and then love for God's creatures is still different than the last two. But the love I feel for this woman is mystifying, and it also enchants and invigorates me. It's altogether pleasing and yet an unfamiliar pain is attached.

"Though I strive to control my thoughts and feelings, I lose control when I'm in her presence. It's quite strange because it's the only time I don't mind losing control. When I'm near her, bliss engulfs me, and when I'm away, I'm shrouded in anguish, and thoughts of her beauty and gracious voice haunt me. What mystifies most is that I didn't choose this love, but rather, it chose me and beckons me to reveal my secret to the one who is its source."

Bernadette's heart raced as she pulled her journal to her chest and asked, "The woman you love doesn't know you love her? What if she doesn't feel as you do? What will you do then?"

Nicholas stopped and turned to look down at her. "I'm so naïve about this kind of love that I never thought of that question. I must try to find out about her feelings. What do you think I should do, Bernadette?"

Bernadette was confused. She hoped and believed it was she who won his heart, but what if it was not? She replied with care. "Nicholas, I'll help if I can. Why not create a gift and place it by her in secret? You'll know how she feels by the way she responds. The gift should be simple. Just attach your heart to it and you'll receive an answer."

"Thank you, Bernadette. I'll think on this tonight. In the meantime, when we return to the Mission, you should prepare for Joseph's arrival. Tonight you will witness something very special."

Bernadette knew Nicholas was not only naïve but quite innocent when it came to the subject of love and women. All she could do was to trust in her hope that she was the object of his love and that she would be strong enough to love and support him in his lifelong mission.

After walking Bernadette to the Bellicini home, Nicholas packed his personal belongings and headed to his new house to take up residence. Even though it was not complete, he decided to stay and help with the final construction. He unpacked his clothing, and pondered the special gift he would make for Bernadette. It must be a simple gift with his heart attached, and what better form could it take than a poem? He would fashion the words in a way that would let her know his feelings, and at the same time give her a means to express hers in return, without ever speaking a word.

He lit the fireplace for the first time, then perched on a half-constructed staircase and made his gift. He wrote the lines in his best hand, folded the sheet and sealed it with red wax. He knew she'd be busy with Joseph later that evening, so he returned to the Bellicini house and secretly placed his gift in her room.

CHAPTER 46. A MIRACLE IN THE DEAD OF NIGHT.

Joseph lay in his bed hollow with hunger as he approached the third day of his fast. Unable to sleep before his encounter with the palsied twins, he decided to dress and go down to the Mission to hear Giovanni sing to the children. As he stepped outside the cabin, a thick cloud engulfed him. He'd never seen a fog so dense, so he stepped back inside and lit a lamp to guide him down the jagged stone stairs. The light of the Mission's gate torches was not visible, but he made his way slowly in what he trusted was the right direction.

Ten minutes later, he went through the gate, directly to the Bellicini house. Lund was waiting as Joseph emerged from the fog holding his lamp.

"Is that you, Joseph Solo?"

"Yes it is. I've come to hear Giovanni sing. Am I too late?"

"Not at all. He has just begun to strum his guitar. I'll take you upstairs so you can be alone and hear what angels must sound like."

Lund took Joseph to the second level where a sitting table overlooked the stairwell into the grand room. The moment Joseph sat back in a cushioned chair, Giovanni began to sing to the children surrounding him by the fireplace. His voice was so soothing that before he began the second stanza, Joseph was enchanted. He sat motionless with his eyes closed, moved to tears by the spiritual words and perfect vibrato. The lullaby carried Joseph into a deep sleep.

Sometime in the middle of the night, Bernadette woke him. Touching his arm, she said, "I see you took up Nicholas' invitation to hear Giovanni?"

Rubbing his eyes, Joseph answered, "Yes, it was wonderful. I don't remember falling asleep."

"We should have warned you of the effect he has on people. Three tunes will usually get the job done."

"I fell asleep at the first one. What an amazing voice he has! It felt I was in Heaven itself."

"Joseph, before we go in to see Daisy and Rose may I ask you a few questions for the journal?" Bernadette asked.

"Go right ahead."

"When did you first realize you had the gift of healing?"

"When I was about seven I was out playing in an open field just behind a bakery. I used to go there with my brother and sister to smell the fresh-baked bread. One day we saw a dead bird under a tree behind the bakery. Out of curiosity, we went over to look, and when I stooped down to pick it up, I felt it stir in my hands. I thought it might not have been dead after all. My brother and sister looked at me as if they'd seen a ghost, but I thought nothing of it and released the bird into the air.

"After they swore the bird was dead and I had some kind of magic, an old man came out the back door of the bakery and approached us—actually, he approached me. He said he had seen everything and that he knew the bird was dead, as it had been lying there since the day before. Then he asked what kind of spell I cast to revive the bird. I told him I only picked it up and it stirred in my hands. It was at that moment I knew whatever this strange occurrence was, it would bring hardship and pain as long as I lived.

"The old man accused me of having a demon inside, and said he would inform the community and ask the church for an inquiry into my family. I was so scared, I ran away to my uncle's house. My father brought me home to make his own inquiry, and he and my mother forbade me from ever dabbling in witchcraft again. From then on trouble came on a daily basis as the gift of healing began to reveal itself."

"What happened after that," asked Bernadette not looking up from the journal.

"As time went on things grew worse. Every time a family member became ill, I would come down with the same illness. My parents thought I just wanted attention, but they couldn't have been more wrong. I became so confused that as soon as I was old enough, I moved out with my books and a small inheritance, and from that time to now I've been alone."

Bernadette frantically scribbled notes into the journal. "When did you first lay hands on someone, knowing they would be healed by your touch?"

"That's an important question, so be careful to write accurately, Bernadette. When I was twenty-five, I couldn't cope with living so close to so many people. I lived in a cave on the outskirts of Rome, until fate let me find a deserted cabin not far away. I lived in that cabin for five years, knowing if I moved back into the city all sorts of strange maladies and sicknesses would overcome me.

"I realized that being near other people had something to do with it all. As I began to get comfortable with the cabin and solitude, I made trips to Rome in search of books that might help me find out about the strange life I led.

"One day, while in Rome, I found a copy of the New Testament and studied everything it contained. After only a month, I came to believe the writings were the truth and that God utilizes His Holy Spirit to affect this world. My life suddenly made some sort of sense, and I began to think everything that happened up until then was ordained of God, and somehow now finally I would discover my destiny.

"Not long after that, while searching the scriptures, the world around me became uncommonly still. I looked out the cabin widow and everything seemed normal, only exceptionally quiet. I rose from my desk and accidentally knocked my tin cup to the floor. It crashed without a sound. As the cup rolled silently across the wooden planks, I knew I'd lost the ability to hear. I cried out, even more terrified at the absence of the sound of my own voice.

"I was afraid, so I gathered what I needed to make the trip to Rome and sought the counsel of the Church. I spent an hour with a local priest pleading for an answer to my deafness. He made gestures with his hands indicating he would pray for me. Then, reaching down, grabbing the back of my neck, he smiled, gently guiding me out the door. I can't say I blame him, because I must have seemed mad in my desperation.

"After leaving the Church, I roamed the streets in a panic for an answer to my now silent world. When I turned a corner, I peered down an alley behind an inn and saw a large man with a leather strap, lashing a young girl. She was hunched on the ground with her arms around her head protecting her face. In between lashes, she moved her hands in an odd way as if to communicate something. Not knowing what to do to stop the beating, I ran down the alley and confronted this man knowing, in the end, I might receive the same fate as the girl.

"When I stopped at the end of the alley, and he noticed me standing there, his expression went from angry to fearful in an instant. He looked at me in terror, then dropped his strap and ran into the back door of the inn. Looking behind me to see what'd frightened him, I saw nothing except a flash of light ascending into the sky. When I approached the young girl, she sat up, reaching out to me, moving her hands about as though they were speaking. Somehow I understood what she was trying to say, even though I couldn't hear.

"All at once, my hearing returned as she wept, making motions with her hands to thank me for rescuing her. By her incoherent speech and hand movements, I believed she was deaf and dumb, and probably being punished for a minor offense. As tears fell down her beautiful face, I knelt and held her hand, compassion welling up in me as never before. I knew firsthand what her world was like and suddenly realized God had directed me to her for a purpose.

"For some reason I thought back to the dead bird that stirred in my hand when I was a boy. As she wept and laid her head to my chest, I brushed her hair back and laid my hand on one of her ears. 'Receive your hearing in the name of Jesus Christ,' I said. The words came out as if it were not I who spoke them. At that very moment, she stopped weeping and stayed very still, resting her head on my chest. Then, all at once, in words barely comprehensible, she uttered, "Soun! I hear soun. I can hear! How can dis be, ma Loord?"

"She rose to her feet, pointing to the birds and sounds in the city streets. I explained that it was not I who healed her but the power of God. I said I was only His instrument and that she should give thanks to the Lord and glorify Him with a devoted life from that day forward.

"She approached me, and reaching for my hands began kissing them, praising God for her miracle. She said she thought her name sounded like Constance. I told her my name, charging her not to point me out as the one responsible for her miracle, wanting to remain anonymous.

"Several days ago I asked one of the monks to deliver a message to Constance, describing Hope Mission and what we do here. I left an open invitation for her to visit if she ever felt inclined to teach the deaf her clever hand signs, giving them an opportunity to communicate with the world and with each other."

After finishing her notes, Bernadette wiped her pen, and with a smile she stood. "Thank you, Joseph. I've got it all down. Now, do we need to do anything before you see the twins?"

"All the preparation has been done. I only need to see them now."

It was the dead of night, and the house was as silent as a church after prayer. Joseph and Bernadette walked downstairs to Daisy and Rose's room. Just before they entered, a door squeaked open down the hall and Maria's head popped out. Bernadette pleaded with Joseph to let Maria be a part of this wonderful event. Joseph stopped and, looking back at her, said, "You, Miss, are as stubborn as the man who loves you."

"And who might that be, sir?"

Joseph smiled. "Who would it be but the one whose eyes sparkle at the mention of your name?" He motioned for Maria to join them.

As they entered the room they found the palsied twins awake, quietly whimpering in discomfort. Joseph positioned the women on the opposite side of the bed, while he knelt at the bedside in silent prayer for a long time. Then, as the women looked on, he rolled Daisy onto her belly and placed one hand on her spinal cord and the other on her head, whispering, "I will, Lord. I will, so now in the name of Jesus Christ be thou whole, child."

Daisy seized up into a convulsed ball of muscle, but when Joseph stretched her arms and legs away from her body, she relaxed. The women stood transfixed as Daisy slowly turned her head with perfect control, locking eyes with her mother for the first time in years. Maria lunged toward her, embracing her smiling child.

Joseph repeated the same steps with Rose, while Bernadette stood watching as if trapped in a surreal dream. Within ten minutes, both children sat relaxed, moving their bodies with perfect precision, giggling with their new ability to move and play with the greatest of ease and control.

Maria couldn't stop weeping as she pulled Joseph's face to hers, kissing his forehead, then his eyes and nose, and then his hands.

Bernadette wept as well at the sight of such joy, then burst into laughter as Joseph's face turned red from all the kissing.

"I knew I should have made you stay in your room until I'd escaped, Maria," Joseph complained. "You must understand, I'm only God's servant. It is He who cured the children. Now please stop kissing me as if I'm someone special."

"Joseph," Bernadette protested, "she's besides herself with joy. She can't help herself. We have just witnessed a miracle. I'm absolutely positive God is such that He wishes you to share in the wonder of this moment."

The children rose from the bed and ran toward Joseph, knocking him backwards onto the floor, smothering him with kisses and hugs of gratitude. They wouldn't stop until he was overcome with their affection and laughing with delight. Soon everyone was laughing, so much so that they woke the other children. They burst into the room, touching the twins as if they could not believe they were the same Daisy and Rose.

As the sun rose, a breakfast celebration ensued and, as Joseph tried to slip out the back door, Bell stopped him, handing him a large basket of food. "Mr. Nicholas told me you been fastin'. Now take this food up to you cabin, and when it empty, Bell makes more for Mission healer. You heal good, Mr. Joseph."

Joseph bristled, grabbing the basket. "It's not me, Bell! It's not me who heals...Uhh... they just don't see it!"

Chapter 47. The Slaughter Begins.

After the breakfast celebration for Daisy and Rose, Bernadette went to her room, exhausted from the night of journal writing, and miracles. As she sat down at her desk to enter final notes in the journal, a letter resting against the inkwell greeted her. Hope filled her heart as she broke the red wax seal and unfolded the single sheet.

> *The Color of Love*
> *Her fearful life was slain but lives,*
> *With new resolve in love's abode,*
> *And grace her maid nay fails to give*
> *New strength to fly with wings of hope.*
> *And as she glides on currents high,*
> *Her eye doth search for kindred soul.*
> *And all at once in distant sky*
> *A stealthy lover sends his call*
> *To join him till his mission's end,*
> *Or till the injured cease to be.*
> *And she replies her life to lend*
> *To all beneath despair's decree.*
> *And reaching him she turned and said,*
> *'What pleases thee, what suits thine eye?'*
> *And he replies, 'The color red',*
> *While gazing at the crimson sky.*
> *And as he spoke with love's repose*
> *Her wings transformed to pinkish hues,*
> *With deepened tints on every word*
> *Until their glory seized his view.*

Bernadette's heart burned within, and she read the poem over and over until she had it memorized. The message in the poem spoke clearly of Nicholas' desire for her total dedication to the hurting of the world, and then his unexpected affinity for the color red. Thoughts of how she'd answer his poem greatly increased her desire for him as she slipped into bed and fell asleep holding the poem to her breast.

The rain had ceased, but an eerie stillness took its place, when Captain Ficci stepped outside his tent to review the situation. Waving his brother and Sergeant Vance to come give their report, he glanced toward the mountaintop and noticed an unusual dense fog blanketing the summit.

Sergeant Vance approached. "Sir, we've completed the first stage of the plan. I sent a patrol to see the effectiveness of the traps and poisoned meat. They've reported nine dead wolves and a dead wildcat. On their return, three more wolves were shot. The footmen have seen others run up into the fog."

Sergeant Ficci trotted up and dismounted. "Captain, I ordered my men east, where we located a trail bypassing the mudslide. We saw a dead bear and four dead wolves from the poison and traps. I found a wildcat still alive and shot it."

"How steep is the incline on the trail?" asked Captain Ficci.

"It's about the same as the other, but there's no way to be sure. I only went up fifty paces or so."

The Captain immediately ordered a single-file march on the new trail. With the many muskets discharging, the air was soon filled with smoke, as the soldiers killed or chased away everything in their path. After an hour of slaughter, they came to a ravine just before a steep incline.

Captain Ficci was out in front when he lifted his hand, bringing the soldiers to a halt. Staring at the end of the incline, about thirty paces away, he removed his feathered hat, and dismounted, walking to the edge of the ravine. A thick cloud shrouded everything from the top of the tree line up, putting an abrupt end to their surge forward.

Pacing with his arms crossed, the Captain kept looking up, shaking his head.

Sergeant Vance dismounted and approached. "What is it, sir? What's bothering you?"

Sergeant Ficci rode up and joined them. "I'll tell you what's bothering him, that cloud up there. There will be no visibility once we enter."

Captain Ficci nodded in agreement.

"But, sir," said Sergeant Vance, "we've already killed a dozen wolves, and poisoned and trapped many others. How many more could there be?"

"Good point, but I still don't trust the situation," the Captain said. "We'll wait until tomorrow and see if the weather clears."

There they set up camp and posted a heavy guard around the campsite for the night.

Justus sat on the other side of the fog, spying down from the steep incline. After counting Ficci's men, and seeing them begin to set up camp, he surmised they were waiting until it cleared before continuing.

While watching the soldiers pitch tents and gather wood for their campfires, Justus was tempted, and considered how easy it would be to kill both the Captain and his brother from where he sat. He reasoned that if the brothers were off the scene, the others might abandon the mission and return to San Marco, but he was unsure. Not wanting to jeopardize Nicholas' plan, he mounted his horse and rode up the mountain, fighting off vengeful fantasies of wreaking a final justice for his family. What Nicholas had taught him about hate and un-forgiveness helped, but his flesh was still weak, and it took all his will not to ride back and satisfy his desire for vengeance.

As he drew closer to the Mission, the fog became even thicker, so much so, he could only see several steps ahead. He dismounted and walked his horse the rest of the way. He thought, *If I didn't know the way as well as I do, I'd be disoriented. This cloud is heaven-sent with the soldiers in pursuit.*

When he reached the Mission's west gate and stepped through, he went directly to Nicholas's new home to give his report.

"Do you see how thick that fog is? It's incredible, Nick. I could only see a few feet in front of me."

"That can only work to our benefit," Nicholas answered. "It couldn't have come at a better time. Welcome back, son, what's the situation down there?"

When Justus stepped into the great room, the Bellicini family, who were visiting Nick, greeted him as he took a seat by the fireplace. "There are fifty soldiers in all, ten on horseback including the Ficci brothers. I happened to notice another sergeant among them I've never seen before. Hidden in the fog, I watched them kill many wolves. Some were in traps, others poisoned... I think. There were chunks of raw meat next to their bodies.

"Nothing stopped them until they came to the ravine where the cloud begins. One thing more, they were heavily armed. Each soldier had more than one firearm. I think they're going to camp there until the cloud lifts, then continue killing everything in their path until they arrive here."

"Let's pray that cloud remains for a while," Nicholas said. "Tomorrow, at first light, Justus and I will go down to the fog line and assess the situation while there's still time. If I have to, I'll speak to Captain Ficci in private and try to persuade him to return to San Marco. That is, if he doesn't want the Italian government to find out about his traitorous relationship with the Duke of Guise.

"Justus, if I have to talk to him, you'll stay hidden in the cloud with your crossbow trained on the Captain and his brother. This will be your most difficult test to date; to face the Ficci brothers with complete restraint and control. Only if my life is in danger should you release an arrow, and only then to wound or divert their attention. Should you have to fire, I'll try to make it back into the cloud. If I don't make it, you must return to the Mission and tell the Bellicinis to begin their journey down the back side of the mountain."

Walking to his cabinet, Nicholas retrieved four sacks of gold coin and handed them to Ox. "If they get past the ravine, take this gold and head down the hidden mountain pass. Don't forget to conceal the trail entrance on your way down. When you get to the bottom, ride west towards the Tyrrhenian Sea. When I was in Cosenza, I saw several merchant ships in port, so try to gain passage on one of those."

"What about you, Nicholas?" Ben frowned. "We can't just leave you, knowing you might be hurt or captured or both."

His brothers agreed, but Nicholas was determined. "I appreciate how you feel, but we have very little choice here. If they arrest me, they won't stop and take me back to San Marco. They'll continue their drive to reach you, and then we'll all be in a fix. If they get past the ravine and make it to the Mission, they must not find you. At that point, they would probably leave the Mission and take me back to San Marco to stand trial for harboring a fugitive. If it goes that far, Justus will follow in stealth, and while they're camped that night, he'll figure a way to get me out."

The four brothers reluctantly agreed and returned to their home for the night. Justus stayed with Nicholas to plan their strategy with greater detail. It was clear the following day would be a turning point for the Bellicini family and the Mission.

While Nicholas lay in bed that night, a mighty faith rose in his spirit, convincing him that God had created the cloud on the summit to protect them. Tomorrow, when facing the Ficci brothers, would be no different. God would intervene somehow, and on that he rested his faith.

CHAPTER 48. BERNADETTE'S RESPONSE.

Bernadette awoke late in the afternoon, having been up all night journal writing and witnessing a miracle. After a visit to the kitchen, she returned to her room with a tray of Bell's leftovers and a bowl of chicken broth. She decided to work as long as needed to sort out notes and detail everything that had happened to the twins with a formal entry into the journal.

As she sipped her broth and reviewed her notes, she heard chirping and a rustling just outside the open window. Stepping to the windowsill, she glanced down at the bush below, seeing a bird trapped in the branches.

Slipping on a shawl, she went around the outside of the house. A young robin was snared in the branches. The bird must've been there for quite some time, appearing to have very little fight left.

She gently removed it and returned to her room. After filling a bowl with water, she set the young bird on the rim, leaving it to drink its fill. As she stared at its red breast, Bernadette's mind returned again to the poem, *'What pleases thee, what suits thine eye. And he replies the color red while gazing at the crimson sky.'*

Inspired by the young robin, Bernadette plotted a way to respond to Nicholas' poem. What she'd experienced during the past two weeks was so compelling that thoughts of doing anything else with her life seemed pale in comparison. To witness a miracle and see the joy that ensued thereafter, affected her spirit to the point of bliss, not to mention the ache in her heart to be ever closer to Nicholas.

The tiny robin pecked at the water, while Bernadette stood across the room holding treats in her palm, teaching the bird to come to her. It flew from the bowl to her hand, and then back again several times, until it was well acquainted and unafraid, finding a safe resting place on Bernadette's shoulder.

After feeding yet more treats to her little friend, she picked up the broken red wax seal that'd fallen off the poem, placed it in a spoon, and held it over a lit candle until the wax melted. She then placed the tail end of her pen into the wax pool and turned it about, covering an inch of the quill.

With the end of the pen waxed red, she went to her dresser and pulled out her favorite white cotton lace dress and a spool of red ribbon. Cutting the ribbon to size, she sewed a thin strip above the lace on the sleeves, hem and neck, which came to a V just above the breast line. After the ribbon was sewn in, she fashioned a tiny bow with the red ribbon and sewed it where the V met, finishing her response to Nicholas' poem.

What pleased her most about his romantic poem was that Nicholas had never been influenced by the world regarding other woman. He was innocent and totally sincere in his endeavors with her. He'd never been hurt by unrequited love, and she was determined life should remain that way for him. All she had to do now was choose when and how she'd approach him with her response.

The next day, just before sunrise, Nicholas went the guest room and woke Justus. This was the day they'd confront the Ficci brothers and, if all went as planned, end Ficci's attempt to arrest the Bellicini family.

After Justus dressed, they made their way through the ever-present fog to the Bellicini home for breakfast before their trek down the mountain. As they sipped cider, Ox, Ty and Lund entered the kitchen and rehashed the plan, hoping they'd left nothing to chance. Before they realized it, an hour had passed and the entire house was stirring with activity.

Nicholas stopped Makande on his way to the grand room. "What's going on, Makande? What's everyone in a rush to see?"

"We have new teacher, Mr. Nicholas. She give her first class to children in great room. Bell and me go now to learn some new things." Then off he went without another word.

Nicholas turned to the others. "Does anyone know who the new teacher is?"

They all smiled simultaneously as Ox replied, "You should see this for yourself, Nick."

Nicholas adjourned the meeting and asked Justus to saddle the horses while he took some time to see what all the fuss was about. When he entered the grand room, Bernadette stood in front of a class of twelve children and a host of curious onlooking adults. His heart raced when he saw the tiny robin perched on her shoulder, and her beautiful white dress, trimmed everywhere in red ribbon. Bernadette gazed at Nicholas with a loving smile, pointing her red-tipped pen at him.

"Good morning, children. My name is Bernadette LaViono, and after speaking in length to Brother Taylor, he's graciously allowed me to teach you all to read and write. My class will be the first of many different classes you will attend in the coming weeks and months. There will be a day of history, a day of mathematics and a day of learning about God. Your teacher for that class will be Brother Taylor. As for this class, thanks to Joseph Solo, half of our library is already in place to begin learning to read and write."

Bernadette turned toward a large easel holding up an oversized blank husk of paper, writing letters relating the fundamentals of language.

Nicholas looked on in amazement and great satisfaction. Bernadette had not only overcome the fears she'd held for so long, but had chosen a public vocation as an added position at the mission. Her example caused him to believe people were able to excel beyond their own expectations, given the right experiences and atmosphere.

Watching her instruct the children with a smile in every sentence, Nicholas was overcome with emotion and gratitude. Everyone in the room was taken with her gracious voice and movements, to say nothing of her resounding beauty. As the young robin flew from Bernadette's shoulder to his, her response to his poem was verified in the most delightful and meaningful manner.

Overcome with the need to be near her, he walked to the front of the class. "Forgive me, children, but I must have a word with your new teacher before I leave for the day. I promise to return her in only a few minutes."

As the children moaned, Nicholas led her into the kitchen and shut the door.

"What's wrong?" wondered Bernadette. "Have the soldiers come?"

"No, not yet. First, let me say how radiant you are today, and how you continue to surprise and confound me on a daily basis."

Bernadette reached for his hand. "Your poem was most beautiful. Thank you."

Nicholas lifted her hand to his lips. "Your response to my poem has enthralled me, and continues to move me as I speak. It will reside in my memory as the single most beautiful experience of my life. I should like very much to continue this conversation when I return, but for now Justus and I must ride down the mountain to meet Captain Ficci. I've left instructions with Brother Taylor and the monks regarding the Mission. If I don't return today, it will probably mean Captain Ficci has found a way to reach the Mission through the fog.

"The Bellicini family will escape down the other side of the mountain. If they're not here when the soldiers arrive, the Captain has no need to disturb the Mission and will most likely leave without bringing harm to anyone. However, the Ficci brothers have a taste for beautiful women. If they see you, they will have no mercy. One of the monks will come with a warning before they enter the gate. At that point, you and Bell need to escape through the south gate and go to Joseph Solo's cabin."

Bernadette trembled. "Why must you confront them? They're murderers! What they did to Justus' family—my God, don't go, Nicholas!"

Nicholas pulled out the document indicting the Captain and explained there was no other way. Drawing her near, he kissed her lips. "Don't worry, Bernadette, I'll be fine. I have a plan that's sure to keep the Captain at bay, but we must go down there before he gets any closer."

Bernadette pleaded, "I'm afraid again, Nicholas. I'm afraid to lose you. Before we met, I was only afraid for myself, but now everything has changed. I wanted to respond to your beautiful poem in subtle creative ways, but now I cannot but speak my heart to you. For the first time now, life has meaning and I have joy as never before, and I owe it all to you. I feel a love for you as I never have with anyone, and that's why I don't want you to go."

Kissing her again, Nicholas peered deep into her eyes. "In the past I've tried in vain to deny my feelings for you, doubting that our lives would ever be compatible, but I was wrong. After reading your journal and seeing you work with everyone, I'm convinced God will bless us. I've never felt a love like this before and am mystified by it in your presence."

Embracing her, he whispered in her ear, "I love you with all my heart, it's clear. Say you will be my wife and end this ache in my being forever."

Bernadette drew back for a moment and put her hands on his face, then drew his lips to hers. "With all my heart, I will."

Just then there was a knock on the door. Justus burst in and, seeing them embrace, quickly turned his back. "Nicholas, the horses are ready and so am I. The fog outside is even thicker, if you can believe it."

"I'll be right out, son."

When Justus left, Nicholas kissed Bernadette again and told her to be strong and have faith God would see them through. Bernadette's eyes welled, and her hands shook as she pulled the strap on his travel bag over his head onto his shoulder. "Should the soldiers make it here, you will find me at Joseph Solo's cabin. I shall not cease speaking to God until your safe return."

CHAPTER 49. NICHOLAS CONFRONTS CAPTAIN FICCI.

A third of the way down the mountain at the fog line, Sergeant Vance and eight well-armed foot soldiers made their way across the ravine, up the steep incline into the cloud. Sergeant Ficci stood next to his brother, silently watching as the last soldier disappeared into the mist. Less then a minute later, several shots echoed down the mountain.

Everyone's eyes were fixed to the cloud, when horrifying screams pierced the air. The soldiers looked at each other in fear at the fate of the Sergeant Vance and his men. Captain Ficci mounted his horse and ordered two men on horseback to ride toward the screams in an attempt to rescue anyone emerging from the cloud.

When they were twenty paces from the mist, Sergeant Vance burst through on foot, running with another soldier right behind, but the one that followed never made it fully out. Two wolves clamped down on his legs, dragging him back into the mist, snarling and growling.

Moments later the screaming stopped, replaced by a foreboding silence.

The soldiers stood ready, their flintlocks trained toward the fog, when Vance collapsed before Captain Ficci.

"What happened, Sergeant?" the Captain barked.

Breathing heavily, pale as a sheet, Vance stood, wiping his brow. "Wolves... uhh... everywhere." He crossed his arms to hide his shaking. "Even got... my horse."

"Why are you the only one to make it out unharmed?"

"I don't know, sir," he said, his eyes distant. "I just don't know."

"Captain," Sergeant Ficci called. "Someone's coming out of the fog, to the east."

As the rider slowly came into view, mist still clinging to him, the Captain cried out, "Who are you, sir? What is your business here?"

"I'm Nicholas Kristo and I've come on behalf of the Bellicini family."

Sergeant Ficci put spurs to his horse and rode to his brother's side.

"Mr. Kristo," the Captain shouted, "ride down here at once and explain your position, because as I see it, you also are a fugitive."

"The truth is, Captain, there are no fugitives on this mountain, and I think it would be in your best interest to have a word with me in private. But if you prefer it another way, I will simply slip back into the fog and reconsider your relationship with the Duke of Guise."

Captain Ficci turned to his brother. "Do not fire on this man no matter what. He is the key to the gold. I'll get him into a vulnerable position, then we'll arrest him."

As the Captain rode up the incline to the fog line, Nicholas backed his horse slightly into the mist.

When they were ten paces from each other, and out of earshot, Nicholas began, "Captain Ficci, I wanted this meeting alone, because if your men ever knew about the document my man is holding, across the road from the Judge Magistrate in San Marco, they might desert you."

"And what document might that be?"

"Do you remember a visit from a man named Oscar Grosseto?"

"Yes, I do. He bought three of my finest slaves. Are you his employer?"

"Yes, I am. I'm sorry we had to be so deceptive, but your reputation precedes you."

"So what of this deception and Oscar?"

"I'm pleased to say your former slave, Bell, is now with her husband Makande, and the two young girls have been escorted back to Barcelona. Your main concern is, while Oscar was a guest in your home, he obtained a purchase order stating the sale of ten well-bred racehorses. It seems the purchase was made with Government securities, and the deal finalized with the Duke of Guise's signature right next to yours. Now, the last time I heard, the Duke of Guise was invading our country, which would make you a traitor. To make things worse, you paid for the horses with government monies, which would now make you, pardon the expression, a traitorous thief."

Smiling, Captain Ficci removed his black-feathered hat. "Mr. Kristo, if what you say is true, it seems my career is finished. Unless, of course, the Judge Magistrate is my very close friend and on my personal payroll."

"I might have guessed that would be the arrangement, so as insurance I endowed my messenger with enough gold to make the Judge Magistrate a rich man if he could be assured the document would find its way into the right hands."

"Well, Mr. Kristo, that would be a checkmate if I didn't think you valued your own life more than my demise. I can have you killed on the spot by simply raising my hand."

"Captain Ficci, again, I thought something like this might happen. There is a man in the fog, very close by, who has a rare, uncanny ability with his crossbow. He would like nothing more than to end your life should something unkind happen to me."

Captain Ficci's face twitched in defeat. Straining a smile, he grunted, "What is it you want, sir?"

"The first thing you should know is, if I do not reach my man in San Marco in a week, he will go forward with our plan. So, that means I will escort you and your men back to San Marco, call my man off and destroy the document. But I will do that only after you give a complete and thorough account of what really happened when your soldiers maliciously attacked the Bellicini family at their place of business."

Captain Ficci hesitated, then met Nicholas' eyes. "May I ask what keeps the wolves calm in your presence? How do you gain safe passage with so many of them roaming about?"

Nicholas turned his horse into the fog. "Call it a gift, Captain. It's been this way since I was a child. So, do we have a deal?"

Turning his horse, walking it down the incline, the Captain put on his hat. "I will be at the base of the mountain with my men at first light. It will take a full two days to journey back to San Marco." As he rode away, he began to scheme various ways to seize not only the damning purchase order, but the secret place where Nicholas kept his gold.

Halfway to his men, as the Captain approached his brother, a large white wolf shot out from the fog, moving so fast all who watched could only marvel at its grace and agility. Picking up speed as it ran down toward the ravine, it took a sharp unexpected turn headed straight for Captain Ficci.

When it was only paces from the Captain, the soldiers opened fire, but the wolf turned again and jumped onto a large rock and then onto the Captain, knocking him off his horse. As the wolf took a grip of the Captain's forearm, Sergeant Ficci saw the opportunity he'd been waiting for. Reaching into his saddlebag, he drew out a pistol loaded with grape shot and extra powder for maximum effect. Aiming at the wolf first, he quickly raised his aim to his brother's chest and fired.

"Hold your fire!" Sergeant Vance shouted to the others. Taking aim, he fired his flintlock at the heart of the wolf. He hit his mark, and the wolf yipped and fell over dead as several soldiers ran to the Captain's aid.

The Captain lay unconscious, bleeding profusely from his chest and arm.

When Nicholas heard the shots, he returned to see what happened and told Justus to remain in the fog as his rear guard. When he reached the soldiers, several men were putting bandages on the wounds. Sergeant Vance angrily accused Sergeant Ficci of aiming high when the wolf attacked. One of the soldiers attending the Captain broke in, "He has two pellet wounds in his chest. I can't stop the bleeding."

Sergeant Vance glared at Sergeant Ficci. "May I ask what type of load you had in your pistol, Sergeant?"

"A grape shot load with extra powder, in case a bear or large cat might've needed to be put down in a hurry. It was an accident. The wolf was too close to Andrea."

Sergeant Vance grimaced. "It was no accident, Manuel, I saw you raise your aim."

Chapter 50. Justus Saves Captain Ficci's Life.

As Nicholas approached the angry Sergeants, sorely upset at the loss of his great white she-wolf, Captain Ficci lay on the ground unconscious, bleeding profusely from his chest.

Sergeant Ficci growled, stabbing his finger at Sergeant Vance's face, "My brother was moving erratically when I fired. When we return to San Marco, I will see to it that you are written up, and spend time in the stockade for making these bizarre accusations."

"Whatever you do when we return will be met with a complete investigation of this incident. I know what I saw and in my opinion, sir, you tried to kill Captain Ficci. Looking at him now, I fear you just may have succeeded."

Nicholas rode between them and dismounted. "Gentlemen, we must get this man medical attention at once. He'll never make it down the mountain alive. We have people not far away who are skilled in medical procedures. If you want your Captain to live, I suggest you allow me to take him."

Sergeant Ficci pulled a pistol from his belt, aiming point blank at Nicholas. "You will take my brother and be escorted by me or I'll kill you where you stand!"

"Sergeant, lower your weapon and stand down," Sergeant Vance demanded. "This man is trying to save your brother's life. Force is not an appropriate option here."

Sergeant Ficci turned his pistol on Sergeant Vance. "And since when have you become ranking officer on the mission?"

Sergeant Vance calmly turned his back and faced the rest of the soldiers. "I am officially relieving Sergeant Ficci of his command until the Captain is able to return with orders to the contrary. Should the Captain die as a result of the gunshot wounds, I will remain senior officer until our return to San Marco, where there will be a full inquiry."

Five soldiers aimed their flintlocks at Sergeant Ficci as Sergeant Vance ordered several others to construct a travois and tie it to Nicholas' horse.

"You will be in prison a long time when this is all over, Vance!" Sergeant Ficci hissed. "I promise."

"When this is all over, I'm sure one or two of the other soldiers saw what I did, and will bear witness to the Judge Magistrate. Take heed,

Sergeant, I will have you placed in irons if you raise your weapon or incite any trouble while the Captain is away."

Turning to Nicholas, he said, "Mr. Kristo, we will be camped at the base of the mountain until we hear word from you. If we can be of any help while the Captain is with you, send word. In the meantime, I suggest you make haste while the Captain still has breath in him."

Nicholas mounted his horse. "Sergeant, we'll do our best to save Captain Ficci, but when he is recovered, will you commit to a full and thorough inquiry into the Bellicini case?"

"Indeed I will, sir. You have my word and my honor."

Sergeant Vance called the soldiers to attention and ordered the march down the mountain.

Nicholas rode quickly through the cloud and met Justus, who was already on his horse, leading the way up the mountain pass. Twenty paces behind, Nicholas prepared Justus for the most difficult task of his life.

"Justus, take the back path. We need to get those pellets out of Captain Ficci if he has any chance at all."

Justus turned in his saddle and barked, "Will you tell me why you're so intent on saving his life? He got what he deserved, and from his own brother to boot. I don't understand you. Was this not justice?"

"He's in our hands for a reason, son. We must try to save his life with all we've got."

A white dove swooped down and rested on Justus' saddlebags. Nicholas trotted beside Justus, speaking softly. "Listen, son, you've been a tremendous help this past month. I don't know what I would've done without you. But now you must face the greatest challenge of your life."

"And what might that be?" Justus asked facetiously. "Let me guess. You want me to somehow save his life and redeem myself to Heaven, right?"

"You're already redeemed, Justus, but I do think you're better qualified to save his life than anyone in the Mission."

"What in the world would make you think that?"

"Because you're the only person who knows how to extract grape shot from a man's body. Remember the twelve year-old boy who was shot in the leg in a hunting accident several years back? Remember how you helped your foster mother dig that pellet out and save the boy's life?"

"That's not fair. Anna did all the work. I just helped. Besides, to be quite honest, I'm not the least bit motivated to help him. I can't help it, he murdered my family."

"I know, but that's what'll make your efforts so extraordinary. Think about it! You will put aside your personal feelings and save a fellow human being. Let your drive to save a human life motivate you. I promise you one thing, if you do save him, your life will be greatly changed as a result."

Approaching the west gate of the Mission, they saw Ben and Ox standing outside. After taking the horses and removing the Captain from the travois, Nicholas filled them in on what happened.

They rushed him into the Bellicini dining room, placed sheets on the banquet table, and undressed the Captain from the waist up.

Raven came immediately to assist as the nuns boiled hot water and searched for clean bandages.

Justus gazed silently at the Captain's chalk white face, realizing for the first time that Nicholas was right. This was a dying human being and there was no other option but to make an effort to keep him alive and let God do the judging over his twisted dark life.

Justus asked Nicholas to fashion long tweezers from whatever he could find in his workshop, and bring them to him at once. Nicholas smiled widely and hurried away.

Sisters Mary and Margaret cleaned the blood from around the two holes in the Captain's chest. They were two inches apart, just under the collarbone.

When Nicholas returned with a ground down pair of pointy tongs, Justus set the tip over a flame in a nearby lamp for a minute. When it cooled, everyone present froze as Justus slowly pushed the tongs down into the largest hole until he could go no farther without force. Holding the shaft with both hands, he felt the point tap something metallic. After several attempts, Justus managed to grab the pellet and pull it out.

A great sigh filled the room as Raven sopped the blood, and blew Justus a kiss.

Justus then went to the smaller hole, easily retrieving the pellet only an inch below the surface. Taking his dagger to the stove, he held it over the fire until it turned red, then returning to the Captain, cauterized both wounds.

When Justus seared the Captain's skin, Ficci woke temporally, gasping in pain. All those present wondered whether he would make it through the night, with such a loss of blood.

CHAPTER 51. CAPTAIN FICCI WAKES.

After the Captain had been carried into a guest bedroom, Brother Taylor and the nuns offered to spend the night watching over him. Justus and Raven made their way onto the porch for some fresh air.

Before Justus sat in one of the chairs, Raven leapt onto his back and kissed his neck in sheer delight at the heroic effort of the man she loved. Moving to his ear, she whispered, "I wouldn't have believed it unless I saw it myself, and I did. How did you manage to muster enough forgiveness to save the Captain's life?"

Justus pulled her around and kissed her. "To be perfectly honest, I don't think I've forgiven him. I simply did as Nicholas suggested. I put my personal feelings aside and tried to save a human life. Once I was involved with the task, I saw him only as a man."

Nicholas appeared with Bernadette by his side. "Bravo, Justus. I saw the whole operation. You did a wonderful job. Did I hear you say you put your personal feelings aside?"

"Yes, and it worked long enough for me to get the job done."

"Without knowing it, you followed one of the greatest commands our Savior and King ever gave. He said, 'Whoever will deny himself, pick up his cross and follow me will be my disciple.' When you put your hateful feelings aside you were denying yourself—and that act was very painful for you—which means you picked up your cross. Then you demonstrated an act of compassion and kindness on a person who is perhaps least worthy of it. This is what Christ did for every one of us, for we all fall short of perfection. You've done exceedingly well, Justus."

"Not well enough, Nicholas. My heart has not forgiven him at all. I think I am incapable of forgiving him or his brother."

Nicholas put a hand Justus' shoulder. "Let's take a walk and talk about it."

As the two walked towards the western gate, the fog dissipated, and the crystal blue sky was a welcome sight as an orange sun sank low onto the mountains in the west.

Raven sat next to Bernadette on the porch. "Do you think he'll ever find forgiveness for the Ficci brothers?"

Opening her journal, Bernadette leaned in. "If Nicholas stays as close to the situation as he is right now, anything is possible. He has a way with people and their problems. It's because of him and what he taught me, that I was able to come away from my fears and live again."

Bernadette glanced at Nicholas with his arm over Justus' shoulder, nearing the west gate. "You know, it's interesting, Raven. After reviewing my journal from the beginning, I've come to believe that Nicholas is as much interested in spiritual giving as he is in physical gifts. He said not long ago, for Justus or anyone else, the gift of forgiveness is perhaps the most important gift of all. If we're unable to forgive, God will not forgive us. That's why Nick is so focused on Justus' problem. Now, with still more guidance, it will be interesting to see what Justus does next with regard to the Ficci brothers."

The next evening, Ox and Ben relocated the Captain to Nicholas' home, placing him in one of the larger guest rooms. Bernadette and Raven took turns tending to his wounds and changing his bandages.

Captain Ficci lay unconscious for two full days, burning with fever and sometimes shouting in states of delirium before he woke at the touch of Bernadette changing the cool, damp cloth on his forehead. The Captain peered up, and with a strained whisper, begged for water.

Bernadette soaked a fresh bandage in a bucket of water, squeezing drops onto his lips. As he whispered, 'more', she repeated the process until he revived enough to speak.

Still with a parched whisper, he asked, "What happened? Where am I? Who are you?"

"Don't you remember, sir? You were attacked by a wolf and then shot in the chest. You lost so much blood we all thought you would not live through the first night, but by some miracle you did."

"Where am I?"

"You are at Hope Mission and a guest in the home of Nicholas Kristo. It is he, among others, who helped save your life. Do you remember what happened now?"

"The last thing I remember," moaned the Captain, his face wrinkled in pain, "is...uhh...oooww... an enormous white wolf jumping off a rock and knocking me to the ground. Then I felt a burning in my chest—and that's all until now. Who...uuhh... are you?"

"My name is Bernadette LaVino, the betrothed of Nicholas Kristo. Raven Bellicini and I have been caring for you these last two days."

"Raven Bellicini is here? I was told she had leprosy. Is it true?"

"No, Captain. It's not true. Your brother was deceived about that, among other things."

As their conversation ensued, Nicholas passed by and heard them, with the door ajar. Hurrying to the railing leading down into the grand room, he motioned to Justus, Ben, Ox, Lund and Ty to come quickly, putting his index finger to his mouth as a signal to be silent.

He went into the adjoining room, waving at the men to follow him. Once inside, he pointed to a portion of the ceiling construction that was not yet complete, allowing the conversation within the room to be easily heard.

"So how is it that I ended up...uuhh... with grape shot in my chest?" asked the Captain.

"Captain, try to remember what happened just before you passed out. It's very important."

"Well," said the Captain, adjusting his pillow, "as I went down, the wolf held fast to my forearm while—wait a minute, I remember seeing my brother raise his pistol towards the wolf and then—yes, I remember now...uuh...ooo... he raised his aim at me and then—yes, I remember now. I knew he was up to something but I never thought—"

"Nicholas tells me Sergeant Vance saw your brother raise his aim at the last second and fire," she said, handing him a cup of water. "Vance has relieved Sergeant Ficci of his command and placed him under house arrest until they return to San Marco. In the meantime, your men are at the base of the mountain awaiting word on your condition. What message would you like us to give them?"

Ficci gulped down the water and handed Bernadette the cup. "I will write a message to Sergeant Vance."

Bernadette handed him an empty page and quill.

Sergeant Vance,
I will meet you at the base of the mountain in two days. You will remain there with seven soldiers and Sergeant Ficci. Send the rest of the men back to the San Marco Command Post.
Captain Andrea Ficci.

Folding the page in half, the Captain handed the message to Bernadette. "How many days do you think before I'll be moving about?"

"If I were you, Captain, I wouldn't try to move out of bed until those pellet holes stop oozing blood."

"Tell me, Miss LaViano, how did a beautiful woman like you get stuck on the top of this mountain?"

Bernadette froze for a second. "What makes you think I'm stuck here?"

"Because I've never met a woman half as beautiful as you who voluntarily chose to keep herself hidden from the world. Some fortunate suitor, like myself, could make you a very wealthy woman."

Handing him a small tray of bread and cheese, Bernadette said evenly, "I was born into wealth, sir, but chose to leave it all behind to be with Nicholas. You are very bold indeed to dare suggest I would ever remotely consider such a thing. It is an understatement to say you are most wholly disrespectful to me, and to the man who helped save your life. There you lie, in *his* bed, under *his* roof, attempting to undermine his honor only minutes after waking from the grip of death. Your reputation precedes you, sir."

With a mouthful of bread, Ficci pointed at her. "You cannot stand there and tell me you're motivated to be with this man because of honor and love alone. It's his gold you're after, right?"

"What gold? I have no knowledge Nicholas has any assets except this Mission."

"And how do you think he built it? With honor? With love? No, Miss LaViono, Nicholas has gold and lots of it. My brother found a grinding wheel in his barn embedded with gold. It seems he's grinding gold nuggets."

Hearing the Captain mention gold, Justus tried to speak, but Nicholas put his hand over his mouth and smiled. Justus pushed it away and whispered, "What are you smiling about? That man is an insect! I should have never pulled that grape shot from his chest."

"I'll explain later, son. Let him finish unloading what's on his mind. Did you hear how she defended me, men? I just love that woman."

Bernadette was silent for a moment, then glared into the Captain's cold black eyes. "Sir, I think you're blind as well as deaf. You have not heard a thing I've stated, and are unable to see anything beyond your own selfish ambitions. Nicholas is indeed rich, but not with worldly goods. If he does possess gold, it is used to benefit people or advance the Mission."

As Bernadette turned to leave, Captain Ficci reached out and grabbed a piece of her skirt. Bernadette turned, stretched her arm toward his chest, placing her palm firmly over his wound.

The Captain cried out in pain and released her.

"Sir, if you are truly taken with my beauty, take a very long look right now, because it will be the last time you will ever see me." At that, she turned and hurried from the room.

Chapter 52. All The Mission Men Finally Forgive.

After hearing Bernadette scold Captain Ficci for his lewd manner, Nicholas and the men quickly left the adjoining room and regrouped in the study on the first floor. As Justus and the Bellicini brothers began taking seats around the table, Nicholas said, "Tell me what you're all thinking."

Justus spoke immediately. "I don't know how you kept still while that sorry excuse for a man violated Bernadette with his crass behavior. Please tell me there was a reason you let him go on."

"There is a reason, Justus, but first tell me what you think of the Captain."

"He's an animal," shot Justus. "I'm sorry, but that's what I think. He's an animal predator."

Nicholas asked the Bellicini brothers, "What do you men think of him?"

Ox spoke first. "Well, we were in the other room when he first awoke and it's what I didn't hear that shocked me. I didn't hear any words of gratitude or thankfulness for anyone who helped save his life. It was as if either he knowingly held it back or he's as Justus described."

"I agree," Lund broke in, "but it was how quickly he resumed his evil ways that alarmed me. He wasn't awake for more than five minutes and he was lusting for gold and groping your woman, Nick."

"What is it you're after, Nick?" Ty asked.

Nicholas clasped his hands on the table. "He revealed himself for who he truly is. All of you summed it up very nicely. What we all take for granted in ourselves is missing in Captain Ficci. We all possess a degree of compassion, mercy and gratitude. All of us have conscience and love, which drives us to act in ways we deem 'decent and normal.' But our guest, Captain Ficci, seems to lack many of the finer attributes and virtues.

"To some point, Justus hit the mark. He's like a self-made animal predator. When we see a wildcat attack a smaller animal, kill it, then eat it, we're not shocked, even though the slain animal is innocent. We know the cat's instincts drive its behavior. The only difference between the wildcat and Captain Ficci is that the Captain chose to abandon the God-given attributes that make humans a noble creature. In effect, he's abandoned many of the virtues that separate human behavior from the animal, thus leaving a very shrewd human animal."

"When you put it like that I feel pity for him," said Justus. "It's like seeing him in a whole new light. Nicholas, does forgiving him mean I have to be close to him as well?"

"Not at all, Justus. You can choose not to have a feeling one way or the other. Would you approach a wildcat before his evening meal? No, you wouldn't, because you know what his nature is. It's the same way with the Captain. We all know he has no intention of changing his life, even in the face of death. So, he seems pretty determined to remain as the wildcat. But you can forgive him and free yourself as well, while avoiding him in your daily life.

"You can rest assured that he'll face judgment for the misery he's brought into this world, and one day there will be justice, but on God's terms. Only God knows the secrets of men's lives. Only He can judge in perfect truth and mercy."

"You mean God will be merciful to him?" Justus asked.

"I mean that it is God alone who knows exactly how to judge him, but the key is in the belief that He will do what he says."

"When I see it, I'll believe it," said Ty.

Nicholas paused and replied very softly, "You know, most people feel that way, Ty, but when it comes to our faith and God we turn it around the other way. We submit that, most of the time, *believing* is seeing. The moment you take God at His word, and really believe it, everything changes. Do we all believe that God exists?"

They all nodded.

"Do we all stand before Him in judgment on the last day?"

They all agreed.

"Now comes the big question. Will He judge each one according to his deeds and be absolutely perfect in that judgment?"

Fixed to his every word, they all agreed once again.

"Then you're all free to forgive the Captain with full knowledge that even though you have forgiven him, he must still face the consequences of his deeds while he was alive on Earth. When a criminal is captured, he must pay for his crime even if we, as a society, are moved to forgive him. He must still be imprisoned or even put to death so that justice is measured out for all to see. The only difference in the Captain's case is, he's a government official, so he may elude judgment temporarily. The Captain was placed in a position of public trust, to protect and defend our country's citizens, and he used that position to murder and steal with impunity. How grave his judgment will be."

"As you were speaking," said Ben, "I understood it all in a much deeper sense and I found myself forgiving him for sending soldiers to kill our parents. The moment I forgave him, a great peace came over me and now I stand here dumbfounded by it all."

Ox put his arm on Ben's shoulder and said, "I felt the same, Ben."

Lund and Ty agreed, saying, "We went through the same process Ox—the very same process."

Everyone turned to Justus, only to find him wiping tears, nodding his head in agreement. Then, with his voice cracking, Justus said, "Today I have renounced the name Justus, for I now leave justice in the hands of the Eternal. I have taken back the name my parents gave when I was born: Ricardo Alfonzo Cruz.

"As with you all, the moment I believed God would bring that man to justice, a great burden was lifted and a peace I've never known is now flooding my heart. These tears you see on my face are tears of joy. But Nicholas, the Captain must leave the mountain, true?"

"Yes, Jus—, I mean Ricardo—yes, he must leave the mountain because we know what his nature is. The Captain has let evil reign in his heart, and unlike the wildcat, which kills on instinct, Captain Ficci revels in evil intent. As soon as he's able to stand and move about, he will leave, I promise. In the meantime, I need you to go down the mountain and bring the Captain's message to Sergeant Vance. On your way, prepare yourself to see the face of Sergeant Manuel Ficci, the other man who caused you so much anguish and hatred. When you come back, I want to know how you fared."

When the men left the room and went their separate ways, Nicholas decided to visit the Captain and probe his intentions. Taking a deep breath, he knocked on the door.

"I knew you would change your mind, Bernadette. Come in, please, and let's talk," answered the Captain.

Nicholas entered with a warm smile. "Sorry to disappoint you, Captain, but it's only me, Nicholas. I can't say I blame you for hoping it was Bernadette, for everyone loves to be around her. I must say I'm truly blessed to have her as my betrothed. May I ask what you knew she would change her mind about?"

"Oh, it was nothing," the Captain lied. "I hear it was you who brought me here and saved my life."

"I did bring you to the Mission, but it was a team effort to keep you alive."

A knock on the door came. Ricardo walked in with a bowl of chicken soup. "Sorry to interrupt, but Makande stopped me before I left. He said you were awake and thought this soup might help you gain strength. He wanted to bring it to you, but I insisted."

The Captain motioned with his hand. "Just put it on the end table until it cools."

When Ricardo set the bowl down, Nicholas reached out to his shoulder. "Ricardo, don't run out just yet. I want the Captain to meet the man who took those pellets out of his chest. Captain, this is Ricardo Alfanzo Cruz, previously known as Justus. He did the most to save your life."

Ricardo turned toward the Captain, and when their eyes locked, the Captain froze, staring at him as if he'd seen a spirit. "Your name is Cruz, is it? I knew an extraordinary woman who lived near San Marco many years ago who was also named Cruz— Elizabeth Cruz."

Ricardo hesitated a moment, took a deep breath, then lied, "Yes, sir, I was born in Barcelona and the woman you mentioned was my aunt. She was murdered many years ago and the man who killed her was never brought to justice."

"The family resemblance is remarkable."

Wanting to change the subject, Nicholas broke in. "Does our agreement remain as we discussed? When you're able, we ride to San Marco to clear the Bellicini family?"

"I will keep my word as long as your man in San Marco destroys that document. But you have another problem."

"What's that?"

"My brother Manuel. He found a grinding wheel in your barn with gold embedded into the stone. He knows you have a large sum of gold hidden. No matter what I do, he will not rest until he has his hands on it. And if you think he will be arrested for trying to kill me, think again. I wouldn't be surprised if Sergeant Vance is dead by now and Manuel has control of the men. If I were you, I would come up with something to appease him, because it's clear to me, he not only plans to kill me and take all my property and assets, but to kill and rob you as well, if he can."

"Has he gone mad?" asked Ricardo.

"Apparently. Manuel has been on the edge his whole life. I never wondered *if* he would snap, only when."

Nicholas walked to the window and, looking out, said, "Ricardo will bring your message to Sergeant Vance, and come back with a report. We'll see how to handle your brother after that."

CHAPTER 53. NICHOLAS MAKES A DEAL.

While the Captain finished his bowl of soup, Nicholas stood by the window developing a plan to use Ficci's greed as a means to drive him and his brother away for good. Ricardo, knowing Nicholas was up to something, sat down at the desk beside him.

"What motivated you to build this place and help people free of charge?" asked the Captain, setting the bowl on the nightstand.

"God."

The Captain laughed, without a shred of joy attached. "God? Jesus? He's nothing but a crutch to the weak."

"No, no, Captain... He's not a crutch... He's the whole hospital! People are sick from the effects of original sin, but I don't expect you would understand that."

Flustered by the answer, the Captain's next words shot out like ice. "There is no God, Kristo. You are not only wasting your time and money, but your life. You are living on this wolf-infested mountain with a crowd of pathetic do-gooders, thinking the help you give will somehow make the world a better place. But trust me when I tell you, this world will never be a better place. I've seen the cruelty of men up close, and that includes Manuel and myself. As long as the world allows people like us to have power and live out our lives, this world will remain as miserable as it's always been. Just one more question though."

"What is it, Captain?"

"How do you come and go around the wolves?"

"You've asked me that before and I say the same thing. I was born with the gift. It has helped us to keep the Mission a secret from the world."

"What's to prevent me from telling the world all about it?"

"Nothing, Captain, nothing at all. But I believe the God you say doesn't exist can cloud your mind just as he brought the cloud on this mountain when you tried in vain to reach us. You had a small army and were stopped dead less than twenty minutes from the Mission. Whether you believe it or not, there *is* a higher power on Earth right now that all the armies of the world cannot defeat. Now, based on that belief, I'm proposing a deal with you regarding the gold."

"What is it?"

"Would I be correct in assuming you and Manuel are no longer interested in arresting the Bellicini family, but really came for the gold?"

"Go on."

"In two days, if you're able to travel, I'll give you one-hundred-and-seventy pounds of pure gold nuggets, but you have it only if not another person or beast is harmed."

"How can you so easily give up your fortune?" asked the Captain, his eyes shifting.

"All the money in the world cannot replace one life. And besides, once you have the gold, I can't see anything of value here that would cause you to want to stay a day longer, or ever want to return."

"How will you continue your Mission without money?"

"This Mission would have been built regardless of what gold I had. It might have taken a little longer, that's all."

"If I'd known it was going to be this easy, I would have mentioned it sooner."

Nicholas walked to the bed. "If I'd known you were after the gold when we first met, I would've made the deal right there. Ricardo will leave immediately and deliver your message to Sergeant Vance. The gold is buried somewhere at the base of the mountain. In two days, you and I will travel down the mountain with Ricardo. He and I will remain far enough up the trail to feel safe while you join your men. When you meet them, you'll have to wait only long enough for Ricardo to deliver an arrow to a nearby tree with a map of the location of the gold tied to the shaft. Once you dig up the nuggets, there shouldn't be any reason to want to continue your pursuit of the Bellicini family. Besides, you know what really happened that day at their lumber company, don't you?"

"I suspect my men pressed too hard and ended up dead as a result—it was Ox who killed them, right?"

"Yes, Captain. He came home and found the soldiers standing in a pool of blood. When Ox saw his parents lying there dead, he lost control."

"I'll take you at your word. But what will the Bellicinis do with their land in San Marco?"

"Ox has already told me the family no longer wants the land. They want to build a new life up here on the mountain. When you're able, look to the south gate, where you will see their beautiful house. It was the first one we built here. So, their land is all yours if you make it back to San Marco."

"What makes you think there's any doubt I'll make it back?" asked the Captain, stroking his beard.

"Gold does strange things to a man's mind. Your brother has tried to kill you once already, and you said you think he might have already killed Sergeant Vance. The wolves on this mountain are like sheep compared with the human wolf awaiting your arrival."

With a crooked grin, the Captain grunted, "I know Manuel's weakness. I'll be the one who'll ride back to San Marco with my men and the gold. We'll bury my brother somewhere on the way."

Nicholas and Ricardo left the room, and as they descended the stairs to the grand room, Raven appeared. Latching onto Ricardo's arm, she stole him from Nicholas, walking in the other direction.

Nicholas called out, "Ricardo, you must deliver the Captain's message at once if our plan is to go smoothly."

Ricardo reached out around Raven's neck and drew her close, kissing her cheek several times. As she giggled, he called back, "My horse is saddled; I'll be on my way in two minutes."

When the couple stepped outside to the hitching post, Ricardo saw another saddled horse next to his. "Whose horse is that?"

"It's mine," said Raven. "I need you to take me to Pizal after you deliver the message to Sergeant Vance."

"It's out of the question. No Miss—it's too dangerous!"

"Justus...I mean, Ricardo, how dangerous could it be with Captain Ficci still up here recovering and Sergeant Vance in charge? They won't do anything with the Captain in our custody. Besides, I must get to the tailor to buy material for Bernadette's wedding gown. She asked me to make her a dress, so when they decide to get married, she'll be ready."

"I'll take you, but on one condition. I want you to buy enough material to make two dresses, one for Bernadette and one for you, if you'll be my wife."

Raven's eyes sparkled as she screamed with delight, jumping up onto Ricardo, wrapping her arms around his neck, and turning him around. "Yes, yes! I promise I'll love you forever. Thanks be to God this revenge thing is over and you've found forgiveness. Now I know your heart is no longer divided and belongs to me alone!"

Laughing, Ricardo swept her onto her saddle, then mounted his horse. As they made their way down the mountain trail, he reached into his travel bag and retrieved three gold florins. Handing them to Raven, he smiled. "Make the most beautiful dress for the most beautiful bride."

Raven took the money, giggled, then kicked her horse to a canter, challenging him to give chase.

Chapter 54. Murder at the Base of the Mountain.

Camped at the base of the mountain, Sergeant Vance had not received word from the Captain, but was wise enough to order his senior corporal to return to San Marco with most of the men. He knew that whatever happened regarding the Captain, the original mission they'd begun a week previously had come to an end. If the Captain lived, Vance's objective was to insure his recovery, then bring Sergeant Ficci up on charges when they returned to San Marco.

Vance chose five horsemen to stay behind and keep Sergeant Ficci under constant guard. Unbeknown to him, the men he chose were secretly loyal to Manuel, save one, a young soldier with a secret mission of his own.

An hour after the foot soldiers began their march to San Marco, Sergeant Ficci gave the signal to his men to seize Sergeant Vance. Vance put up a valiant struggle, managing to wound one of his assailants before the others disarmed him. After securing him to the ground, Sergeant Ficci approached with dagger in hand. Kneeling in front of him, Manuel placed the tip of the dagger onto the base of his throat.

Sergeant Vance grunted, "You're all cowards and a disgrace to your uniform, and the country you serve."

Sergeant Ficci twitched an evil smile and pushed the blade slowly into the man's neck, causing maximum suffering before Vance finally died, choking on his own blood. If the men holding Vance down had feared Sergeant Ficci before, their dread was twofold now.

Standing over the body, Ficci giggled at his evil deed, and then asked why Private Cruz was missing. When no one had an answer, he ordered his men to take Vance's body into the bush and bury it beneath stones.

Twenty minutes later, while the soldiers piled the last of the stones, one of them motioned to Sergeant Ficci, pointing down the trail. Private Cruz, appeared, holding his stomach as he approached.

"Where have you been?" Sergeant Ficci barked.

"I must have eaten something bad, because I've been ill. I had to seek a stream to clean the vomit from my clothes. Where is Sergeant Vance?" asked the private.

"It doesn't matter," sneered Manuel, "I'm in charge now, and you need to get in line with the rest before I send you back to San Marco in irons."

Private Cruz nodded in fearful compliance as they broke camp, mounted their horses and made their way to Pizal for ale, home cooking and to await word from the Captain.

As they drew close to the village, Sergeant Ficci thought about the accusations that would be filed against him when they returned to the Command Post. Those in charge, that Vance had sent back, were also loyal to Sergeant Ficci, and would give a fuzzy account at best when they arrived.

When Ricardo and Raven reached the base of the mountain and the smoldering fires of the soldiers' deserted camp, they dismounted to investigate.

Ricardo remembered hearing Sergeant Vance tell Nicholas he would wait, no matter what, but apparently something had changed his mind.

Not far from Ricardo, Raven gasped, pointing at the ground near one of the fire pits.

"What is it?"

"Blood!" cried Raven.

Joining her, Ricardo stooped down. A pool of blood soaked the ground, with drops trailing off into the bush. They followed the blood trail to a pile of rocks behind the bush.

"What do you think?" Raven asked.

Ricardo removed a half-dozen rocks, revealing the head of Sergeant Vance.

"Who is it?" whispered Raven, reaching for Ricardo's arm.

"It's Sergeant Vance. Looks like someone wanted him to die slowly by the way the hole in his throat had been inserted so cleanly. I told you it was dangerous. Now please, get on your horse and return to the Mission, Raven."

Tears rolled down her cheeks. "Please, no. I'm afraid to go back alone, Ricardo. Please don't make me go!"

"I must deliver the message to the highest in command, and that will undoubtedly be Sergeant Ficci. My guess is that he rode into Pizal to wait, now that he's in charge again. Raven, if I allow you to come, you must do exactly as I say. If anything ever happened to you, I'd go mad."

"I will. I promise, I promise," pleaded Raven.

"We'll ride into Pizal, get the message to Sergeant Ficci, and get out of there as quickly as possible. He's probably at the inn drinking ale. He's bound to question us about the last time we encountered him and deceived him into thinking you had leprosy, so let me do all the talking."

"I have no problem being quiet," said Raven. "I don't want to speak. I'm afraid of him. He's a rapist as well as a murderer."

Pulling rocks off the chest of Sergeant Vance, Ricardo searched his inside jacket pocket for identification, but instead found a small, leather-bound journal. It held a complete account of the soldiers' mission from the outset.

Sergeant Vance described every event in a brief but thorough manner, and most importantly, he had documented the attempted murder of Captain Ficci by his own brother.

Ricardo resolved that as soon as he returned to the Mission, he'd give it to Nicholas for a closer look.

After replacing Vance's burial stones, the two mounted their horses and set off for Pizal, hoping their encounter would be over before sundown.

Avoiding Pizal's main avenue, Ricardo took the back streets until he figured out where the soldiers were and how to approach the inn. When they entered the back door of the tailor shop, Ricardo hurried to the front window, looking down the street toward the inn. Sitting directly in front was a wagon he knew all too well, with the name 'Assanti' painted on the side panel. His heart skipped a beat. If his gypsy nemesis, Rosalina, was somehow connected with Ficci, it would make his task to deliver the Captain's message even more hazardous.

Raven smiled and seemed to forget about their mission as she looked through various satin and lace products the tailor brought out for her inspection. After she had made her choices and paid the merchant, Ricardo nervously urged her towards the front door.

Glancing out the window again, he saw four soldiers stagger out of the inn toward the old boardinghouse across the street. He waited until they were inside before he grabbed Raven's hand and went out the back to the horses, walking them around to the main street toward the inn.

"Raven, do you see that painted wagon behind the horses in front of the inn?"

"Yes, what about it?"

"It belongs to a very dangerous gypsy family; two brothers and a sister. They stole the Mission gold when I was in Pinzola. It was the sister, Rosalina, who shot me and released the poisonous snake that bit me after I followed them into the forest. When I recovered the gold and returned, Rubin brought me to your house before I passed out from the poison still left in my arm. That's the night you took care of me."

"She's the same one who left the lip paint on your arm when she drew out the poison?" asked Raven, arching an eyebrow.

"There was lip paint on my arm?"

"Yes, and that's not all. There was lace torn from an undergarment wrapped around your head and your arm."

Reaching for her hand, as they hurried to the hitching post, Ricardo grinned. "Oh yes, I can explain about all that, but right now let's just get in there, deliver the letter and get out. Oh, and don't be fooled by Rosalina's beauty, she's wicked to the core."

Raven's voice deepened. "Is that how she almost killed you? You were fooled by her beauty?"

CHAPTER 55. RICARDO CONFRONTS MANUEL FICCI.

ying their horses to a post, Ricardo unhooked his crossbow and walked into the inn, with Raven close behind. "Remember, let me do the talking," he said pulling an arrow from his quiver.

Stepping up to the innkeeper, Ricardo asked, "Sir, would you be kind enough to tell me if Sergeant Manuel Ficci is registered here?"

The old, toothless innkeeper's smile turned to a frown. "Unfortunately, he is. If he wasn't a government official, I would've paid someone to throw him out. He's in the back room with a gypsy woman, who seems as wild as he."

"Did you happen to see any other gypsies with her?" asked Ricardo, craning his neck to see the back room.

"Yes, two men, but they left an hour ago, barely making it to their wagon, where I suspect they passed out."

Ricardo thanked the innkeeper and walked with Raven to the back room, his crossbow ready in case the situation became unstable.

In the nearly-deserted room, Rosalina Assanti sat on Manuel's lap helping him sip ale, laughing with every little spill onto his jacket.

Manuel glanced up, apparently drunk. "Well, look who it is... Mr. Crossbow and Little Miss Leprosy."

"You know that pretty boy?" Rosalina asked.

"I met him on the mountain. Do you know him from somewhere?"

"Oh yes, indeed, my sweet Manuel, he's the one with God's gold."

"God's cold...gold?" slurred the Sergeant.

"Yes," said Rosalina, stroking his face, "my brothers and I managed to take at least fifty pounds from him. What we didn't realize is how skilled he was with that crossbow."

"Boy, why don't you lower that weapon?" said Manuel, kissing Rosalina's neck. "What happened next, Rosy?"

"He followed us into the woods, and after he shot my brother in the hand, pinning it to the wagon wheel, he made me return the gold."

Turning to Ricardo, the Sergeant asked, "Why are you here, boy?"

"I have a message from Captain Ficci for Sergeant Vance. Is he here at the inn?"

"Noo..oo," slurred Manuel, "he took... the sholdiers back to... Shan Marco. I'm in command now. Is... ma brother still alive?"

"Yes, sir, he is. He's recovering quickly. Here is the message he wrote to Sergeant Vance."

Holding his crossbow in the Sergeant's general direction, Ricardo approached and handed him the paper. As Manuel opened it and began to read, Raven stood behind Ricardo, peeking out, to get a better look at Rosalina.

Rosalina noticed and gave a wicked smile.

Sergeant Ficci crumpled the paper. "Tell my brother... the Captain... while I was trying to shave him from the wolf, he was moving... toooo much... my grape shot somehow found his chest. Tell him... I'm grrrr...ieving over the whole thing and I'm relieved that he lives...now. I ride to the base of the mountain in two days as he wishhhes. What is your name, boy?"

"I am Ricardo Alfonzo Cruz." Ricardo moved back as he spoke.

"Tell me, pretty boy," Rosalina smiled, leaning out to see Raven. "Is this young girl your toy for today? Did you tell her about us? I'll bet anything you didn't."

"There's nothing to tell except you stole the Mission's gold and tried to kill me twice."

Moving to his side, Raven laid her hand on Ricardo's arm.

Rosalina strode forward and pushed Ricardo's crossbow down, her devilish beauty rivaling Raven's. "But you're leaving out the best part. Have you forgotten what you did before you left our camp that day? I hope your little girl toy can handle your appetite for women."

Ricardo glanced at Raven. "She's lying, Raven. Don't believe a word she says...you know I would never..."

"Oh, I beg to differ," said Rosalina, addressing Raven with a wicked laugh. "Your handsome devil is just that...a devil. Before he left that day, I ripped a few pieces of my undergarment to stop his bleeding, that much is true. But when he saw my legs, the look on his face changed and I knew he was trouble. While one of my brother's hands was impaled to the wagon wheel, he tied my other brother to the same wheel and then came after me. He took me inside the wagon and overpowered me. I must say he was so sweet that I didn't struggle very long. It seemed like only moments and I forgot all about the gold. Yes, he is quite the lover, little girl. And I might add that you are so beautiful, he may keep you twice as long as the others he told me about."

Raven gulped.

Ricardo sighed. "All right, you've done your wicked deed for the day, Rosalina. Sergeant, we'll meet you at your old campsite in two days." At that, he backed out of the room as Raven turned and ran for the horses. Stepping out the front door, Ricardo heard laughter in the back room.

Raven had a handkerchief to her nose and refused to even look at Ricardo when he mounted his horse.

Riding out of the village, he turned to her. "You can't tell me you believed a single thing she said in there? I've never thought about her. It's you that I love, Raven."

After a long pause, Raven replied, "She is a beautiful woman. How can I believe you never thought of her?"

"The only pleasant thing she's ever done was dance. Outside of that, I only thought of her as a dangerous women who happens to be...well... stunning."

Surprised, Raven huffed, "Oh, she danced for you as well?"

"When I was in Pinzolo, she danced in the town square for at least fifty people. It was a public show, Raven."

"All men. I presume?"

"Most were men. But after that, I swear I didn't ever think of her again in a kind way."

"You mean as soon as you recovered the gold, you forgot about her?"

"Yes, Raven, I swear to you."

"Well, if you forgot about her, how is it that when I was caring for you after the snakebite, you called out her name twice in your fever?"

"I did? It was probably because she left an impression on me. Most *men* that I meet aren't as dangerous as her."

Raven considered his words. "I must admit, when she first said you did those disgusting things, it pierced my heart and I wanted to run away. But then when I thought back to what she said exactly, I do believe she was lying about everything. The last thing she said was that you told her about all the other lovers you've had, and I know for a fact there were no other women in your life before me."

"How'd you find that out?"

"I asked Nicholas about it once and he said you never had time for women with all the hunting and practicing with your crossbow and dagger."

"Thank God for Nicholas. So, do you believe me, Raven? Can we just put all of this behind us?"

Raven kicked her horse to a canter. "It's all behind, Ricardo, but I'll keep an eye on you..."

Chapter 56. A Dinner Conversation.

$\mathcal{L}$ater that evening, at the Bellicini home, everyone sat around the banquet table enjoying Bell's superb dinner. On the table was every variety of vegetable, picked daily from the garden, with fresh baked, hard-crusted bread. The main course was roasted duckling and baked trout.

Passing a basket of bread across the table, Ben asked, "So, Nicholas, do you think we're nearing the end of this drama with Captain Ficci?"

"I really hope so. I'm looking forward a time when we can live without having to look over our shoulders every day. We have a lot more work to do here, and as soon as the charges are dropped against your family, we'll finish the construction and get to the business we were called to do."

Resting her salad fork, Bernadette broke in, "You know, people of the world have the impression Mission work is boring and laborious, but after being here some time now, I know that couldn't be further from the truth. While it's true we have some challenges ahead, the Mission is anything but boring. Nicholas and I were just reviewing the journal, and we were amazed at how much has happened in such a short period. Coming here was the biggest surprise of my life, and thinking back, I have only one regret."

"What's that?" Maria asked.

Smiling, Bernadette replied, "Being in the Captain's room when he awoke."

"Whatever he said to offend won't happen again." Nicholas grinned, resting his hand on hers. "You won't have to tend to him any more. I asked Brother Taylor to see to him until he leaves. I know the Captain isn't prepared for a monk like Brother Taylor, and will be ruffled in short order."

Ben asked, "How so?"

"I see it like this," said Nicholas as he buttered his bread, "Brother Taylor is a man who is filled with love, while the Captain is filled with greed and hate. Pure love cannot understand hate, but will acknowledge its presence in the world. On the other hand, hate and evil cannot fathom what love is all about, and acknowledges its presence only as a weakness.

"My guess is they'll both suffer somewhat as a result, but our favorite monk will suffer less. Although the Captain may mock and humiliate Taylor, thinking him pathetic and weak, Taylor will not return insults or vile words. He'll only return love, which will totally befuddle the Captain and cause his mind to spin in confusion. I'll venture to say that before the

Captain fully recovers, he'll ask that Brother Taylor be removed and replaced by Makande, his former slave."

Makande looked up from his vegetables. "I will watch him. I make him feel better, but he must know I am free man."

"By all means, Makande, by all means. I want to know everything he says to you when the time comes. And remember, there's no need for fear, as there was in the past. He has no authority here, and he's still very weak, so speak your mind."

"I'm not hating him, Mr. Nick, but freedom beats drum in my heart next to Love God. I will beat freedom drum to him." Then Makande called to his wife, who'd gone into the kitchen, "Bell, guests want to taste that pie you make."

Bell entered the room with a berry pie in each hand. As she divided the dessert, serving the helpings, she shot Makande a look of caution, "You won't ask me to go to Captain, Makande."

Shaking his head, Makande answered, "No, my Bell, only Makande goes to Captain."

Nicholas glanced at the front door, smiling, when he saw Brother Taylor enter the room talking to himself. "Come join us, Brother," said Nicholas, "you're just in time for Bell's berry pie."

Taking a piece from Bell, the despondent monk seated himself next to Ox. "No one has ever made me feel like this before. I always used to think there was hope for everyone, but I have my doubts after tending to the Captain today."

"Why do you say that? What happened?" asked Bernadette, tasting the pie.

"I can't go into detail, because I'm afraid it would cause me to repeat some of the things he said. I will say, having spent the day with him made me examine just how black darkness can be. I pity him, because I think he sees his own darkness as light. I will pray for the man."

"Did he happen to mention Makande?" asked Nicholas.

"As a matter of fact, he did."

At that, everyone at the table chuckled.

"Did I say something funny?" asked Taylor.

"We're laughing because only a minute ago I mentioned that the Captain might be annoyed I asked you to look after him. I also mentioned that he might ask for Makande in the end."

"He asked for Makande right out. I'm positive he would be more comfortable with him. I had an urge to leave the room when he asked me if I had ever had a woman. I finally left when he started boasting about his fleshly escapades. I had to, Nick. I hope you don't mind."

"Not at all. If all goes well, he'll leave the Mission sometime tomorrow. Makande said he'd be willing to relieve you. It will be interesting to see how everything turns out when the Captain has to meet his brother and share the gold."

"Why did you give him all that gold, Nicholas?" Ty asked. "There must be a fortune buried down there."

Swallowing a bite of pie, Nick answered, "I never wanted anyone to know about it, but unfortunately the Sergeant found the grinding wheel with the gold embedded in the stone. I told the Captain I would give him all the gold in my possession. He doesn't know about the original vein of gold though. Its location will die with me."

"How ironic is this life of mine," said Bernadette, laying a hand on Nicholas' arm. "I leave an opulent, affluent life to fall in love with a preoccupied, humble man of God with only one mission in life. As it turns out, he's wealthy beyond belief, but doesn't like to mention it."

Nicholas' eyes sparkled as he addressed Ty. "Don't be so sure I've lost the gold. After we separate from the Captain, Ricardo and I will follow them from a distance using the magni-tube. It's as I've said before, gold can cause a deadly fever in a man once his thoughts are fixed on it."

Just then, Ricardo and Raven came through the front door. Nicholas called out, "Ah, just the man I wanted to see. I'm glad you've returned unscathed. What happened down there today?"

Raven reached for Ricardo's hand as they stepped up to the table. "Ricardo ran across someone even more treacherous than the Captain. It was a beautiful gypsy woman, Rosalina. She was sitting on the lap of a most drunken Sergeant Ficci when we entered the inn. After Ricardo gave the message to him, Rosalina took revenge on Ricardo and accused him of having his way with her, but I knew it was lie."

"You saved my life, Nick," Ricardo chimed in. "Thank God you told Raven that I never saw another woman before her. Rosalina is a very skilled liar. She almost had Raven convinced I was a philandering dog.

"As for what went on down there, Sergeant Ficci killed Sergeant Vance. We found him beneath a pile of stones in a shallow grave near one of the fire pits at the soldiers' campsite. When I searched his jacket for identification, I found a small journal instead. I think you'll find it very useful if we are to clear things with the authorities. I didn't read it all, but what I did see will be very helpful to us. Sergeant Ficci has five soldiers, but there's no telling where their loyalties lie."

Thumbing through the notebook, Nicholas smiled. "Great job, son! I'll read this little jewel later. So tell me, how did you get out of there without a confrontation?"

"The whole time my crossbow was drawn and continually aimed at Ficci's chest. But to tell the truth, I believe he knew he was too drunk to get away with anything. At the time, I was more suspicious of Rosalina."

As Ricardo sat down and split the last piece of pie with Raven, Nicholas leaned over to speak. "Ricardo, I need you to visit Joseph Solo early tomorrow before we leave. Tell him we need to borrow the magni-tube for a time. Bring my musket case and put the tube in it before you return to the Mission. I don't want the Captain to know we have a magnifying device."

Nicholas kissed Bernadette and excused himself, saying he needed a good rest before what he hoped would be his last day of dealing with the Ficci brothers. Before he reached the door, Makande called out, "I come with you, Mr. Nick. I go to the Captain to see if he in need."

When they arrived at Nicholas' house, Makande went to his room and pulled a navy blue suit from the closet. After changing clothes, he slid into a pair of shiny boots. Looking in the polished metal mirror to make sure he looked the part of a free gentleman, he made his way upstairs to the Captain's room. Pausing a moment, he gently tapped on the door.

The Captain barked, "If it's you, monk, go back to your cell. I'll be fine tonight."

Makande entered and stood staring at his former owner.

The Captain complained, "Who'd they send me now? Who are you?"

"I am Makande, sir. You no remember?"

"What! That's you, Makande? Yes, it *is* you. I didn't recognize you in that suit. I must say you look quite distinguished. It makes all the difference. Why, if you weren't a slave, you might be taken for a gentleman."

"I am gentleman, sir. A *free* gentleman."

"Oh yes, that's right. Manuel told me how the boy bought you from the slave trader. Also, how you came together with your wife again is certainly another story. Your friend Nicholas was quite clever sending that young boy Oscar to deceive me and buy Bell for you. That boy has potential; he was one step ahead of me every moment."

"Bell is free woman also. We have new baby. Name her Hope."

"Do you like living way up here on the mountain?"

"This is special holy place. Makande and wife will live here forever. We let Hope decide to what she want when she older."

The Captain turned in his bed the wrong way, causing the wound in his chest to ooze blood. Racked with pain, the Captain grunted, "Makande, go get some new bandages. When will this cursed hole stop bleeding?"

"I happy to help you, sir, but first you need to know you must never command a free man anything. If you ask free gentleman, he glad to help you."

"What? I can't believe this! All right, all right. Makande, PLEASE change this bloody dressing. Or maybe you'd like me to be your guest for another week?"

"When you say like that, I change in quick time."

Makande hurried to the kitchen for clean bandages.

Captain Ficci laid in his bed, planning each step he'd take to confront his brother about the shooting. He'd convince Manuel that he thought the shooting was a terrible accident and believed he never meant any harm. After he was sure Manuel believed him, he'd assess the other soldiers, and test their loyalty. When the balance of power shifted to his advantage, he'd kill Manuel first, and then anyone else he thought might prevent him from returning to the Command Post without the gold or his health.

CHAPTER 57. CAPTAIN FICCI LEAVES THE MISSION.

The next morning, when Nicholas woke, he went to the bedroom window and caught a glimpse of Ricardo heading to Joseph Solo's cabin to borrow the magni-tube.

After dressing, he hurried downstairs to the kitchen, loading his travel bag with the foodstuffs they'd need for the next few days. While searching the pantry for bread, nuts and any other dried foods, an idea of how he might bring the matter of the Ficci brothers to a speedier conclusion popped into his mind.

With his travel bag filled, he returned to his bedroom and pulled two sacks of gold coins from his closet, and a sack of gold dust from his desk. His intension was to infect the captain with gold fever early on. Once Ficci had possession of a hefty sum of gold, with the mother lode still ahead, he was sure to begin making decisions based on his lust for more.

His timing was perfect. Makande had just left the Captain's room after having helped him get dressed when Nicholas tapped on the door.

"What did you forget, Makande? Come in," called the Captain.

With his hands full, Nicholas maneuvered to lift the door latch. "It's Nicholas, Captain. Are you well enough to ride?"

"I'm on my feet and that's all I care about."

Nicholas entered, smiled at the Captain and went directly to the sitting table and set down the gold. Opening a sack of coins, he spilled out the contents for visual effect. A shaft of sunlight hit the gold with such intensity, that it seemed to glow. The Captain stood speechless, gasping with delight.

"I told you I'd give you all the gold in my possession, so here's what I had stored at the Mission."

"There's a fortune on that table," smiled the Captain.

"Lots more too. This is only a small part of what's buried down there."

"Exactly how much more?" asked the Captain, fingering through the mound of coins.

"As I said yesterday, as least a hundred and seventy pounds. You're going to need a supply horse just for the gold."

"I'm impressed. Where did you get it?"

"A total of one-hundred-and-eighty-pounds of solid gold is not enough for you, sir?" asked Nicholas, clearly irritated.

"I know you don't deal with people like me on a daily basis, but if you did, you'd know the answer to that question is always no, there's never enough."

Nicholas put his hands on his hips, glaring at the Captain. "The location of any other gold will die with me, Captain. You must just take what I've offered and go in peace. There's enough gold buried down there to keep you rich for two lifetimes. Have we not saved your life as well? Will you please stop now?"

"You and your people did save my life. For that I'll not press any further. Is my horse saddled?"

"Yes, sir, Makande took care of that earlier," said Nick, breathing a sigh of relief.

"All right, let's go before I run into that monk again. Why did you send him to me anyway?"

As they gathered the gold and headed downstairs, Nicholas explained, "I thought you would be a sort of education for him, and as it turned out I was right. You made him re-think some of the more interesting questions about worldly men, and why they act as they do."

"A worldly man is exactly what I am, and he would have learned a great deal more if I had the stomach to put up with his pathetic outlook on life. He thinks like a woman. Now, can I get a bite to eat before we leave? I'm famished."

"Yes, of course. I believe Makande's preparing, if I had to guess by the aromas, steak, biscuits and fried eggs."

The men joined Makande in the kitchen and ate breakfast in silence. The Captain seemed starved for protein and shoveled the food down as if it were his last meal.

Nicholas glanced out the window and saw the west gate swing open. Ricardo walked his horse through, the musket case with the magni-tube strapped securely to the saddle. By the time he reached Nicholas' house, the Captain had finished and they were standing by their horses.

Nicholas looked around, then took off his red cap. Scratching his head, he declared, "That's funny, by this time of morning everyone is usually busy with the gardening and construction, but I don't see a soul."

Looking up at the guest rooms on the second floor, Nicholas saw Bernadette, Bell and Raven peeking past the curtains to get a glimpse of the Captain leaving, for what they hoped would be forever.

The Captain laughed aloud as he shoved the sacks of gold in his saddlebag. "You don't think they're all hiding on my account, do you?"

"Well, Captain," Nicholas smiled, "you *have* made a lasting impression on quite a few people, but having said that, I bet you're just as happy to be leaving."

"That, Nicholas Kristo, is the understatement of the century. A place like this belongs in the mountains, far away from the rest of the world. All I see in this place are misfits, cripples, and feeble-minded holy men. Help me mount my horse and get me out of here, then maybe we'll all be happy."

As the three men mounted their horses and made their way toward the south gate, people emerged from everywhere. Monks came out of the church housing, and children from the Bellicini house. They all walked toward Nicholas' house as Bernadette, Raven and Bell emerged from the front door.

When the men were on the other side of the fence and Ricardo closed the gate, a thundering applause broke out. Nicholas did all he could to hold back the smile.

The Captain turned to him with a wicked grin. "Well it looks like I *did* make an impression after all, but if they'd done that when I arrived, it would have made all the difference."

"I get the feeling it would take a lot more then their applause at your leaving to offend you," joked Nicholas.

"I do believe you're getting to know me, Nicholas. If I had any respect for what they do, I might have been upset. But as it stands, you and your people are simple sheep who have escaped the rest of the real world down there. You've created a make-believe utopia that coddles you and makes you think you will actually do the world some good in the end. It's a dream world you've created, and when you wake up to the cruelty this world will eventually impose on you, maybe then you'll see the truth of what I'm saying."

Turning onto the main trail, Nicholas rode beside the Captain. "Our worlds are very different, Captain, and so are our views on what we think is valuable and meaningful. I never really expected you to understand or even like what we do here. And as it stands, we were all very pleased to have helped save your life, and that, you must admit, was not a dream. You are alive because we believe in the worth of human life, even if we are diametrically opposed to the things you stand for."

"Well spoken, Nicholas," said the Captain. "That was profound, and I thank you for saving my life, but you already know I'll never change."

"I know that, Captain, but I wasn't called to judge anyone. I don't judge you for who you are."

Ricardo called from behind, "I thought you would never say that, Captain."

"Say what, boy?"

"*Thank you.* I've been waiting to hear you say 'thank you' just once before you left, and praise God, you just said it."

Hearing Ricardo's rebuke, the Captain kicked his horse to a canter, intentionally riding ahead.

"Don't get too far ahead, Captain," Nicholas called out, "this mountain is teeming with dangerous animals."

No sooner had Nicholas spoken, than a giant black bear ran out of the bush directly toward the Captain. When his horse reared back, Nicholas galloped to him at once. Upon seeing Nicholas, the huge bear stopped in its tracks, snorted, then lay on its belly.

When his horse settled, the Captain trembled, keeping his eyes fixed to the bear.

Nicholas dismounted and walked to the massive creature. While it shook its head, rolling onto its back, Nicholas squatted and rubbed its belly vigorously. The Captain's mouth dropped open. "If I didn't see it myself I would've never believed it. Is it the same way with the wolves and wildcats?"

"Yes, it's been this way since I was a boy, but don't ask me why, because I don't know myself."

"So that's why you chose the mountain for the location of your Mission. You have a natural way to prevent intruders. But how do your people get around the problem?"

Nicholas urged the bear to its feet and directed it off in another direction. "That's a trade secret, Captain, sorry."

Continuing down the mountain trail, the Captain was careful to stay close to Nicholas.

The sun was high past noon when they heard voices coming from beyond the trail. Ricardo pointed to the soldiers' camp, which was now visible at the bend in the road.

Nicholas stopped the Captain. "This is as far as Ricardo and I go, Captain Ficci."

"Where will I wait for the map?"

"There's a large oak tree at the entrance to the mountain trail. It has a warning sign regarding the wolves. Ricardo will release an arrow to that sign some time within the hour. You'll find the map to the location of the gold attached to the arrow. Farewell, Captain."

CHAPTER 58. GREED IN THE PIGPEN

icholas and Ricardo remained silent as they watched the Captain turn his horse and ride the rest of the way down the trail.

Nicholas motioned for Ricardo to follow him back up the trail, around an alternate path leading to a clearing where they had a clean shot at the sign. After dismounting, Nick pulled the magni-tube from the musket case and quickly found the best spot for Ricardo to fire his crossbow.

They moved to the ground and lay on their bellies looking over a cliff to a large oak tree at the base of the mountain. Nicholas pointed the scope directly at the sign, then moving his focus left, saw Sergeant Ficci cantering toward the entrance of the mountain trail, where the Captain had just dismounted.

"What's happening, Nick?" asked Ricardo.

"Nothing yet. The big oak is at least two hundred paces from here. Do you think you can reach it? The warning sign looks so small from here."

Peering through the scope again, Nicholas saw Manuel leap from his horse and embrace his brother the moment he reached him.

"Of course I can hit it," Ricardo said. "The question is, will I hit it on the first shot?"

Nicholas smiled. "All right then, give me an arrow." Rolling a small paper map around the shaft, he went to a nearby pine tree, broke a branch and scraped sap from the core, rubbing it on the edge of the map, gluing it to itself.

Handing the arrow to Ricardo, he asked, "Are you sure your crossbow is powerful enough to make the distance? It looks farther than I thought, but this is the only spot we can see the sign clearly."

"I built my crossbow with a custom feature for long shots. The catch for the bowstring can be adjusted to go back another half-thumb. The arrow should travel at least another hundred paces. Don't worry, Nicholas, I'll hit it."

Ricardo cranked back the bowstring as Nicholas took the scope and fixed his eye on the Captain and his brother. By now they were walking toward the warning sign and waving at the soldiers to follow. When they were about forty paces from the oak tree, the Captain pointed to the sign, then ordered the soldiers to the side of the road to wait.

Ricardo rested the crossbow on a small log and lay on his belly ready to fire. "Is there wind movement in the trees down there?"

Turning the scope to the treetops, Nicholas replied, "Yes, there is. It's mild, blowing steadily to the east."

Ricardo took aim. "If I aim to the left side of the sign, with any luck, the wind should nudge the arrow to the right a hair." Holding his breath, Ricardo fired.

Nicholas heard the whiz of the arrow, keeping his scope fixed on the sign. Seconds later he leapt to his feet. "Great shot, Ricardo! The arrow barely caught the right side of the sign just as you predicted. Bravo!"

"I told you I'd hit it, but you'll never know just how difficult a shot it was. Even though we know that sign is three feet across, it looked like a thimble in my sights."

Nicholas trained the scope back to the sign and saw Sergeant Ficci trying to pull the arrow from the thick wood. It was embedded so deeply that he gave up and unrolled the map right there. As soon as he came down from the tree, the Captain approached and they read the map together.

Seconds later, the Ficci brothers ran to their horses and set off in the direction of Nicholas' farm, with five soldiers galloping behind. Nicholas was relieved that the farm remained deserted since their move to the mountain.

Ricardo hooked his crossbow to the saddle and mounted his horse. "Nick, if we have any chance to see what happens when they start digging, we'll have to ride the narrow mountain trail that follows the base of the mountain all the way to your place."

After securing the telescope to his saddle, Nicholas mounted up. "All right, son, you lead the way. If we hurry, we can make it there before them. We'll come around on the forest edge just behind the farm where we'll have a plain view of everything they do, without being detected."

When they entered a small clearing about a hundred paces behind the farm, they tied the horses to a tree and walked to the beginning of the tree line, behind Nick's house. Resting the tube on a fallen tree, Nicholas saw several soldiers in the pigpen already digging. Others were chasing the pigs out of the pen.

It wasn't long before one of the men came up with a nugget the size of his fist. Thrusting his hand into the water trough, the soldier washed the mud off and held the nugget out to the Captain.

"What's happening, Nick? Did they find it?" Ricardo asked, squinting in vain.

"Yes, they found it. One of the soldiers is walking to the Captain with a huge nugget. Wait a minute. It looks like they're hauling it all out now, dumping it in the trough. Sergeant Ficci has put a blanket on the ground next to the trough, and I think he's ordering them to pile the gold there. It looks like they about have it all out now and are standing around laughing. Here, Ricardo, you take the scope. The Captain is walking backwards away from the rest. Something looks strange."

Ricardo moved onto the scope and pointed it directly at the Captain.

Nicholas leaned his back against the tree, chewing on a piece of jerky. "What's happening, Ricardo?"

Ricardo related that the Captain walked to his horse, while Sergeant Ficci and the rest were stuffing saddlebags with the gold. Then Sergeant Ficci stood up with his back to the Captain, reaching for a pistol in his belt. The Captain knew he was up to something and already had his pistol out, aiming at his brother. Manuel turned to fire, but the Captain fired first, hitting Manuel in the face. Manuel dropped down, rolling frantically on the ground, holding his face, while the others looked on.

"Manuel has stopped moving now. The Captain just grabbed a flintlock from his horse and is aiming it at the other soldiers. It looks like he's making them disarm. Yes, they're dropping their pistols and daggers."

"What about Sergeant Ficci?" asked Nick, squinting toward the farm.

"I think he's dead. The Captain is walking to the soldiers, indicating they should all move toward the barn. He stopped at his brother and is turning him over. Oh! Manuel's not dead. He just lifted an arm and fired his pistol point blank at the Captain. Captain's grabbing his stomach... he just fell next to his brother. They're both very still now. The other soldiers are coming now."

Nicholas leaned close to Ricardo and whispered, "I think you've just witnessed your 'poetic justice.' How do you feel now, more satisfied?"

"No," sighed Ricardo, "I don't feel satisfied. I feel pity for them. Had I not forgiven them, I would not have felt satisfaction unless I'd killed them myself. But now, for their greed and lust they will stand before the bar of God. Will He have mercy on them, Nicholas?"

"All I know for sure is they will be judged with perfection, and mercy will be given, to some degree, by the grace of God. You have grown a great deal through all of this, Ricardo. I'm proud of you, but look back to the soldiers, what's happening now?"

Ricardo peered through the scope. "The soldiers are all squatting down around the bodies, talking to one another. They're getting up now and walking toward your house, Nick."

Fifteen minutes passed before the soldiers came out the front door wearing civilian clothes. Nicholas had the scope now, and with a hint of contempt, said, "They just came out of the house wearing my father's clothes. I knew I should have taken them when I moved to the mountain. It appears these men have plans to desert the Italian Army and divide the gold among themselves."

"Well," said Ricardo, "do you think now that the Captain and his brother are dead and these soldiers are off on their own we're out of danger and can return to the Mission?"

"Not just yet. Let's follow them. I don't think we've seen the last of the gold fever."

Nicholas watched as the soldiers stuffed their saddlebags with gold nuggets, being careful to divide it evenly five ways. Afterwards, they tied the Captain and his brother to their horses and took them in tow, riding north toward Rome.

After following for hours, staying a good distance behind, Nicholas noticed the men change direction, riding toward a lake to the east, probably to camp for the night.

Nicholas and Ricardo rode to the high ground, where they could see the soldiers' camp from across the shallow water. As the sun began to sink into the mountains, Nick kept watch while Ricardo set up camp. When he'd finished laying out their bedrolls, the younger man joined him. "What are they up to now, Nick?"

"They just finished setting camp and making a fire on the edge of the lake. One of them is pointing to what looks like a natural ditch. Three of them just got up and took the brothers off their horses and are dragging them toward the ditch. Wait! Something's going to happen again. There are two men by the fire, and one of them just grabbed his musket and put two pistols in his belt. He's headed for the ditch, but the one left by the fire is trying to hold him back. Wait. The soldier with the guns broke free and now he's firing. Oh Lord, he's firing at all of them!"

CHAPTER 59. FERNANDO CRUZ

When the gun-smoke cleared, three more dead soldiers joined the Ficci brothers in a ditch on the mound, leaving only two soldiers to split the fortune in gold.

Wishing to stay unnoticed, Nicholas and Ricardo did not make a fire and ate only the dried foods. When darkness came, Ricardo fell fast asleep, but Nick lay staring at the stars and full moon for hours, thinking of the Mission and the task ahead. He missed Bernadette and began to recall her rebuke to the Captain the day before. After hearing her deep conviction and devotion, his longing to be with her became overwhelming. As he turned on his blanket in an attempt to avoid the ache in his heart, a shot rang out, echoing across the lake. Only a second passed before another shot discharged, but this time a man's screaming and moaning silencing even the crickets.

Ricardo jerked awake. "What's that? What happened?"

"Gunshots from across the lake. Someone was shot. You can still hear him moaning. It won't be long before sunrise. We'll wait until we can see exactly what's happened before we go near their camp."

Ricardo lay back and fell asleep, while Nicholas tried in vain to get a glimpse of the soldiers' camp in the moonlight. He saw movement but couldn't tell which of the men it was. At the first signs of light he tried the telescope again, finally seeing the camp clearly. Waking Ricardo, Nick nudged his shoulder. "Come on, son. I think it's safe to go to their camp."

"Can you see them?"

"Yes, it appears one is dead and the other badly injured, but still alive. Let's get the horses and ride around the lake. Before I ride into the camp, take a hiding spot with your crossbow ready to fire, but don't shoot unless you see me raise both my arms. I really think we can manage this situation now without any more bloodshed."

They rolled up their blankets and hurried to the horses. After riding around the lake, when they were close to the camp, Ricardo took his position in a tree. Nicholas walked his horse calmly to the smoldering campfire.

A soldier sat with his back against a tree, moaning. One of his feet was wrapped in a blanket. Catching sight of Nicholas, he raised a pistol. "Who are you, sir? What do you want?"

Nicholas did not respond, but dismounted and walked even closer.

"Stop right there, sir, or I *will* fire."

At twenty paces, Nicholas stopped. "I don't mean to harm you. I've come to help. Don't you recognize me? I'm Nicholas Kristo. I was the one who took the Captain up the mountain after he was shot."

Sweating profusely, the soldier lowered his pistol and moaned, "Can you bandage my foot properly? I'm in agony. I'm missing two toes."

"Put your pistol aside, and I'll do what I can for you."

The soldier dropped the weapon and lay back. Nicholas called for Ricardo to join them, and pulled a water sack from his saddle. Searching his saddlebag, he retrieved bandages, and a jar of the Chinese powder Anna used to kill pain.

When Ricardo arrived, he dismounted and went directly around the tree, removing the pistol from the soldier's reach.

Nicholas unwrapped the blanket on the soldier's foot, and drizzled water on it. He'd rarely seen a man in so much pain, but he washed the sticky blood off and quickly assessed how much damage had been done. Halfway through the cleaning, the soldier passed out and Nicholas opened the jar of Chinese powder, sprinkling a hefty amount over the soldier's two stumps. After wrapping the foot in a clean bandage, he restarted the fire.

Turning to Ricardo, Nicholas asked, "You any good at fishing with that crossbow, Ricardo? We could have a decent breakfast when the man awakes."

Ricardo smiled widely, grabbing his crossbow. "That's what I love about this job. Right in the middle of our most important assignment I get to go fishing. I won't be long, Nick."

Thirty minutes passed before Ricardo returned with four good-sized trout, and herbs he'd found along the way. Dropping the fish next to the fire, he asked, "Did he wake at all?"

"No, not yet, but when he does we'll find out everything. Let's get those fish over the fire and have something cooked before the patient wakes."

Just then the soldier rolled on his blanket and sat up, with a most unusual grin.

"By your smile, might I presume you're feeling better?" asked Nicholas.

Rubbing his eyes and looking at his bandaged foot, the man asked, "What did you put on my foot?"

"A special Chinese powder that kills pain. It is an extract of the poppy flower. Did it make your foot numb?"

"Not just my foot, but my whole body," said the soldier. "I feel like I'm floating on air."

"I'll leave the rest of the jar with you to keep. You'll need more when the numbness wears off. Tell us your name."

"My name is Fernando, and I wish to thank you both for coming to my aid. I know the gold in those saddlebags belongs to you. I want to tell you straight away, I never came on this assignment for gold. My father is a wealthy man and I have a substantial inheritance. I joined the Army in search of a certain man. I thought by having a degree of authority I'd be able to acquire information of his whereabouts, but that's another story. For now I'll tell you the events that led up to last night."

As Nicholas gutted the trout, and Ricardo poured cider, the soldier said he'd gone to San Marco with Sergeant Vance two months earlier. They'd just finished fighting the French in Genoa when he put in a request to be transferred with Vance. San Marco was the city he would begin the search for his missing relative. But much to his chagrin, when he joined the ranks of Captain Ficci's soldiers, he knew they were a different breed from the heroes of Genoa.

Nick threw the fish onto the sizzling skillet, and asked, "When do you think things went out of control?"

"It was after you brought the Captain up the mountain. Sergeant Vance was in command and things were fine until he sent most of the men back to San Marco with the corporal. I thought that was a mistake, because I knew the men he chose to stay behind. Even though they were the most experienced, they were loyal to Sergeant Ficci.

"With seven of us remaining, one of the soldiers must've given me tainted water. I was sick and searched for a steam to clean myself, and when I returned, Sergeant Vance was gone. When I inquired about him, the Sergeant said it didn't matter, and threatened to have me thrown in jail if I didn't fall in line with the others. Right then I knew they'd killed Sergeant Vance, and I'd be next if I didn't follow Ficci's lead."

Turning the fish in the skillet, Ricardo asked, "What happened when the Captain finally arrived?"

"They unrolled the map on the arrow and went right to the gold, ordering us to start digging. After all the gold was removed, the Captain and Sergeant shot each other. Before I realized what happened, Corporal Vitelli took over and declared we were all in this together and there was enough gold to make us rich for the rest of our lives. So we broke into the deserted house and found civilian clothes. After splitting the gold, we rode north toward Rome. At that point, I knew my life was in extreme danger, and I searched for a way out, but it was impossible. I was stuck with them.

"When we finally made camp here, Vitelli told three of the others to dump the bodies of the Captain and his brother in an open ditch. As they dragged the bodies onto the mound, the corporal grabbed his weapons and went after them while their backs were turned. I tried to stop him, but he pointed a pistol in my face, so I let go. He killed them all, and I realized I was next. I surmised he needed me only long enough to help him bury the bodies and transfer the gold to his horses."

Nicholas glanced at Ricardo as if to confirm the soldier was telling the truth, having been accurate in his description from the time they were watching through the magni-tube.

Finishing his cider with one last gulp, Nick asked, "What happened last night?"

"By the time night fell, and we could only see by the light of the fire, Corporal Vitelli seemed to say less and less. I was sure when I dozed off he would kill me, so I made sure he saw me load two pistols and set them next to my blanket. I lay down and turned toward the fire, keeping an eye on him.

"Every minute seemed like an hour as I began to imagine he could see me shivering in fear under my blanket. I lay there wondering how fate had cast this evil shadow on me in spite of my good intentions. Then, I pretended to sleep. I kept my eyes closed until I heard footsteps coming my way. I leapt from my blanket with both pistols and, seeing him looming over the fire with a log in his hand, I fired, hitting him in the neck. My other pistol went off by accident, taking my toes off.

"When I realized Vitelli was dead, I grabbed my dagger and cut off my boot. By the time I managed to stop the bleeding, I thought back to when I saw him hovering over the fire. It occurred to me that he might have been only feeding flames with the log he held. I guess only God knows what his real intentions were, but there you have it."

"So, Fernando, what are your plans now that you're the only soldier left that knows the truth?" asked Nicholas, plating his fish.

"First, I'll turn the gold over to you and be glad it no longer influences my life or my health. Then, when my foot is healed, I'll return to San Marco, turn in my report and hope the higher authorities find my story credible. If all goes well, I'll continue the search for my cousin."

"Eat some of your breakfast, then tell us about this man you seek," said Ricardo, handing him a plated trout.

Fernando seemed to inhale the fish, then, rinsing it down with more cider, he continued, "My family lives in Barcelona, and my father is a very successful businessman who took over his brother's business when he disappeared eight years ago. When my uncle did not reply to my father's letters for many months, he sent several of his workers to find out what had become of him and his wife and child. When his workers returned from San Marco, they told my father the authorities didn't know anything about my uncle, his family, or his business.

"They investigated further by going to the house my uncle rented each year while he conducted business with government officials. When they found the house, it was deserted, and no one in the surrounding properties knew what had happened. My father's workers didn't give up and went into the city asking everyone for the whereabouts of the family, but no one could help. It was as if they just disappeared. Over the next three years my father launched two more investigations, but still nothing. And then something unexpected happened six months ago."

Ricardo suspected that Fernando was his long lost cousin, especially when he mentioned the house just outside of San Marco where his mother was murdered. He had known he'd had a cousin named Fernando, but they two had never met. Could this young man be him? Hope began to awaken in his heart as he listened.

"One day while my father and I were in the field, tending our olive trees, we saw a man enter the gates of our property, but he was too far away to tell who it was. As he came closer we realized it was my uncle, and we ran to him and embraced him with many tears. He told us that eight years earlier he had been arrested on false charges and put in jail without a trial or even the opportunity to contact his family or anyone else. As time passed he gave up hope of ever being released, until a jail guard befriended him, enabling him to escape several months later.

"After his escape it took over two months for him to make his way from central Italy to our home in Spain. After he rested a week, he made plans to go back to San Marco and search for his family.

"My family discouraged his plan, warning him that he would eventually face the same authorities who had unjustly imprisoned him the first time. That's when we decided I would join the Army in Genoa, make my way to San Marco, infiltrate the soldiers, and find out what I could. But as it turned out I'll have to return to my father and uncle without any information, and missing some toes."

Smiling, Ricardo asked, "Is your last name Cruz? Are you Fernando Cruz?"

"Why, yes. How did you know that?"

"And is your father's name Roberto, and your uncle's name Raphael Cruz?"

"Right again! How could you know that?"

"You have found your cousin, Fernando. I am Ricardo Alfonzo Cruz, son of Raphael and Elizabeth Cruz. I can't believe this is happening. Nicholas, I have found my family! My father is alive! Oh good God, he's alive!" Wiping tears with his sleeve Ricardo walked on his knees to Fernando, and embraced him.

CHAPTER 60 A NEW ASSIGNMENT FOR THE COUSINS.

After their trout breakfast, Nick and Ricardo broke camp and helped Fernando saddle his horse and prepare to ride. With all the gold in his possession again, Nicholas was determined to keep its existence a secret from now on. Before they arrived at the base of the mountain he reminded the cousins what men might do if they knew such a fortune in gold was hidden somewhere in the Mission.

As they traveled, stopping just once to water the horses, Nicholas watched the cousins laugh and bond with each other all the way to the warning sign at the base of the mountain. Ricardo's arrow was still solidly fixed in the upper right hand corner. Nick stopped, wondering if Fernando was well enough to travel back to San Marco with Ricardo and end the Bellicini ordeal once and for all.

As Ricardo climbed the signpost and removed his arrow, Nicholas asked, "Fernando, how is your foot? Can you travel still farther today?"

"Oh yes, the pain in my foot is only now beginning to return. If I change the bandage again, and put on more of the powder, I'll be fine to travel. What would you have me do, sir? I owe you my life."

Turning to Ricardo, Nick asked, "Are you willing to escort your cousin on an assignment?"

"What is it, Nick? I'm ready for anything now."

After jotting some words on a scroll of paper and pulling a sack of gold coins from the Captain's saddlebags, Nicholas said, "I'd like you to go back to my farm and get Fernando into his uniform again. Then take this sack of gold and your cousin to Pizal and visit Anna. Have her take a good look at his foot, and prepare him for the ride to San Marco. Go directly to the inn closest to the Command Post. You'll find a monk there named Santos. He is the one who has the document that indicts Captain Ficci. Tell him who you are and what happened and he'll release the document, and the gold I gave him, to you."

Handing Sergeant Vance's journal to Ricardo, Nicholas explained that he had read it all at the lake while the cousins were getting acquainted. Vance had recorded everything, so the journal would exonerate the Bellicini family and put the rest of the Mission family in the best possible light.

Fernando was to report to the Judge Magistrate, and if asked what happened to Captain Ficci, say nothing. He'd tell the judge he'd release the gold to his care after an audience with General Emeliano. The General had a reputation of being an honest man, and also, Vance mentioned he had fought with him in Genoa.

Ricardo asked, "What will I do?"

"Watch over your new cousin, son. Get to know him. Help him get around until his foot heals. Besides, haven't you had enough adventure in your life these past weeks?"

"I guess you're right. I'll take a vacation for a while."

"It won't be a vacation dealing with the Judge Magistrate, Fernando," said Nicholas. "He was on the Captain's personal payroll. Just remember, when you deal with him, be gentle but shrewd. Do not let the gold go before you see the General. Oh, and you might want to send a messenger to Barcelona with a word to your father."

Fernando maneuvered his horse close to Nicholas, reached for his hand and placed it on his heart. "Thank you, sir, for turning around a situation that, in my own eyes, was hopeless. I will honor your mission with my life, and I will always thank God for sending you to save me, and deliver my cousin, Ricardo, into the arms of his family."

"God placed me in the world to give hope, Fernando," smiled Nicholas. "That's what my life is all about. I trust I'll see you again some day, but if not, I pray God smiles on your life and gives you peace." Then, turning to Ricardo, he asked, "And what about you, Ricardo? Will you go directly to Barcelona and your father after Sam Marco?"

"After we're finished in San Marco, I intend to come back for Raven. I'll want her to meet my family before we're married. She'll love my beloved Spain and I know she'll love my father. It will be a season of great celebration and a time to put adventure in my saddlebags for a while."

When Ricardo and Fernando said farewell and turned their horses, Nicholas watched them until they were nearly out of sight.

Looking north, to the mountains beyond Rome, he spotted a man and woman riding his way. While he waited, thinking they might be in need, he thought about the past few days. A deep sense of relief and gratitude filled his heart. He was thankful the bloodshed was over, and that none at the Mission had been injured through it all. Moved to tears when he realized how God had provided for him, he dismounted and dropped to one knee, giving thanks to the Lord and praising him aloud. He rose to find the riders waiting in silent respect.

Wiping a tear from his cheek, Nick smiled, "Good day to you, friends. Can I be of service? Are you lost?"

They were a handsome couple, dressed rather modestly, but by no means in need of anything material. Both had the same bright countenance, with a packed supply horse in tow and fine looking shepherd dog trailing behind.

The young woman spoke first, moving her hands gracefully with every word. "Good day, kind sir. My name is Constance Aviono, and this is my husband Pino. We are friends of a man called Joseph Solo, who has invited us to his home on the top of the mountain. Do you know our friend?"

"Indeed I do. My name is Nicholas Kristo, and I can take you to his home. We work together at the Mission. I'm glad you didn't try to travel to the summit without a guide. The animals aren't very kind to strangers. But if you are friends of Joseph's, you are no longer strangers to me. I will be happy to be your escort."

"You are the same Nicholas that founded the Mission?" asked Pino.

"I am. Did Joseph mention that?"

"Yes," Constance replied, "but he said to keep your identity and the Mission's location a much-guarded secret. We haven't mentioned our pilgrimage to anyone, and we were not going to attempt to travel the mountain trail until someone came down to escort us. Joseph gave us strict warning in his letter about that."

"How did you come to know our favorite healer?" asked Nicholas.

Constance moved her hands again as she spoke. "I was once deaf and left by my parents in the hands of a wicked innkeeper to slave for my room and board. One day, when I was seventeen, being lashed for trying to communicate hand signs to one of the customers, Joseph appeared from out of nowhere. I rushed to him and fell at his feet, when the innkeeper fled without reason. While I wept, Joseph sat on the ground holding my head to his chest, and as he wiped my tears, he laid a hand over my ear. All at once, I heard a faint sound that kept getting stronger with every breath. Suddenly I could hear. He charged me not to tell anyone that he was God's instrument for my healing. A year later he came to see my progress, and by then I was fortunate enough to have partial ownership of the inn and then to fall in love with and marry my partner's son, Pino."

Pino reached for her hand and continued, "Not long ago we received a letter from Joseph delivered by a monk. After reading it, my wife couldn't contain her joy at the possibility of helping the deaf communicate with hand-signs. This is something she's been talking about since we were married. We've been fortunate these past years and made a handsome profit from the inn, but now my wife wants to bring meaning to her life, and so do I. So here we are, clay in the potter's hand."

Beaming with delight, Nicholas said, "You could not have come at a better time. Let's make our way to the summit. I'll explain what our mission is all about. After you see our village and visit Joseph in his lookout tower, we'll talk more about how best to use your God-given talents."

As he spoke, the shepherd dog crawled its way to Nicholas and rolled onto its back.

Pino said, "That's remarkable! I've never seen our dog act that way to a stranger."

Nicholas smiled. "I have that effect on many animals. I was born with a gift. Your dog looks like she's about to give birth to a litter. What's her name?"

"Her name is Sun," Constance answered, "because she's the brightest dog we've ever known. Yes, it's true, she will soon go into labor. I pray we make it to the Mission in time."

"Oh, I think we'll make it just fine. Let's get started. We should arrive at the Mission by sunset."

On the mountain trail, Nicholas explained the purpose of the Mission and detailed its history. The newcomers asked many questions, and by the time they reached the southern gate, they were beaming with enthusiasm and more than ready to hear what Nicholas thought about their helping in some way. But that would have to wait. Bernadette and Joseph appeared outside the southern gate as they came to a stop.

Joseph called to Constance, "My child, my child, how good it does my heart to see you! Is this your husband who rides by your side?"

"That he is, my dear friend," said Constance, "and I must say I've missed your visits these past years. But tell me, how is it you are comfortable in the company of other people. No more solitude?"

"Oh, I wouldn't go that far, but I do get along much more comfortably with Mission folk. It helps when people around me are likeminded. Come, let's bring the horses to the stable and get you a home-cooked dinner. You must be famished after your journey here."

Joseph retrieved the magni-tube from Nicholas, then greeted Pino, while Constance dismounted and kissed Joseph's cheek.

Before Nicholas had fairly hit the ground, Bernadette met him, embracing him in silence. Closing her eyes, she drew in his scent, relieved beyond words that he'd returned unharmed.

Their embrace went on until Bernadette broke the silence. "I prayed every moment for your safety. What happened with the Ficci brothers? And where is Ricardo? Has he been hurt?"

"Ricardo is fine. I'll tell you the whole story when we sit down to that home-cooked meal Joseph was talking about. In the meantime, has anything new happened since we left?"

"So much has happened," Bernadette replied, leading him to the Bellicinis' house, "I don't know where to begin.

CHAPTER 61. THE MISSIONARIES UPDATE NICHOLAS.

$\mathcal{W}$alking hand in hand with Nicholas, Bernadette exploded with excitement as they made their way across Mission grounds from the south gate.

"So much has happened, I don't know where to begin. I guess it all started the day you left with the Captain. After that rousing applause for his departure, Daisy and Rose, and the older boy Ben brought from Rome, Roberto, began working with Ben on several projects for Mission gifts. They were secretive about what they were doing, not wanting anyone to see until you returned. Perhaps after dinner we could take a peek in their workshop. I'm dying to see what they've done.

"The morning after you left, your traveling missionary monks returned. Dominic, Thomas, James and Jude are such a witty bunch; they had me laughing all afternoon. They said they have plenty of names and would give their report as soon as you returned. They'll be at dinner as well.

"Last but not least, Mario Fuso has been seen going in and out of the northern workshop, right next to yours. He seems to be undercover as well, locking the door every time he wheels his chair in or out. So my dear, you have much to catch up on and many secrets to uncover."

Putting his arm around Bernadette's shoulder, Nicholas gently drew her close and kissed her. "I love you, sweet, and I can hardly wait to see and hear what our Mission's been up to. Where will the dinner be this evening?"

"At the Bellicinis'. They have the only dining room large enough until the Grand Hall has a roof on it. Can you smell the garlic and seafood, and fresh baked bread wafting over from their house?"

Pulling her hand to his lips, Nicholas said, "Indeed. I'm so thankful you're in my life, Bernadette. At this very moment, I don't remember ever being more happy or content."

Taking his hand to her lips, Bernadette kissed him. "My feelings are a mirror to yours. The love you give is sublime, and if you love me one tenth as much as you love God, I am truly blessed more than any woman."

Arm in arm they entered the Bellicini home.

The dining room table had two additional tables set at the far end to accommodate the thirty seated missionaries, busy in conversation and laughter. Makande stepped in from the kitchen and, seeing Nicholas with Bernadette, grabbed Ox's cane and sternly rapped it to the floor. The room became quiet until they turned to see Nicholas standing in the doorway with Bernadette.

When applause broke out and everyone stood, Nicholas blushed, holding up his arm as if to request they not make a fuss over him.

Ox approached first and asked, "Is it over, Nicholas? Is it finally over?"

"Yes, Ox, it's over," Nick replied. "When Ricardo returns from San Marco, we will know for sure if the Italian government has exonerated you and your family. But trust me, we had enough evidence to put the Ficcis in jail for two lifetimes...if they were still alive."

A silence came over the room, all eyes on Nicholas as he motioned for them to be seated.

After Brother Taylor said a blessing, and several monks brought in the food, Nicholas related the story. When he told of how greed had caused the soldiers to systematically shoot one another until only one remained, the dinner guest were struck silent, riveted to the story. But soon applause broke out when they heard of Fernando's search for his long lost cousin, ironically discovering it was Ricardo, one of the men who saved him.

"Ricardo is now on his way to San Marco with Fernando to see General Emeliano. According to what Sergeant Vance wrote in his notebook, the General is an honorable man, who fought beside Vance in Genoa. If all goes well, the Bellicini family should be acquitted of all charges by the end of the week."

"Will Ricardo return to Barcelona with Fernando after they've seen the General?" asked Raven from across the table. "He must be beside himself to see his father."

"No, Raven," said Nicholas. "He told me he'd come back for you and take you to his beloved Spain to meet his father. He said he wanted a season of celebration."

"Did he say we would make our home in Spain?"

"He said he loved his work here, and the two of you have made plans to build a home by the north gate."

Giddy with delight, Raven rose from her seat and danced her way to Nicholas, kissing him on the cheek. "Thank you for everything, Nicholas. If it weren't for your wise advise, I know both Ricardo and I would never have come this far."

Blushing again, Nicholas grinned. "It was my pleasure, Raven. Now, will someone please tell me what's been going on in my absence?"

Brother Taylor indicated four young monks at the far end of the table. "Yesterday, our traveling mission team returned from their assignment, a little prematurely if you ask me, but I must say they brought enough names to keep us busy for quite some time. I'll let Brother Jude explain."

Washing his bread down with a gulp of cider, Jude stood. "Nicholas, I'm sure you're aware that, even though we all know heavy competition is sinful, my brothers Dominic, Thomas, James and I stand here guilty before you. Being as young as we are, our zeal to excel, and ambition for success has negated, and even blinded us to the negative effects of competition."

Nicholas chuckled and broke in, "So this is the future, is it? I can't wait to hear the entire explanation. Go on, son."

"To add to the sin of competition, both teams became prideful as well. Even though Dominic and Thomas went north and James and I rode south, both teams wanted to return first with the most names of people in need, and to better the other team. Somehow, we all met on the road to Pizal two days ago and realized how we all shared the same sin. But then after we discussed it in depth, we felt the end justified the means and none of us feels the slightest bit guilty any more, only that we didn't bring enough names."

Nicholas glanced at Brother Taylor, who was rolling his eyes by now, and then to the young monks, who were smiling; confident Jude made their case well. Nicholas grinned and said, "You should've been a lawyer, Jude. In your explanation, you start off saying you all stand guilty before me, and then, before you finish, you're not the slightest bit guilty of anything except not bringing enough names. Although I'm not exactly sure how you arrived at innocence from confessed guilt in the same paragraph, I do believe you are all thinking responsibly about your actions. I wish I had had the drive to do good with as much enthusiasm as the four of you when I was as young. Though the sins you speak about are minor ones, I have no doubt they are forgiven and have, in an odd way, managed to entertain everyone here at the table. Now that this is all behind us, tell me about the people you met."

As the young monks bolted from their chairs, pushing each other to bring their lists to Nicholas first, Bernadette held back her laughter and laid her hand on his. "I told you they were characters, Nicholas. Was I right?"

Nicholas nodded, then after reading the lists, he looked up and found Constance and Pino across the table. "For everyone who has not been intro-duced, here are Constance and Pino Aviono. They have come to help teach the deaf to speak in hand signs. After reading the list the boys brought back, I see there are at least three people on the list who are deaf and in need of instruction."

Leaning across the table, Nick spoke to them more privately. "We'll talk about this more tomorrow, but for now you can think about the possi-bility of staying at the Mission for a while and teaching several monks and nuns how to sign. Pino, perhaps when those pups are born, you might teach them to be guide dogs for the blind. I see here on the list at least two names. If your dog Sun is as intelligent as you say, the pups would learn very quickly. And then when they're grown, you could plan your own Mission trip. What do you think?"

Constance leaned over, kissed her husband and said, "Thank you, Pino, for sharing my vision. Do you like his idea about Sun?"

Pino reached for her hand and kissed it. "It's brilliant. I don't know why I didn't think of that myself. Sun went into the stable when we came to dinner. This might be the night she delivers."

Nick invited the couple to stay at his home for the evening until they were set up with more permanent lodging. The couple agreed, then left to check on the condition of their dog.

After dinner, Nick saw Mario Fuso at the other end of the table and waved his hand, catching his attention.

Mario rolled his chair back and joined him. As Bernadette pulled her chair to the side a bit, Mario squeezed in between them. "What do you need, Nick?"

"Everything I need is right here at this table, Mario," said Nicholas. "I just wanted to see what you've been up to."

Ben appeared and sat across the table in Pino's empty chair.

Mario reached for a piece of bread crust and nibbled it as he said, "I finished all the plans for the Mission a week ago, and now I've begun something new. If you've finished your dinner I'd like to show you, and see what you think."

"My curiosity won't last another minute. Let's go, Mario!"

As he and Bernadette rose from the table, Ben stood as well and said, "I have something to show you also. May I join you?"

"By all means, my brother," said Nick. "I'm starting to get the feeling the Mission's moving forward again now that we're not running any more."

Chapter 62. Toy Makers.

*A*s the group walked to the northern section of the Mission grounds, Mario wheeled his chair, telling them what inspired him to return to his work as a silversmith. "It all started when I began to have dreams again, soon after I finished the plans for the Mission. This time I had the same dream night after night.

"The dream begins with me sitting on a stool in front of my old silver shop in Pizal. As I glance up the street, Nicholas appears about twenty paces away with a curious smile, holding a little red sack. As he approaches, I glance in the silver shop window and see a necklace, a ring, a bracelet, and a formal silver stewpot on a red doily. Then I wake up.

"The dreams are such that I see the designs on the four objects clearly and cannot dismiss them from my thoughts. Anyway, I took all my wages and gave them to Ben, asking him to go to the bank in Pizal and exchange the gold florins for silver bars. When he returned, he not only came with the silver, but also with all the hardware from my burnt-out silver shop, including my smelting oven."

Bernadette asked, "So what do you think the dreams mean, Mario?"

"I don't quite know, that's why I need your help."

After he unlocked the door and everyone stepped inside, Mario lit two lamps and guided the group to his workbench. Reaching onto a shelf under a table, he came up with a hand-engraved, wooden jewelry box. He opened it, and pulled out a rolled black velvet cloth. As he undid the cloth, Bernadette gasped with delight as a thin silver necklace with a delicate oval pendent in the center was revealed. On the pendent, Mario had engraved an orchid with swirling leaves and stem.

"Someone please say something," Mario urged.

"It is so lovely, Mario," said Bernadette. "This necklace is perfect for any woman to wear at any time. It is beautiful and simple, yet elegant... very charming indeed."

"Let me ask you a question, Mario," said Nick. "Whose life, in your opinion, would benefit most, having possession of the necklace? Think carefully."

Mario paused a moment, then replied, "This may sound strange, but I have a friend in Pizal who would do just about anything to give a necklace like this to his wife. He is a very hard-working man whose life never seems to settle from troubles. He works as a blacksmith day and night, and if it's not someone robbing from his business, it's his children getting sick or his landlord complaining about back rent. I've never known a time he wasn't struggling. He loves his wife more than anything, and he told me, one Christmas Eve, how wonderful it would be to give his wife a gift of some value. Something that would make her think he was not born to lose in every step of life, but something small enough to be easily hidden from thieves if necessary. Yes, Nicholas, my friend could really use this necklace."

"May I make a suggestion?" asked Nick.

"Please, go right ahead."

Nicholas reached for the necklace and held it by the lamp. "Well, first I'd like to say I'm thrilled the workshops are already producing such quality items, especially in view of the fact that it wasn't too long ago the Mission was only an idea floating around in my head. But with regard to your necklace, I think it would be in line with the spirit of the Mission if you gave your friend the necklace before Christmas this year. The custom of giving gifts during Christmas is spreading, and this Christmas season we will partake in that custom, only our gifts will be given anonymously."

Mario interrupted. "I'm glad you said that, because my friend would never accept the necklace if I offered it to him. He would feel he needed to pay for it." He smiled. "That is why I never made him anything before. How do you think we could get it into his hands?"

"That's the fun part, Mario," said Nicholas, admiring the craftsmanship of the necklace. "If he happens to find it in a little red sack that's sitting on the seat of his supply wagon when he returns from his errand, well, then he'll just have to open the sack and see what he's found. And when he realizes it was a gift from who knows who, he'll start to believe God meant him to have it. And then he'll believe the gift was a blessing from Heaven, and if you can get a person to believe in any capacity...well, then, anything can happen."

"That's a great plan, Nick," said Mario. "You took the red sack idea right from my dream. It all makes so much sense now. But I still need to make the ring and bracelet and stewpot. What will I do with them?"

Nicholas replied, "Rest assured, by the time you're finished making them, you'll know exactly who to give them to and why. If you just think in the same way when you told us about your friend, you can't go wrong. And besides, if you become confused, you can talk it over with any one of us."

"He's right, Mario," added Ben. "If you need us, just say the word, and when the time comes I'll take your necklace myself and secretly put it in its proper place. Then I'll follow the man home and tell you everything that happens."

Ben turned to Nicholas. "Now, you must come with me to your workshop. I've been working with my soon-to-be daughters, Daisy and Rose, and also Roberto, the boy I brought back from Rome."

"What a day this has been," said Nick, "and now you tell me there are more surprises."

After locking Mario's door, the group set off to Nicholas' workshop.

"What you're all going to behold now is just plain remarkable," said Ben, leading the way. "Something extraordinary has happened to Daisy and Rose, after their miracle. Though the girls are small for their age, they are making up for it in talent. Two days ago I visited Maria to discuss our upcoming wedding, and she came to the door in tears, leading me into the girls' room. I wept too as we sat on the edge of the bed watching the twins cut rows of dolls and butterflies and flowers from folded paper. They cut the paper with the skill and agility of a grown adult. We marveled when in a matter of minutes they opened the folded paper and stretched out a row of birds in flight. When they saw the dumbfounded look on our faces, they laughed.

"Without a moment's hesitation, I took the girls to your workshop and introduced them to your tools and raw materials. Within minutes, Daisy created the most beautiful rag doll I've ever seen, rosy-cheeked smile and all. Then, when I turned to Rose, she'd created a matching boy doll that worked together with Daisy's perfectly. The most remarkable thing about it is that no one taught them anything. When they finish a piece, they always giggle the cutest way you've ever heard."

Arriving at the door to the workshop, Ben continued, "They've been in here at least twelve hours a day since you left with the Captain. They say it's too much fun to stop, or they have too many ideas and not enough time. They're only eleven-years-old. What do you think?"

"I think we should go in and look at the work," Nicholas replied, "and then we'll see."

As Ben opened the door the twins screamed with excitement, scurrying to cover their latest creations. Bernadette laughed, but then quickly became solemn in prayer, remembering the first day she'd met the palsied twins, convulsed and twisted without a shred of hope.

After they spread kisses to everyone, the twins ran to the worktable.

"I want to show him," Daisy demanded.

"No, I want to show him," Rose argued.

Ben broke in, "Now don't fight. Show us together."

They lifted up one end of the blanket and picked up a male doll, bringing it to Ben. As he took the doll into his hands, Bernadette cried out, "Will you look at what we have here? That is the most remarkable doll I've ever seen!"

The doll was a replica of Ben, with his mask, his hat, and even a hand-sewn miniature copy of his uniform, complete with the black leather sash and red trim falling down across his chest. Ben paused for a moment, then asked, "Is this doll for me?"

The girls chuckled at the same time. "No, silly, it's for Mommy."

Daisy added, "We want her to know who our hero is."

Unable to speak, Ben simply squatted down and embraced them both. After kissing his mask over and over, the girls turned and ran to the worktable. "Come see, come see all the other toys."

When the group reached the table, the twins threw off a sheet and revealed a stuffed lamb, a hand-made painted flowerpot, and a host of painted paper cutout decorations.

Nicholas took his cap off and scratched his head, squatting down in front of the girls. "This is a great day for Hope Mission. Daisy, Rose, you have been given a very special gift from God. How do you get the ideas to create these dolls?"

Holding a doll of Makande, Daisy replied, "We don't know. They just come into our thoughts, and then we have fun making the ideas come to life."

Nicholas stood, turning to Ben. "I think it's a wonderful idea for them to come here and be creative, as long as they attend their time at school and they have some guidance in the workshop."

"I've been here with them from the beginning," Ben said. "I kept myself busy with them by making something entirely new. When I was in Pizal last, I saw our friendly dove swoop down and fly into an alley behind the village bakery, so I followed it. I found it sitting on a garbage heap, pecking at the remains of an old broken violin. The dove flew onto my shoulder and I really felt I should take the broken instrument back to the Mission and make a new one. Don't ask me why, but does that make any sense?"

"The dove has never made any worldly sense," said Nicholas, placing a hand on Ben's shoulder. "After you finish making the violin, go back to where you found it and try to find out how the old one was broken and why it was thrown out. By now, I know our friendly dove always has a good reason to intervene in human affairs. Now, if you would, please tell me about young Roberto. What's he been doing?"

"Come to the table on the other side of the room, folks," Ben replied. "He has an uncanny ability to make games of skill and other interesting toys. On this side of the table are tops, colored blocks, and game sticks. And over here you can see a board game and a wooden sword."

Tickled by the variety of toys laid out before them, Bernadette said, "Nicholas, imagine taking a sack full of these toys down to the orphanage this Christmas Eve. Imagine the look on all those precious faces when they wake up and find a toy by their bed, created just for them."

Nicholas turned to Ben and Mario, pointing to Bernadette. "Has God not blessed me with the perfect match, men?"

As Ben and Mario affirmed his question, Nicholas kissed Bernadette, then continued, "This Christmas will turn out to be very special indeed, but we must also be diligent in working through the rest of the year, finding where the most need is and addressing it."

After walking Bernadette to her room at the Bellicini home, Nicholas returned to his house to make sure Constance and Pino were comfortable. Makande had already prepared the guest room and the couple had gone to sleep, weary after their long journey from Rome.

Not long after, Nicholas slid into bed content and fulfilled, as images of the toys he'd just seen popped into his mind. His vision of the Mission was emerging into reality with surprise and delight. Now he would begin to work on the list the young monks had given him at dinner. In the morning, he'd review the list and begin to organize the work. But for now, sleep beckoned, while visions of the coming Christmas carried him into flamboyant dreams.

Chapter 63. The Rescue of Three Maidens.

arlier that day, Ricardo and Fernando had arrived at Anna's house while Nicholas was on his way up the mountain with Constance and Pino. Helping Fernando off his horse and into the house, Ricardo stopped at the doorway, showing his cousin the panel Ben had carved for Anna and Michael, telling him the story of the wolves.

When Anna came out, she kissed her foster-son, and led Fernando to the kitchen, changing his bandage immediately. Ricardo related the fantastic story of his reunion with his cousin, and the thrilling news of his father's survival. Anna was beside herself with joy for them, but warned Ricardo not to travel with Fernando any more that day. She wanted to make a temporary open-toe shoe for him before they journeyed to San Marco.

Ricardo agreed and set out to the village tanner's shop to buy leather for Fernando's special boot. On his way, he stopped at the inn for lunch.

While sipping ale and waiting for his meal, he overheard a conversation at the table behind him. Two men were discussing the price to be paid for the sale of the daughters of one of the men. As soon as Ricardo heard the word 'bankruptcy', he surmised the man selling his daughters was a nobleman whose business had finally failed, leaving no dowry for his children.

When the men struck a deal and left, Ricardo followed the nobleman to his home. He peered through the parlor window at the side of the house, and saw the dismay with which the man's three daughters heard the news. Tears ensued, and they fell to his feet begging for any other fate.

Ricardo's heart sank when the father left the room in tears at having brought this disgrace upon his own household. He mounted his horse and rode to the tanner, purchased the leather and returned briefly to Anna's house, where he told Fernando he had to attend an urgent matter and would return by morning. After taking his leave, he set off to the mountain trail. If anyone had a solution to the problem it was Nicholas Kristo.

Arriving just after dinner, Ricardo looked into the dining room and caught Nicholas' attention. Seeing his urgent expression, Nick took him to a guest room where Ricardo told him about the dowerless maidens. Nick paused a long moment, then said, "And you're sure you heard the nobleman say his daughters did not have a dowry and he was bankrupt?"

"Yes, sir, exactly," said Ricardo, "but you had to see their reaction when their father told them he had no other recourse but literally to sell them. Those maidens were so distraught, it tore my heart to witness it."

"How did you manage to witness it?"

"I rode to their house and sneaked to the side window."

"I can see it will take quite a bit more time to quell that adventurous nature of yours, but you were right to return and find a way to prevent this tragedy. This is one time when gold might save those maids from a cruel fate.

"Go to the stables at the southern gate and look for Captain Ficci's saddlebags. You'll find sacks of gold coins. Take three and return to the house of the nobleman. You must find a way to get the gold into the house before morning. Use you imagination, son, but get the gold in there secretly before the sun comes up."

Ricardo thanked Nicholas, embraced him, then left in haste, riding straight to the stable for the gold. He made his way back down the moonlit mountain trail, hoping he'd find an opened window or door waiting when he arrived.

He made it to the edge of the village in just over two hours, and tied his horse to the hitching post at Anna's house. Throwing the saddlebags over his shoulders, he hurried to the nobleman's house. Every sound echoed in the deserted streets, so he was careful not to stir a dog or make a sound that might bring attention to his mission.

When he reached the front gate, he followed a stone wall around to the side of the house and climbed over. He sought a way inside, but the house was locked down.

Hearing a chirp, he glanced up and saw the shadow of a bird fly to the roof and land on the chimney. All at once it came to him; he'd get the gold into the house through the chimney! Since it was summer, no live coals were likely to be in the fireplace.

He assessed the size of the chimney. It was long and wide enough to allow the gold to drop straight down. Ricardo crept to the back of the house, finding a lattice that led to the second floor, and then a small angular roof directly connected to the upper roof. Quiet as a scout, he began his way up until he arrived at the base of the chimney, where he quickly removed the gold from the saddlebags. Perched on the top of the chimney, the Mission's friendly white dove was revealed by the moonlight. Ricardo thought, *Divine guidance indeed.*

After taking off his calfskin jacket, he removed his burgundy cotton shirt and laid it onto the roof, placing the gold sacks in the center, using the sleeves to tie it off. Next, he put his jacket on and looked down into the chimney. He felt neither smoke nor heat, so he dropped the package. When it hit the bottom, he was surprised to hear so little noise. Apparently, the sack had hit a large pile of ash and half-burnt wood.

Ricardo hurried down, and when he made it back to the lattice, he looked into the window that faced the fireplace. Staring back at him on the other side was a young girl, who screamed at the sight of him.

Ricardo jumped the rest of the way down and ran as fast as he could to Anna's.

After the maiden awakened her father, her sisters joined them in front of the fireplace. The heavy gold had thrown ash and woodchips halfway across the parlor when the sack landed, so they saw it at once.

The nobleman pulled the burgundy sack out and opened it, revealing the gold. He wept, surmising a rich, saintly merchant had heard of his dilemma and decided to save him and his family.

As the daughters danced in celebration with their mother, the nobleman asked the daughter who had awakened him if she had seen anything after the gold had been dropped.

"Yes, Father," said the eldest daughter. "After I heard the thump in the fireplace, I went to the window and saw a man climbing down the lattice."

"Was it someone we know? Did you recognize him?"

Taking the burgundy shirt from the floor, the maiden replied, "I didn't recognize him, but this must be his shirt, for when I saw him through the window he wore only his jacket and a bare chest. He was exceedingly handsome, with black silken hair and a thin mustache with a small patch of hair under his lip."

On hearing her description, the nobleman remembered seeing a young man like that at the inn earlier that day. He must have overheard the conversation and decided, for whatever reason, to save his family. Overwhelming gratitude swelled in the father's heart. He decided that, come morning, he'd to go into the village to seek and thank the young man, offering a lifetime of service.

It was past noon when Ricardo woke to a smother of kisses from Raven. She'd come down from the Mission in the early morning, wanting to surprise him, and to ask if she could travel with him and Fernando to San Marco.

Still half asleep, Ricardo smiled as the kisses kept coming like rose petals falling onto his face. When he opened his eyes fully, he saw Raven standing over him, smiling, holding a breakfast tray with fruit, biscuits, and berry juice.

"When did you arrive, love of my life?" he asked.

Placing the tray over his lap, Raven answered, "About an hour ago. You never sleep this late. You must've been up half the night on a mission for Nicholas?"

"How did you know about that?"

"Because, when you returned to the Mission last night, I saw you run from the guest room after talking to Nicholas. Judging by how quickly you left, I presumed he sent you on an urgent assignment."

"You're right, my love, and I was up half the night. But I managed to get the job done. Have you met my cousin Fernando?"

Fernando limped into the room and joined them. "Raven and I are old friends by now, Ricardo. We thought you would sleep the rest of the day. I must say, cousin, you have chosen the most beautiful women in all of Italy to be your wife."

"Thank you," said Ricardo as he reached for Raven's hand. "She is truly the most beautiful, and her heart is as pure as she is lovely."

Raven blushed. "My love, I brought enough money and supplies for us to travel to Barcelona after you finish your business in San Marco. Please say you're not angry, but Nicholas told us everything last night, and he said that you would return and take me to Spain to meet your father."

"I'm not angry at all, Raven," Ricardo said. "This will save me a trip back to the mountain after we're done in San Marco. But we're not out of danger until we've dealt with the Judge Magistrate."

When Ricardo finished his breakfast, he rummaged through his old clothes and found a shirt to replace the one he'd left at the nobleman's house. After saying farewell to Anna, the group mounted their horses and rode through the main street in Pizal toward the north road.

As they passed the nobleman's house on the far side of the village, a rider approached from behind and called out, "Young man, will you yield for a moment? Please, I must speak to you."

Ricardo slowed to a stop, knowing it was the nobleman's voice. Turning to Raven and Fernando, he said, "I must speak to this man in private. It was him I had business with yesterday and I'm not sure Nicholas would have anyone know how we helped him."

Raven and Fernando agreed and rode ahead, while Ricardo waited for the man.

Taking his hat off as he approached, the nobleman smiled. "Thank you for yielding, sir. I'll only take a bit of your time."

"How can I be of help to you, sir?"

With his voice cracking, the nobleman stretched out his hands and said, "You have already helped as if you were sent from God Himself. My daughter saw you after you climbed down from my roof last night. I don't know why you chose to help my family, but I'm eternally grateful, and commit my services to you in any way for the remainder of my life."

"It was not my gold that has released you from the dilemma you faced regarding your daughters," replied Ricardo, struck by the man's emotion. "I was only the messenger who overheard your problem at the inn yesterday. Your daughters' benefactor wishes to remain anonymous and would have you consider the dowries a gift from God. He knows your heart was torn and that you were driven to despair, and that's one reason he decided to help. Another reason had everything to do with keeping your daughters chaste; their dignity intact."

"And that to my eternal shame, is something I should have managed for myself," said the nobleman. "Please tell the man of God, I owe him my life, and I will die before ever again jeopardizing my children. And if he is in need of anything from this day forward, please send word through you and I will respond."

"Sir, the only request he has right now is to charge you and your family with an oath of silence regarding the gold."

The nobleman put his hand over his heart and said, "On my life I promise."

Smiling, Ricardo turned his horse and cantered after Raven and Fernando.

Chapter 64. Fernando Confronts the General.

After joining Fernando and Raven in the dining room of the San Marco Hotel, Ricardo handed his cousin a document and Sergeant Vance's journal. "I just met Brother Santos in the stable. He gave me the purchase order and said he'd hold the gold until he hears from us. He said he would've loved to join us but is fasting."

As the innkeeper brought in bowls of venison stew, bread and cheese, Fernando presented an idea to Ricardo. "I think it'd be wiser if I went alone to the Judge Magistrate and General Emeliano. This whole matter has to do with official government business. If you and Raven are present, it'll look suspicious."

"But . . ." Ricardo broke in.

Fernando pressed on, "You must trust my plan to deal with the Judge and General alone, cousin. It'll end the matter once and for all. You and Raven can meet me here tomorrow. If I don't show up, you'll know something went wrong, and at least you'll be free to bring others to help."

Though reluctant to miss any adventure, Ricardo gave way to Fernando's reasoning. He told his cousin that in the morning he'd bring Raven to the same house his father stayed when they visited San Marco on business. They'd return to the hotel before evening and wait for word from him.

The next morning, several hours after sunrise, Fernando was dressed and out of the hotel on his way to the stable. With sweaty hands he saddled his horse, put his good foot in the stirrup, and mounted up. The thought of maneuvering past the Judge Magistrate, knowing he was on Captain Ficci's payroll, put a knot in his stomach.

On his ride to the command post, soldiers began to appear. He recognized some that were sent back by Sergeant Vance, and they waved, beckoning him to stop and tell what happened after their departure. Fernando brushed them off, telling them he had to make his official report before speaking to anyone.

After tying his horse to a fence at the Command Post, he kept silent in spite of the barrage of questions from soldiers surrounding him. More nervous than he'd ever been, Fernando pushed his way through to Judge Impastato's office, straightening his feathered hat, and pulling his jacket taut.

As he entered the room, a gravelly voice called out, "What is it, who are you? I don't see anyone until 11 o'clock. Well, speak up, soldier."

"Judge Impastato," squeaked the young soldier, "I'm Private Fernando Cruz, and I've returned from Pizal with urgent news concerning Captain Ficci and Sergeants Ficci and Vance."

"Well, it's about time," barked the judge, stroking his white beard. "Come closer, man, and speak up. Where is Captain Ficci? Is he on his way to San Marco?"

Fernando stepped up clearing his throat. "Forgive me, Judge, but I've been instructed by Captain Ficci to give my official report to General Emeliano only."

"Is that so, Cruz?" said the judge, leaning back, scratching his bald head. "Why would the captain ever want to bypass the chain of command? I think you'd better hand in that report before I have you put in irons and thrown in jail until you're ready to cooperate."

"Put up with me only one more minute, Judge," said Fernando, laying a hand on his heart. "The captain told me you might not understand this strange request, then handed me twelve pounds of gold coins for you to keep until his return. He said he'd explain everything very soon, only you must allow me to report to the General."

The Judge twisted his mustache and lowered a brow, mumbling, "Why in the world would he ever seek Emeliano? He's on the other side of the fence."

"If I may, Judge, the Captain said you might be confused by his tactics, and if so, to ask you to remember the game of chess you and he were playing with the rest of the world."

After a long pause the Judge motioned for Fernando to come closer. "All right, Cruz, bring the gold to my office and I will set up a meeting with the General this afternoon."

"Bear with me this one last time, Judge Impastato," begged Fernando. "The Captain said the gold should remain in my possession until after I've seen the General so others might not become suspicious of collusion between him and you. He said only then will his strategy have a chance to succeed. Quite frankly Judge, I can't say that I understand anything about the chess game or anything I've told you, but the Captain said you would."

"Well, then, Cruz. I trust you've written your report already?"

"No, sir," replied Fernando. "The Captain said I should give a verbal report directly to the General from memory."

Pausing a long moment, staring at Fernando, the Judge rose. "Come along with me, Cruz. I'll take you to the General myself. As soon as the report is given, I want you to report back to me and we'll get that gold in a safe place."

Wiping sweat from his brow, Fernando followed him to the top floor and waited outside the General's office, while the Judge entered and updated him. After what seemed like eternity, the Judge came out, and held the door open, motioning for Fernando to come in.

He rubbed the moisture from his hands onto his breeches and hobbled past the Judge, who left him alone with the General.

The General leaned against his desk. "Come in, soldier. Don't be afraid, I won't take your head off. I hear you've come with a sensitive report regarding Captain Ficci's command mission to Pizal."

While small in stature, the General made up for it in confidence. He had a studied brow and majestic brown beard. His highly decorated uniform fitted to perfection, with his chest lifted slightly, making him look all the more the part.

Sitting on a couch that faced the balcony was a young lady Fernando thought to be quite attractive, until she turned to look at him. An infirmity caused her left eye and the left side of her mouth to droop. Looking farther down he saw that her left hand was withered and limp, frail, without muscle.

Realizing that Fernando had noticed the girl, the General explained, "This is my daughter, Angelina. She was born with some sort of malady no doctor in all of Italy can figure out. Her mother died giving birth to her, and so she's all I have. But, please, Angelina is very quiet, go right ahead and give your report, soldier."

Fernando began at the beginning and told the General everything he'd witnessed, or even heard, while on the mission with the Captain. After hearing about the slaughter of the wolves and the shooting of the Captain by his brother, the General interrupted. "You mean to tell me Sergeant Vance saw Sergeant Ficci aim his weapon directly at the Captain?"

"Yes, General Emeliano, and afterward, Sergeant Vance accused Sergeant Ficci of trying to murder his brother. Sergeant Ficci then raised a pistol towards Sergeant Vance and threatened him. That's when Sergeant Vance announced he was relieving Sergeant Ficci of his command."

"What happened to the Captain? Was he dead?"

"No General, but wounded very badly. A man named Nicholas Kristo emerged out of the fog and said there were people on the mountain not far away that might be able to save him. Sergeant Vance allowed Nicholas to take him, realizing the mission he'd been sent on had drastically changed."

"What about the Bellicini family?" asked the General. "Were they up on the mountain? And who is this Nicholas, where did he come from?"

"Nicholas is a man of God who was hiding the Bellicini family somewhere on the mountain. He believed the family to be innocent, and now so do I, sir." Fernando took Vance's journal out of his jacket and handed it to the General. "I think you'd better read this before I continue my report, sir. It's Sergeant Vance's daily journal."

The General, now curious by the turn of events, took the notebook and walked to balcony window, sat down in a cushioned chair next to his daughter, and read. After several minutes, he stood. "Did you read this notebook, Fernando?"

"Yes, sir, I did."

As he stared at the book, the General's voice softened. "I fought with Vance in Genoa, and I knew him to be a man of honor; a real patriot. The journal says the Bellicini family had been unjustly pursued for the murder of three soldiers several months ago. Do you know any more than what he's written?"

"Before my return to San Marco, I spoke with Raven Bellicini, who was an eyewitness to the ordeal. She said after the soldiers shot her parents, her brother Ox walked in, saw them lying in a pool of blood, and lost control."

The General stood and began to pace, frowning. "What happened to the Ficci brothers?"

After Fernando explained all that had happened, the General poured two glasses of port wine, handing one to Fernando, inviting him to sit.

Fernando took a seat next to Angelina and, sipping his port, reached into his jacket, pulling out the purchase order that proved the Captain a traitor. "One more thing, General. When several men lifted the Captain's dead body onto his horse, this document fell out of his pocket. I think it may explain a few things."

The General finished his drink and reached for the paper, walking to the balcony window. After a quick examination, he massaged his forehead, then rubbed his eyes. "Do you realize what you've found, son?"

"I'm not sure of all the names on the document, sir, but even though the Captain is dead, it looks like he's better off that way rather than to have to face the Italian authorities as a traitor."

"You're right, soldier, but there's more," said the General, pacing excitedly. "Although the document doesn't mention the amount the Captain was to pay the Duke of Guise, I would guess that ten race horses would be worth the gold he had in his saddlebags. One of the reasons I was sent to this command post was to find the traitor who's been leaking information to the French. This document proves it was Captain Ficci. But what we didn't know was who'd been dipping his hand into the Italian treasury. Did you notice the signature at the very bottom of the document?"

"I did, sir, but the signature was scribbled."

"It's the signature of Judge Impastato. He's the one who brought you to my office. So, with this one document, you've helped us pinpoint the traitors and expose a high-ranking judge, corrupting our justice system to the extreme."

Watching Angelina stand and limp to her father's side, Fernando joined them. "May I change the subject, General?"

"Go right ahead, Fernando, we're through with this investigation anyway."

"Raven Bellicini spoke of a man on the mountain who has the gift of healing. She told of a blind man who received his sight, and palsied twins who were healed completely. Perhaps a visit to Nicholas Kristo and his friend the healer might end in a normal life for your daughter."

Angelina reached for her father's hand, staring at him desperately.

"I have never been a religious man," the General replied. "But at this point, we just might pay him a visit."

The General put his arm around Fernando's shoulder. "You've done a fine job, son, a fine job indeed. I'll put you in for a promotion at once."

"If it's all the same to you, sir," said Fernando, pointing to his missing toes, "I would like to return to my father's olive trees in Barcelona. I've had enough adventure for two lifetimes."

"Well, then, you're discharged as of this day. Before you leave, see my secretary and he'll draw up the appropriate papers. In the meantime, you need not bother reporting to the Judge. He'll be too busy explaining how his name found its way on that purchase order. And when he's finished lying about it, he'll smell the stench of the same jail he sent so many possible innocent souls to. I'll launch an investigation and find out who was unjustly imprisoned."

Fernando stood and saluted the General. "General Emeliano, if only I could've served under a great man like you from the start, I might have wanted to stay in the Army for life."

The General smiled. "Fernando, if these recent events had not unfolded exactly as they did, the Ficci brothers would still be alive to murder the innocent. And evil judges like Impastato would still be fixed in their positions of power, and good people like you and the Bellicini family would still be subject to their random treachery. Go to your father's olive trees now, and begin a new life in peace, son."

Fernando turned and limped his way out of the General's office, going directly to the secretary to receive his discharge papers. Not having waited more than five minutes, the secretary's door opened and Judge Impastato walked in looking for Fernando. Before he could say a word, the secretary reached for his sleeve, saying "Excuse me, Judge Impastato, General Emeliano wishes to see you at once."

Surprised, the Judge glared at Fernando suspiciously. Fernando removed his feathered hat, locked eyes with the Judge and said, "Checkmate!"

Chapter 65. Christmas is Drawing Near.

Four months passed, and the Christmas season made work at Hope Mission a joyous activity, with production of specialized gifts spreading to every workshop. All the building construction was complete, except for Raven's and Ricardo's home, which would be built according to their plans upon their return from Spain. Many of the monks who had worked on construction returned to their churches, and the Mission community had become considerably smaller but more intimate as a result.

Ben and Giovanni amazed everyone when they teamed up and made two violins, a wooden flute and a cello. Ben planned to give a guitar he'd made in secret to Giovanni on Christmas Eve.

Mario rarely left his workshop. He had finished the silver ring and bracelet of his dream, but the silver stewpot was still a work in progress.

Daisy, Rose and Roberto had created dozens of toys and games; more than enough to provide for the orphanage on Christmas Eve.

A month earlier, Maria and some of the nuns had persuaded Nicholas to send three monks to Rome to purchase a loom. This they had brought up the mountain in pieces and assembled in a workshop designed solely for fabric manufacturing.

Constance spent all of her days teaching the nuns to hand sign, and Pino was befriending the six pups of Sun's litter while he waited for them to be mature enough to begin their training as guide dogs for the blind.

Nicholas worked tirelessly to complete the list of prostheses and wheelchairs needed before the young brothers came back with a second list. After a short stay, the traveling missionaries were on their way again to deliver the newly-completed items.

Bernadette was becoming a master journalist as well as a prolific teacher, encompassing many subjects. She and Nicholas planned to marry on Christmas Day along with Ben and Maria. It would be a day no one would ever forget.

The first snowflakes of the year began to fall as Ricardo, his father Raphael, and Raven rode onto the main street in Pizal. After the couple married in Barcelona, and the celebration was over, Raphael decided to return with the newlyweds to see what Mission life was all about. He couldn't bear being away from his only son again after spending so many years in prison. For him, every day he saw the joy in his son's eyes was a miracle. He would live out his days spoiling his grandchildren and fishing in the mountain lake Ricardo talked so much about.

After stopping at Anna's house to introduce Raphael to the woman who had cared for him as her own, Ricardo led the way up the mountain trail. Several inches of snow had accumulated, so Ricardo decided not to stop until they reached the summit. He remembered the snowstorms that had dominated the weather the previous winter.

Pointing to the arrow hole in the warning sign at the foot of the mountain, Ricardo told his father the story of how he made the now-famous 'impossible shot' from so far away. The moment he finished the story, they heard a voice call out from a rider on the road ahead.

"Ricardo, is that you?" the voice echoed down.

The falling snow diminished visibility as Ricardo called back, "Yes, it's Ricardo. Is that you, Ben? What are you doing out in this snow? You know it could be a storm."

"If it becomes heavy and I can't make it back I'll stay in Pizal, but no matter what I'll be back in two days, in time for Christmas, and my wedding with Maria."

After Ben joined them, Ricardo lifted his arm toward Raphael. "Ben, this is my father, Raphael Cruz."

"So nice to finally meet you, sir," said Ben warmly. "You must be thankful to be reunited with your son."

Raphael glanced at Ricardo and Raven. "I've never been more thankful for anything, Ben. I not only have my son again but have also added the most beautiful daughter-in-law to our family. Ricardo told me so much about you, it's an honor to finally meet you, sir."

"I am honored as well, Raphael." Turning to Ricardo and Raven, Ben grinned under the mask. "We all knew you'd be married upon your return. How is life after matrimony, Raven?"

Raven smiled widely, her countenance glowing. "I am with child, Ben. Next summer I will give birth. If it's a boy, his name will be Justus, and if it is a girl she will be Elizabeth, to honor her grandmother."

"Ben, what brings you down the mountain in the snow?" asked Ricardo.

Indicating the sack he carried on the side of his horse, Ben replied, "The Mission made special gifts that need to be in the hands of a few deserving people before Christmas Eve. As soon as the gifts are delivered, I'll return. I'm so happy that you all returned when you did. This Christmas will be a very special one. But don't let me hold you up any more, I'll tell you everything on my return."

With that, Ben turned his horse onto the road to Pizal, as Ricardo's group continued the two-hour journey to the summit.

Chapter 66. The Broken Violin.

*T*he snow-covered cobblestone streets of Pizal were bustling with shoppers and merchants as Ben rode to the stables at the edge of village. When the blacksmith appeared, Ben recognized him as the man whose life Mario had described whose as a continual struggle. By the way the man carried himself, Ben discerned he was severely depressed. He was of a small, husky stature, with a long beard and no neck, and his back hunched a bit. His gaze never left the ground, as if his soul were lost down there.

After taking Ben's horse in and putting a feed-bag on its head, without once looking up, the blacksmith asked, "Will you be long, sir?"

"I may have to spend the night if the snow doesn't let up. I'll be back in an hour to tell you my plans."

With that, Ben walked into Pizal directly toward the alley where he'd found the broken violin. On his way, he wondered how to get the jewelry Mario created into the hands of the blacksmith and his wife in the required secrecy. In the meantime, he wanted to investigate the story of the violin.

An inch of snow covered the garbage in the alley where the dove had landed months earlier. As Ben walked to the spot where he'd found the violin, a strong wind blew in behind him, forming a snowdrift in the doorway of a stonemason's back door. Painted on the window, he read, "Mortar, Bricks, Ceramic Tiles, Expert Stonemasonry."

Stepping onto the stairs, Ben looked through the door window, seeing bricks and bags of mortar inventory stacked to the ceiling. To his left was a tile storage room, with a tall teenager standing next to a lantern resting on a pile of ceramic tiles.

The young man held a two-foot flat board under his chin, and his hand moved on the other end as if he were pretending it had the strings of a violin. As he pressed the board's imaginary strings, his voice provided the notes his fingers imagined. Wearing mason's gloves, his fingers flew up and down the board with great familiarity. He had curly black hair down to his shoulders, and his clothes were embedded with mortar dust. Tied around his knees were rags, most likely kneepads for laying tiles.

Ben tapped on the window, but the boy was too enchanted with his virtuoso performance to hear anything else. Ben gave the door a good kick and the boy turned, seeing Ben's mask peering through the window. The imaginary violin now became a club as the startled teenager called out, "Who are you? What do you want?"

"I mean you no harm, young man. May I have a word with you? I promise I won't take much of your time."

Taking the lantern to the door, the young man held the light to Ben's face. "You say you mean me no harm yet you wear a mask. Why do you hide your identity?"

"Underneath this mask is a face so mangled and scarred by fire, my only recourse is to wear a mask. Just give me a few minutes and I'll be on my way."

Opening the door and stepping back, the young man reeled as Ben ducked under the door and entered the room. His huge body and mysterious appearance caused the young man to keep his distance as he held the violin-club ready for anything.

With a soft voice, Ben asked, "Are you a stonemason for hire?"

The teenager strained a laugh. "No, sir. Sadly, I'm not for hire. I'm worse off than a slave. But that's *my* problem. How can I help you?"

"My name is Ben Bellicini and I am affiliated with Hope Orphanage. It's a brand new home built in the countryside of Pizal."

"You mean that building they put up last summer on the Pallone farm?"

"Yes, that's it," said Ben, moving closer. "When spring comes we may need some masonry done before we bring the children there to live."

"Are you with the church?" asked the young man, laying the board down.

"I work with a group of people who are very close to God, but we are not directly linked to any one church or denomination. Why do you ask? What is your name?"

"My name is Benito Mendoleni, and I'm finished with religion. Religion got my family arrested and will eventually have them killed. Religion also made me a slave to this stonemason."

Ben glanced at Benito's gloves, seeing the tips of the fingers worn through, and the skin on his fingertips cracked and bleeding. "I can't say that I blame you, Benito. It was religion that nailed Christ to the cross. Religious hypocrisy is at the root of every vile act that claims to represent true spirituality. May I ask why your parents were arrested?"

Benito craned his neck toward the hallway, checking for privacy, then, shutting the door, he answered. "I'm totally taken by your response, Ben. I don't know anyone with a view like that, but I can tell you I like it."

"I have a great teacher; he's the founder of Hope Mission," said Ben with a smile.

"My parents were arrested by the Roman Inquisition a year ago. They were accused of spreading the Protest Religion into Roman provinces.

When they refused to give in and confess to their so-called heresies, they were condemned to death. I was placed in the custody of this stonemason until I worked off the fine that was imposed on my family for their crimes against the Holy Roman Empire."

"When are your parents scheduled for execution?"

Benito's eyes welled with tears. "On the last day of this year. I've lost all hope that anything can be done to alter their fate. Whoever placed me in this miserable situation might as well have given me the same sentence. I work every day from sun up till sundown, laying bricks and breathing in this deadly mortar dust. Lately, I wake up at night wheezing and occasionally spit up blood. If there is a God, He is far from this place, and even farther from me."

"That's where I have to disagree with you, my young friend," said Ben. "Never give up hope. God has sent me to help you. I can't explain everything about that now, but tell me first about the fine."

"I can't say how much money I owe, but it comes to three more years of hard labor. I know I'll never even make it one more year."

"If you were released from your debt, what would you do with the rest of your life?"

"Find a decent job, perhaps teaching music. Then, after I made enough money, I'd buy a violin and continue composing original music."

"Is that what you were doing when I saw you with that board under your chin? Were you practicing?"

"Yes, precisely. I lost my right to play, or even to have, a violin, several months ago. That old violin was the only pleasure I knew until the master stonemason said I spent too much time on such nonsense. With one swipe he smashed it to pieces."

"Where did you learn to play?" asked Ben, sitting down on the worktable.

"My mother was a cellist and my father a conductor of the university orchestra in Milan. That's how they met. They taught me music from the time I could walk, and that's what grieves my soul to near death. Music is all that I've ever loved and now I'm forbidden to play. Even if I were free to play, my fingertips are so calloused and cracked it would take months to return to the skill and sensitivity I had before my parents were arrested."

Ben adjusted his mask and smiled. "If I were able to get you out of this place for good, would you consider teaching our people music at Hope Mission?"

"If you could help me out of here, kind sir, I'd be willing to do just about anything you asked. I'd owe you my life, because if I'm forced to work as I have been straight through the winter, I'll surely die."

"Are you willing to trust what I say and leave this place tonight?"

"Yes, sir, but how will..."

Ben broke in, "Just leave everything to me, and when the time comes allow me to handle the explanations."

"I have nothing to lose," said Benito, "so I will follow your lead."

Ben went to the back door and picked up the sack he'd brought from Mission. Placing it on a chair, he pulled out the beautiful, new violin he and Giovanni created, holding it out to Benito. Gasping, Benito took hold of it, saying, "Where did you get this instrument? It's extraordinary! It must have cost a fortune."

"It was created at Hope Mission, and will be yours to keep and use to teach our people. Why not try it out?"

Holding it as if it were a living thing, Benito said, "I dare not. If the master hears the music he'll come down in a rage and destroy this master-piece."

Suddenly, the storeroom door was flung open and in came the master stonemason with a face so ridged it looked harder than the bricks that surrounded him. He was a large man, completely bald, but appeared small standing next to Ben.

Before Benito could say a word, the stonemason barked, "You have time for friends, do you? You'll be up until midnight if you expect to finish the day's work." Turning to Ben, he asked, "And who are you? What business do you have with Benito? He's only a worker here. I'm the owner."

Ben's eyes bored into him. "Forgive my intrusion, sir, but it's not important who I am, but rather why I've come."

Benito handed Ben the violin.

"Well, why have you come?" the stonemason demanded. "To sell Benito a new violin? If that's the reason, he doesn't have the time or money for that. And why do you hide your identity? Are you running from the law?"

The brow on Ben's mask ruffled. "My business here is with you, sir. My employer is an anonymous benefactor who has an interest in Benito's welfare. And for your information, I am running from no one. Like my employer, I also wish to remain anonymous. My question to you is, how much money will it take to pay off what the boy owes?"

"He has three full years here before he can leave."

"That's not what I asked, sir," said Ben, in a firm voice. "Let me put it another way. How much would you pay a hireling to do the same job over a three year period?"

"One gold florin every two months. That's six a year. Let's see, that would be eighteen gold coins in all. I suppose your employer is rich enough and willing to waste his money on this skinny runt?"

Ben reached in his coat and pulled out a sack of gold florins. Pouring the coins onto the worktable, he counted out eighteen pieces, stacking them neatly in three piles. Then, moving closer to the stonemason, Ben said, "You can have this gold if you release the boy to me right now."

With his eyes fixed on the coins, the stonemason replied, "I'll need six more florins to cover his room and board."

After Ben laid the added coins down, the stonemason said, "Take him. Glad to be rid of him. He has a weak back and the hands of a woman."

Resting a hand on Benito's shoulder, Ben whispered, "Go and pack your things, Benito. I want a word with the master stonemason."

As Benito ran up the stairs to his room, the stonemason collected the coins into his apron.

Ben moved within inches of the man's face, pushing him against the wall with great force. "Normally, after any business transaction, I would leave without a word, but I feel compelled to give you a piece of my mind, sir. The only thing you're a master of is cruelty. Your treatment of that fine young man is despicable, and I believe you had every intention of literally working him to death. It appears your heart is harder than the bricks you make. If you say another word to Benito before he leaves with me, I may forget who I am and give you a taste of what you gave him."

Without a word, the stonemason backed out of the room and disappeared.

When Benito returned with his bag, they left and walked to Anna Borrelli's house. Ben wanted immediate attention for Benito's hands and also to find him decent clothes and to give him a home-cooked meal from Anna.

Benito wept tears of joy all the way, thanking Ben, holding his new violin to his chest like a newborn.

Chapter 67. Ben Executes Justice & Mercy.

The snow stopped falling by the time Ben and Benito arrived at Anna's. Leading them in from the porch, Anna took them into the kitchen where Ben explained everything. Reaching for Benito's chapped and bleeding hands, she cut off his gloves and went right to work.

While soaking his hands in warm water, Ben explained he had one more task to complete before they began their journey to the mountain. He thanked Anna, and walked straight to the blacksmith's stable, wondering how to place Mario's jewelry near the husband and wife without being noticed. He stopped about fifty paces from the stable, laid down his sack of gifts and watched from behind a wagon.

The blacksmith was taking his leave of a woman, with a farewell kiss. As she walked away, smiling, Ben assumed she was the man's wife, so he followed her to the center of the village. She stopped along the way several times to browse in the windows.

Entering a Pawn Shop, she reached into a shopping sack and pulled out two bronze objects that appeared to be tableware of some sort. Less than a minute later, she came out with her head down, still holding the tableware.

Ben approached her and asked in an urgent voice. "Ma'am, please, may I have a word with you?"

Startled by his mask and size, the woman stood as if frozen.

Ben stopped ten paces from her, the snow crunching under his boots. "Don't be afraid, ma'am. I was passing by and noticed you go into the pawnshop. Were you trying to pawn that beautiful bronze pitcher and serving plate?"

Comforted by his kind voice, she replied, "Yes, sir. I was really hoping I could fetch a good price for these items. This year I'm determined to buy something wonderful for my husband. He works so hard all year but trouble never seems to leave his side. This Christmas I want him to feel that blessings have finally come instead of more curses."

"Well, this may be your blessed Christmas, ma'am," said Ben, moving closer. "I work with a dozen lovely folks who would indeed enjoy using your tableware this Christmas. May I know how much you're asking?"

The woman smiled, holding out the items. "The pawn shop owner said two silver coins was too much, but I know they are well worth that and then some."

"How about one gold coin, ma'am? Will that cover it?"

The woman smiled. "Oh, that's so generous, sir. Yes, please take them."

Ben handed her the coin and took the tableware, purposely dropping the pitcher onto the snow. As the woman bent to pick it up, Ben slipped a small red sack containing a silver ring into her basket, then reached for the pitcher. "Thank you, ma'am. I pray you have a blessed Christmas this year, and I hope you find that special gift for your man."

"And a wonderful Christmas to you," said the blacksmith's wife as she clenched the gold coin in her fist.

Ben put the bronze tableware in his large sack and quickly returned to the blacksmith's stable.

When he arrived, he glanced down the road leading out of the village, and saw the blacksmith with a man walking toward a wagon a good distance away. A white dove swooped down out of nowhere and landed on Ben's shoulder. Then it flew up and across the street onto a lamppost next to the stable entrance.

Following its lead, Ben knew he was receiving heavenly aid in his pursuit to deliver Mario's gifts to the troubled family. The moment he arrived at the lamppost, the dove flew into an alley next to the stable. Ben continued to follow all the way to the rear entrance. Sitting on a stack of barrels next to the back window, waiting for Ben to arrive, the dove illuminated in the darkness. As soon as Ben stepped behind the barrels, the dove flew up onto his shoulder and turned its head toward the back window.

Peering through the window, Ben saw a man of small stature enter from a door on the east side of stable. He had a burlap sack in his hand and went directly to a storage bin, emptying its contents into the sack. It appeared to Ben that the man was stealing the blacksmith's inventory; horseshoes, nails, and even some gear for wagons and horses.

Ben thought, *The man does not appear as a thief. He's dressed in a suit and hat befitting a gentleman.* But he continued to watch, and after the sack was full, the man reached into his pocket and pulled out a tiny flask. Pulling the cork out, he emptied the contents into a tin cup next to the blacksmith's unfinished dinner. A chill came under Ben's mask as he quickly made his way to the other side of the stable where the man had entered. He waited behind the open door until the little fellow made his escape.

As soon as the man stepped beyond the door, Ben took hold of him by the back of his neck and lifted him completely off the ground, causing him to drop the sack. Ben hurled him across the alley onto the cobblestones, into the garbage. Standing over him, with his hands on his hips, Ben tapped his boot to the man's shoe. "You look like a gentleman, sir, but I would bet anything your actions for the last five minutes were anything but gentlemanly. Who are you?"

Trembling, the little man sat up. "You won't hurt me, sir, will you? Why do you wear that mask? Do you want my money?"

"Answer my question. Who are you?"

With his hands shaking, as pale as the snow, the man stood up. "My name is Salvatore Minutti. I am the owner of the stable."

"Well, then," said Ben, backing him into a corner, "I guess you won't mind my asking why you took the blacksmith's inventory?"

Gaining some confidence, Salvatore argued, "Everything in there belongs to me. You have no right asking me anything more."

Ben reached down and seized him again, dragging him into the stable to the tin cup to which he had added the powder. Picking up the cup, he pushed it to Salvatore's face and said, "In about two seconds I'm going to force your mouth open and make you drink what's in this cup. That is, unless you tell me what you put in the blacksmith's drink, and why."

"No, please, sir, don't make me drink it. I'll tell you anything, only don't make me drink it."

"Start talking," said Ben, as he poured the drink to the floor. "And if I catch you in a lie, I promise, you'll end up with broken bones."

Ben released his grip and ordered Salvatore to put the blacksmith's inventory back in the storage bins. Afterwards, the man said he would tell him everything, if only they might leave the stable before the blacksmith returned. Ben agreed and followed him across the alley to his home.

After adjusting the wood in the fireplace, and offering him a glass of sherry, Salvatore asked Ben to sit as he explained. "Believe it or not, sir, I'm quite relieved I was caught in that act of treachery. It all began when I met Camille, the blacksmith's wife. Although I'm a very successful businessman, I've never known a woman, but when I set eyes on Camille, I instantly loved her and lusted to know her. The more my desire increased, the more desperate I became to have her in my life somehow. So, I began to bring trouble into her Carlo's life in an effort to turn her affection away from him. But it seemed the more trouble he had, the more she clove to him until I devised a way to be rid of him forever."

"So, it was you all along who made his life so miserable? You own the stable, and rent it to Carlo with intentions of sabotaging every step of his life because you covet his wife?"

"Yes, it's detestable, I know," said Salvatore. "But my desire for her consumed me and even now I'm tormented by knowing what type of person I've become. I've become so self-absorbed that my own sister might die because of my indifference."

"How is your sister tormented?" Ben asked, sipping his sherry.

"Several years ago I purchased the stonemasonry business in the center of Pizal. When I hired a new master stonemason to manage the place, my sister became enchanted with him and they married. Soon after, he began to shout at her, and then I noticed bruises on her face, arms and legs. I know I should have helped her in some way, but I was too busy with my own plans and schemes."

"Earlier today I met the 'charming' stonemason," said Ben grimly, "and he said that he owned the business."

Gulping down his drink, Salvatore replied, "He lied to you. He likes to think he owns it because he's married to my sister, but it'll never happen. If I ever manage to make up for the damage I've done to Carlo, I'll figure a way to rescue my sister from the hands of that beast. You must believe what I'm trying to say, Ben. I repent of the evil I've done and planned, and if you don't have me arrested, I'll do everything in my power to restore Carlo's dignity. I'll never again let my eyes look upon his wife in an inappropriate manner."

Ben went to the fire. Squatting, he rubbed his hands for warmth. "I'd like to believe you, Salvatore, but I don't know if your will to do good can compete with the lust in your heart for your neighbor's wife, so I'll go half way. I'll forget what I witnessed on one condition."

"Anything. I'll do anything to feel like the man I was before these desires ensnared me."

Ben finished his sherry. "You must follow my instructions in every detail regarding Carlo and his wife, and also your brother-in-law, the master stonemason."

"You can trust me," pleaded Salvatore. "I swear... I'll follow every instruction to the letter."

"Well, just to ensure you don't lose your way again, I should tell you that I have close ties to the Italian Government through General Emeliano. I'll return to Pizal after Christmas and look in on Carlo's family and also the stonemasonry business. If I find that you've returned evil for good, and have not followed my instructions, I will report you to the General and you'll be arrested and imprisoned for a good long time."

Tears of gratitude and relief welled in the man's eyes. "I'll do everything you say. On my life, I promise. I thank God you turned me from evil today."

Ben put a hand on Salvatore's shoulder. "All right then. Go to the master stonemason tomorrow and fire him. Perhaps you can pay him something to leave your sister and this country altogether, but make sure he's gone before Christmas. Then, take your sister to your home and have someone tend to her health. After I leave tonight, go back to the stable and invite Carlo to your house to discuss what a fine job he's doing, and then increase his status...enormously."

Reaching into his sack, Ben pulled out a black satin handkerchief tied into a bundle. Untying it, he let Mario's silver necklace and bracelet fall onto the coffee table. "This necklace and bracelet were made at Hope Mission exclusively for Carlo to give to his wife for Christmas. Give the pieces to him as a bonus for a job well done over the past years. Tell him you were wrong to have treated him so harshly and want to make up for it with the jewelry. Then, bless him with a new life working together to build up your businesses."

"But he'll think it was my generosity that gives him the jewelry, when in fact I'm guilty of the worst kind of selfishness. How can I let him think me a good man?"

"If you have truly repented of the evil you intended, you've already been forgiven by God and me. Consider this your first act of goodness and consider the silver jewelry as God's way of renewing and blessing not only Carlo's view of life, but your view of God's grace."

Hardly able to hold back his tears, Salvatore cried out, "I can see the goodness of God now. I see His grace very clearly now. And I vow to you this day, I will do everything you say, and more, to make up for the pain I've caused that family, and the pain I've allowed my sister to endure."

Ben looked into the man's earnest face and believed him. "Remember, I'll return after Christmas and see how it all turned out," he said, "but I feel sure all will be well."

Ben left Salvatore's house and went directly to Anna's to prepare Benito for the ride to the Mission.

Chapter 68. The First Christmas Tree.

At nine in the evening, Ben and Benito rode through the southern gate of the Mission. The hours traveling up the mountain trail provided plenty of time to inform Benito about the Mission's purpose, and of the oath of silence when it came to their location. After listening to Ben's heartfelt love for his commission, he knew the Mission was no den of religious hypocrites, but rather a spirit-filled work force for the living God. Still, because of his experience with the Roman Church, he wanted to see for himself.

As they rode to the stable, Ben spotted Nicholas running toward the Bellicinis' house. Nick called out, "Ben, something has happened to Joseph Solo. Meet us inside."

After their horses were unsaddled, in the stable for the night, they joined the others at the Bellicini home. Joseph sat on a ledge by the fireplace in the grand room. He struggled to speak, but only mumbled, having lost control of the left side of his face. Also, his left eye drooped and his left arm and leg fell limp.

Nicholas squatted next to him. "Can you understand me, Joseph? Don't try to speak, just nod your head."

Joseph nodded.

"Is it God telling you someone is to be healed?"

Joseph mumbled, "Maybe. Yea, pobbaly."

"Can you walk?"

Joseph shook his head. Ox lifted him and asked Nicholas where to take him for the night.

"Take him to his cabin, Ox. Bernadette and I will look in on him soon."

The moment Ox left with Joseph in his arms, Ben joined Nicholas and introduced him to the young musician. Nicholas invited them to his house for the night, eager to learn how Ben managed to deliver the Mission gifts. With journal in hand, Bernadette pleaded with Nicholas to let her come along, only long enough to hear Ben's story and take some notes. Nicholas agreed, and after arriving at his house, Ben told the story as the group gathered around the fireplace.

Benito was amazed that Ben not only managed to give the gifts in a self-effacing way, but that he was also able to bless many people in the process. When Ben got to the part where he ordered Salvatore to dismiss the master stonemason, Benito stood and lifted up his shirt.

"The night before Ben arrived, the master came into my room after beating his wife, and gave me the same treatment. I don't know why, but the man is vicious."

"Why are your hands bandaged, Benito?" Nicholas asked.

"My fingertips were raw and bleeding from the constant bricklaying. Anna put salve on my hands that helped ease the pain, but I can't wait until they're healed so I can play the violin again. Ben gave me a wonderful new violin to teach anyone interested."

"So you want to stay at the Mission and teach?" Nicholas asked.

"I'll stay and teach as long as I can be of service to your Mission. After all, I owe you my life, and everyone I've met up here seems different than the so-called 'religious' living in the world down there. There is a genuine sense of love in this place."

"We only pray you recover from the past year of cruelty and begin to enjoy life again, composing and teaching music," said Nicholas, smiling.

"I'll never enjoy life while my parents are in jail, sentenced to be executed."

"Ben mentioned that when you arrived. I was informed we have until the end of December to intervene. Is that correct, Benito?"

"Yes, that much is true, but the situation is hopeless. The Pope himself has sanctioned their arrest and has put them in a jail no one has ever escaped from."

"Was it the Pope who went after them initially?"

"No, he sanctioned their arrest only after some of the more stringent Cardinals put pressure on him. Actually, I think the Pope wants to release them, realizing there's no stopping the new Protest sect. It's already spread halfway across Europe."

"And they were arrested for simply evangelizing people to their sect?"

"That's only part of it. The official charges were that they also took authority to teach others the Holy Scriptures. Quite frankly, I'm amazed at the ignorance behind this. How can the Church put people to death over the interpretation of scripture, or a different point of view? In my opinion that's the greatest affront to God, and now my parents are caught in the middle of it all."

"I agree," said Nicholas, stoking the fire. "If religious people would only look at the character of God, it would never dawn on them to bring harm to another believer, let alone to anyone else. We live in a time of political and religious uncertainty, and only God knows what is in the hearts of men. But through all of man's ambiguity, God still has his true believers here on earth. We will begin at once to work on a plan to have your parents released. Don't give up hope. That's what this Mission is all about."

Before Benito could respond, Ricardo burst into the room. "Nicholas, excuse me, but there's a situation developing in Pizal. Raven and I were buying supplies for Daisy and Rose when we saw soldiers enter the village from the north. They went to the inn and rented rooms for the night, then asked around where they could find you. When we entered the inn, the innkeeper introduced Raven and me as the people who could best help.

"The man in charge was with two other soldiers and a young lady with a disorder affecting one side of her body. When I asked why he sought you out he said he was General Emeliano, and he came seeking help for his daughter. I told him to wait at the inn until I informed you of his arrival."

Nicholas scratched his chin, deep in thought. "I had the feeling he'd show up one day seeking Joseph Solo. Tomorrow is the day before Christmas, and we'll be very busy, but somehow we'll make it all work. Leave at once for Pizal, and at first light escort the General and his daughter here. Ask him to leave his soldiers behind for a day or two. The General is our ally now. He may be able to help with Benito's problem before he leaves. In the meantime we'll prepare Joseph Solo for the General and his daughter."

Ben took Benito to a guest room for the evening, leaving one of the monks to keep him company and make him familiar with the house and the Mission compound.

Nicholas and Bernadette walked arm in arm to the west gate, toward Joseph's lookout cabin. At the halfway point, Nicholas stopped, staring at a small lone pine tree on a mound at the edge of the lake.

"What is it, Nicholas?" Bernadette asked. "What do you see?"

Nicholas led her closer to the tree. "The sky is the daily bread of the eyes. Look how bright the stars are tonight. I've never seen so many. If you look at that pine tree long enough you can see the stars right through the sparse branches. It looks to me like the tree is sparkling with stars."

"How right you are, dear. It looks heavenly."

"This has inspired me, Bernadette. On the way back from Joseph's house I intend to cut down the tree and bring it home."

"How has it inspired you?"

"As I look at the tree, in all its natural glory, it appears to me as a symbol for this time of year. The pine tree is evergreen, symbolizing eternal hope and life through our Lord Jesus. Then, the moonlight sparkling in the powdered snow on the branches, and the stars appearing here and there through the tree, speak of Jesus as the light of the world."

Bernadette drew his hand to her lips. "When I view it now, after hearing your thoughts, I'm inspired as well. For the first time, Christmas is alive as never before. What a lovely moment this is."

Nicholas turned to Bernadette and, gazing into her eyes, whispered. "Lovely indeed, but the light of the moon and stars cannot compete with your eyes or the touch of your hand or the sound of your voice."

Bernadette embraced Nicholas, kissed him, then led him toward Joseph's house.

When the wind blew a chilling gust in their faces, Nicholas removed his red scarf and wrapped it around Bernadette's head and neck. They picked up the pace as they crossed an open field that led to a trail just behind the tree line. Having reached the base of the huge rocks below Joseph's cabin, they climbed the crude steps.

A high-pitched voice echoed down, "I saw you coming in the moonlight. Be careful of the loose rocks near the top."

Holding Bernadette's hand all the way up, Nicholas met Joseph at the last step.

"Welcome my friends. Come in out of that wicked wind."

They hurried into the cabin where Bernadette went directly to the fire, took off her mittens and rubbed her hands. "We thought you might still be in that half-paralyzed state, Joseph. Did you lose weight? You look rather pale."

Nicholas agreed, joining Bernadette. "She's right, Joseph. Are you well?"

"I came out of that horrid condition after Ox left, but I'm in perfect health now. However, I did lose some weight on my current fast."

"How many days now?" asked Nicholas.

"I can't recall; I really wasn't counting. But I know this is my last day. I've become too weak. All for good reason, right, Nicholas? You brought word of the one who is afflicted on the left side, true?"

"Yes. The one with the affliction is a young lady named Angelina. She's the daughter of General Emeliano. They have arrived in Pizal. I sent Ricardo to escort them here to meet you."

"Nicholas, I've been praying about this for quite some time now. I would feel more comfortable if you and Bernadette bring Angelina and her father to the open field behind the huge rocks. You must send the girl by herself the rest of the way. She won't have to come far. I will be just beyond the tree line to greet her. I want to stay anonymous from this point on. If anyone could understand the reason why, it's you."

"I understand. She will limp into the tree line with her affliction and emerge from there a new woman."

"Yes, exactly. Her father will not see me, and the mystery of it all will turn his attention to God as the healer. This is what I want more than anything. When you send her to me and she's left walking in that field alone, the General will have to trust and have faith; two things a military man rarely employs, outside the might of his army."

Looking up from her journal, Bernadette smiled. "I have the greatest job in the world. To see and record all of these events as they unfold, fills my heart with gratitude for the majesty of the God we serve."

Joseph turned to Nicholas. "She was made for you, Nick."

"And I for her. How shall we prepare the General and his daughter? When should we come here?"

"I know tomorrow will be a busy day for you, being Christmas Eve and all, but it's the best time. God is going to make this Christmas very special for many people. I just hope you can squeeze it all in."

"I'll be with him every step of the way, Joseph," added Bernadette. "Besides, everyone at the Mission has prepared for Christmas months in advance."

"Wonderful," said Joseph. "Now, when you're with the girl, build up her faith, as she will be frightened and uncomfortable meeting new people and unfamiliar with her surroundings. Tell her about all the miraculous events that have occurred here and introduce her to Giovanni, Ben and Maria, Daisy and Rose. Let her speak in private with them all. It will build her faith to speak with those who've had miracles themselves. When that's been done, bring her here. I'll be waiting from mid-day on."

Putting on his mittens, preparing to leave, Nicholas put a hand on Joseph's shoulder. "Everything will be done as you wish." Pointing to an axe that rested in a corner by the door, Nicholas asked, "Can I borrow the axe until tomorrow? I want to decorate inside my house with a tree, if you can believe that."

"I've never heard of such a thing. Why?"

"Come with us now and I'll explain on the way. By the time you end that fast with Bell's leftovers, I'll have the tree mounted in the grand room and we'll begin to decorate it."

*N*icholas fixed a base to the nine-foot Christmas tree, and stood it opposite his fireplace in the grand room, Bernadette brought in clumps of red berries from the kitchen and tied them here and there on the tree, saying, "These symbolize the bounty that the Lord provides all year long."

Seeing Bernadette freely decorate the tree, Daisy and Rose ran to Mario's workshop with an idea of their own. They found him engraving finishing touches on the formal silver stewpot. Sweeping up the shavings on the table and floor onto a wooded plate, they invited him to come to see the tree.

As Mario headed out the door, Daisy and Rose took the shavings to their workshop and cut two dozen various sized stars from a thin hardened leather sheet, coating them with rabbit's glue. While the glue was sticky, they dipped the stars into the silver shavings. When the glue dried they tied a thread to each star and giggled, watching the glittering silver bounce light in every direction.

Running to Nicholas's house with the new ornaments, the twins gasped when they entered the grand room and saw the tree adorned with trinkets high and low.

Benito had come and sat by the fireplace with his new violin. Ripping the bandages from his hands, he began to play his own rendition of Christmas favorites. Giovanni strummed harmonic chords on his guitar as the twins asked Ben to place some of their stars on the higher branches.

Nicholas sat with Bernadette on his buckskin couch, taken with delight at the effect the tree had on everyone who'd come to see. Bernadette drew close and said, "I've never been more content in life than at this very moment."

"Nor have I, Bernadette. Let us enjoy this moment to the fullest, because tomorrow we'll not even have time to think."

A knock came on the door, and when it swung open, Anna Borelli appeared. Stepping inside, she gazed at the tree and looked about the room, hearing the music and feeling the Christmas spirit glow as never before. "It's absolutely enchanting in here! What a beautiful tree, Nicholas. Whatever made you bring it inside and decorate it?"

Nicholas explained, pointing out all the symbols representing Jesus' birth as light of the world, then asked, "What brings you up the mountain, Anna? Is there an emergency?"

"No, not at all. I have your list for Christmas Eve. Ben told me about your wanting to deliver the toys in the dead of night. What a great idea!"

"It wasn't my idea. Bernadette suggested it, and you're right, it's a great idea."

"I came to help you prepare," said Anna, pulling a sack from her coat. "I wrote the names of all the children on tiny tags. Tonight we'll gather the games and toys, and put a name to each gift."

"That's very thoughtful," said Nicholas, kissing Anna's cheek. "You can spend the night here and come morning, travel down the mountain with Ben. He said he wanted to cut down an evergreen for Hope Orphanage."

After kissing Nicholas goodnight, Bernadette led Anna to the workshops to gather the toys in one place and tag them.

That evening brought more snow, the temperature dropping well below freezing. By mid morning Ricardo was on his way up the mountain trail with General Emeliano and Angelina. No sooner had they reached the first bend in the trail then a pack of wolves appeared, flanking them. The General's horse reared back as he turned, seeing several more wolves approaching from behind.

Ricardo dismounted and shouted, "Don't be alarmed, General. They're no threat to us."

Ricardo squatted with palms up, but the General was too distracted to notice until the wolves moved off the road and lay in the snow on their bellies.

Surprised at their sudden passiveness, the General arched his bushy eyebrows. "They looked aggressive at first. What changed them so fast? They're as meek as a flock of sheep now."

Careful to keep the Mission secret, Ricardo answered, "In a sense, they are trained, General. Don't ask me to go into it, I can't. Just rest assured that you and your daughter are safe as long as I'm with you."

"I've never seen a trained wolf before. It's remarkable."

"When Joseph Solo lays healing hands on your daughter you will not only see something remarkable but rather impossible."

"That is something I've been struggling with since I left San Marco. I'm a military man and miracles never happen in the Army. We are taught to depend on training and the power of our armies to keep things under control. As a matter of fact, I've never seen a miracle. This is one situation I feel totally powerless, and I can't get myself to believe my daughter's condition will improve."

Ricardo maneuvered his horse beside Angelina. "Do *you* believe you can be healed, Angelina?"

Lifting a scarf over her nose she nodded. "I know God lives, and sees, and cares. If He is willing, I will be healed."

"That's the key, General Emeliono; faith. As long as Angelina believes God can do the impossible, there is hope. Besides, you must have had some faith to set out on this journey in the first place."

"It wasn't faith that made me come, but love for my child. She was so sure God would help her that I left my own beliefs aside and chose to believe her. But the closer we get to the Mission the more doubt rankles me."

"You have not made this journey in vain. God has his hand on this Mission. Let's pick up the pace, for we must try to arrive before noon."

Chapter 70. Angelina's Faith.

$\mathcal{N}$icholas and Bernadette were standing outside the Mission's west gate when Ricardo, General Emeliano and Angelina arrived. The General dismounted and immediately went to Nicholas, while Ricardo leapt from his horse to help Angelina dismount.

Extending his hand, the General smiled. "Nicholas Kristo, it's so good to finally meet you. You've been a tremendous help to our government. We are in your debt."

"Welcome, General Emeliano. You owe us nothing. We're just relieved the truth finally came out." Reaching for Bernadette's hand, Nicholas added, "This is my betrothed, Bernadette LaViono."

"Pleased to meet you, General," said Bernadette, smiling. "Was your journey here a pleasant one?"

"Your young man Ricardo seems very capable. He made our way past the wolves seem effortless. The only unpleasantness came from my own doubts concerning my daughter."

Ricardo walked Angelina to the group. Keeping her scarf over her nose, she extended her good hand to both Nicholas and Bernadette. "Despite my father's doubts, I do believe there is hope. What shall I do before meeting Mr. Solo?"

"All you have to do is come to my house for lunch with a few friends who've had similar encounters with impossible situations," said Nicholas, pointing to his house.

When they arrived and removed their coats, Makande and Bell seated them at the dining room table. Already seated were Ben and Maria, Daisy and Rose, and Giovanni.

Bell served barley soup, while Makande followed with roasted ducklings and vegetables. After Nicholas introduced everyone, it wasn't long before they were sharing stories of their former disabilities. The General and his daughter sat transfixed as the twins told of their palsy, making everyone smile when Daisy said, "We were so happy to be healed, we jumped on Joseph, knocking him to the floor, kissing him until he joined in our giggles."

Soon after lunch, the General turned to Nicholas. "So, when will we meet Joseph Solo?"

"Joseph has always been reluctant to put on a public display. Too many times people have given him credit for his gift, which is the last thing he wishes. I know they can't help it but he desires all the glory to go to God. We'll go to the open field behind Joseph's cabin. At that point your daughter will meet with Joseph alone."

"Won't she be in danger, with the wolves roaming about?"

"Not at all. Joseph will be just beyond the tree line. As a matter of fact, he's probably already there. Let's go to the field right now."

Angelina rose from the table, putting a hand to the afflicted side of her face. As she rushed to put her coat on, her withered leg gave way and she fell, weeping.

Bernadette lifted her. "Don't be afraid, dear. Joseph is a kind man."

Wiping tears with her sleeve, Angelina replied, "These are not fearful tears, Miss Bernadette. They are tears of joy for my deliverance. Hearing everyone's story has lifted my faith. I know now for certain God will bless me this day."

"Faith is the key, General," Nicholas said. "Your daughter has much faith."

The General looked confused as the group bundled up and made their way out the west gate and onto the field behind Joseph's cabin. When they were a hundred paces from the tree line, Nicholas stopped and turned to Angelina. "This is where we wait. You must walk just beyond the trees. Joseph will be there for you."

Angelina turned to her father, kissed him, then slowly limped her way across the field. Everyone stood silent until she disappeared into the forest, Bernadette jotting down events as they happened.

General Emeliano turned to Nicholas. "I've never felt so helpless in my entire life. And now I fear I'll lose my daughter if she comes back to me in the same condition. She's had many seasons of depression, and remained detached for months at a time. It's a strange thing, Nicholas. On the battlefield, I've never known a fear as dark as the one that's gripped me this very moment."

"Whatever you do, General, don't lose hope. Even though you've only learned about the power of armies and governments until now, perhaps God wants you to learn about Him. His power resides everywhere in the undercurrents of life. Fear not, General, for today you will see the power of God work on behalf of your daughter."

Twenty minutes passed before Angelina stepped out from the trees. Her arms were outstretched and raised above her head as she hurried toward the group. The General shouted, "She's not limping! Can you see? She's not limping. Could it be? Could it actually be?"

Halfway across the field, Angelina fell to her knees and called out, "Father, praise be to God, I am delivered from my infirmity!" Bowing her head in her hands to the ground, she wept and thanked the Lord aloud.

The General ran across the field and fell to his knees, embracing his daughter. When Angelina turned her head up, her father held her face in his hands. "It is true. Look at you, daughter. Your face is perfect!" Taking her left arm he found the same results. All the muscles and nerves seemed to be in perfect health. He helped his daughter to her feet, and they embraced and made their way to the others. Overwhelmed at the miracle, everyone wept, surrounding Angelina, praising God aloud.

General Emeliano turned to Nicholas. "You were right, my friend. Today I have seen the power of God work on my daughter's behalf. Our lives have changed forever, for the Lord has convinced me He exists and is willing to intercede in man's affairs."

Nicholas leaned toward to Bernadette and whispered, "This is exactly what Joseph wanted. The General is giving God the credit."

Angelina declared, "Mr. Solo is very kind, and charged me to claim God as my healer and Joseph as His assistant. I would have done that regardless, for when Joseph laid hands on me, the Holy Spirit revealed Himself, and I knew it was God's power present in my body. I am filled with gratitude and my soul magnifies the glory of the living God."

Bernadette scrambled to write Angelina's comments verbatim, while Nicholas directed the group back toward the west gate. After finishing her notes, Bernadette ran to catch up with Nicholas, who was a good distance ahead of the General and his daughter.

A minute later, Nicholas turned to find his betrothed reaching out to him. He took her hand, saying, "Did you get it all down?"

Out of breath, Bernadette replied, "Yes...hu...huu... I'm quite sure I did. Why are you walking ahead of them?"

"Because Angelina became overwhelmed with emotion and began to weep uncontrollably. I think her father's intimate support is what will help her right now. Besides, they'll be our guests through Christmas. They'll be plenty of time to be together."

"I wanted to ask about how you're going to get all those gifts to the children at the orphanage and Pizal in one night," said Bernadette.

Lifting her hand to his lips, Nicholas explained, "There are three sacks of toys and games. Ben will take one sack with him early in the evening. He'll hide it in the barn next to the orphanage, and then cut down an evergreen and bring it in for the children to decorate. Later that evening Giovanni and Benito will visit and play Christmas music. After the children are asleep, the nuns will place a toy at the bed of each child. Ricardo and I will leave at midnight and take one sack each into Pizal, where we'll meet Ben. We'll leave the tagged toys at the houses of every child on the list."

"Perhaps we should delay our wedding a few days," suggested Bernadette. "You'll be exhausted by the time you return the next morning."

"I love you too much to wait another day. We'll only delay it until late afternoon on Christmas Day. How's that, my love?"

"Sounds wonderful, Nick. What about Benito's parents freezing in that Roman dungeon? Do you think General Emeliano can help?"

"That's the very next problem we'll address. I'll speak to him the moment they're settled for the evening."

Chapter 71. Giovanni Counsels Angelina

W hen they arrived at Nicholas's house the entire Mission turned out to see the new Angelina. Maria, Bell and the nuns surrounded her, touching her face and inspecting her left leg and arm. Benito stood in the distance, transfixed at Angelina's beauty, while Giovanni stood on the porch watching silently. The women escorted the young girl into the house to search for a mirror and found one in Nicholas's guest room.

Angelina sat silently and gazed into the looking glass. Tears came again as she touched her left cheek and said, "I have been given a miracle today. How can I give thanks and show my gratitude for such a gift?"

Giovanni entered the room and said, "You have a sure way to show your gratitude, Angelina." Nicholas and Bernadette came and stood in the doorway as Giovanni continued. "Unlike other beautiful women, you have had plenty of time to know how the world treats the unlovely. You know the pain of rejection. You know first hand the reproach of people with facial defects. You've heard the cruel accusations of people speculating about your lifelong affliction; their suggestions that you have a demon or that you were cursed at birth because of the sins of your father. Don't let the beauty you possess now make you forget what you've experienced."

Sitting down with his guitar, Giovanni strummed soft harmonic chords and continued, "Some women and even men who were born beautiful never tire of finding ways to become even more so, using that beauty as power to get what they desire. In time it begins to consume them and then very little of anything else matter to them. It's all vanity in the end. You must find ways to glorify God with the beauty you now possess. Consider a flower: its outer beauty is glorious, but its nectar is what feeds the bee. Reveal the glory of God in your heart all the days of your life. Let that be the gratitude for what He has done for you this day."

Angelina put down the mirror, walked over to Giovanni and said, "Sir, over this Christmas I will meditate on all the truths I've just heard. I have not taken what you've said lightly. I will study ways that point people toward God rather than towards me. My heart burns with love for Him."

Giovanni looked towards Nicholas and Bernadette, smiled and nodded in approval. Nicholas gave him a salute and walked back to the grand room to talk with General Emeliano in private.

The General stood before the fireplace, staring into the flames, stroking his stately beard. He was lost in the mystery and wonder of the event that had changed his whole perspective on life.

"May I have a word with you, General?"

"By all means, Nicholas. I'm still befuddled by what has happened to Angelina, but eternally grateful that God chose to have mercy on her. When I return to San Marco I will see to it that your anonymity stays intact on this mountain. And if I can be of further assistance in any regard, all you need do is ask."

"Having a friend in the Italian Military is a welcome relief. All I need at this point is some advice."

"What is the problem, Nicholas?"

"The parents of our new music teacher, Benito Mendoleni, have been arrested for heresy and placed in a Roman jail awaiting execution. We have a week before their sentence is carried out. Is there any way to stay the execution?"

"I doubt it. Once a sentence is handed down by the Vatican it becomes an example to put fear into people, should they stray from the Church's traditional teachings. That's one reason religion has never appealed to me."

Nicholas smiled and said, "Religion is what Jesus opposed since the day he began His ministry. He pointed out the hypocrisy of the highest religious authorities in Judaism, and He did not mince words in the process. In the end it was religion that nailed Him to the cross."

Puzzled by Nicholas's response, the General asked, "You are undoubtedly a man of God, but not religious?"

"I don't consider myself religious at all, and neither do I think Jesus was. He was, and is, Spiritual. His love, like mine and that of many others here, is for God and fellow man, not rules and laws. We have one law, and that's the law of love, for God and fellow man. If you keep this law in your heart it will not only please God but direct you towards a spiritual life."

"I've never heard anyone put it quite that way. Now, to your problem. You say these people are in a Roman jail?"

"Yes. Do you know exactly where they might be? I've been there. If they are sent to the lower levels they might be dead already. Prisoners sent there are tortured, a practice I have never condoned in my own command."

Angelina entered, beaming with joy. "Father, this Christmas is the most wonderful we have ever had. And this place is so enchanting, don't you agree?"

"Yes, dear, it most certainly is, but we are seeking a solution to a grave problem."

As Nicholas explained, Benito stood in the doorway, hardly able to keep his gaze away from Angelina. Nicholas waved him over, saying, "I have informed the General about your parents. Can you add any additional information regarding their situation?"

Forcing his eyes from Angelina to her father, Benito said, "Their names are Santo and Rosetta Mendoleni. The last time I was able to inquire they were located in the west wing of the dungeon near the lower levels."

The General shook his head, stroked his beard and said, "The problem just got worse, if that's possible. Commander Brutti oversees the west wing. If you think Captain Ficci was bad, Brutti makes him look respectable. If they have any chance at all we have to act at once."

"Do you have an idea, General?" Nicholas asked.

"Yes, but I must leave at once."

"But, Father, it's Christmas Eve. Can't it wait just one more day?"

"No, daughter. If you ever saw what they do in those dungeons you would have wished I left an hour ago. Besides, this is the least we can do to show our gratitude to God and this Mission. You must stay here until I return with the couple." Turning to Nicholas and Benito, the military man said, "I have an idea how to get them out, but when I do they must stay hidden for the rest of their lives. The Roman Church will not relent until they are found and executed."

"I will take care of that part of the problem," said Nicholas. "If you can get them up this mountain I can keep them safe. Just remember, General, you'll need an escort when you come to the base of the mountain."

The General kissed his daughter and went directly to his horse. Brother Taylor escorted him down the mountain trail until he was safely on his way to Pizal and the two soldiers awaiting him.

The sun was setting by the time the General had met his men at the inn and discussed their mission to Rome over dinner. The soldiers were loyal to him, for General Emeliano had risked his own life saving them while fighting the French at the front in Genoa.

Their plans laid, they left Pizal and rode through the night, hoping to reach Rome by the next evening.

CHAPTER 72. JOSEPH SOLO'S DEATH.

$\mathcal{I}$ t was Christmas Eve when Joseph Solo peeked in the front door of Nicholas' house just as Benito and Giovanni had begun to play their Christmas music. The evening meal was coming to an end when Bernadette glanced up and waved Joseph into the dining room. Joseph's eyes widened, seeing the entire Mission staff squeezed into the Grand room enjoying their first Christmas together.

Makande came out of the kitchen and handed a plate of food to Joseph, pointing to a place next to Angelina, seated at the dining room table.

After Giovanni and Benito played several tunes, Nicholas tried to slip into the kitchen unnoticed. Joseph saw him from the corner of his eye and followed him. When the door was closed, he said, "I wanted to thank you for the beautiful Christmas present, Nicholas."

"What do you mean, Joseph? I don't recall giving you a gift."

Smiling, Joseph explained, "As I sat in my cabin this evening, reading, I had an overwhelming desire to be with everyone. That's never happened before. I was always reluctant to be around more than one person. But tonight my life has changed. As I listened to the music, I felt like a family member. I'm not afraid any more. You've given me the gift of fellowship. If it weren't for you constantly urging me to trust the missionaries, I might have never experienced their love or enjoy my love for them."

Nicholas laid a hand on Joseph's shoulder. "You know, Joseph, I never saw what I urged you to do as a gift. I only wanted you to get all the good that God intended for you while you were with us. But I'm happy you saw it that way. Many people never consider loving advice a gift."

Just then the kitchen door swung open and in came Ox, Lund, Ty, Ben and Ricardo. Ox gave a hearty laugh. "Ho, ho, ha...happy Christmas, Joseph. We were wondering when you'd come down from that rock."

The top of Joseph's head came to Ox's belt as Joseph thrust his tiny hand upward toward the giant man. "Happy Christmas to you, Ox, and everyone here. I think you will be seeing more of me from this day forward, thanks to Nicholas."

"It's rare that I see you all in the same place at the same time," said Nicholas. "What are you up to?"

"We want to help deliver the gifts tonight," said Ben. "We went to the workshop and were surprised at how many homes were on your list."

Nicholas scratched his head. "I must confess, if you hadn't come and volunteered, I probably would've come looking for you. With all of you to help, we're sure to get the job done tonight."

"I want to help too," Joseph said. "May I come?"

Before Nicholas could answer, Joseph began to sway as if he were dizzy. His eyes rolled to the back of his head and he fell to the floor, face down. Everyone froze for a second, shocked at the turn of events. Bernadette heard him fall from the grand room and came in to investigate. By then Nicholas had turned Joseph over and begun slapping his face and shaking him. Joseph had stopped breathing. His face was blue and although his eyes were open, there was no life in them.

"What happened?" Bernadette cried, crouching next to her man. Still trying to revive Joseph, Nicholas whispered, "I don't know. My God... I don't know. One moment he was talking and the next he was on the floor. How could this happen tonight?"

Ricardo bent down and placed his ear on Joseph's chest. "Everyone be quiet... I can't hear a heartbeat."

Nicholas stood, wiping a tear from his eye. "I don't understand this at all, unless God has a plan to use Joseph in a way none of us would ever suspect." Turning to Bernadette, he asked, "Will you please ask Brother Taylor and all the monks and nuns to meet my bedroom?"

Ben gathered Joseph into his arms and carried him past the grand room into Nicholas' bedroom, the others following close behind. Everyone was silent until prayer broke out, moans of sadness and weeping mingling in.

Lost in grief and his thoughts, Nicholas stood in the doorway wondering how and why all of this could have happened. Was this the providence of God?

Giovanni entered the room holding hands with Daisy and Rose. When the twins saw Joseph's lifeless body, they ran to the bed, weeping. Giovanni joined them, sitting down on the bed, laying his head to Joseph's chest. "You were so good...so loved...so much like the Lord," he mourned.

Twenty minutes had passed before Bernadette approached the bed with a folded sheet, intending to cover Joseph's body and accept his passing. As she laid the sheet over his face, Joseph suddenly sat up. Blinking, he gasped in a gallon of air, and then another gallon, saying, "Glory... glory... I... didn't want to come back."

Everyone froze, eyes wide with shock as Nicholas rushed to Joseph's side. "What do you mean, Joseph? What just happened to you? We all saw you talking one moment and then the next you fell over dead. You were dead for almost a half hour."

Joseph put his hands to his face and rubbed his cheeks. "I was with the Lord. I was with Him."

"What did God say, Joseph?" Bernadette asked. "What happened?"

"He did not speak to me, that is, not in any human language, but I was in His presence and all I know is that I never wanted to leave. It was bliss, only conscious bliss the whole time."

"Did the Lord reveal anything to you?" Brother Taylor asked.

Makande handed Joseph a cup of water and, after gulping it down, he answered, "I seemed to wake in the presence of a great majesty. I couldn't see anything, but I knew I was in God's presence. I knew it could only be our Lord, but what I didn't expect was how very majestic He is. We all view Him as our Savior, but then I realized I was in the presence of a King whose majesty was beyond description.

"I remember asking Him if He would reveal His glory, and before I finished the question, a searing light saturated my being and I was overcome with joy. I understood for the first time the glory emanating from God into and through me is His very character and attributes. You see? That *is* the glory of God...His character! His perfect love, wisdom, justice and mercy!

"The light engulfing me was God's essence revealing His immutability and omniscience. His character is pure, undiluted love. The information I received was not spoken, but rather imparted directly to my understanding. Don't ask me to explain, I can't. I only know, I didn't want to return here, but now that I have, it all makes sense."

All that gathered around the bed were transfixed to Joseph's every word. Nicholas asked, "Do you have a message from the Lord for us?"

"He spoke to my understanding regarding the missionaries, saying, 'Well done thou good and faithful servants'."

Tears of joy swept the room, the monks and nuns overwhelmed the Lord was pleased with them.

Leaping off the bed, Joseph tapped a hand to his chest. "Now, you must not continue to make a fuss over me. Let us resume our plans for the evening."

Bernadette broke in, "Joseph, we couldn't help making a fuss. While you were in the presence of the living God, we were all grief-stricken over your sudden death. Everyone has come to love you so."

Nicholas added, "Yes, we've come to love you, Joseph, but what I can't stop asking myself is why God chose this night to shake things up?"

Joseph laughed as if he knew something special was in store. "The night is only beginning, Nick. Let's go to the workshop and rig up those sacks of toys and games. This will undoubtedly be the most exciting Christmas we've ever known."

With that, laughter and chatter filled the room and everyone's joyous spirit returned. Nicholas and his delivery team went directly to the workshop and tied the sacks to their horses. Ben finished first and rode out quickly, taking Benito and Giovanni to the orphanage for their Christmas concert.

A half hour later, Nicholas was ready. He had divided the two large sacks into six, one for each man.

Mounting their horses, they rode out the south gate. On the way, Nicholas told them to ride directly to Anna Borelli's house. She would direct each man to the right house according to the tags tied to the toys.

The snow on the ground crunched under the horses' hooves as the men descended the moonlit mountain trail. The temperature had dropped alarmingly low by the time they reached Anna's house, and they tied their horses to the hitching post with numb hands and feet.

CHAPTER 73. DELIVERING TOYS ON CHRISTMAS EVE.

Ben, Benito and Giovanni arrived the orphanage by nine p.m. After Ben hid the toys in the barn, he cut down a ten-foot evergreen, nailed a base to the bottom and carried the tree into the parlor. By then the musicians were well into their concert.

Brother Taylor had visited the night before and prepared the nuns in advance for what Ben intended to do on Christmas Eve. After the tree was decorated and the children had eaten their apple pie and pudding, Giovanni sang a Christmas lullaby. One by one the nuns helped the children to bed, eager for them to fall asleep and awake on Christmas morning with a special gift waiting beside them.

After warming up at Anna's house, Nicholas went to the front door and put on his bearskin coat. The other men followed suit and soon they were out on the porch, Anna directing each man in a different direction with their sacks of toys.

Nicholas and Joseph began at the north road to Pizal and would eventually make their way back to Anna's when all the gifts were delivered. Just before arriving at the first house on the list, Nicholas glanced down the snow-covered street and saw a carriage drive up and draw to a halt in front of a gated mansion. A well-dressed man and three ladies emerged, laughing and jesting, probably after having had a grand Christmas Eve with friends or relatives. Nicholas turned to Joseph. "Looks like the Christmas spirit to me, don't you agree, Joseph?"

"Indeed. Do you think they're the nobleman we gave financial support to several months ago?"

"You're probably right. That's the only mansion I know of in Pizal. But look on the other side of the street. What's that woman doing?"

A young woman had stepped out of the shoemaker's shop, pulling something off the side of the building. "I don't know," Joseph replied, "let's go and see."

Crossing the street, the men hurried to inquire but were too late, for the woman disappeared into the side door, sobbing and talking to herself. When they reached the store window, Nicholas peeked in but could see only partially down into the living quarters. Standing on his tiptoes to get a better look, he still couldn't see, so he lifted Joseph onto his shoulders. "Can you see them, Joseph? What was she sobbing about?"

"There are two people huddled around a dimly lit fireplace with a crib between them. The women just put a slab of wood in the fire and she's returning to the crib. The husband is covered with many blankets and coughing. The women just lifted her child's limp arm, wailing in grief. I think the child is dead, Nick."

Nicholas brought Joseph down from his shoulders and asked, "Do you think this has something to do with your dying for that short spell earlier this evening?"

"This is one time I'm not quite sure. God has never directed me to lay hands on a dead person before. But I believe we cannot leave this place before we've done everything possible to diminish that family's suffering. What do you say, Nick?"

Before he finished speaking, Nicholas was at the shoemaker's front door. A minute after they knocked, the door opened and an anguished woman with swollen, red eyes appeared and, in a parched voice said, "If you've come in need tonight, gentlemen, I'm afraid I cannot help you. My two year old has passed on this evening and my husband appears to have the same illness. You would be wise to leave now while you're still healthy."

"We're from Hope Mission and have come to help you. We are not afraid of the disease and want to know what your needs are," said Nicholas, smiling and laying a hand on the woman's shoulder.

The woman's eyebrows arched as she squinted through tears. "Hope Mission? Where is that? I've not heard of it before. What are your names?"

"We are Nicholas Kristo and Joseph Solo; our Mission location must remain secret. But please tell us, what are your needs? We have many resources at our disposal."

"We would be eternally thankful to have some wood for the fire. Since my husband's been ill, we've run out of wood and coal. I've been ripping off the planks from the side of the house all day."

"May my friend Joseph Solo come in and assist your husband?" asked Nicholas. "He's very much like a doctor and may be able to help."

"A doctor? By all means, come in, sir, but I'm afraid you won't be much warmer than you are right now."

Joseph followed the woman inside as Nicholas turned and walked across the street, calling back, "I'll return with everything you need, ma'am."

He went directly to the nobleman's mansion, opened the iron gate and walked up to the giant oak doors. Only a moment after he knocked, a smiling man opened the door. "Good Christmas Eve, sir. What keeps you out so late this evening?"

"Good evening, sir. My name is Nicholas Kristo, and I'm from Hope Mission. Several months ago the founder of our Mission helped a nobleman in this area with a certain financial dilemma. Are you that same nobleman?"

"Why, yes I am. I will be forever indebted to the founder for saving my family. Can I be of service to you?"

Nicholas informed him of the situation across the street and asked, "If you could provide a wagonload of firewood and a basket of food for them, it may ease some of their grief and distress."

Two of the nobleman's three daughters came up behind, anxious to see who had come calling. The man told Nicholas he would load the wagon immediately, and added to the girls, "Please inform your mother of the situation and help her prepare hot soup and leftovers from this evening's meal."

Nicholas thanked him and went to the man's wood supply on the side of the house, selected a bundle, and headed directly back to the shoemaker. When he arrived, Joseph was talking to the man of the house who was now standing, his cough and fever dispelled. Nicholas went to the smoldering ashes and re-ignited the fire. "Your wife told us you were very ill. I see you're feeling better, sir."

"Yes, I can't believe I've recovered this quickly. I thought the illness would surely take my life. But when Joseph came and put his hand on my head to assess the fever, I felt better almost immediately."

Nicholas smiled and said, "As I told your wife, Joseph is very much like a doctor."

Huddling closer to the now blazing fire, the shoemaker and his wife noticed Joseph approaching the child's crib.

"It's too late," said the woman, wiping her swollen eyes.

Joseph smiled at her. "You know, sometimes a sickness can appear as death, but the person may be only sleeping."

Beginning to weep again, the woman said, "Oh, I wish it were so, but my child has not taken a breath all evening."

Leaning into the crib, Joseph put his tiny hand on the child's chest and whispered, "Awake, child, and breathe again, in the name of Jesus Christ. For He has proclaimed, 'I am the resurrection and the life."

Several moments passed before Joseph saw the child's eyes start to roll around under her eyelids. He leaned farther in and picked up the two-year-old, bringing her to his shoulder and patting her back.

The shoemaker and his wife gazed at Joseph oddly, but then they heard the child cough and begin to whimper. The woman screamed, running to Joseph, staring at the child's open eyes, assuring herself that she was not dreaming.

The shoemaker stared at Joseph for a moment, rubbing the goose bumps on his arms. Then he joined his wife, and they sat down by the fire inspecting every inch of the child, weeping with joy.

After seeing his daughter vibrant with life, the shoemaker approached Joseph. "Are you a prophet come from God this Christmas Eve? I know my child was dead, but now, by some miracle, she lives. I'm...overwhelmed... cannot express my gratitude. Whoever, whatever you are, may God bless you all the days of your life. I only wish I could repay your kindness."

Joseph spoke softly. "All thanks and gratitude must be given to the One who gives life and breath to every one of us. It was His power and His will that you've witnessed. Nicholas and I were sent to you, but it was God who restored your family this evening."

Nicholas could not stop smiling as he watched Joseph struggle when the woman, child in arms, kissed his cheeks repeatedly, thanking him a thousand times. He knew that was the last thing Joseph wanted.

Just then the door swung open, and in came the nobleman's daughters with a tray of hot onion soup, fresh-baked bread, meat pie and pudding. The youngest called out, "Where shall we set up your Christmas dinner, sir?"

"The kitchen table is fine. Don't you live right across the street in that lovely house?"

The eldest daughter answered, "Yes, sir, we do. My father is filling your wood shed this very moment. You'll have enough wood now for a year. We feel shamed that we did not know of your hardship much sooner. Not long ago someone helped our family in a time of need, but after we became comfortable again we forgot about those around us who were struggling. You live only across the road and we neglected to notice your troubles."

The shoemaker's wife broke in, "You need not hold any guilt, for tonight we've been given a miracle. Even if you had not come, my husband and I would have rejoiced because my child has life again, and my husband has his health."

By now, the nobleman had arrived in the wake of his daughters. After hearing part of the conversation, he said, "From this night forward our family will make it our business to look in on you from time to time. We should have helped you long ago. Our comfort had given us blinders, like a horse, preventing us from seeing what's going on around us. This evening, Nicholas Kristo came and took off the blinders."

"Is your daughter's name Renee?" asked Nicholas, laying his hand on the shoemaker's shoulder.

"Yes, how did you know?"

With a wide grin, Nicholas answered, "Oh, that's not important. Why don't you put on your coat and follow me out to the horses? I have a little Christmas gift for the child. We had plans to stop here much later in the evening, but I'm glad we came when we did."

The shoemaker slipped on his coat and followed Nicholas and Joseph. After digging to the bottom of the sack, Nicholas pulled out a small rag doll with Renee's name written on the tag. Handing it to the man, he said, "Joseph and I must be on our way. We have a full night's work ahead of us."

Curious, the shoemaker asked, "What will you do with all those toys?"

"In return for what God has done for your family, may I ask you to keep our visit a secret? Will you pretend you never saw that sack of toys? Many children in this village will have a special Christmas gift when they awake in the morning, but we want the giving to be a secret and a surprise."

"Your secret's safe with us, and I'll tell our generous neighbor your wishes as well. You and Joseph have made this Christmas the most wonderful we've ever had. God bless you, my friends."

With that, Nicholas and Joseph mounted their horses and made their way through Pizal to deliver the toys. At every stop they placed the gifts, some on the porch or on the front steps. They'd knock on the door and then flee before anyone had time to discover them. Nicholas had the most fun, feeling as he had as a boy, giving anonymous gifts and making a clean getaway.

It was three a.m. when they finished and met the other men at Anna's house for hot soup and a chance to warm up. After Anna learned what had happened at the shoemaker's house, she began to weep. "That's the most beautiful Christmas story I've ever heard. As soon as the New Year comes, I'll visit all my friends and advise them to look in their closets for shoes that are in need of repair."

Nicholas said, "And we'll do the same at the Mission."

Ty asked, "Forgive me for asking, Nicholas, but with all your gold, why wouldn't you just leave some gold coins when you come upon a family in so much need?"

"Good question, Ty. In some cases I would give gold, but that's not always the wisest choice. In the shoemaker's case, he is the type of man that might think of it as a beggar's alms. He might be insulted by it. By giving him more shoes to fix, he'll be building his business and a strong sense of self-reliance. He is a humble but proud man, and tonight he is also a happy and grateful man. He knows that all the money in the world could never have given him what he was blessed with this evening."

As the men put on their coats and bundled up, preparing to return to the Mission, Nicholas gave Anna a hug and said, "I'll see you tomorrow evening at the wedding?"

"I wouldn't miss it for the world."

CHAPTER 74. THE PLAN TO FREE THE MENDOLENIS.

$\mathcal{J}$t was mid-morning on Christmas Day by the time General Emeliano and his men arrived at the Black Boar Inn on the southern road leading to Rome. The General took a large room, letting his men eat and then sleep several hours before they began the ride to the stockade.

By mid-afternoon it had begun to snow, and the General woke Major Como and Captain Toboso. As they rolled out of bed, fighting off their weariness, the General faced them. "I'll say it once again, men, this assignment is not official business. I'm returning a favor for the man that helped cure my daughter. You can back out now if you like."

Major Como stood to attention. "We are loyal to you, General. We don't care that this is personal. You saved our lives more than once in battle, and this is the least we can do."

"All right then, in order for us to maintain our positions back in San Marco, I must remain here at the inn. You need to disguise yourselves before you go to the stockade."

"Why do you have to stay behind?" asked Captain Taboso.

"I am known by too many soldiers and politicians. They'd track the Mendolenis' disappearance straight back to my visit to Rome. The Black Boar Inn is remote enough to keep our activities quiet."

"What about us, General? What disguise could we possibly wear that would conceal our identity?"

"We'll adjust your uniforms to look like those of prison guards. The guards don't wear feathers in their hats, only Royal Guard have that distinction. Leave off your capes, and then you'll look almost exactly like them. You will also need to shave your beards. Commander Brutti likes his men clean-shaven, because they are so close to the Vatican."

"But, General," the Captain complained, "our beards are our manhood, the pride of every Royal Guardsman."

The General offered a sympathetic smile. "How well I know that, Captain Taboso, since I'm the one who's given the most support to that tradition. But it's the most important part of the disguise. After you've shaved and adjusted your uniforms, you'll ride to the stockade, march to the sub levels and relieve the Sentries on guard. It's Christmas Day, so there shouldn't be more than two men on duty. Tell them you've just arrived to serve under Commander Brutti's command and have come to relieve them for the holiday. Tell them Commander Brutti said they've earned time off. If they start asking questions, play dumb. Also, say you were transferred from the Sicilian Prison Authority, it's the most renowned after Rome. After they turn over the keys and leave, simply walk through the corridors calling out the couple's last name, Mendoleni. Release them and bring them here at once. I will have horses ready for their ride back to Pizal."

"Won't there be an investigation? The guards will recognize us," warned Major Como.

"No doubt there will be, but by the time they send someone to San Marco, the two of you will have grown beards."

The General handed them a razor and adjusted their uniforms, while the men quibbled over who'd shave first. In less than an hour they were on the road to Rome, teasing one another about who looked sillier.

The streets of Rome were nearly empty as they approached the stockade, except for a man begging alongside the building's giant wooden doors. Major Como dismounted and threw a coin onto the blind man's blanket. "Maybe this will bring us some luck."

Captain Toboso reached for the door's giant iron ring and knocked. After a minute, a guard came and pointed them to a corridor that led to the dungeon. A rank smell greeted them as the soldiers marched down the dark stairwell in search of another guard able to direct them to the dungeon cells.

As they descended to the second level, only a few torches lit the corridors, and their boot heels echoed at every step. Just ahead a rat scurried across their path and disappeared under a cell door with no window. The moisture on the wet, black walls and the smell of rotting human flesh in the dank, cold air made them gag, wondering how anyone could survive down there.

Turning onto a west wing corridor, they saw a sleeping guard with his feet over a small desk and the chair on two legs, ready to give way. Major Como called out, "Soldier! You wouldn't be sleeping on your watch now, would you?"

Startled, the guard rushed to his feet, taken with fear by the sound of authority, "Who comes? Identify yourselves."

As they stomped their boots ever louder for effect, the Major approached and explained why they were there and what his orders were, then asked, "Is there another guard on duty today?"

"Yes, there are two more guards another level down."

"Is that where the foul odor is coming from?" Captain Toboso asked.

"Down there are those condemned to die."

Major Como turned to the Captain. "Relieve this man at once." Then, turning back to the prison guard, he said, "Commander Brutti has ordered your return in two days."

With a puzzled look, the soldier said, "He's never been that generous. Are you sure it was Commander Brutti that gave the order?"

"I'm sure, soldier. Or perhaps I should return and tell the Commander your feelings on his generosity?"

The guard scrambled for his things, handed the Captain the keys and, as he walked down the corridor, his voice echoed back. "This is one Christmas Day you'll want to forget, especially if you go down to the third level. The guards down there are more vicious than those they keep watch over. The one in charge is Calibus. Oh, you're just going to *love* Calibus."

Chapter 75. Dealing with Calibus

When the stockade guard hurried down the corridor and out of sight, the soldiers began their way down the dungeon stairwell to the next level. Faint screams from the torture chambers below made the pungent smell of death that much more horrific.

The screeches grew louder when the Major and Captain stepped onto the third level, and marched to a desk at the end of passageway. A guard stood with his hand on his mouth, gazing into one of the cells. Major Como called out, "Soldier, what is your name?"

Surprised at the visitors, the guard walked to meet them, saying, "Corporal Farinelli on guard. Why have you come?"

"Commander Brutti has relieved you of your position and wants you to report to him in two days."

"Did he say why? Am I in trouble?"

"I don't know, soldier. I only know you're not to disturb him this Christmas Day."

"Calibus won't like this at all. I need to inform him about my leaving."

Major Como lowered a brow. "That won't be necessary, Corporal. We'll tell Calibus why Commander Brutti has sent us here. You may leave at once. Where is Calibus?"

The Corporal hurried to the desk, grabbed his hat and sword, and headed quickly down the corridor saying, "Please wait until I'm at the stairs before you tell him anything. He's in the torture chamber with a client, at the end of the passageway."

As the Corporal climbed the stairs, Major Como turned to his partner. "We may have to change plans. This Calibus character may give us more trouble then we thought."

They marched to the end of the corridor and turned into the entrance of a huge room. Several torture tables sat in the center with metal instruments decorating the walls all around. These instruments were designed to produce confessions. Off to the right was a nearly naked man hanging by his arms in chains suspended from the ceiling. His back was turned to them and blood oozed from whip marks that started at the bottom of his legs and connected horizontally up to the back of his neck. The man remained motionless while a man standing next to him stretched his hand toward the open wounds, wiping the blood onto his index finger, tasting it.

Major Como cleared his throat. "Are you Calibus?"

When the man looked up, the hair on the backs of the soldiers' necks stood on end. The man's eyes glared at them in madness. He was naked from his waist up, and hair covered his back and chest. His beard was wild, matted, and food-infested. He stood well over six feet and his bald head shone with sweat and black grease. Before he answered the soldier's question he smiled, revealing a mouth full of rotted, half missing teeth. "I Calibus. Who you are? Where my Corporal?"

The Major's stomach turned. His instincts told him he needed to change his line of reasoning if he and the Captain hoped to leave unscathed. "We have orders from Commander Brutti to interrogate two of your prisoners."

Walking to the western wall, Calibus unfastened the chains that held the prisoner suspended. The man fell to the ground motionless. "Uuhh... went too far," grunted the beast. "I no like when they die so quick. What prisoners you want to talk?"

"The Mendoleni couple. Are they still alive?"

With a grimace appearing, Calibus' face grew fearful. "Yes... gods protect them. I won't enter cell. White god light surrounds them."

"What light?"

"Uhh... not going in. I give you key. Not going in."

While Calibus rambled on, the Major thought of a different plan. "You won't have to worry about going in there, Calibus. We have instructions to ask a few questions and if they answer correctly we must take them to Commander Brutti's headquarters. We're to prepare them for an interrogation with several influential Cardinals. It seems someone important in the Vatican has doubts about their crime of heresy and wishes to revisit their case."

"You follow," said Calibus, heading down the corridor.

As the soldiers followed, a voice cried out from one of the cells. "The gods curse you, Calibus! You will die ten thousand times in your sleep. You are the Devil's whore!"

"Who is that?" asked the Captain.

A wicked smile came to Calibus. "It is Impastato... the judge. He comes here from San Marco. Pay no mind. He want to kill me...bad."

Realizing it was the same Judge Impastato that General Emeliano had imprisoned months earlier, Major Como asked, "Why does he want to kill you?"

Calibus laughed, a vile odor releasing into the air. "I love his hate."

"What did you do to him?"

Turning to them, Calibus explained, "When they arrest him, they took his young wife too. She help in his crimes. I defile and torture her...

make him watch. On fourth day, Impastato go mad. Every day I pass cell, I remind him how I like his wife. He rages when he hear me...ha ha he."

Several paces from the Mendoleni cell, Calibus stopped, handing the keys to Captain Toboso. "I leave now. I fear them again. I must go... I must go away."

With that, Calibus hurried down the corridor, calling back, "Take them away! Don't come back! Leave keys in door."

Judge Impastato heard Calibus and shrieked, "May the gods rot your eyes out, Calibus! Worms shall inhabit your belly!"

When Calibus was out of sight, the Captain opened the Mendoleni cell and found the couple in a corner, shivering in an embrace. The soldiers could see no light surrounding them, only terror in their eyes as they stepped into the cell to explain.

"Don't fear for anything. We've come to help you," said Major Como. "Are you well enough to travel?"

As Captain Toboso unlocked their chains, Santo's eyes widened at his reassuring smile. "Am I dreaming? What day is it?"

Major Como replied, "It's Christmas Day, Santo, and no, you're not dreaming. You and your wife will be free today, but not free from the Vatican's interest in you. We'll make our escape at once. General Emeliano will explain everything. In the meantime, let us make haste."

The couple stood in their rags. On taking her first step, Rosetta fainted, but Major Como caught her and carried her out the cell door. Captain Toboso reached out, holding back the Major. "We can't just leave and let Calibus continue his wickedness. We must stop that beast before we leave this place."

Major Como pulled away and walked down the corridor carrying Rosetta, with Santo limping behind. "I've thought about that already, Captain. I want you to go to Judge Impastato's cell and unlock it. Open the door a crack and then quickly join us. The Judge will think of a way to get even with Calibus. My guess is that Calibus will not go down easily and the Judge will not come out unscathed. Either way, I'm confident justice will be served."

Captain Toboso ran to Impastato's cell, unlocked it, then ran to meet the others on their way up the stairwell.

When they were outside the prison walls, Major Como and the Captain unrolled the bedrolls from the horses and covered Santo and Rosetta. Then, with two riders on each horse, they rode north into the city. Behind, the Captain called out, "Major, why are you going into the city? We need to go south!"

"If someone sees us ride away, I want them to think we're escaping into the city," said the Major. Glancing back at the watchtower, he saw a guard at the top watching them leave. "We've been spotted, Captain. We'll change direction as soon as we can't be seen from above."

Eager to report what had happened, the watchtower guard went directly to Commander Brutti's palatial apartment. It adjoined the stockade, so in a matter of minutes he had the commander's undivided attention. "A prisoner escaped and leapt to his death from the stockade wall, sir. Also, I saw two horses, with two riders on each horse, heading north into the city. They were too far away to make an identification."

"Who was the prisoner that jumped to his death?"

"I don't know, sir. I'm new here and have only served watchtower duty since my arrival."

"Well done, soldier. I want you to go to the prison command post, locate the Sergeant of Arms and bring him to my office at the prison. No one has ever escaped from my jail, and we're going to keep it that way. Tell the Sergeant to bring five of his best guards. In the meantime I'll investigate the situation in the dungeon."

After finding Calibus with his head caved in and a heavy torture instrument lying beside him, Brutti checked the corridor, realizing the suicide prisoner was Judge Impastato. Marching further down the passageway, Commander Brutti saw the Mendoleni cell opened, so he sent for the guards who were supposed to be on watch. When they arrived and explained how two soldiers had relieved them and gone seeking Calibus, Brutti asked, "Didn't you suspect anything?"

"No, sir, they looked just like us. And one of them spoke like he'd been a soldier for a long time."

Commander Brutti turned to the Sergeant of Arms. "The watchtower guard said he saw riders heading north into the city. Take your men, and find them. They must be captured. It seems we have a pair of traitors and a pair of heretics who've grossly underestimated the justice system of the Roman Government."

The Sergeant of Arms and his men mounted their horses and rode into Rome, making inquiries at every intersection. Several hours later, after they returned to the stockade no more informed than when they started, an Army Constable approached the sergeant. He said he'd seen two soldiers with the escapees riding south just beyond the city limits. Before the constable finished speaking, the sergeant put spurs to his horse, yelling back to report to Commander Brutti with word that the search party had found their trail and were in pursuit.

CHAPTER 76. ESCAPE THROUGH THE BLIZZARD.

On the second floor of the Black Boar Inn, General Emeliano glanced out his bedroom window, seeing his men leading their horses to the stable to be watered. Not seeing the Mendolenis with them, he ran downstairs, but stopped in his tracks when he noticed a couple wrapped in blankets sitting at a table eating as if it were their last meal.

Approaching the table, the General asked, "Are you Santo and Rosetta Mendoleni?"

Fear-stricken by the General's uniform, the couple looked up but said nothing. Just then Major Como came into the inn and joined them.

"You've nothing to fear, Santo, Rosetta. Meet General Emeliano, who planned your escape." Turning to the General, the Major warned, "We were spotted riding away from the prison. I don't know how much time we have."

Santo stood, reaching for the General's hand in thanksgiving. "We are eternally grateful to you for freeing us, General, but we don't understand any of this. Soldiers deceiving soldiers, what's this all about?"

"We know that you were sentenced to death for heresy by the Vatican. We also know that what you actually did to offend the church is hardly worth a lashing, but some ambitious Cardinals chose to make you an example."

Santo asked, "But why did you plan our escape?"

As the couple continued their meal, the General told of his daughter's miraculous healing, and also Benito's rescue from the stonemason. "And then there's Nicholas Kristo and his Mission. He's the one behind the effort to rescue you. I'll explain everything on our journey there, but now you must go up to my room. I've bought new clothes and boots for you, also winter coats. We have to be on the move if we ever expect to make it to the Mission before Brutti's men gain on us."

Santo rose from the table with a piece of bread, took his wife's hand and hurried up stairs to the General's room. Major Como and Captain Tomoso sat down and ordered a quick meal before the journey to Pizal.

The General settled up with the innkeeper for the rooms and horses and went to the stable. Not long after, the others joined him and they set off on the road to Pizal.

Snow began to fall heavily when the Sergeant of Arms and his men arrived at the Black Boar Inn. Seeing the tracks of horses, they knew they weren't far behind, and were determined to return to San Marco with the escaped prisoners and traitors.

Bypassing the innkeeper, the sergeant went directly to the stable. The blacksmith told him four men and a woman had ridden south on the road to Pizal less than an hour earlier.

"Are you sure there were four men, not three?"

"Yes, a high ranking soldier led the way with two other soldiers, and two civilians, a man and woman."

Without thanking him, the sergeant turned his horse into the ripping wind and motioned his men to follow.

General Emeliano grew concerned as the snow deepened and the temperature dropped. He thought the only advantage to the inclement weather was that the heavy snow would surely cover their tracks.

Riding into the wind-blown snow, the night seemed to go on forever before the village lamps of Pizal came into view. The General gathered the group together. "Can everyone manage another two hours? I don't want to risk coming all this way only to be trapped at the most obvious refuge. If we bypass Pizal, we can make it up the mountain in less than two hours."

Rosetta spoke first. "I will make it, General. This storm is a relief compared to even one hour in that evil dungeon."

"What about the wolves?" Major Como asked. "You said we needed an escort on our way to the summit."

The General grabbed his beard, shaking away the ice and snow. "I forgot about that. We need to think of an alternative plan."

Santo moved his horse beside the General and reached for his arm. "We don't need another plan, General. This is a situation where I know I can be of service. The good Lord has given me a gift when it comes to animals."

"What do you mean?"

"It's true, General," Rosetta added. "From the time I met Santo he's had a way with animals. Once a bear came upon us in the forest, and when it saw Santo it lay on its belly and rolled over. Santo had no fear, and when he approached the bear, it licked his hands. No, we won't be in any danger, General. Not from the animals."

The General turned his horse to the others. "If Nicholas taught me anything, it's that God's ways are above our ways. With that thought, and a prayer that Santo has not lost his gift, let us proceed up the mountain."

When they reached the base of the mountain, the wind calmed and the falling snow thinned. Howling wolves could be heard in the distance as the group began their ascent. The moon had broken through the clouds by the time they reached the first steep incline.

Major Como glanced back down the trail. "General, I can see horses through the trees at the base of the mountain. If that's Brutti's men, they're not far behind."

The General stopped and turned. "Who else could it be? Let's just continue and hope those howling wolves are not as friendly to them."

As they reached the halfway point the General came to a stop. "Did anyone hear that? Everyone be still a moment."

Calming the horses, the group listened, and heard a screeching wild-cat and then two gunshots. A human scream echoed up the mountain and then three more gunshots rang out.

"It sounds like there's more than one animal attacking them," said Rosetta, shivering.

Other screams joined the first and then a few moments later, there was silence. Major Como turned his horse. "General, it sounds as if there's no one left in pursuit."

"I think you're right, Major. Let's continue up the mountain, we've not far to go."

General Emeliano breathed a sigh of relief when he saw the torches on either side of the Mission's southern gate. But his relief turned to fear when he spotted three wolves standing in front of the gate. Moving in either direction, the beasts flanked them.

Santo leapt off his horse and walked directly to them. At thirty paces away, the wolves sank to their bellies, and one rolled onto its back, yipping. The soldiers stood motionless, unable to accept what they were witnessing.

Santo approached a large black male, knelt down and vigorously scratched behind its ears. "You can come to the gate, General. They are no threat to us."

The group dismounted and walked the horses past Santo and the wolves. Rosetta jumped back when the Mission gate suddenly swung open.

Brother Taylor stepped out. "Ah, General, welcome back. It looks to me like your mission was a success."

"Good to see you, Brother. I'm pleased to introduce Santo and Rosetta Mendoleni. Standing behind them are the heroes who were able to remove them from the dungeon safely. Meet Major Como and Captain Toboso."

Brother Taylor greeted them, then reached for Rosetta's shivering hand. "Come into the Mission at once. We'll get you warmed up in no time."

Walking toward Nicholas's house, the General asked, "How did you know we were at the gate? It's the middle of the night."

The monk turned and smiled. "It's five-thirty in the morning, General. I milk the cows every day at this time. I heard your voices over the fence. Besides, Nicholas asked me to look out for your return. He wanted me to bring all of you to his house upon your arrival."

"Isn't this the day he and Bernadette are to marry?"

"No, that was yesterday. It was a wonderful Christmas wedding. Both couples were married at the same time. Bernadette and Maria never looked more beautiful. But you didn't miss it all. The newlyweds wanted to wait and celebrate late this afternoon when everyone is rested from the Christmas activity."

Bernadette was at the door waiting when the group arrived. "Please come in out of the cold. You all must be half frozen."

As they filed in, shaking off the snow, Brother Taylor asked, "What gets you up so early, Bernadette?"

"I wanted to help Bell with some of the baking needed for the wedding celebration this afternoon."

The group went directly to the huge fireplace, removed their coats, hats and mittens, and stood silently, defrosting their hands and feet. Bernadette and Brother Taylor went into the kitchen and prepared barley soup, bread and cheese.

The silence was broken as a voice called from the second level. "Bravo, bravo!" Nicholas descended the stairs, wrapped in a red blanket, wearing his favorite crimson sleeping cap. "Is everyone unharmed?"

Putting his arms around Major Como and Captain Toboso, the General replied, "Yes, Nicholas, thanks to these outstanding soldiers."

The General went on to commend his men for their bravery. Then he introduced Santo and Rosetta. The couple approached Nicholas, Santo reaching out his hand. "We don't have the words to tell you how very thankful we are. Is our son here at the Mission?"

Nicholas smiled, turned and pointed to a guest room. "He's in there, sound asleep, but something tells me he won't mind if you wake him."

The couple rushed into the room and in moments laughter mingled with weeping could be heard throughout the house. Bernadette came from the kitchen with a tray of food and gathered the soldiers to the dining room table. As Brother Taylor poured the soup, Nicholas joined them. The General sat and related everything that happened from the time they left the Mission.

"How did you gain passage up the mountain without an escort?" Nicholas asked, sipping his soup.

"It was Santo who helped with the animals. Rosetta told us he has a God-given gift. When we were confronted by wolves at the southern gate,

Santo leapt off his horse and went directly to them. I've never seen anything like that before. When he approached them, they went down on their bellies. Santo reached out and scratched behind the large black one's ears."

Nicholas' eyebrows arched. "Is that so? I think Santo and I have a great deal in common. As soon as the family's finished reuniting, I have an idea that will not only keep them safe from Roman authorities, but will bring them blessings for the rest of their lives."

CHAPTER 77. THE NEW WORLD.

When the Mendoleni family joined everyone at the dining room table, their eyes glowed with the hope of a new life. As they began their meal, Bernadette sat next to Nicholas with her journal and started writing.

"So, could it be true, Santo?" Nicholas asked. "You and your wife were arrested for merely teaching scripture to someone?"

Santo was a stocky, big-boned man with a round face and a burly, partially gray beard, ending just below the neckline. With a deep, husky voice, he explained, "It's a little more complicated than that. We were on holiday in Rome when a priest wearing common clothes joined a group discussion we were having in the square. Not knowing he was a Roman priest, Rosetta corrected him when he pressed his point about penance being the only way to Heaven. When she said that 'we are saved by faith, and not by works, lest anyone should boast', his face turned red and he proclaimed us heretics on the spot. Things became worse when I cited where it was in scripture. According to him, we had no authority or even any right to interpret scripture, to say nothing of us teaching it."

"When did they arrest you?"

"They came to the inn where we were staying that very evening. After spending the night in the stockade, we were brought before the Vatican council and accused as heretics by the priest who first sighted us in the square. We were sentenced to death without a chance to defend our position, and our son was given a fate not much better than ours."

Rosetta added, "But God has answered our prayers. We are free once again, and so is our son. We owe all of you so much. How can we ever repay you?"

"You owe us nothing," Nicholas answered. "Please remember, you're only free as long as you remain on this mountain. Rome will not soon forget your escape. They'll send others to find you."

"Brutti will not relent. When his men do not return, he will be incensed," the General warned, sopping bread in his soup.

Leaning in, Santo asked, "What shall we do, Nicholas? We cannot impose on you forever."

"Don't lose hope. God will make a way for you. Now, tell me what happened to you in the dungeon. Did they torture you?"

"No, thank God, and we cannot say why," Rosetta answered, leaning back. "When we first arrived, Calibus came to our cell. When I looked into his eyes, the hair on the back of my neck stood up. I knew he was mad and by the way he ogled, I knew he intended to defile me. But then the strangest thing happened. After he unlocked my chains, a strange light appeared around us. Calibus grunted and looked at us in horror, then ran out of the cell. From that day on we saw no one except our guard until the Major and Captain opened the door to free us."

Santo added, "We did not waste the time spent in that horrid place. Even as we heard prisoners being tortured we prayed and drew near to God. As the days passed and our execution drew ever closer, the meaning of our lives became crystal clear. We considered just how corrupt and evil the world is, and how it had infected the church and church authority. We reasoned the same spiritual disease that blinded the Jews in Jesus' day had reemerged and caught up to us. The scripture that kept coming to mind was, '...we fight not against flesh and blood, but against principalities and powers in high places.'"

"How true that is, Santo," said Nicholas. "Please continue."

"Rosetta and I agreed that, if by some miracle we were ever released, we'd spend the rest of our lives fighting against those evil 'principalities and powers' in the name of the Lord."

"And how would you wage that war?" asked Nicholas with a twinkle in his eyes.

"We'd start by loving the unlovely. Then, we'd feed the poor with bread and the rich with truth. We'd speak up for those who cannot speak for themselves, and be willing to suffer the consequences. We'd give truth and light to those in need, rich and poor alike, for many that are rich cannot see spiritually, neither can they hear. We'd spend the rest of our days defining the light of truth to this darkened world, but with anonymity this time."

"Why would you stay anonymous?" asked Bernadette.

"Not because we're afraid of upsetting the powerful, but only to be able to continue until we've given as much as we can while we still breathe. My wife and I were imprisoned at the very beginning of our mission efforts. We shall be wiser this time."

"So, if I understand you correctly, you want to spend the rest of your lives giving selfless, Godly gifts to as many who are in need, anonymously?"

"That's it, Nicholas."

Before Nicholas could respond, he noticed Captain Toboso nodding off across the table. "I'm sorry about that," the General apologized, "but my men have hardly slept in two days. We'll take some rest now before the celebration this evening."

Nicholas agreed and after Bernadette showed the soldiers to the guest rooms, he resumed his conversation with Santo and Rosetta. "The General tells me that you have a way with the creatures of the forest. He said the wolves went down to their bellies when you approached."

Santo replied, "It's been that way since I was a boy. I'm just thankful I was able to help after what everyone did for us."

"We have much in common, Santo," said Nicholas, smiling. "I am blessed with the same gift when it comes to animals. That's why I chose to build the Mission on this mountain. It ensures our privacy and anonymity. The mountain is teaming with wolves and other wild creatures. There are warning signs everywhere."

"How do the others at the Mission come and go in safety?"

"I'll explain that tomorrow. You must be exhausted from the journey here. You'll be guests at my house for as long as you wish. Bernadette will show you to your room."

Bernadette's heart went out to the petite, redheaded woman as she helped Rosetta from the table. "While you were eating I asked one of the nuns to heat bath water for you."

"I can't think of anything I would enjoy more," said Rosetta with a sigh. "You are an angel, Bernadette, an absolute angel!"

Santo remained seated and continued, "Nicholas, please answer just one more question."

"What is it, my friend?"

"We are fugitives from the Roman government. How can we expect you to harbor us, knowing if they ever make it up here they'd surely put us in chains, arrest you, and then maybe destroy this blessed place?"

"This type of situation has happened before and the Lord has seen us through. Tomorrow I'll show you exactly what we do here and then propose an idea I think you might like."

"Please forgive me, Nicholas, but I won't sleep until I know there's a way to keep this place safe. I need to figure out a plan of escape."

"All right then, just to give you peace of mind, I'll tell you what I'm thinking."

Nicholas summarized the story of how and why Hope Mission came to be, and then went on to explain how similar their faith and goals were. By then, Bernadette had rejoined them and had begun writing.

Nicholas explained that Brutti would not relent in his effort to recapture them, so they had two choices. They could either remain at the Mission for the rest of their lives, or leave the country and start their own Mission on an entirely different continent.

"Well," said Santo, scratching the back of his head, "I don't want to remain here for the rest of my life, constantly thinking some day they'd find us. We'd be jeopardizing all of your hard work. What about leaving the country?"

Bernadette stopped writing, patted the ink dry and closed the journal, handing it to Santo. Nicholas smiled at his wife's discernment. "My wife has kept a journal of everything that's happened here since the Lord gave me this commission. Over the next few days we would like you to review what is written and then consider taking your family to the New World. I'm speaking about the new continent Admiral Columbus discovered over sixty years ago. By now the settlers have begun building cities and farms and churches all over the land. You could search for a mountain like this one and remain anonymous for the rest of your life. I'll show you how to deal with the forest animals so that your people will have the same freedom to come and go as you do. Remember, even in the New World, Rome can see and find its enemies. You'll have to send out people secretly after you're settled and the Mission is built."

"It all sounds very promising, but how would I build anything? The Roman government has seized all of our possessions. My house and land, livestock, everything."

"God will provide what you need from His storehouse. If you decide to build the Mission in the New World, Hope Mission will provide your needs."

"How could I accept monies from you when you've done so much already?"

"God has provided me with enough resources to build many Missions. You would not be traveling with my gold, but God's. It all belongs to Him. Besides, you and your wife were willing to give your lives for our King. You have indeed earned a second chance to advance the Kingdom of God."

"You've lifted a great burden from my shoulders, Nicholas. You've brought hope to a hopeless situation."

"That's exactly what you could bring to others if you establish yourself in the New World. For me 'hope' has always been the most meaningful gift to offer this world. Many are lost in the darkness of social, political, and religious corruption. Somehow innocent people always suffer for it."

"I'm inspired and honored to accept your commission," said Santo, his eyes welling. "We'll start a new life in a new land. We will study how you've managed to build this place, and then learn about God's commission to you."

Delighted, Nicholas stood, went around the table and sat next to Santo. "It won't be easy getting you out of the country. By the time we find a trade ship scheduled to leave for the New World, Commander Brutti will have alerted every western port on the Italian coastline. The first thing we'll do is to change your identity. Santo is a common name, but we'll have to change your surname."

"What about your surname, Nicholas? Under the circumstance, I think it's appropriate," suggested Santo.

"Santo Kristo, yes. Very good, but Rosetta should change her first name as well, just until you leave the country. Then we'll have to disguise you, and give you enough gold to build the Mission."

Santo leaned in, stroking his beard. "With all due respect, Nicholas, there's a problem with that."

"Oh? With the disguise or the gold?"

"The gold. In the course of my work, I've come to know about commerce and trade. The ships leaving from Portugal and Spain are mostly destined for a place called Mexico. They've found goldmines there. The point is that gold has little value in the New World. It's when they bring it here that it takes on its value. Over there industrial goods and hardware, fabrics, spices, and the like, have the most value."

"Excellent point, Santo," Nicholas said. "I guess I've been up on this mountain too long. What do you propose we do then to get you started?"

"The change of identity and disguise will work well. We'll just take it one step further. We could buy several shiploads of goods to bring to the New World, then set up a business in a populated area where we'd trade for land and lumber and all the things we need to build our Mission."

"But what if you're discovered and word gets back to Rome?"

"Once we arrive in the New World, we'll stay behind the scenes. I'll play the eccentric, wealthy businessman and hire trustworthy people to conduct my affairs. Now that I think of it, we can bring all of the equipment and tools needed for us to be in a position to help the struggling population. With my expertise in industry and Rosetta's knowledge of botany, our Mission will help people survive that brutal environment. When all is established, we'll introduce them to our Savior. After we're settled, we'll build a church in the city and then a mountain retreat, similar to this, where we'll finally reside."

Smiling, Nicholas spread his arms out. "You're the man for the job, Santo Kristo! I like the way you think."

Santo stood and paced around the table. "I'll make a list of everything we need. Then, perhaps we could send missionaries to Rome, buy the goods and have them delivered to ships in Cosenza. While there, they can book a charter."

Nicholas pointed to a closet in the grand room. "You'll find the gold in three saddlebags on the bottom shelf. We need to be ready by the beginning of spring, since that's when the first trade ships leave for the New World. Now, my brother, go and rest before the grand celebration begins. Besides the weddings, we'll celebrate a new Mission in the New World with the new Kristo family."

CHAPTER 78. THE MIND OF GOD.

The sun had just begun to set when Ben rode through the Mission's south gate, late for his own wedding celebration. With everyone in the Bellicini home, Brother Taylor appeared on the porch, waving him over. As Ben dismounted, Maria stepped out wearing her simple but elegant wedding dress, and a glowing smile. "Hello, husband. We were hoping nothing happened to you. Everyone is inside and Makande is beginning to bring the food out. What a grand evening this will be."

"I'm sorry for holding things up, but it took longer than I thought to take care of all my business."

Leaping from his horse, Ben swept Maria into his arms, lifted her off the ground and carried her through the doorway.

When they saw the couple in the doorway, Nicholas and Bernadette began to applaud, and soon everyone joined in.

Earlier that day the monks had baked loves of bread and pastries. Bell cooked every variety of fish and plenty of pasta. Makande helped the nuns prepare three different salads with a wide variety of vegetables. Ox had extended the dining room table enough to accommodate everyone and then some.

After Brother Taylor gave thanks, Makande plated the pasta and the monks streamed out of the kitchen one by one with trays of food and drink. As soon as Benito and Giovanni had their fill, they picked up their instruments and filled the air with lively rhythms of a perfectly joyous occasion.

Reaching for Nicholas' chin, Bernadette turned his head toward Anna and Michael Borelli. They had come with all their children.

Anna pointed to the open floor in front of the fireplace and directed May Rose to go out and dance. May Rose giggled with her hand on her mouth and ran out twirling and spinning in perfect time to the music, then curtsied. Everyone laughed with delight and applauded for her to continue. As she spun with unusual elegance for a child so young, her sisters joined her and soon everyone had a smile and a warm comment.

Nicholas put his arm around Bernadette and remembered that only a year ago he and May Rose had struggled through the harshest snowstorm he'd ever experienced. He thought back to the miraculous glowing anvil that saved him and the child. Then, looking to Anna and Michael, who had now joined their children in the dance, he recalled how Ben's sculpture of their family helped rekindle their marriage. Nicholas realized this wedding celebration not only defined a new experience in Bernadette's and his life journey, but also a new beginning for almost everyone there.

Curiosity joined his festive spirit as he turned to Ben and Maria. "So, Ben, what does the future hold for you and Maria, now that the Mission is almost complete? Will you venture out and make a new life with Maria and the children?"

"Only if I want my head handed to me."

Maria stood up, walked behind Ben, unhooked his hat, and kissed the back of his neck. "We want to stay right here. Ben and I love the work, and so do our children. If it's God's will, we intend to have more children."

Ben added. "If we do have more, they'll eventually join Daisy and Rose in the workshop. It's a thrill to watch them create toys."

Sitting across the table, Ricardo and Raven lifted their glasses. "Here's to the newlyweds!" said Ricardo." Raven and I have the same love for this place. When our son is born he won't learn the skills of the workshop though. He'll hunt and fish with me."

"And who says it's a boy?" Raven asked.

Everyone smiled and waited for Ricardo's answer. "Because I ate plenty of cabbage this past year."

"What does cabbage have to do with anything?" asked Raven with a curious smile.

"Before we left for Spain to visit my father, I asked Ox if there was anything I could do to ensure we had a son after we were married. He said, 'Eat lots of cabbage.'"

Laughter filled the room as Ox called from across the table. "But was the cabbage raw? It only works with raw cabbage."

Ricardo smiled and joined in the laughter, realizing he was the brunt of the joke.

Raven stabbed a piece of cabbage with her fork and lifted it to Ricardo's mouth. "Girl or boy, we'll still be happy. Right, my love?"

Turning his attention down the table, Nicholas grinned at the General, then asked Ox, "What about the Bellicini family, Ox? You know our good friend General Emeliano has exonerated all of you. You can restart your lumber company again if you like."

"Lund and Ty said they were thinking about it, but as for me, I only intend to leave here long enough to ask Nanette to be my wife. If she says yes, and agrees to live here at the Mission, then this is where we'll make our home. Those monks are the best men I've ever worked with, outside of my brothers."

"You have a lady friend, Ox? I didn't know."

"Before the ordeal with the Ficci brothers we were quite fond of each other. I only hope she hasn't found another in my absence."

Brother Taylor stood, motioning for the monks and the nuns to do likewise. "Another toast to the newlyweds!"

Everyone lifted their glasses. Nicholas kissed Bernadette, then turned to Brother Taylor. "What would we have done without all of you? You have truly made this Mission the dwelling place of God."

Smiling, Brother Taylor replied, "As well as you, Nicholas. This coming year we'll have four more monks and two nuns. In the underground church, this Mission is already famous. The younger brothers and sisters want to come because it's unique, and the elders see it as a retreat. Either way, we're expanding."

"It's a welcome expansion, Taylor. When our lively group of young monks come back with another list of people in need, we'll have our hands full. We'll need all the help we can get."

Just then, Mario Fuso wheeled himself in from the front door carrying a large box with a bow on it. Rolling his wheelchair in front of the newlyweds, he lifted the box onto the table. "This is a wedding gift for the four of you from everyone at the Mission. May the Lord bless you all the days of your lives."

Bernadette and Maria smiled and stood to open the gift. As they undid the huge red bow and opened the box, two more boxes were revealed, one marked Kristo and the other, Bellicini. With everyone looking on, the women opened their boxes and gasped, pulling out custom-made formal silver stewpots. On the lid Mario had engraved their surnames and on the sides, the first names of each of the couples, adorned with scrolls and flowers. Then, on the lip, he engraved, "Christmas, 1556."

Handing the stewpots to their husbands, the women ran to the other side of the table and smothered Mario with kisses.

As the men admired Mario's skill, Nicholas asked, "What gave you the idea to make these masterpieces, Mario?"

"It was that dream I had several months ago. Do you remember I told you I saw a stewpot on a red doily?"

"Yes, what did it mean to you?"

"Everyone knows how you love the color red. To me, the dream meant that the stewpot would go to you and Bernadette."

"How come you made one for us as well?" Ben asked.

"I knew you'd be married on the same day, so I made them at the same time. Nicholas and you have been my best friends through the hardest times of my life. It was the least I could do."

Just then, Joseph Solo came through the front door with a white dove perched on his hand. "Sorry I'm late, folks. I couldn't sleep last night, and by the time I began to doze the sun was coming up."

Nicholas asked, "How is our friendly little dove?"

As the bird flew to Santo's hand, Joseph said, "When I awoke this afternoon it was perched on my bedpost. How it got in I'll never know, but right after I wiped the sleep from my eyes, I heard a voice in my head say, "Go with Santo." Is Santo going somewhere, Nick?"

"He sure is Joseph, but I'll tell you all about it tomorrow. For now just have a seat and join the celebration."

As Joseph sat down next to Santo, Bell came from behind with a plate of fried bass and salad.

Nicholas rose with his cup raised. "My friends, I lift my cup to you in honor of everything you've done for the Mission this past year. We have come such a long way in so short a time. Most of the buildings are up except for Ricardo's and Raven's house. But I'm sure we'll finish come spring.

"The Lord has filled our cups and quenched our thirst, enabling us to give the needy gracious gifts from His abundance. But this is only the beginning. Through experience we'll learn deeper ways to impact people's lives with Godly gifts. This year we'll discover new ways to share Spiritual gifts with those in need, such as giving and receiving forgiveness, along with faith, mercy and compassion.

"Each time we see a person in need, we must always make sure to find a way to warm their spirit first, by physically demonstrating the loving kindness of our Lord and Savior. For too long evil minds have misled the masses regarding gifts. Some give to get, others give to gain and boast, still others give to extort.

"We are here to help change that, and with the help of God we will. Or at least our work will bring enough light to show a stark contrast. I would be content with that until the Lord comes, because the reality is that until that glorious day, evil minds will always find ways to slither into a man's heart, intent on teaching him new underhanded ways to present a gift. Gifts with soiled strings attached, given for selfish gain. Let us commit ourselves now to take arms against that enemy with the sword of the Spirit, which is the word of God. Let us also commit never to grow 'weary in well doing', and thus personify the very essence of the King we serve and worship."

And so it was that Nicholas continued to inspire and motivate all who dwelt on the mountain, repeatedly finding new and creative ways to reach out to societies far and wide. So well did he protect his beloved anonymity that every extraordinary gift for which he became famous became attached to the legend of the third century St. Nicholas. Nicholas Kristo wouldn't have had it any other way... that is, except if and when people finally realized that all the goodness to be found in man and woman originated in the mind of God.

THE END

Printed in the United States
200133BV00005B/1-90/A